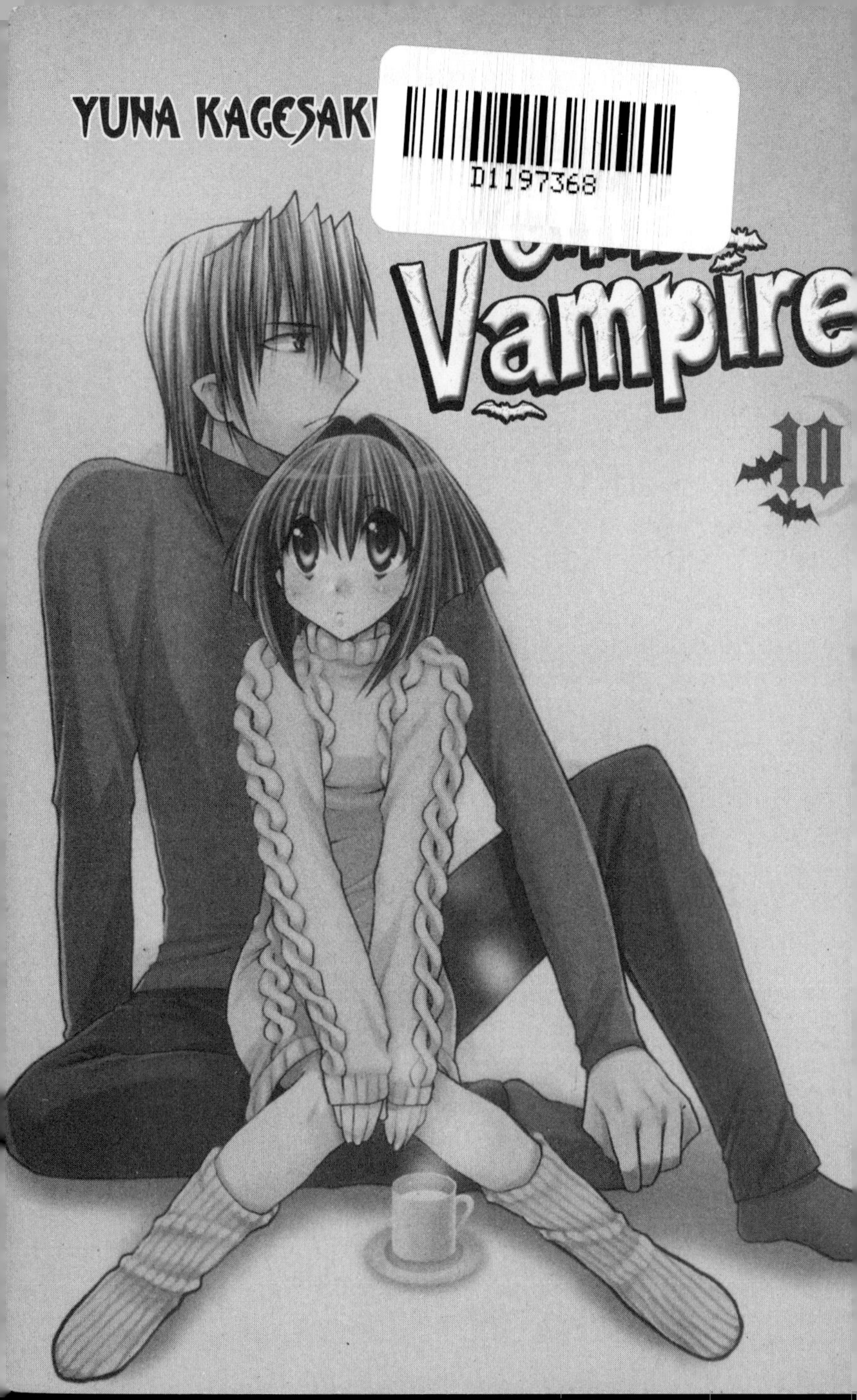
YUNA KAGESAKI
Vampire
10

Chibi Vampire Volume 10
Created by Yuna Kagesaki

Translation - Alexis Kirsch
English Adaptation - Christine Boylan
Retouch and Lettering - Star Print Brokers
Production Artist - Courtney Geter
Graphic Designer - Colin Graham

Editor - Nikhil Burmman
Digital Imaging Manager - Chris Buford
Pre-Production Supervisor - Vicente Rivera, Jr.
Production Specialist - Lucas Rivera
Managing Editor - Vy Nguyen
Art Director - Al-Insan Lashley
Editor-in-Chief - Rob Tokar
Publisher - Mike Kiley
President and C.O.O. - John Parker
C.E.O. and Chief Creative Officer - Stu Levy

A  Manga

TOKYOPOP and  are trademarks or registered trademarks of TOKYOPOP Inc.

TOKYOPOP Inc.
5900 Wilshire Blvd. Suite 2000
Los Angeles, CA 90036

E-mail: info@TOKYOPOP.com
Come visit us online at www.TOKYOPOP.com

KARIN Volume 10 © 2006 YUNA KAGESAKI
First published in Japan in 2006 by FUJIMISHOBO CO., LTD.,
Tokyo. English translation rights arranged with KADOKAWA
SHOTEN PUBLISHING CO., LTD., Tokyo through TUTTLE-MORI
AGENCY, INC., Tokyo.
English text copyright © 2008 TOKYOPOP Inc.

ISBN: 978-1-4278-0674-1

First TOKYOPOP printing: September 2008
10 9 8 7 6 5 4 3 2
Printed in the USA

Chibi Vampire

Volume 10

Created by
Yuna Kagesaki

TOKYOPOP®

HAMBURG // LONDON // LOS ANGELES // TOKYO

OUR STORY SO FAR...

KARIN MAAKA ISN'T LIKE OTHER GIRLS. ONCE A MONTH, SHE EXPERIENCES PAIN, FATIGUE, HUNGER, IRRITABILITY—AND THEN SHE BLEEDS. FROM HER NOSE. KARIN IS A VAMPIRE, FROM A FAMILY OF VAMPIRES, BUT INSTEAD OF NEEDING TO DRINK BLOOD, SHE HAS AN EXCESS OF BLOOD THAT SHE MUST GIVE TO HER VICTIMS. IF DONE RIGHT, GIVING THIS BLOOD TO HER VICTIM CAN BE AN EXTREMELY POSITIVE THING. THE PROBLEM WITH THIS IS THAT KARIN NEVER SEEMS TO DO THINGS RIGHT...

KARIN IS HAVING A BIT OF BOY TROUBLE. KENTA USUI—THE HANDSOME NEW STUDENT AT HER SCHOOL AND WORK—IS A NICE ENOUGH GUY, BUT HE EXACERBATES KARIN'S PROBLEM. KARIN'S BLOOD PROBLEM, YOU SEE, BECOMES WORSE WHEN SHE'S AROUND PEOPLE WHO HAVE SUFFERED MISFORTUNE, AND KENTA HAS SUFFERED PLENTY OF IT. MAKING THINGS EVEN MORE COMPLICATED, IT'S BECOME CLEAR TO KARIN THAT SHE'S IN LOVE WITH KENTA... SOMETHING THAT CAN ONLY BRING TROUBLE. LOVE BETWEEN HUMANS AND VAMPIRES IS FROWNED UPON IN VAMPIRE SOCIETY, BUT KARIN'S FAMILY ALLOWS HER TO CONTINUE SEEING KENTA IN EXCHANGE FOR HIM HELPING HER DURING THE DAY. KARIN AND KENTA'S LOVE FOR EACH OTHER IS GETTING STRONGER AND STRONGER BUT NEW IN TOWN IS YURIYA, A HALF-VAMPIRE WHO HAS SIMILAR TRAITS AS KARIN. YURIYA SEEMS TO BE HIDING SOMETHING IMPORTANT BUT SO FAR, KARIN IS NONE THE WISER...

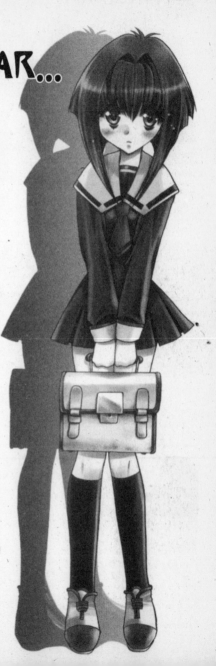

THE MAAKA FAMILY

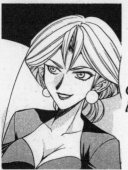

CALERA MARKER

Karin's overbearing mother. While Calera resents that Karin wasn't born a normal vampire, she does love her daughter in her own obnoxious way. Calera has chosen to keep her European last name.

KARIN MAAKA

Our little heroine. Karin is a vampire living in Japan, but instead of sucking blood from her victims, she actually GIVES them some of her blood. She's a vampire in reverse!

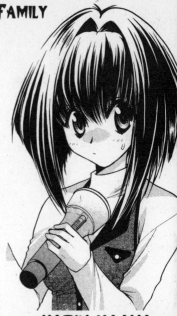

HENRY MARKER

Karin's father. In general, Henry treats Karin a lot better than her mother does, but Calera wears the pants in this particular family. Henry has also chosen to keep his European last name.

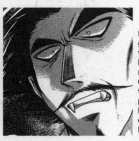

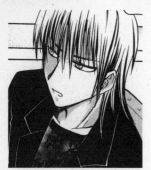

REN MAAKA

Karin's older brother. Ren milks the "sexy creature of the night" thing for all it's worth and spends his nights in the arms (and beds) of attractive young women.

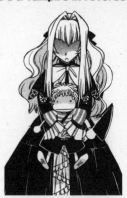

ANJU MAAKA

Karin's little sister. Anju has not yet awoken as a full vampire, but she can control bats and is usually the one who cleans up after Karin's messes. Rarely seen without her "talking" doll, Boogie.

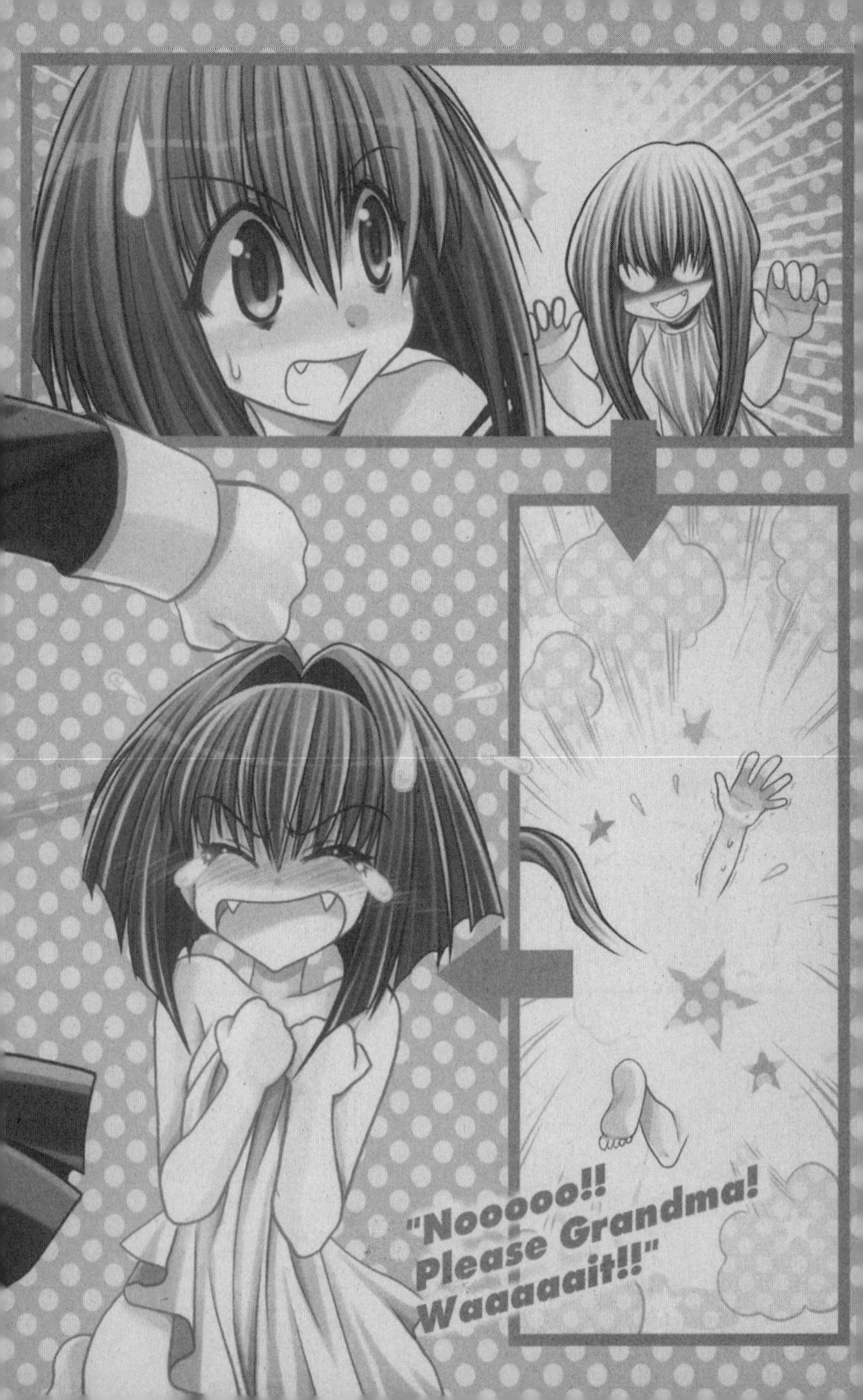
"Noooooo!! Please Grandma! Waaaaait!!"

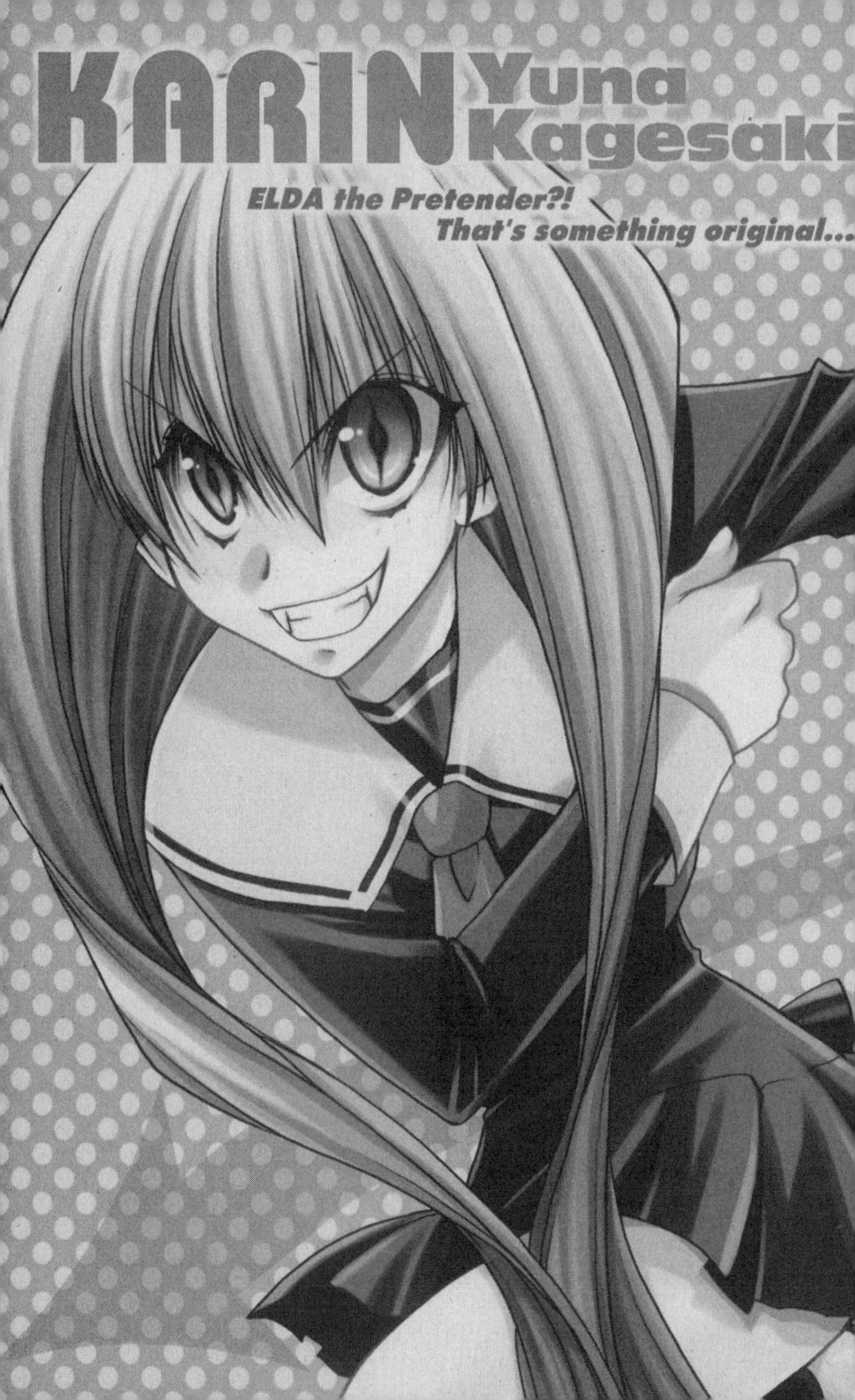
KARIN
Yuna Kagesaki
ELDA the Pretender?!
That's something original...

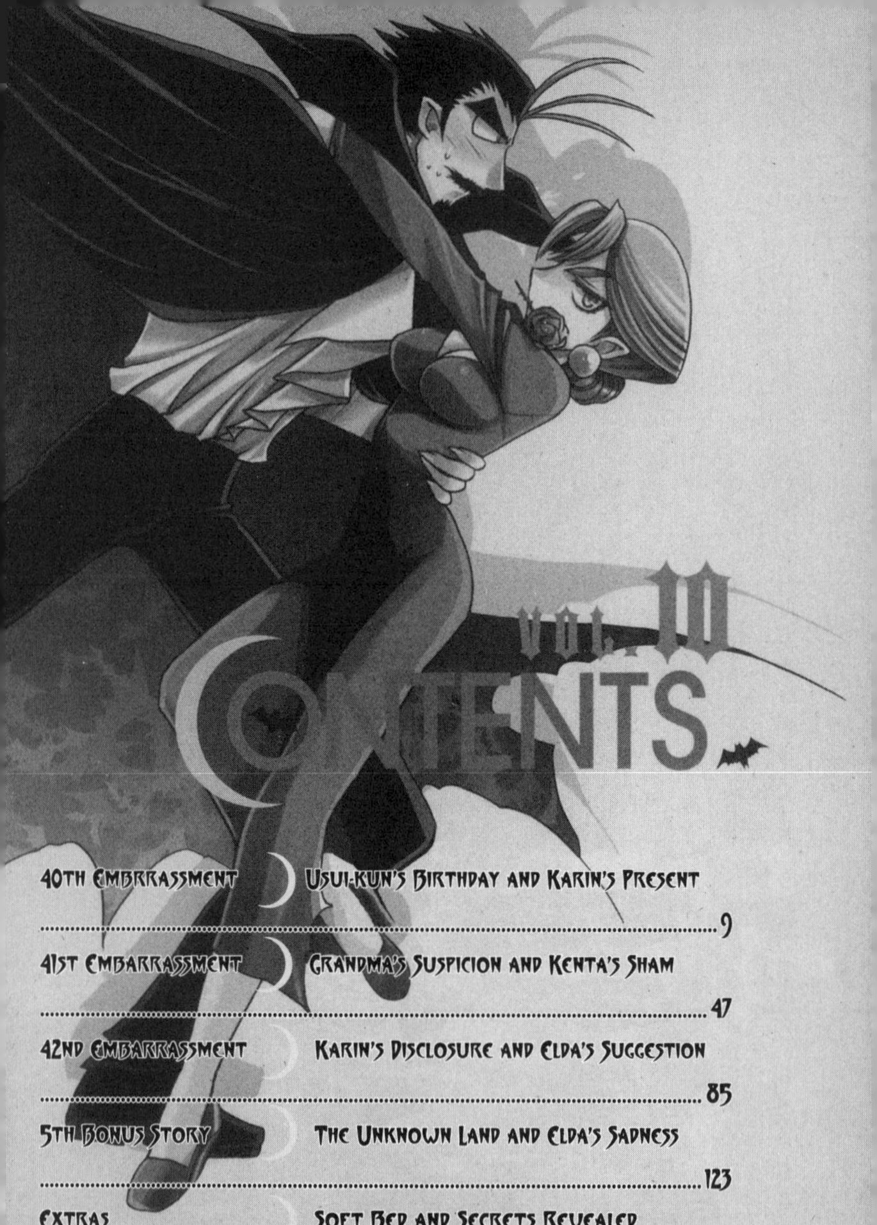

Vol. 10 Contents

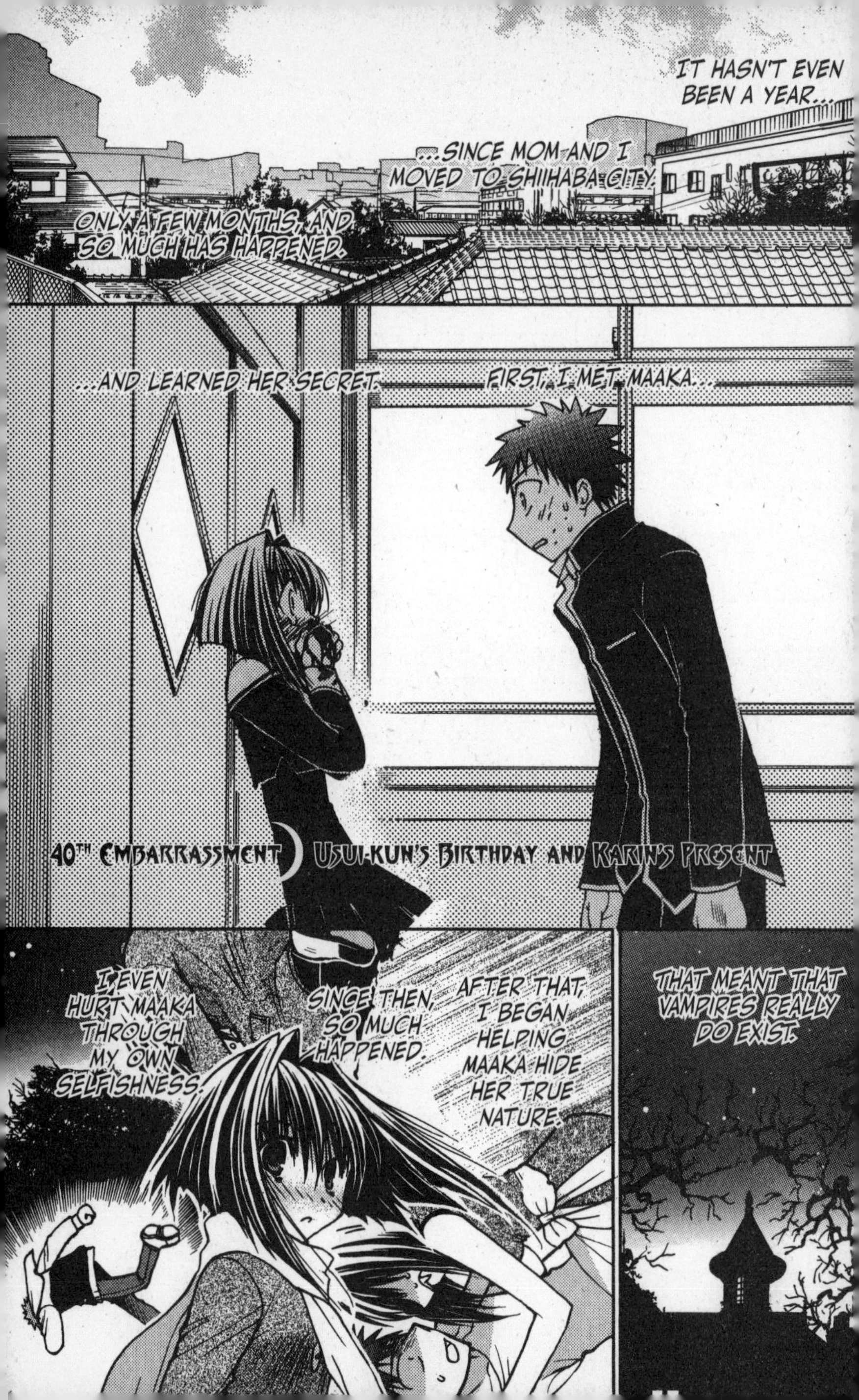
IT HASN'T EVEN BEEN A YEAR...
...SINCE MOM AND I MOVED TO SHIIHABA CITY.
ONLY A FEW MONTHS, AND SO MUCH HAS HAPPENED.
FIRST, I MET MAAKA...
...AND LEARNED HER SECRET.
40TH EMBARRASSMENT USUI-KUN'S BIRTHDAY AND KARIN'S PRESENT
THAT MEANT THAT VAMPIRES REALLY DO EXIST.
AFTER THAT, I BEGAN HELPING MAAKA HIDE HER TRUE NATURE.
SINCE THEN, SO MUCH HAPPENED.
I EVEN HURT MAAKA THROUGH MY OWN SELFISHNESS.

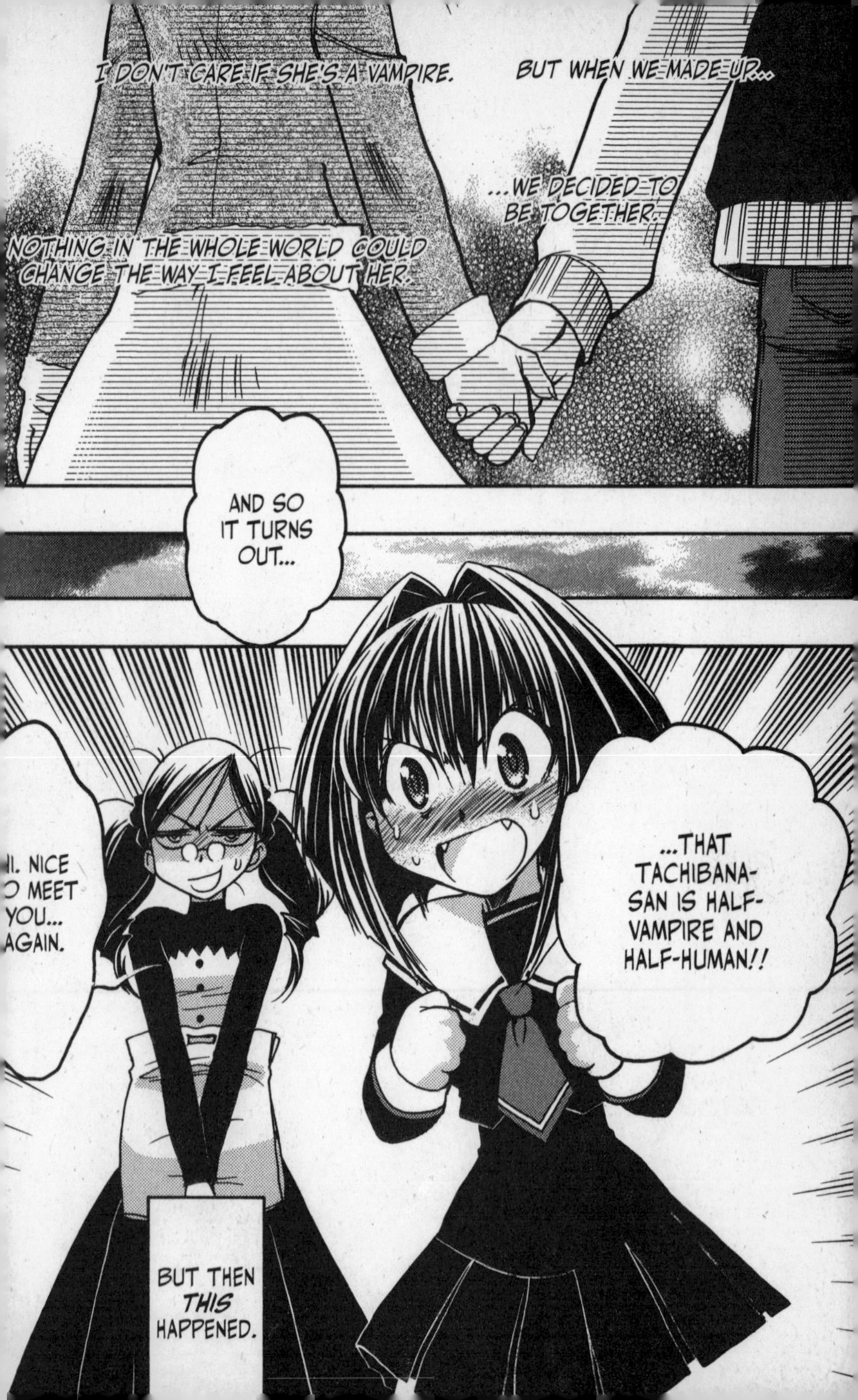
BUT WHEN WE MADE UP...
...WE DECIDED TO BE TOGETHER.
I DON'T CARE IF SHE'S A VAMPIRE.
NOTHING IN THE WHOLE WORLD COULD CHANGE THE WAY I FEEL ABOUT HER.
AND SO IT TURNS OUT...
...THAT TACHIBANA-SAN IS HALF-VAMPIRE AND HALF-HUMAN!!
I. NICE O MEET YOU... AGAIN.
BUT THEN *THIS* HAPPENED.

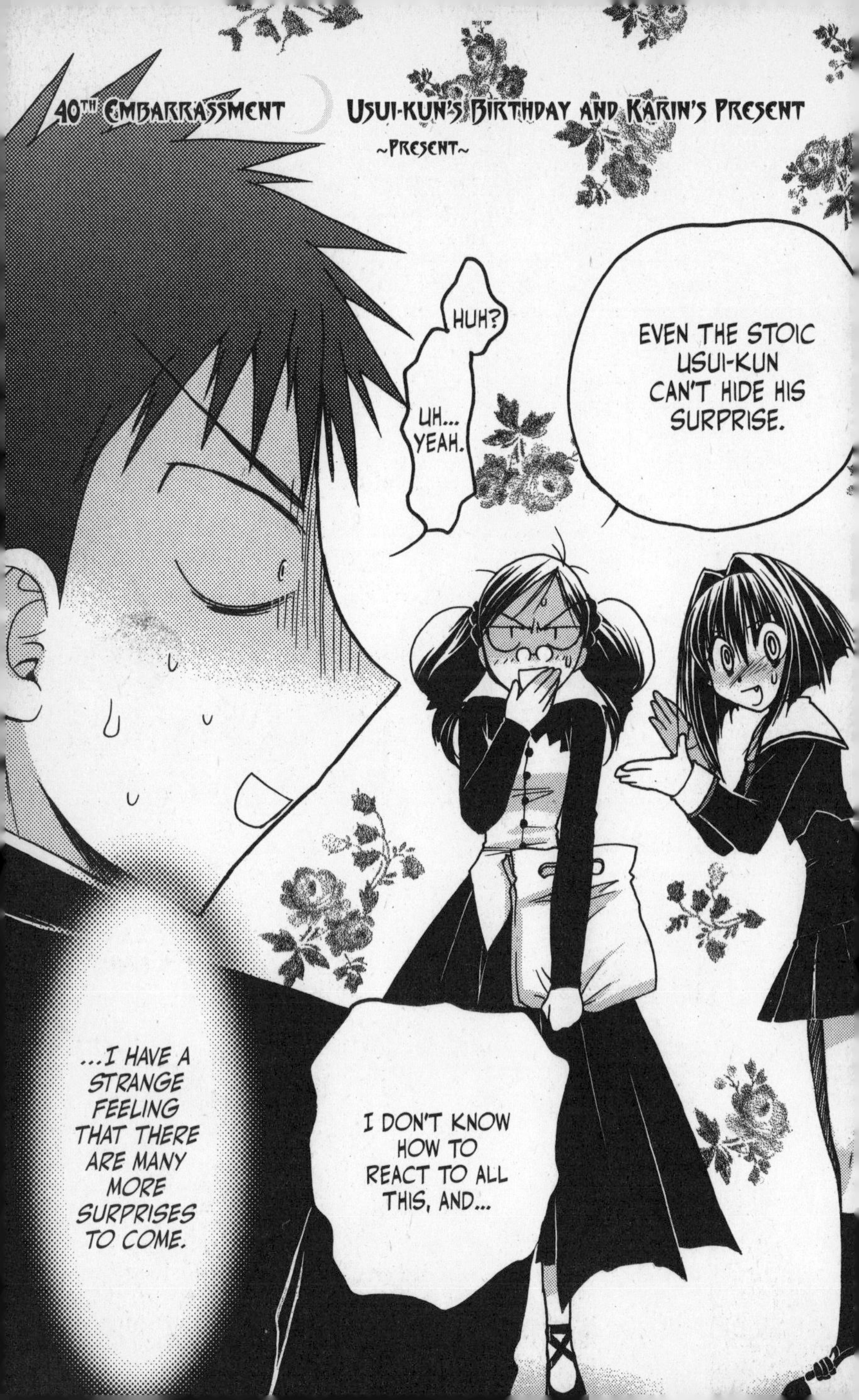
40TH EMBARRASSMENT USUI-KUN'S BIRTHDAY AND KARIN'S PRESENT
~PRESENT~
EVEN THE STOIC USUI-KUN CAN'T HIDE HIS SURPRISE.
HUH?
UH... YEAH.
I DON'T KNOW HOW TO REACT TO ALL THIS, AND...
...I HAVE A STRANGE FEELING THAT THERE ARE MANY MORE SURPRISES TO COME.

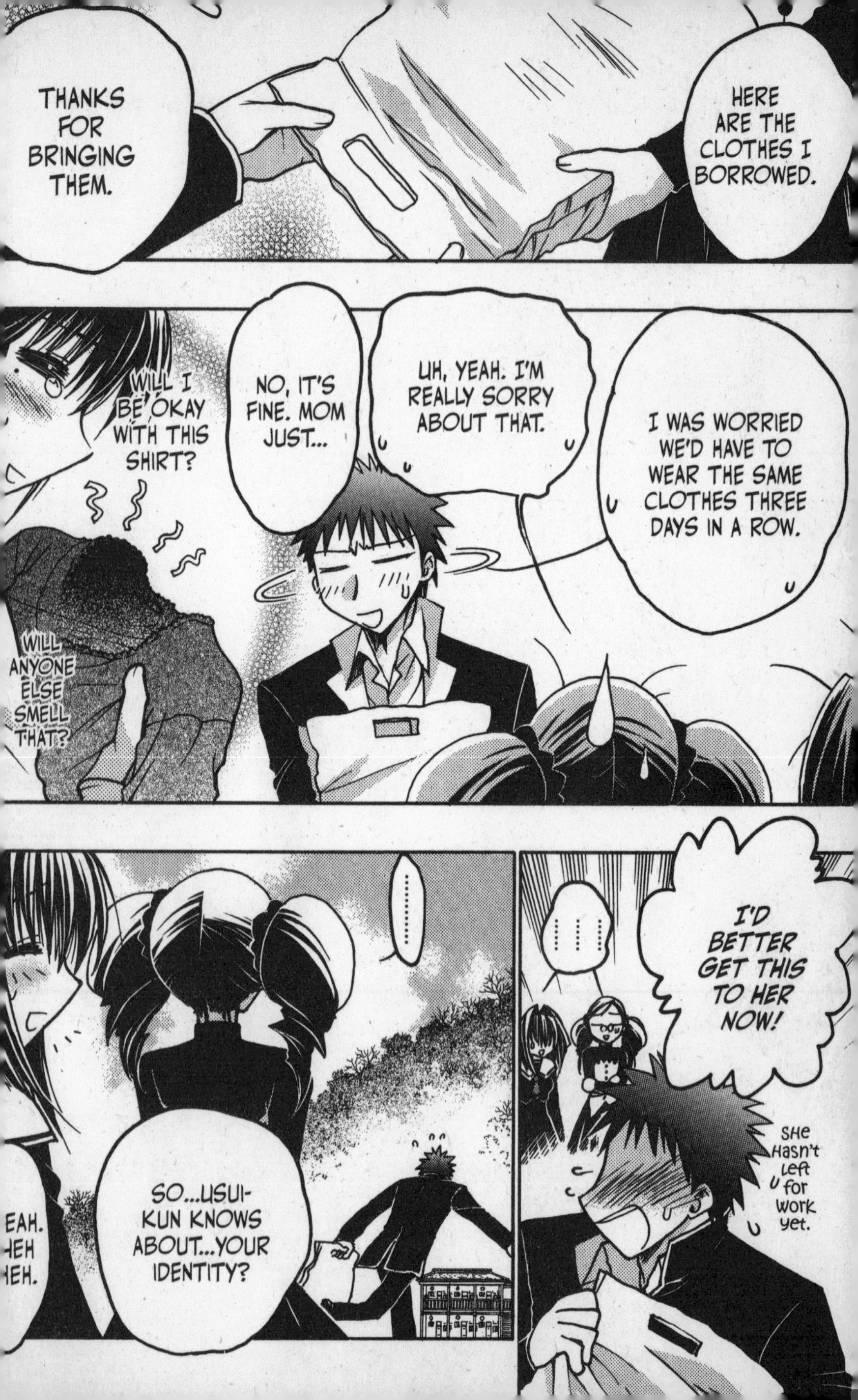
HERE ARE THE CLOTHES I BORROWED.
THANKS FOR BRINGING THEM.
I WAS WORRIED WE'D HAVE TO WEAR THE SAME CLOTHES THREE DAYS IN A ROW.
UH, YEAH. I'M REALLY SORRY ABOUT THAT.
NO, IT'S FINE. MOM JUST...
WILL I BE OKAY WITH THIS SHIRT?
WILL ANYONE ELSE SMELL THAT?
I'D BETTER GET THIS TO HER NOW!
......
SHE HASN'T LEFT FOR WORK YET.
......
SO...USUI-KUN KNOWS ABOUT...YOUR IDENTITY?
EAH. HEH HEH.

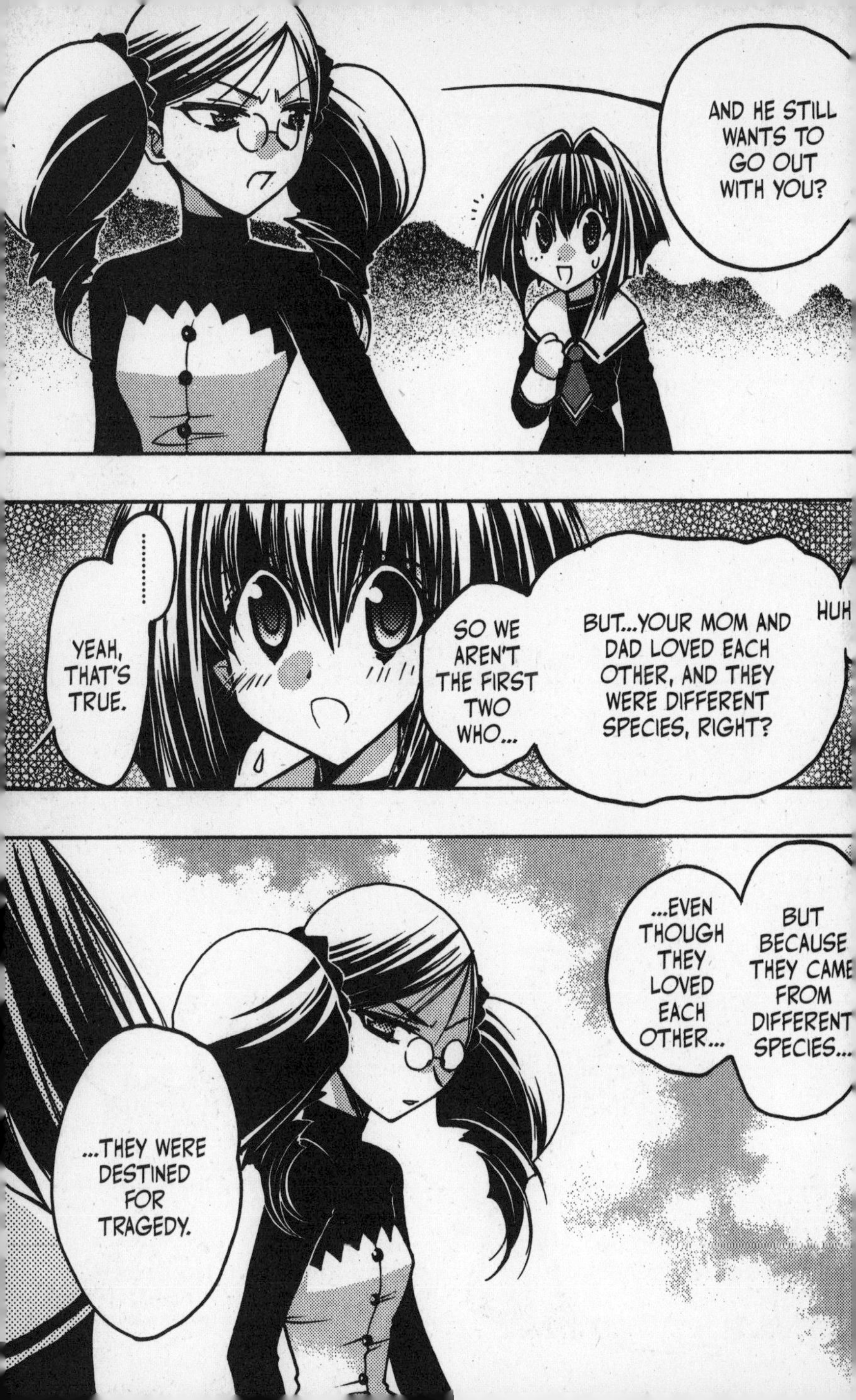
AND HE STILL WANTS TO GO OUT WITH YOU?
HUH
BUT...YOUR MOM AND DAD LOVED EACH OTHER, AND THEY WERE DIFFERENT SPECIES, RIGHT?
SO WE AREN'T THE FIRST TWO WHO...
......
YEAH, THAT'S TRUE.
BUT BECAUSE THEY CAME FROM DIFFERENT SPECIES...
...EVEN THOUGH THEY LOVED EACH OTHER...
...THEY WERE DESTINED FOR TRAGEDY.

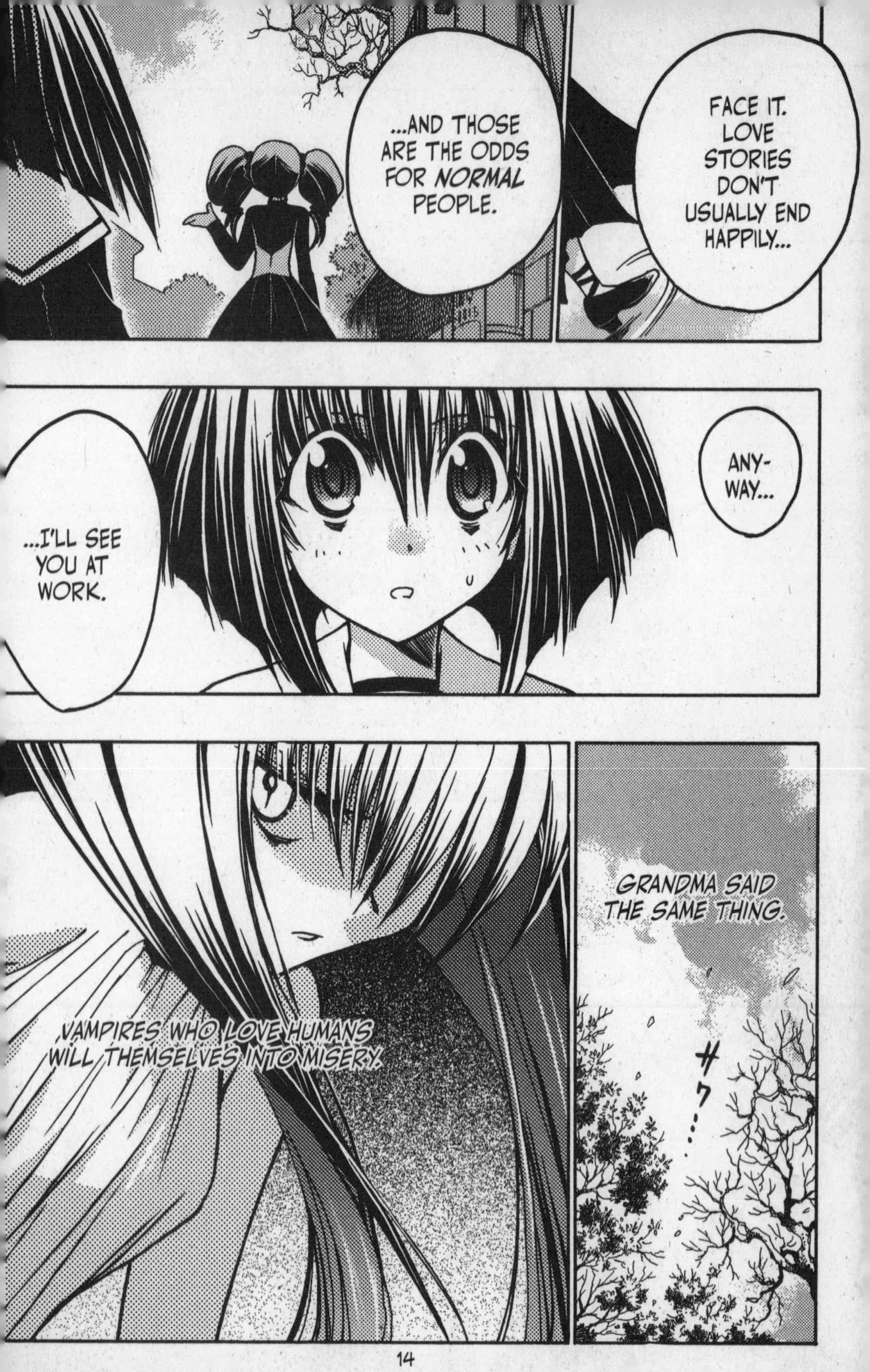
FACE IT. LOVE STORIES DON'T USUALLY END HAPPILY...
...AND THOSE ARE THE ODDS FOR *NORMAL* PEOPLE.
ANY-WAY...
...I'LL SEE YOU AT WORK.
GRANDMA SAID THE SAME THING.
サク...
VAMPIRES WHO LOVE HUMANS WILL THEMSELVES INTO MISERY.

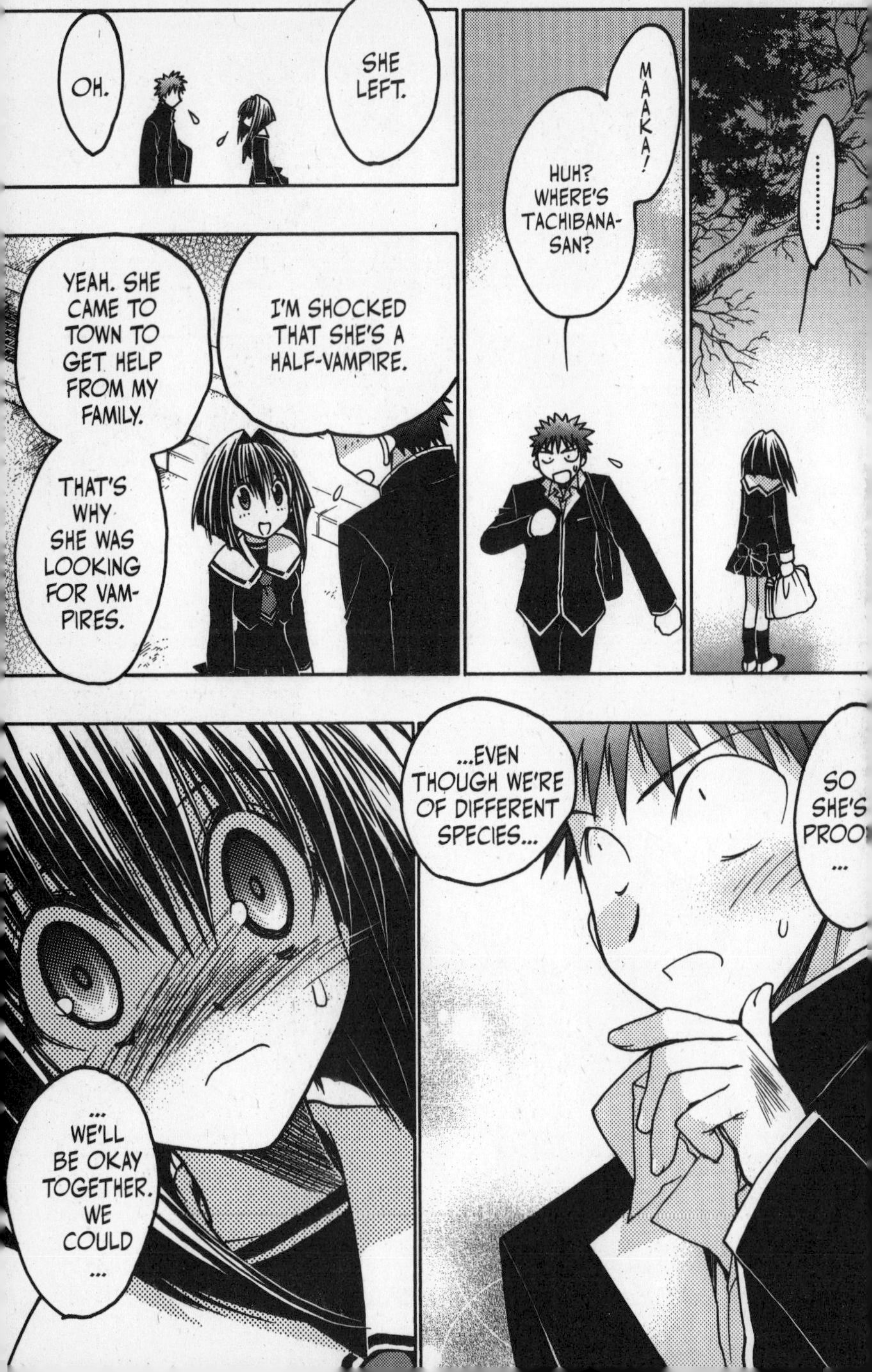
......
MAAKA!
HUH? WHERE'S TACHIBANA-SAN?
SHE LEFT.
OH.
I'M SHOCKED THAT SHE'S A HALF-VAMPIRE.
YEAH. SHE CAME TO TOWN TO GET HELP FROM MY FAMILY.
THAT'S WHY SHE WAS LOOKING FOR VAMPIRES.
SO SHE'S PROO ...
...EVEN THOUGH WE'RE OF DIFFERENT SPECIES...
... WE'LL BE OKAY TOGETHER. WE COULD ...

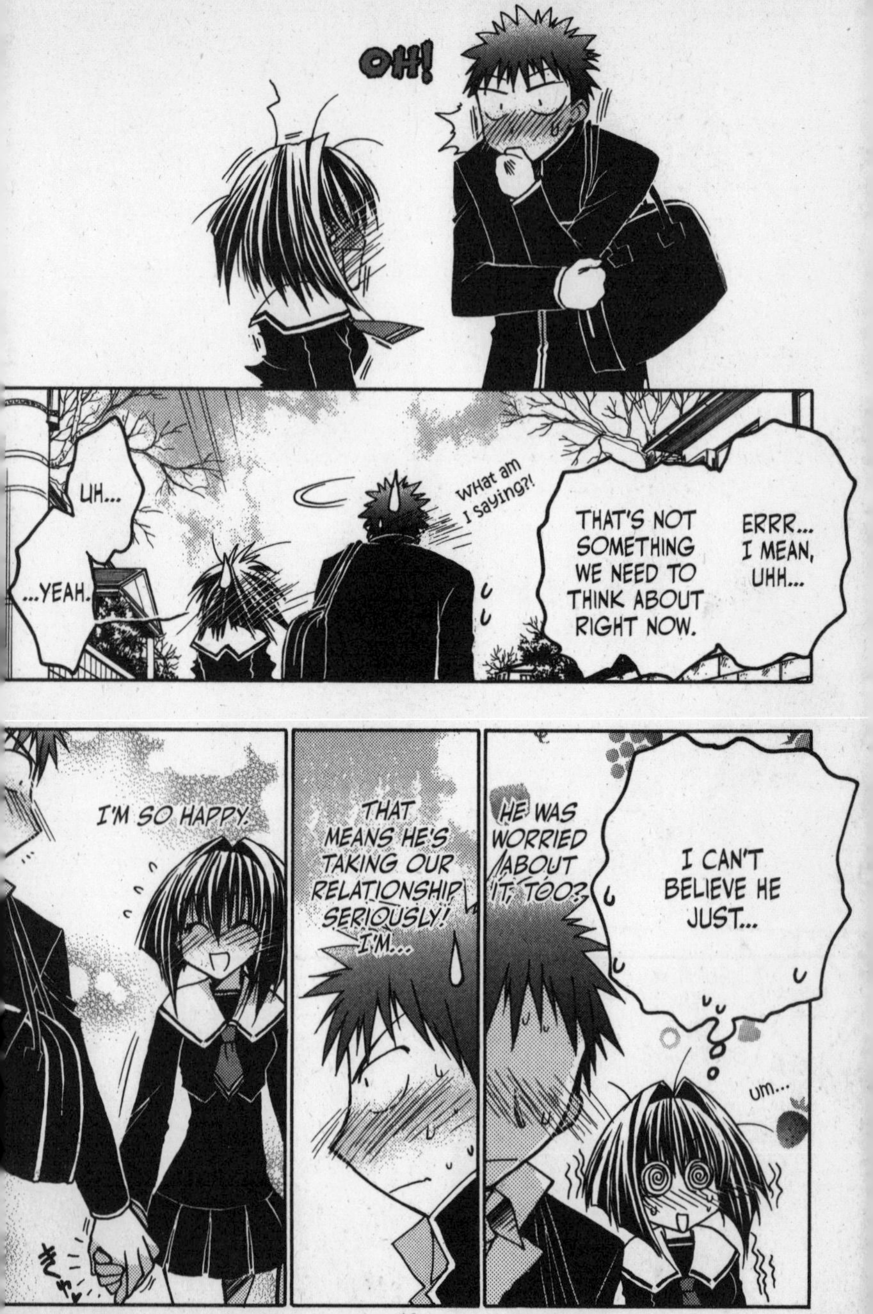
OH!
THAT'S NOT SOMETHING WE NEED TO THINK ABOUT RIGHT NOW.
ERRR... I MEAN, UHH...
What am I saying?!
UH...
...YEAH.
I CAN'T BELIEVE HE JUST...
HE WAS WORRIED ABOUT IT, TOO?
um...
THAT MEANS HE'S TAKING OUR RELATIONSHIP SERIOUSLY! I'M...
I'M SO HAPPY.

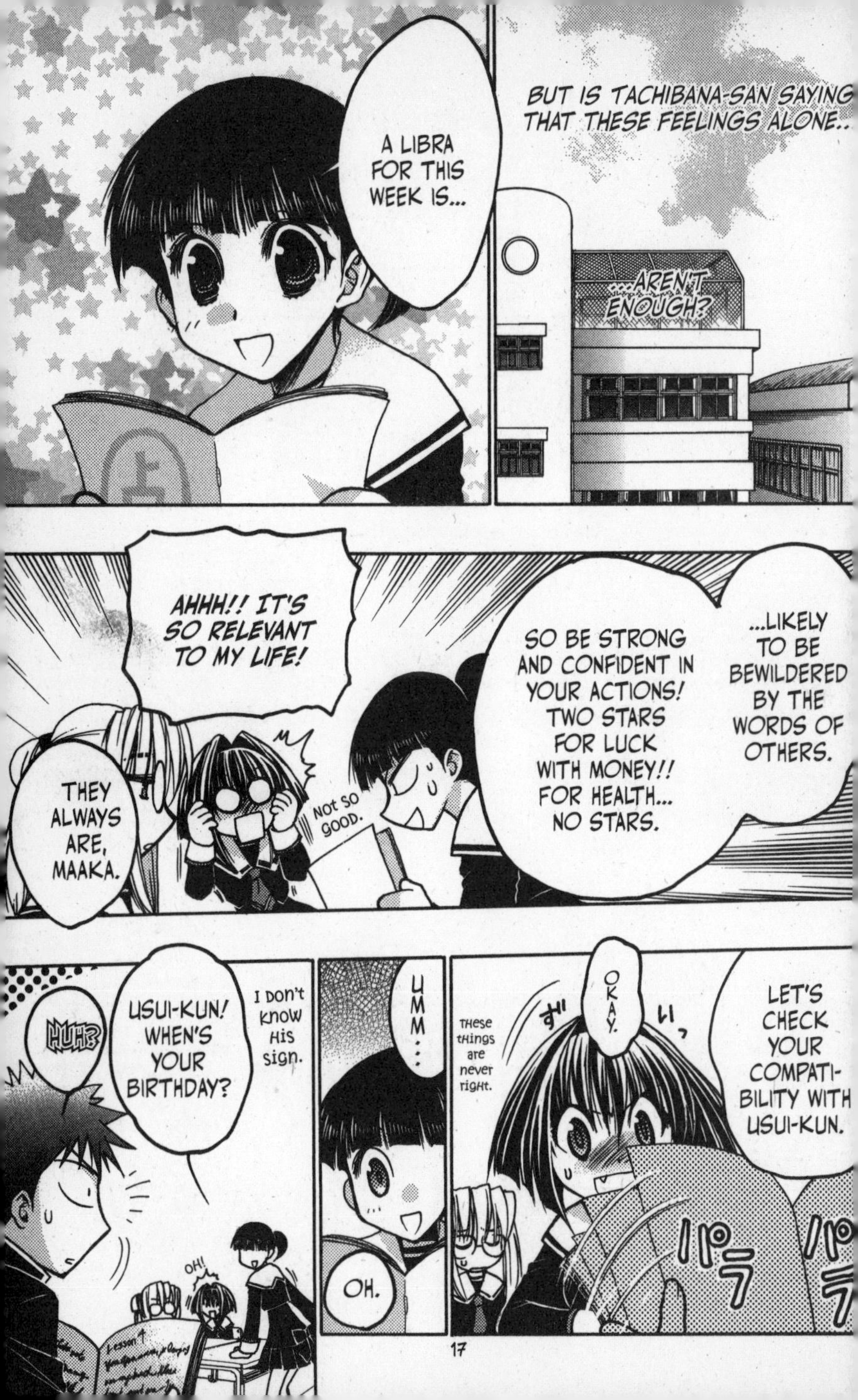
BUT IS TACHIBANA-SAN SAYING THAT THESE FEELINGS ALONE...
...AREN'T ENOUGH?
A LIBRA FOR THIS WEEK IS...
...LIKELY TO BE BEWILDERED BY THE WORDS OF OTHERS.
SO BE STRONG AND CONFIDENT IN YOUR ACTIONS! TWO STARS FOR LUCK WITH MONEY!! FOR HEALTH... NO STARS.
Not so good.
AHHH!! IT'S SO RELEVANT TO MY LIFE!
THEY ALWAYS ARE, MAAKA.
LET'S CHECK YOUR COMPATIBILITY WITH USUI-KUN.
OKAY.
ずい
パラ パラ
These things are never right.
UMM...
OH.
I don't know his sign.
USUI-KUN! WHEN'S YOUR BIRTHDAY?
HUH?
OH!

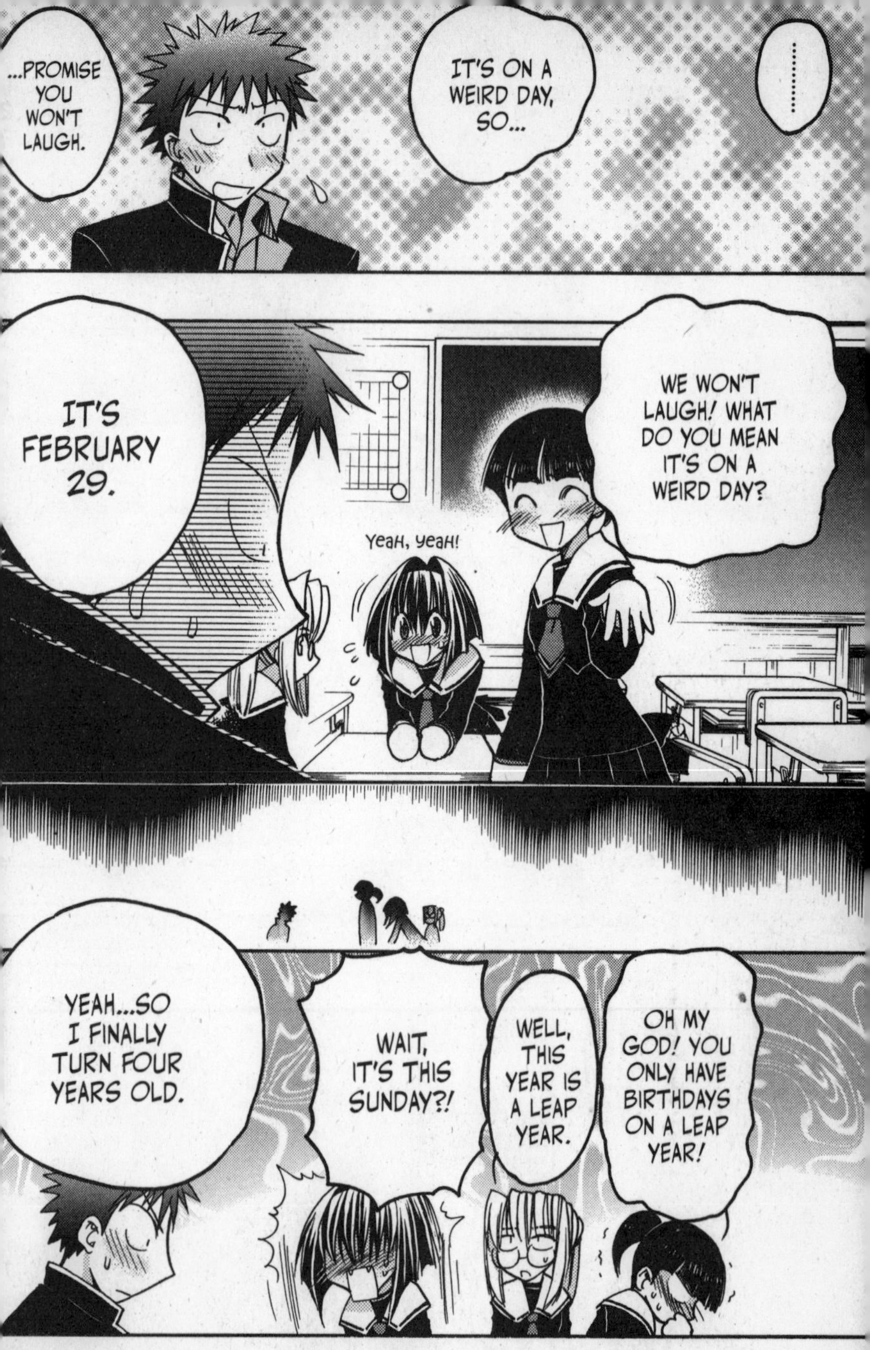
……
IT'S ON A WEIRD DAY, SO...
...PROMISE YOU WON'T LAUGH.
WE WON'T LAUGH! WHAT DO YOU MEAN IT'S ON A WEIRD DAY?
Yeah, yeah!
IT'S FEBRUARY 29.
OH MY GOD! YOU ONLY HAVE BIRTHDAYS ON A LEAP YEAR!
WELL, THIS YEAR IS A LEAP YEAR.
WAIT, IT'S THIS SUNDAY?!
YEAH...SO I FINALLY TURN FOUR YEARS OLD.

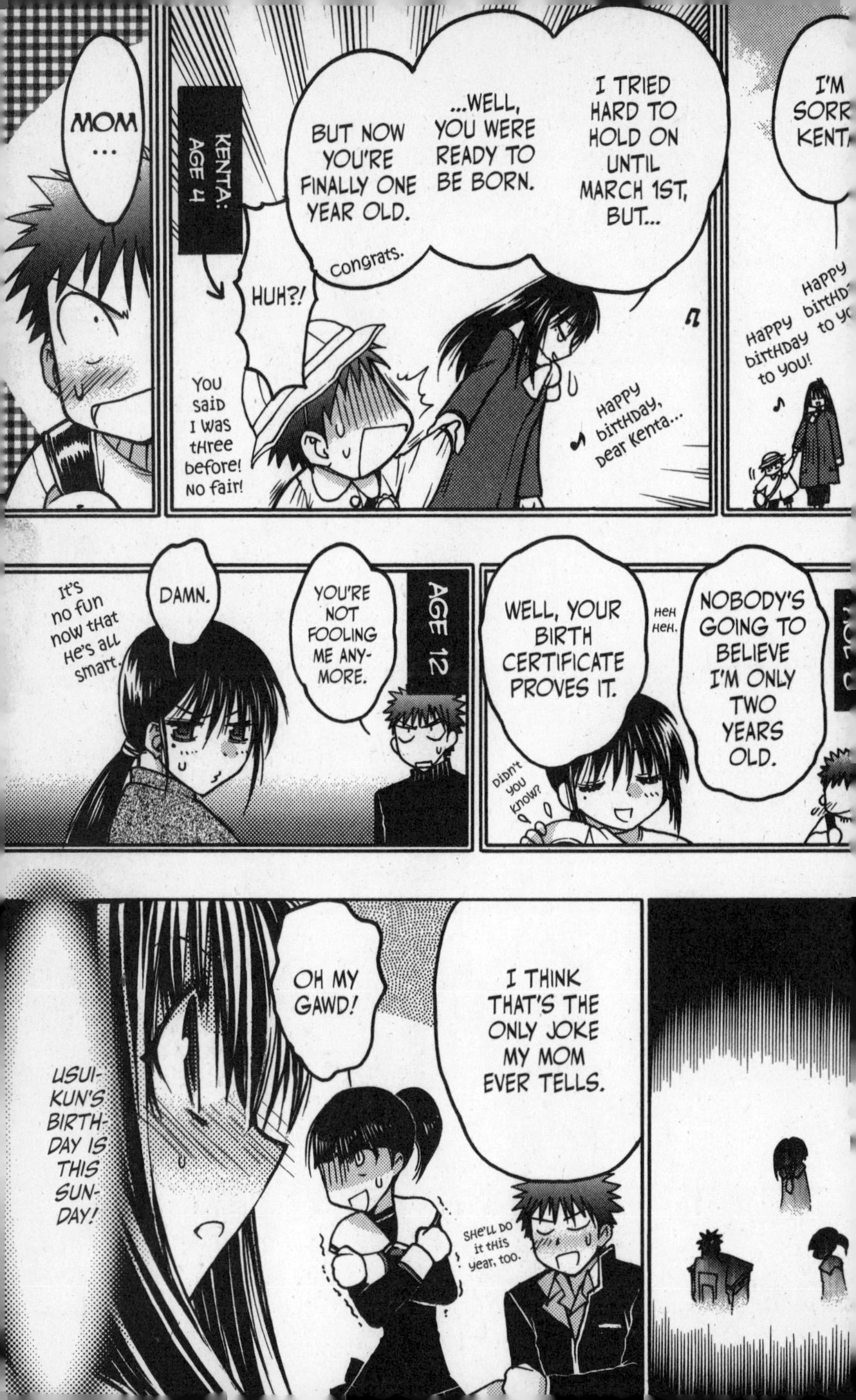
I'M SORR KENT
Happy birthday to yo
Happy birthday to you!
KENTA: AGE 4
I TRIED HARD TO HOLD ON UNTIL MARCH 1ST, BUT...
...WELL, YOU WERE READY TO BE BORN.
BUT NOW YOU'RE FINALLY ONE YEAR OLD.
Congrats.
Happy birthday, dear Kenta...
HUH?!
You said I was three before! No fair!
MOM...
NOBODY'S GOING TO BELIEVE I'M ONLY TWO YEARS OLD.
Heh heh.
WELL, YOUR BIRTH CERTIFICATE PROVES IT.
Didn't you know?
AGE 12
YOU'RE NOT FOOLING ME ANYMORE.
DAMN.
It's no fun now that he's all smart.
I THINK THAT'S THE ONLY JOKE MY MOM EVER TELLS.
She'll do it this year, too.
OH MY GAWD!
USUI-KUN'S BIRTHDAY IS THIS SUNDAY!

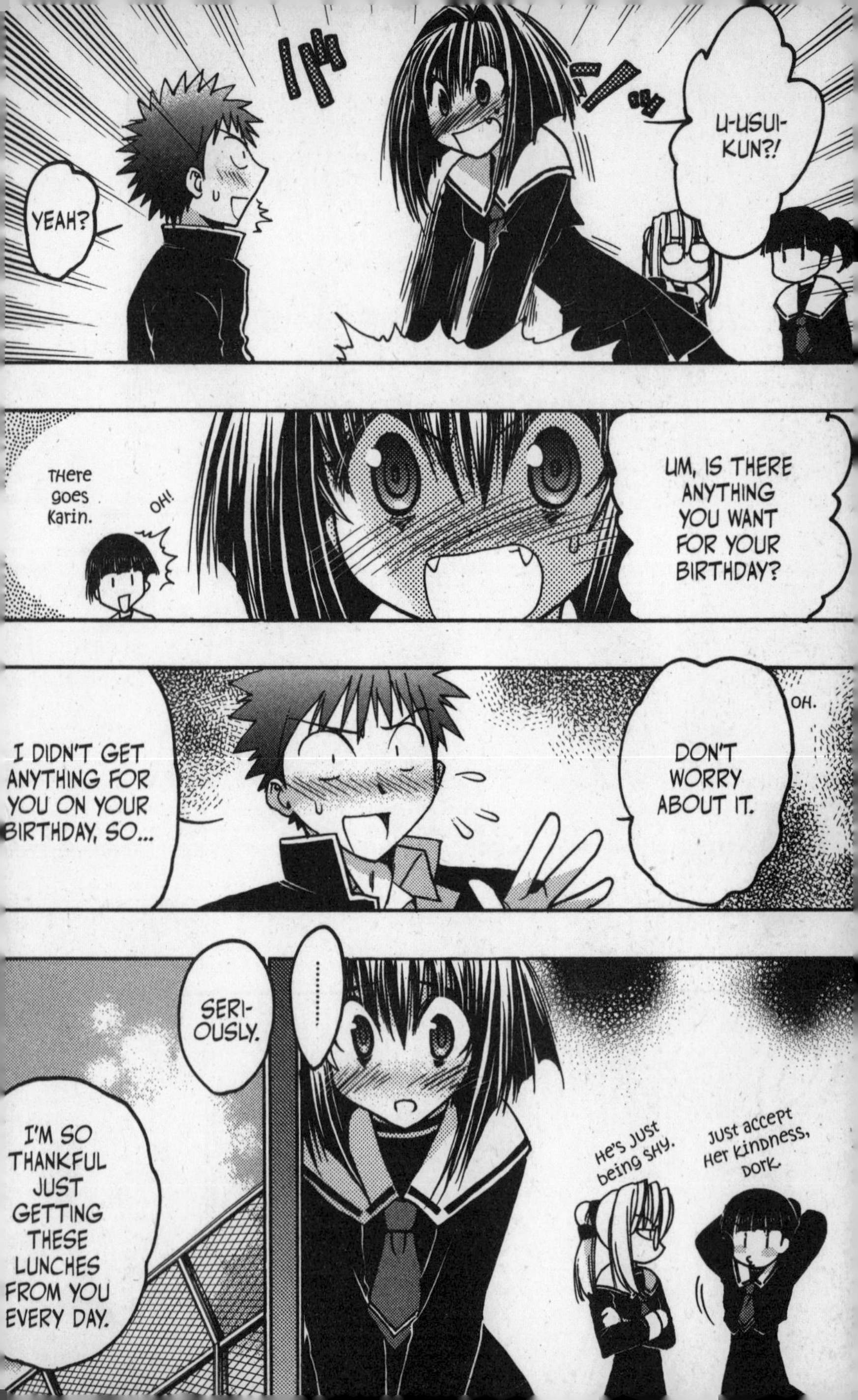
U-USUI-KUN?!
YEAH?
UM, IS THERE ANYTHING YOU WANT FOR YOUR BIRTHDAY?
OH!
There goes Karin.
OH.
DON'T WORRY ABOUT IT.
I DIDN'T GET ANYTHING FOR YOU ON YOUR BIRTHDAY, SO...
......
SERI-OUSLY.
Just accept her kindness, dork.
He's just being shy.
I'M SO THANKFUL JUST GETTING THESE LUNCHES FROM YOU EVERY DAY.

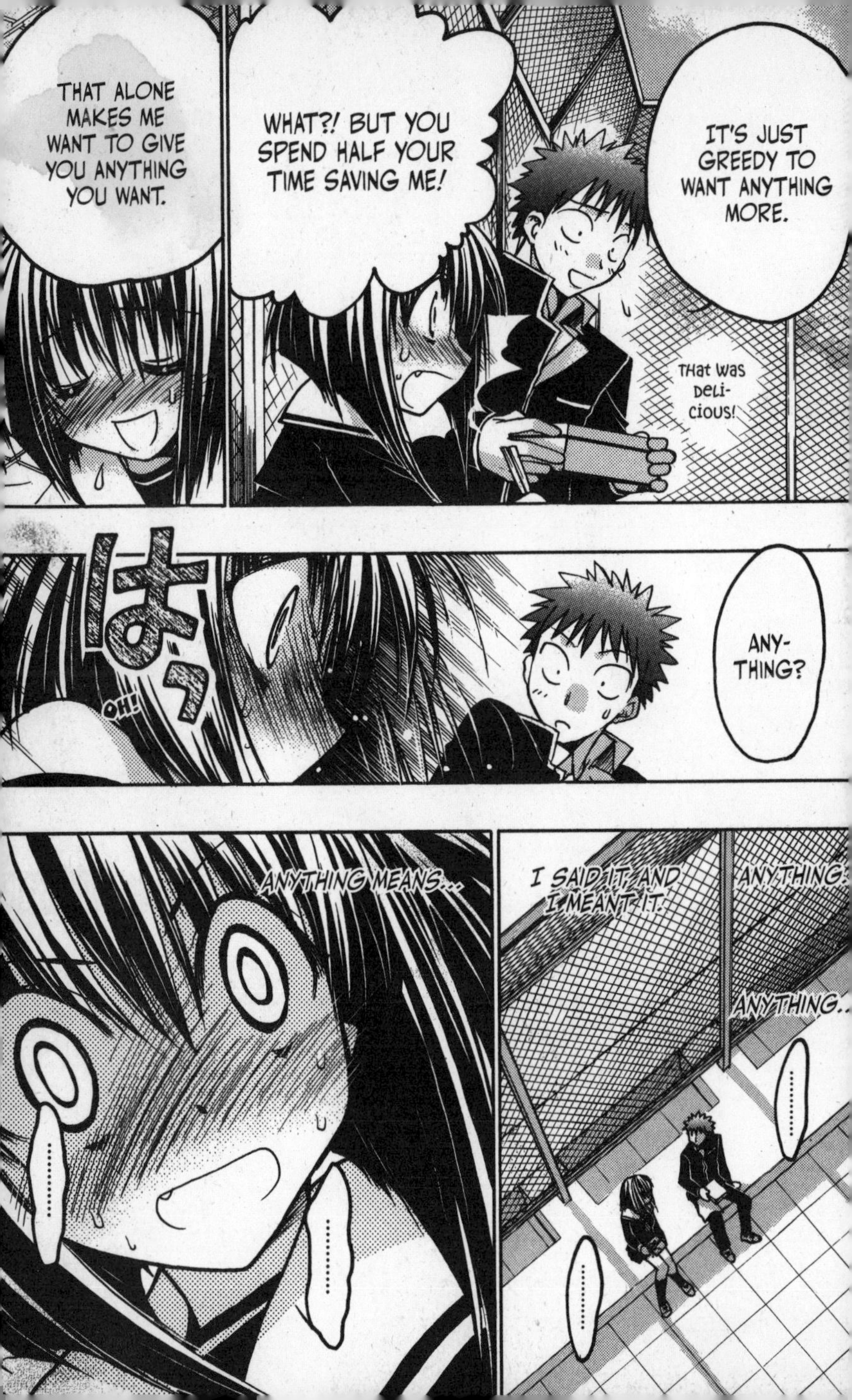
IT'S JUST GREEDY TO WANT ANYTHING MORE.
That was Deli-cious!
WHAT?! BUT YOU SPEND HALF YOUR TIME SAVING ME!
THAT ALONE MAKES ME WANT TO GIVE YOU ANYTHING YOU WANT.
ANY-THING?
はっ
OH!
ANYTHING.
I SAID IT AND I MEANT IT.
ANYTHING...
......
......
ANYTHING MEANS...
......
......

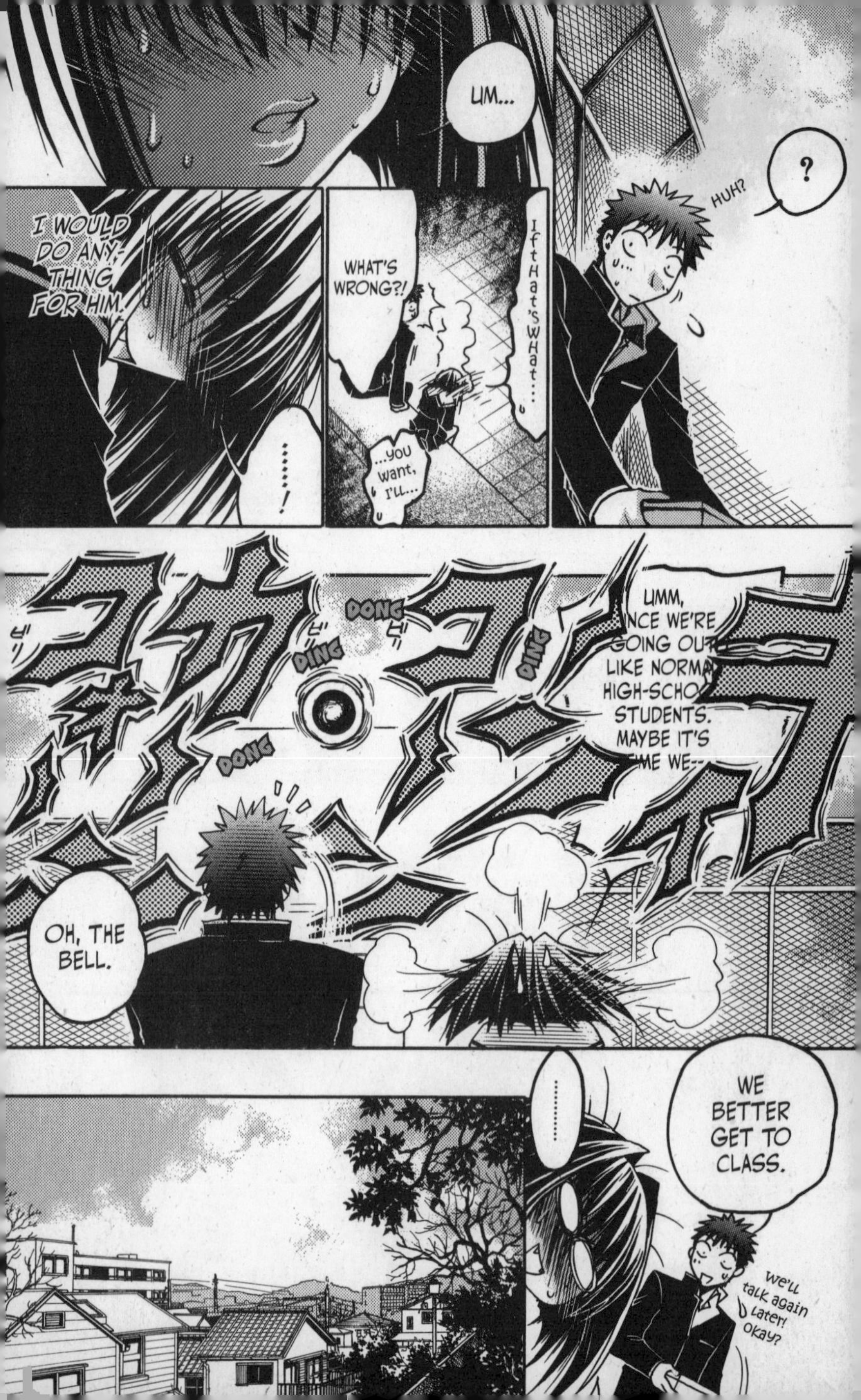
HUH?
?
UM...
WHAT'S WRONG?!
If that's what...
...you want, I'll...
I WOULD DO ANY-THING FOR HIM.
.....!
UMM, NCE WE'RE GOING OUT LIKE NORMA HIGH-SCHO STUDENTS. MAYBE IT'S ME WE--
DING
DONG
DING
DONG
OH, THE BELL.
......
WE BETTER GET TO CLASS.
We'll talk again later! Okay?

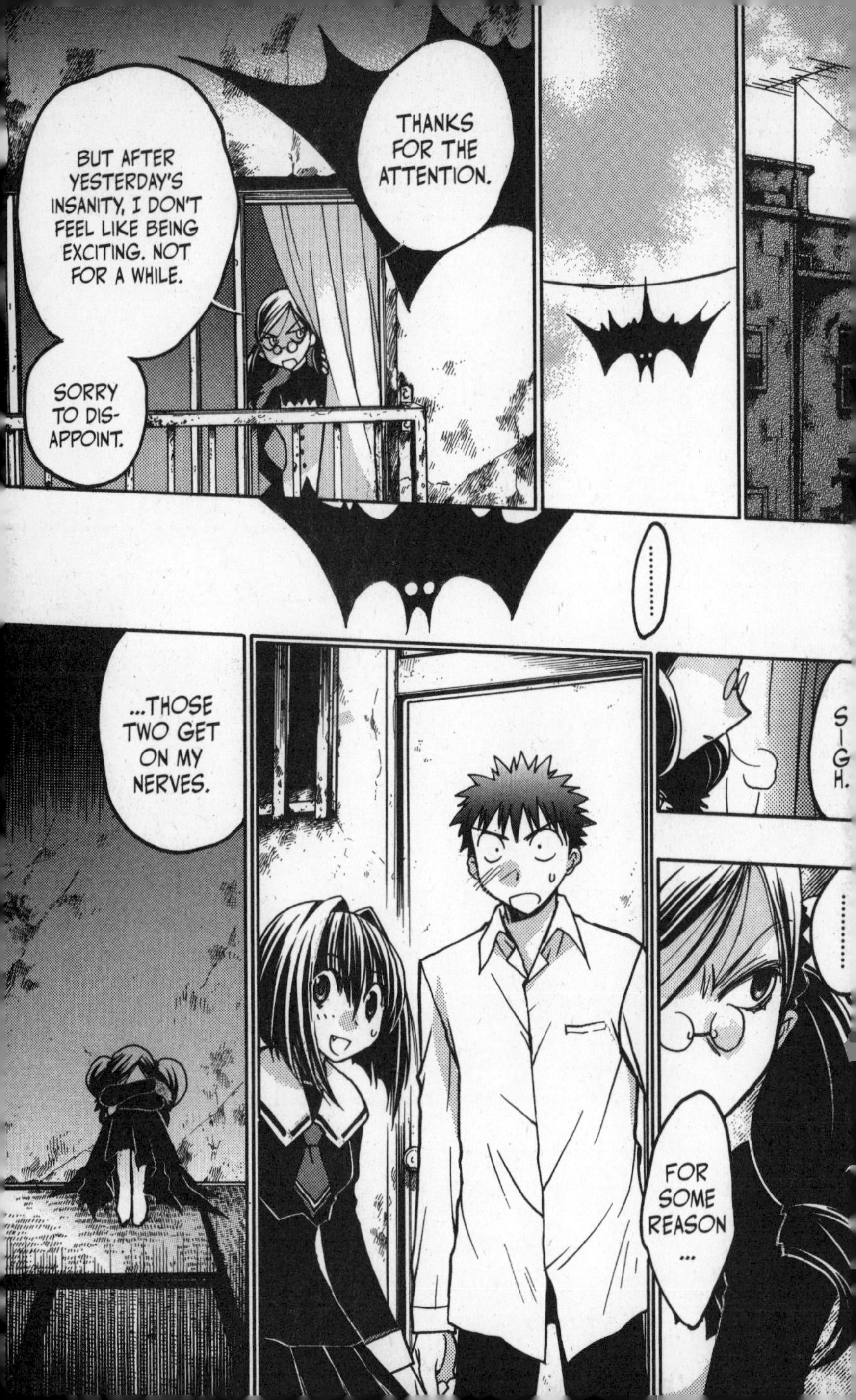
THANKS FOR THE ATTENTION.
BUT AFTER YESTERDAY'S INSANITY, I DON'T FEEL LIKE BEING EXCITING. NOT FOR A WHILE.
SORRY TO DIS-APPOINT.
......
SIGH.
......
FOR SOME REASON ...
...THOSE TWO GET ON MY NERVES.

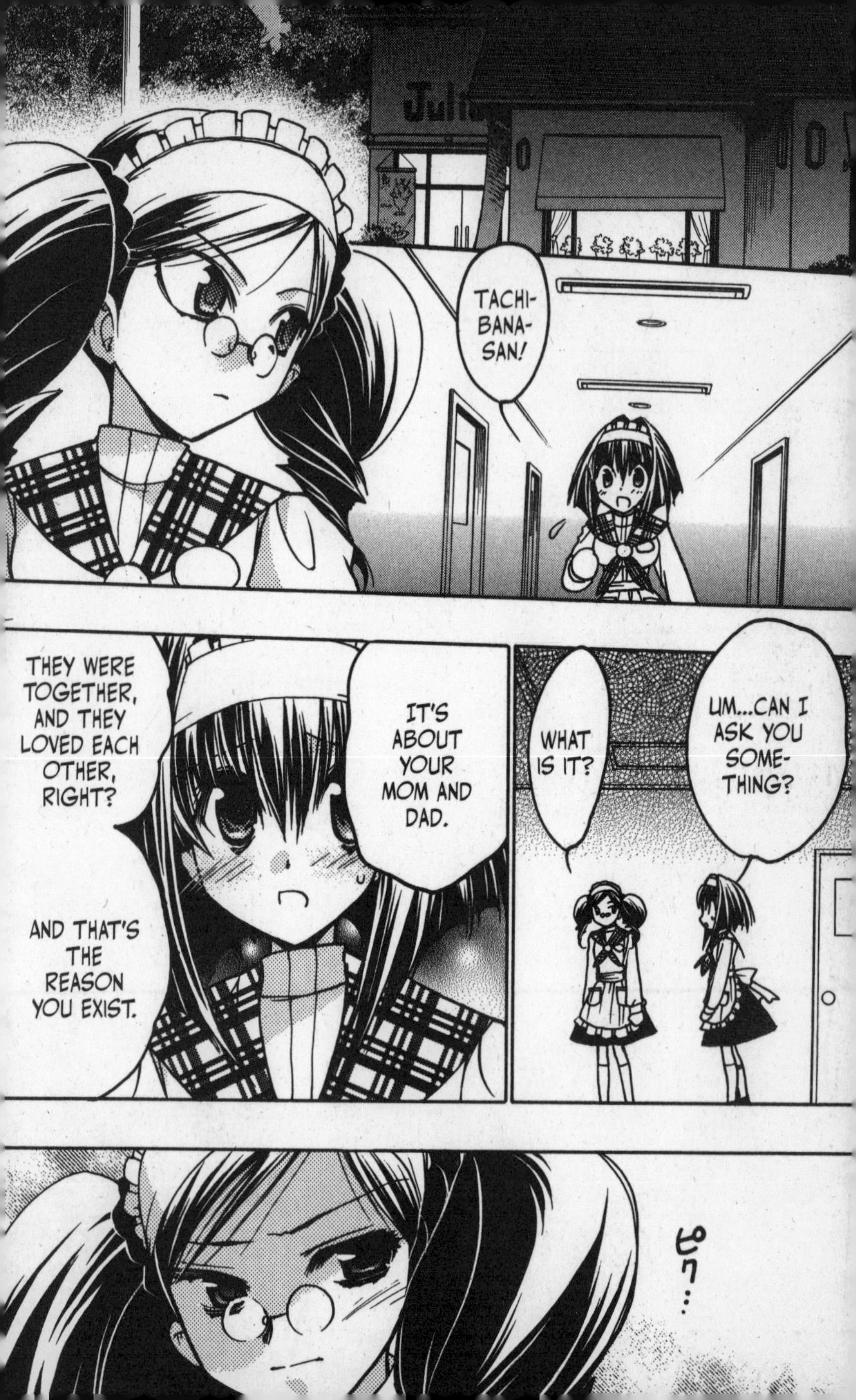
TACHI-BANA-SAN!
UM...CAN I ASK YOU SOME-THING?
WHAT IS IT?
IT'S ABOUT YOUR MOM AND DAD.
THEY WERE TOGETHER, AND THEY LOVED EACH OTHER, RIGHT?
AND THAT'S THE REASON YOU EXIST.
ピク…

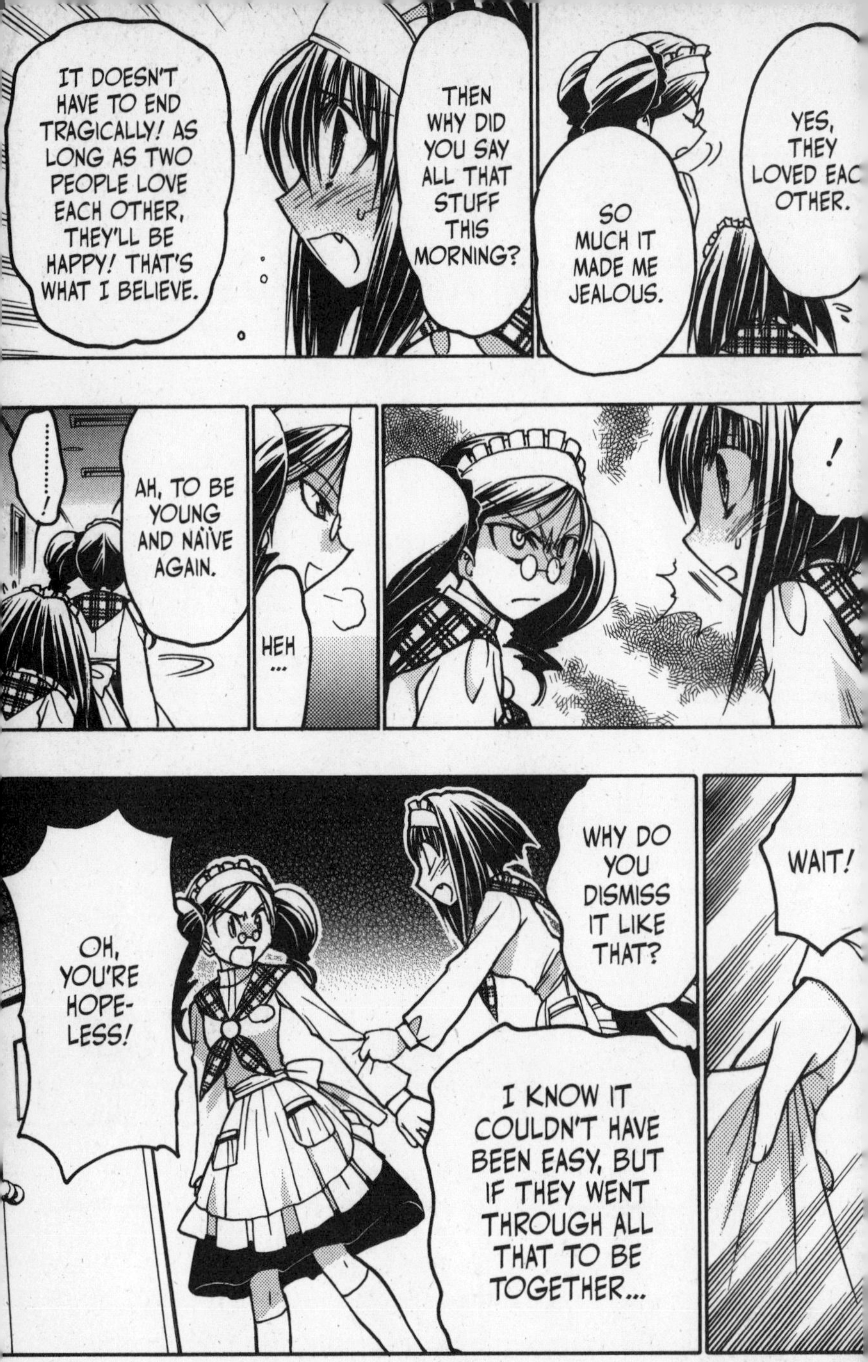
YES, THEY LOVED EAC OTHER.
SO MUCH IT MADE ME JEALOUS.
THEN WHY DID YOU SAY ALL THAT STUFF THIS MORNING?
IT DOESN'T HAVE TO END TRAGICALLY! AS LONG AS TWO PEOPLE LOVE EACH OTHER, THEY'LL BE HAPPY! THAT'S WHAT I BELIEVE.
!
HEH...
AH, TO BE YOUNG AND NAÏVE AGAIN.
......!
WAIT!
WHY DO YOU DISMISS IT LIKE THAT?
I KNOW IT COULDN'T HAVE BEEN EASY, BUT IF THEY WENT THROUGH ALL THAT TO BE TOGETHER...
OH, YOU'RE HOPE-LESS!

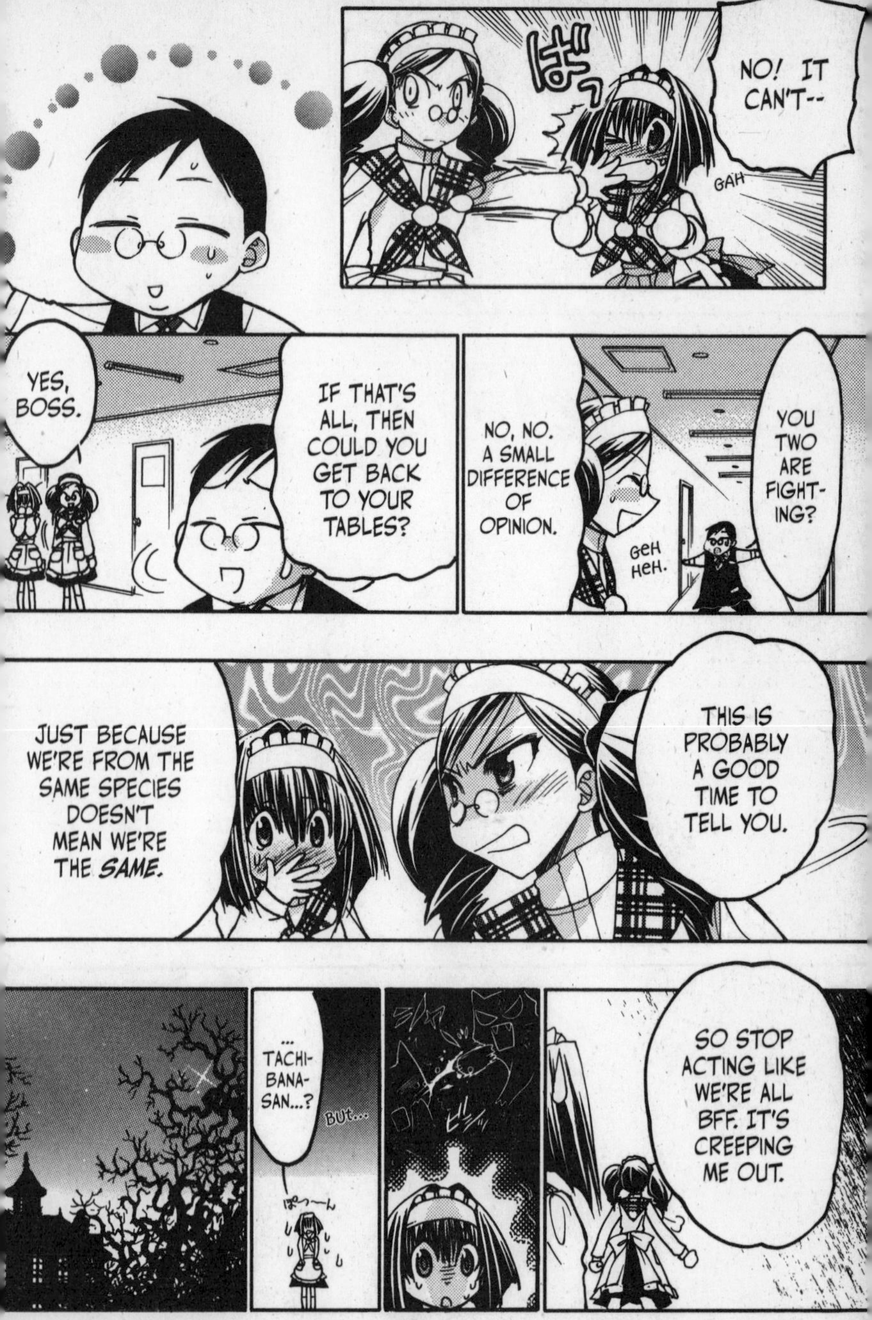
NO! IT CAN'T--
GAH
YOU TWO ARE FIGHT-ING?
NO, NO. A SMALL DIFFERENCE OF OPINION.
GEH HEH.
IF THAT'S ALL, THEN COULD YOU GET BACK TO YOUR TABLES?
YES, BOSS.
THIS IS PROBABLY A GOOD TIME TO TELL YOU.
JUST BECAUSE WE'RE FROM THE SAME SPECIES DOESN'T MEAN WE'RE THE *SAME*.
SO STOP ACTING LIKE WE'RE ALL BFF. IT'S CREEPING ME OUT.
...TACHI-BANA-SAN...?
BUT...

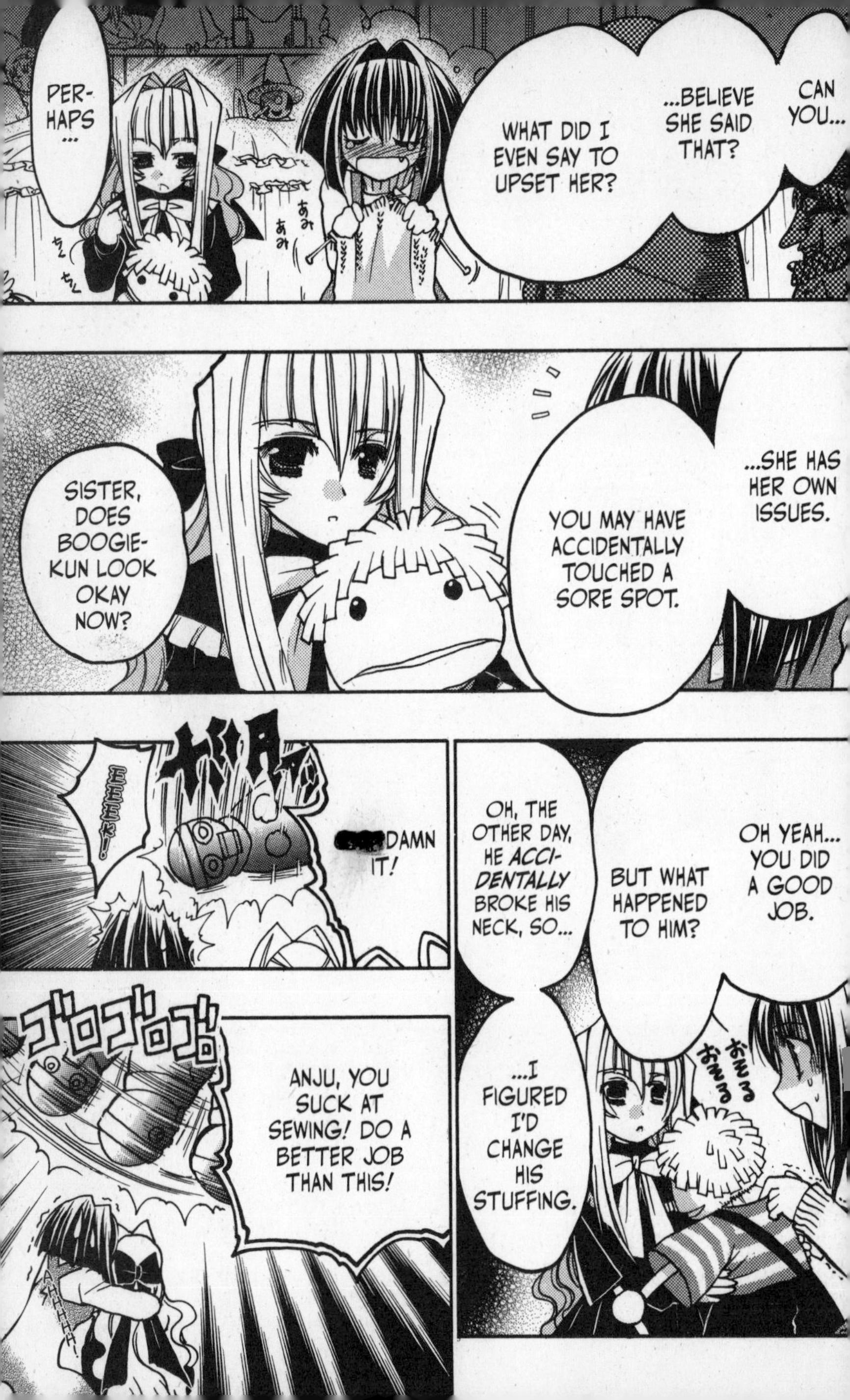
CAN YOU...
...BELIEVE SHE SAID THAT?
WHAT DID I EVEN SAY TO UPSET HER?
あみ あみ
PER-HAPS...
ちく ちく
...SHE HAS HER OWN ISSUES.
YOU MAY HAVE ACCIDENTALLY TOUCHED A SORE SPOT.
SISTER, DOES BOOGIE-KUN LOOK OKAY NOW?
OH YEAH... YOU DID A GOOD JOB.
BUT WHAT HAPPENED TO HIM?
OH, THE OTHER DAY, HE *ACCIDENTALLY* BROKE HIS NECK, SO...
...I FIGURED I'D CHANGE HIS STUFFING.
おそるおそる
[redacted] DAMN IT!
EEEEK!
ゴロゴロゴロ
ANJU, YOU SUCK AT SEWING! DO A BETTER JOB THAN THIS!
AHHHHH!

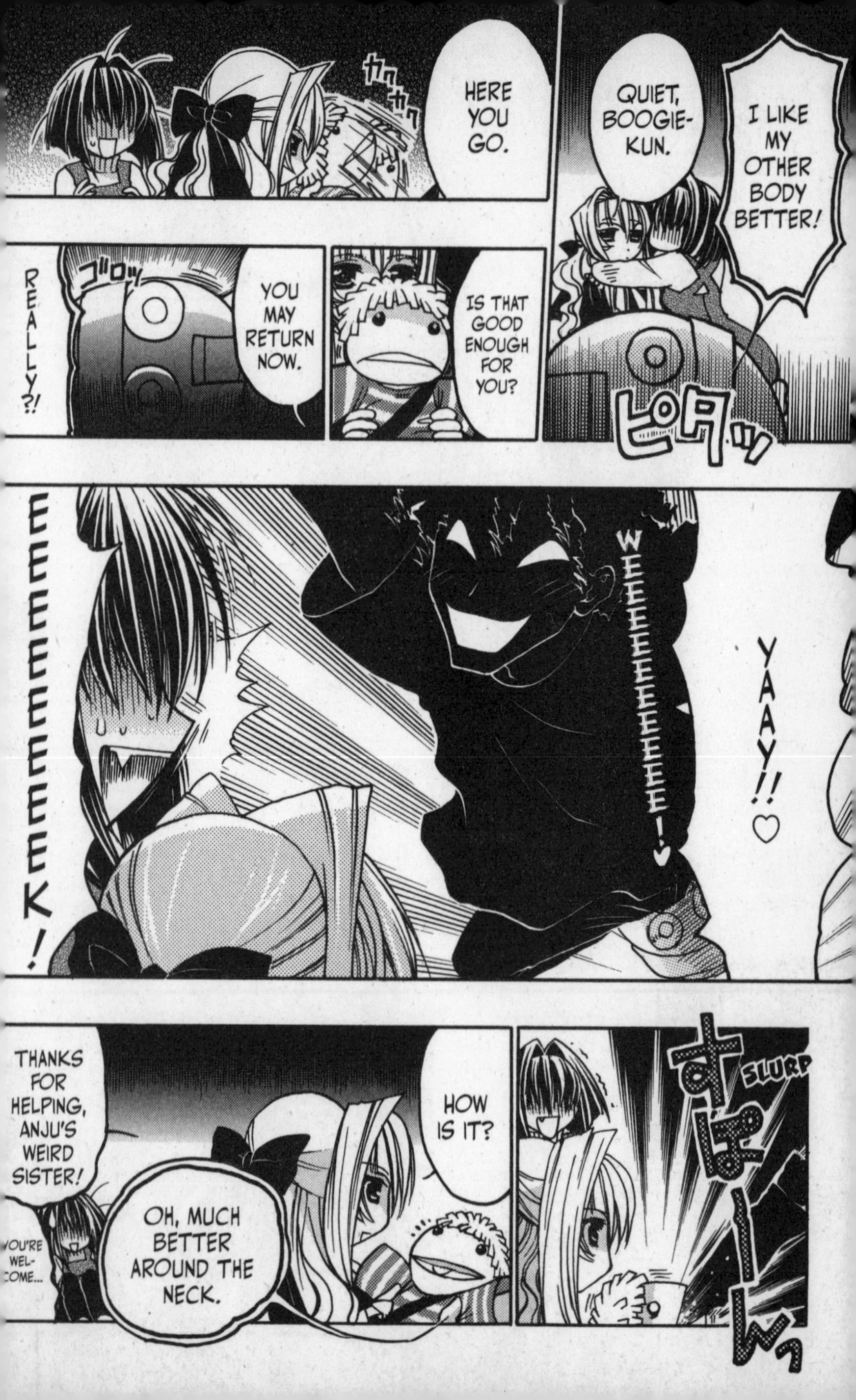
I LIKE MY OTHER BODY BETTER!
QUIET, BOOGIE-KUN.
ピタッ
HERE YOU GO.
IS THAT GOOD ENOUGH FOR YOU?
YOU MAY RETURN NOW.
REALLY?!
YAAY!! ♡
WEEEEEEEEEEEE!
EEEEEEEEEEEEEK!
すぽーん
SLURP
HOW IS IT?
THANKS FOR HELPING, ANJU'S WEIRD SISTER!
OH, MUCH BETTER AROUND THE NECK.
OU'RE WEL-COME...

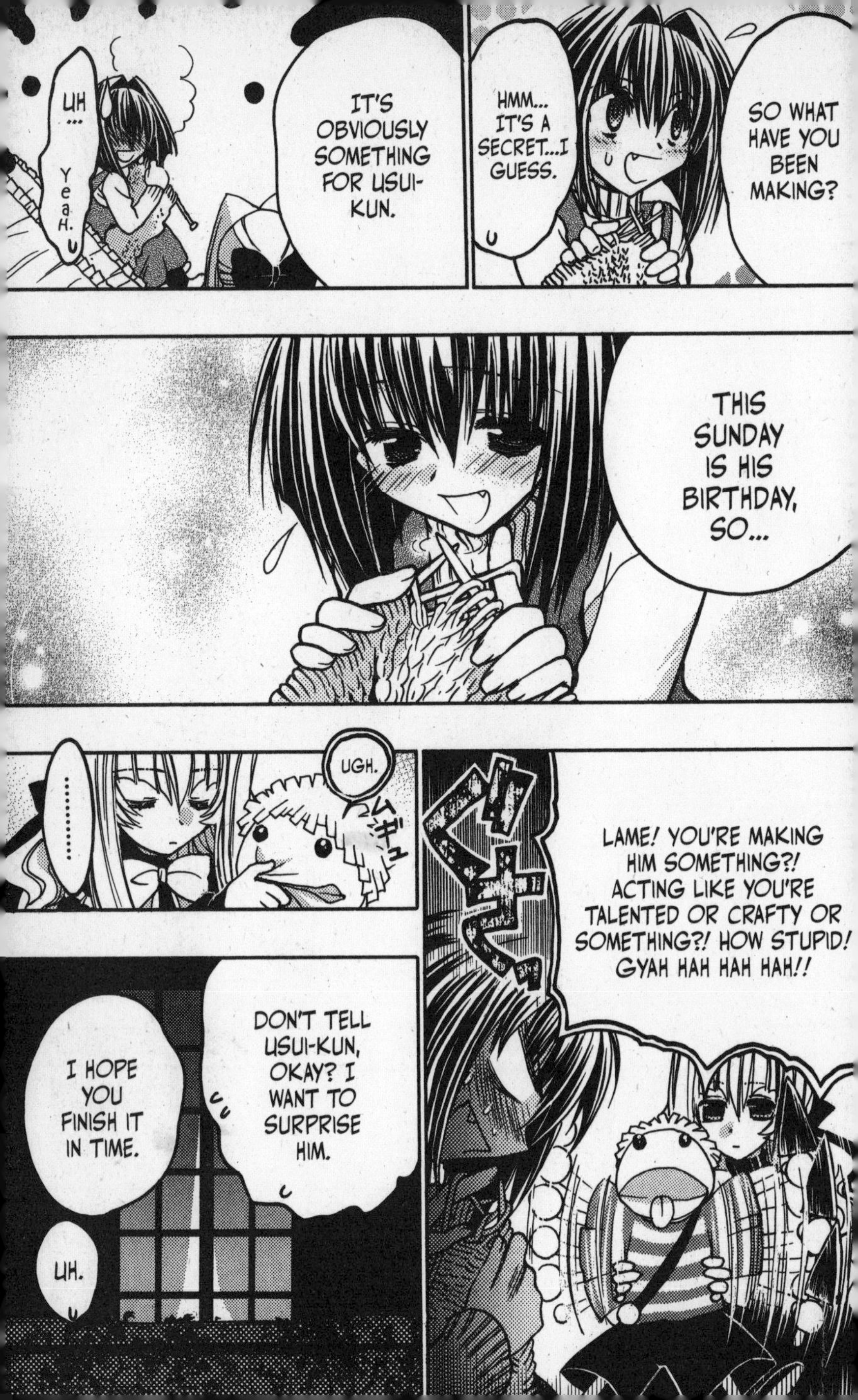
SO WHAT HAVE YOU BEEN MAKING?
HMM... IT'S A SECRET...I GUESS.
IT'S OBVIOUSLY SOMETHING FOR USUI-KUN.
UH... Yeah.
THIS SUNDAY IS HIS BIRTHDAY, SO...
LAME! YOU'RE MAKING HIM SOMETHING?! ACTING LIKE YOU'RE TALENTED OR CRAFTY OR SOMETHING?! HOW STUPID! GYAH HAH HAH HAH!!
UGH.
....
DON'T TELL USUI-KUN, OKAY? I WANT TO SURPRISE HIM.
I HOPE YOU FINISH IT IN TIME.
UH.

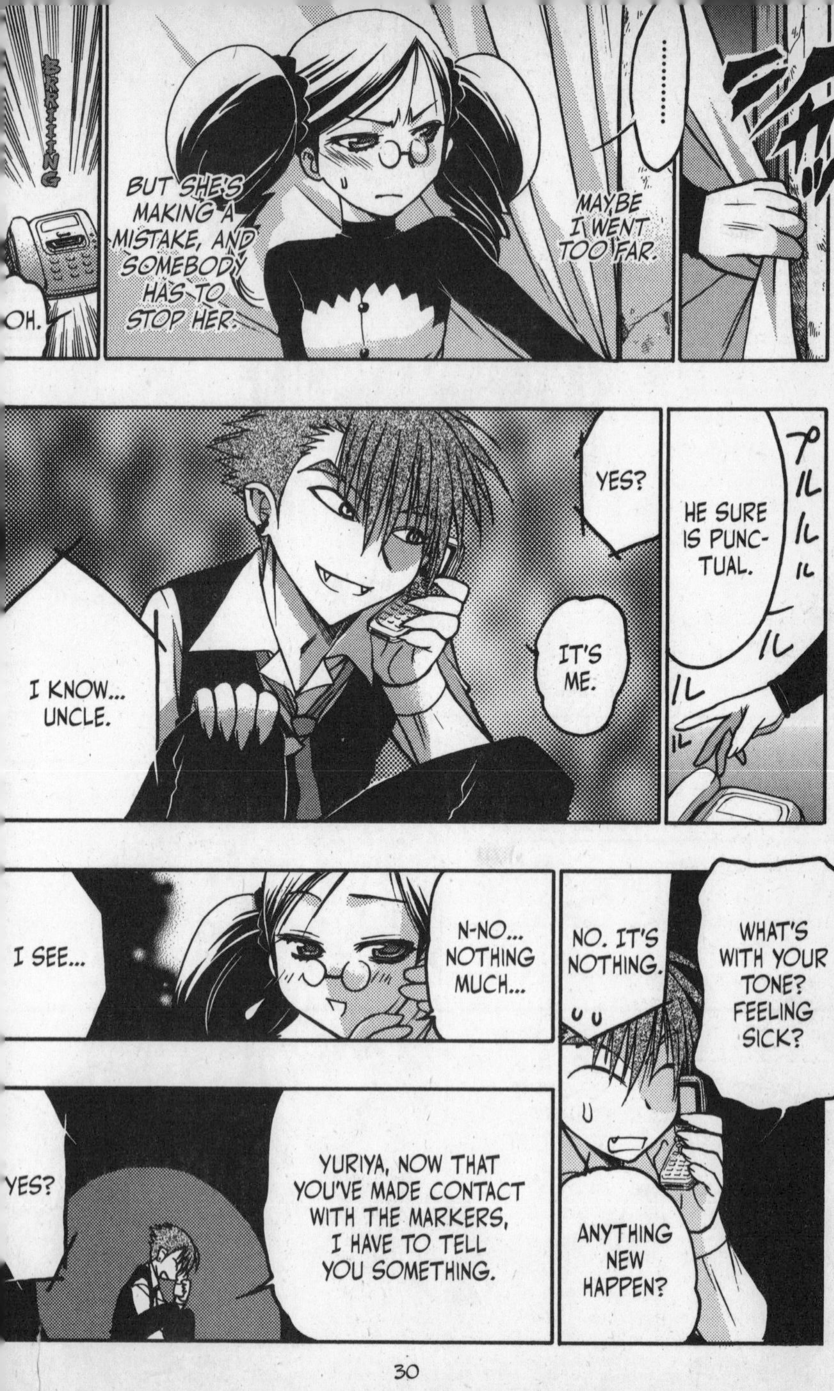
......
MAYBE I WENT TOO FAR.
BUT SHE'S MAKING A MISTAKE, AND SOMEBODY HAS TO STOP HER.
BRRIIING
OH.
HE SURE IS PUNCTUAL.
YES?
IT'S ME.
I KNOW... UNCLE.
WHAT'S WITH YOUR TONE? FEELING SICK?
NO. IT'S NOTHING.
ANYTHING NEW HAPPEN?
N-NO... NOTHING MUCH...
I SEE...
YURIYA, NOW THAT YOU'VE MADE CONTACT WITH THE MARKERS, I HAVE TO TELL YOU SOMETHING.
YES?

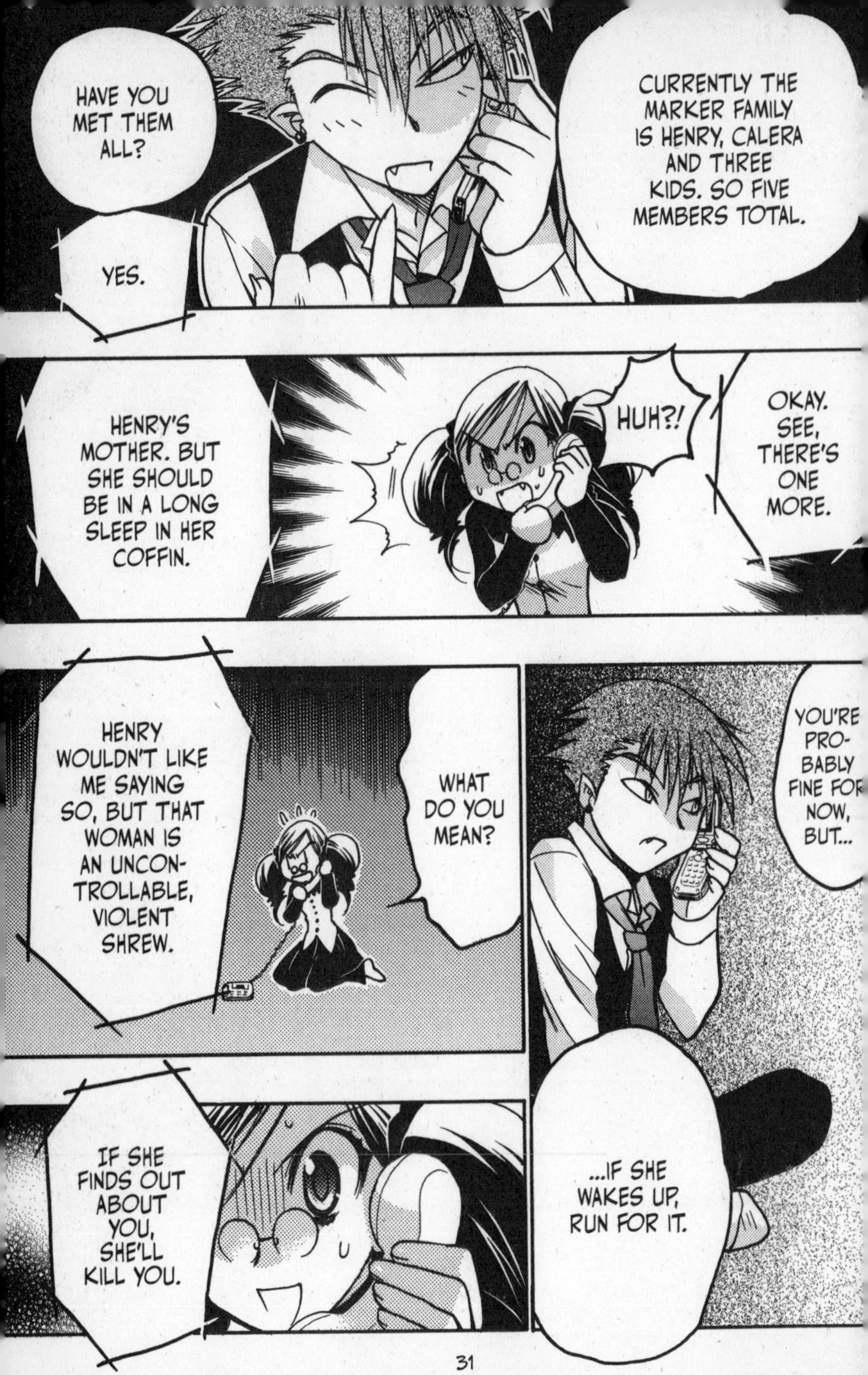
CURRENTLY THE MARKER FAMILY IS HENRY, CALERA AND THREE KIDS. SO FIVE MEMBERS TOTAL.
HAVE YOU MET THEM ALL?
YES.
OKAY. SEE, THERE'S ONE MORE.
HUH?!
HENRY'S MOTHER. BUT SHE SHOULD BE IN A LONG SLEEP IN HER COFFIN.
YOU'RE PRO-BABLY FINE FOR NOW, BUT...
WHAT DO YOU MEAN?
HENRY WOULDN'T LIKE ME SAYING SO, BUT THAT WOMAN IS AN UNCON-TROLLABLE, VIOLENT SHREW.
...IF SHE WAKES UP, RUN FOR IT.
IF SHE FINDS OUT ABOUT YOU, SHE'LL KILL YOU.

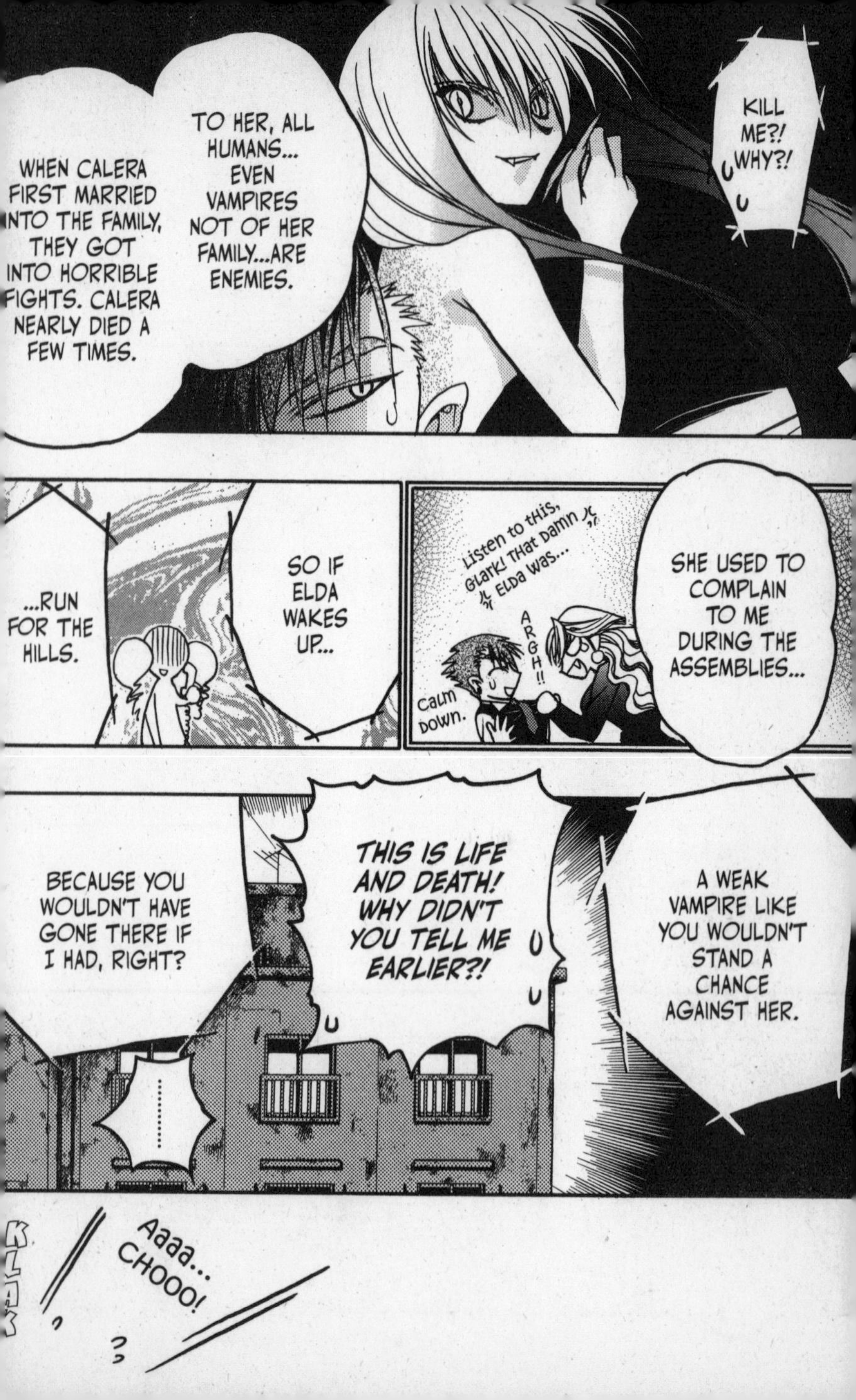
KILL ME?! WHY?!
TO HER, ALL HUMANS... EVEN VAMPIRES NOT OF HER FAMILY...ARE ENEMIES.
WHEN CALERA FIRST MARRIED INTO THE FAMILY, THEY GOT INTO HORRIBLE FIGHTS. CALERA NEARLY DIED A FEW TIMES.
SHE USED TO COMPLAIN TO ME DURING THE ASSEMBLIES...
Listen to this, Glark! That damn Elda was...
ARGH!!
Calm down.
SO IF ELDA WAKES UP...
...RUN FOR THE HILLS.
A WEAK VAMPIRE LIKE YOU WOULDN'T STAND A CHANCE AGAINST HER.
THIS IS LIFE AND DEATH! WHY DIDN'T YOU TELL ME EARLIER?!
BECAUSE YOU WOULDN'T HAVE GONE THERE IF I HAD, RIGHT?
......
Aaaa... CHOOO!
KLAK

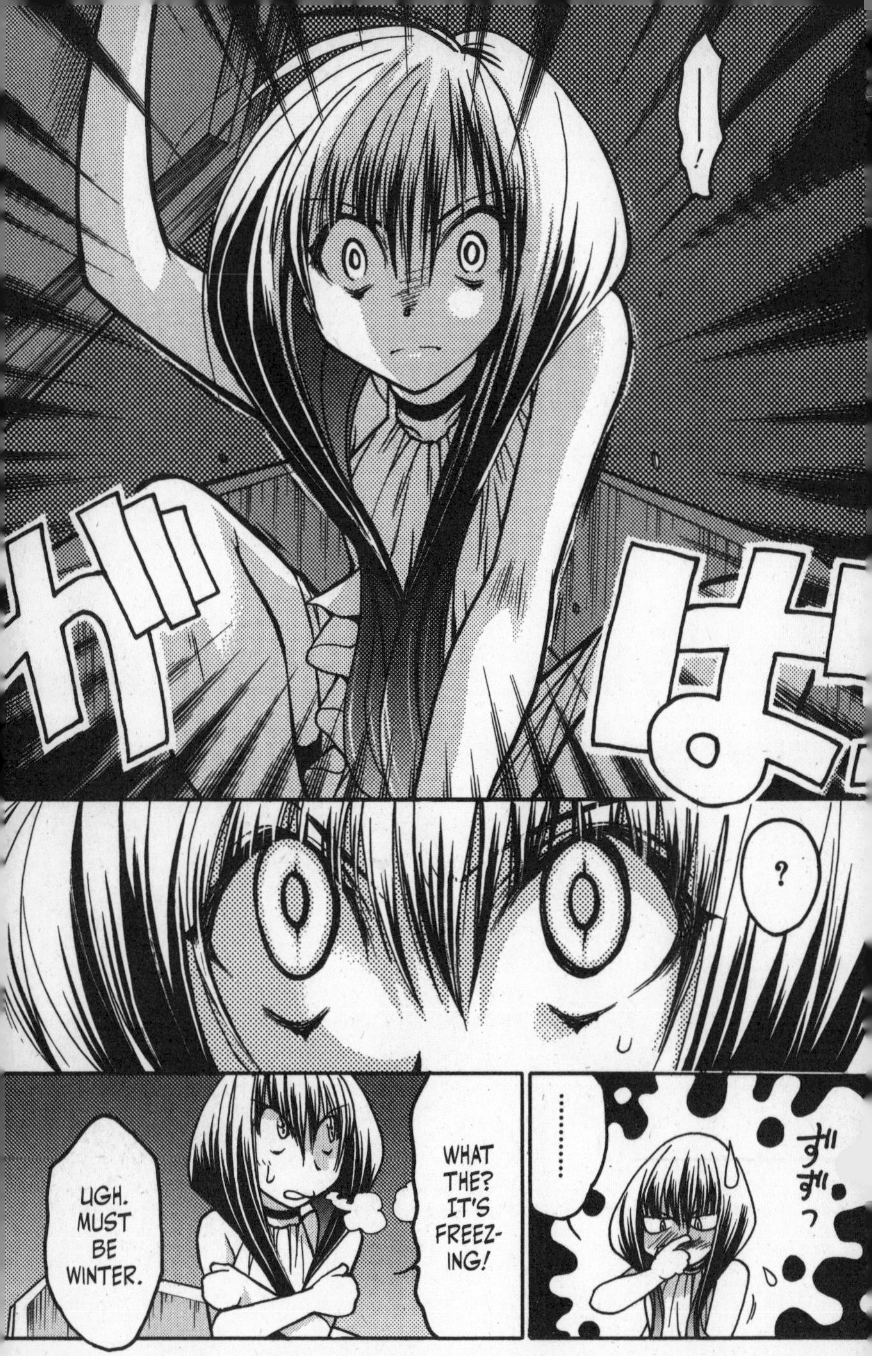
!
?
......
ずずっ
WHAT THE? IT'S FREEZ-ING!
UGH. MUST BE WINTER.

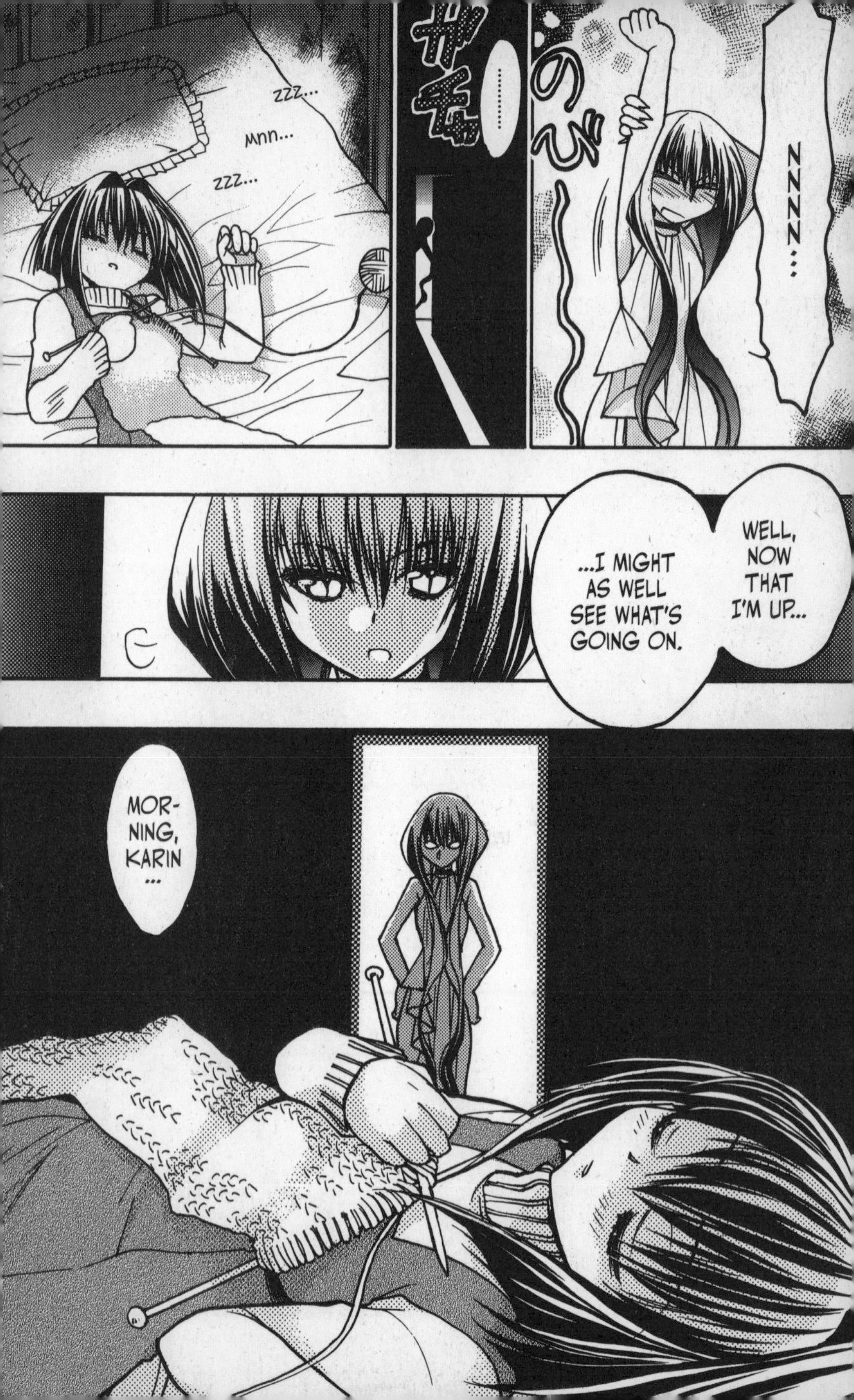
NNNN...
......
zzz...
mnn...
zzz...
WELL, NOW THAT I'M UP...
...I MIGHT AS WELL SEE WHAT'S GOING ON.
MOR-NING, KARIN...

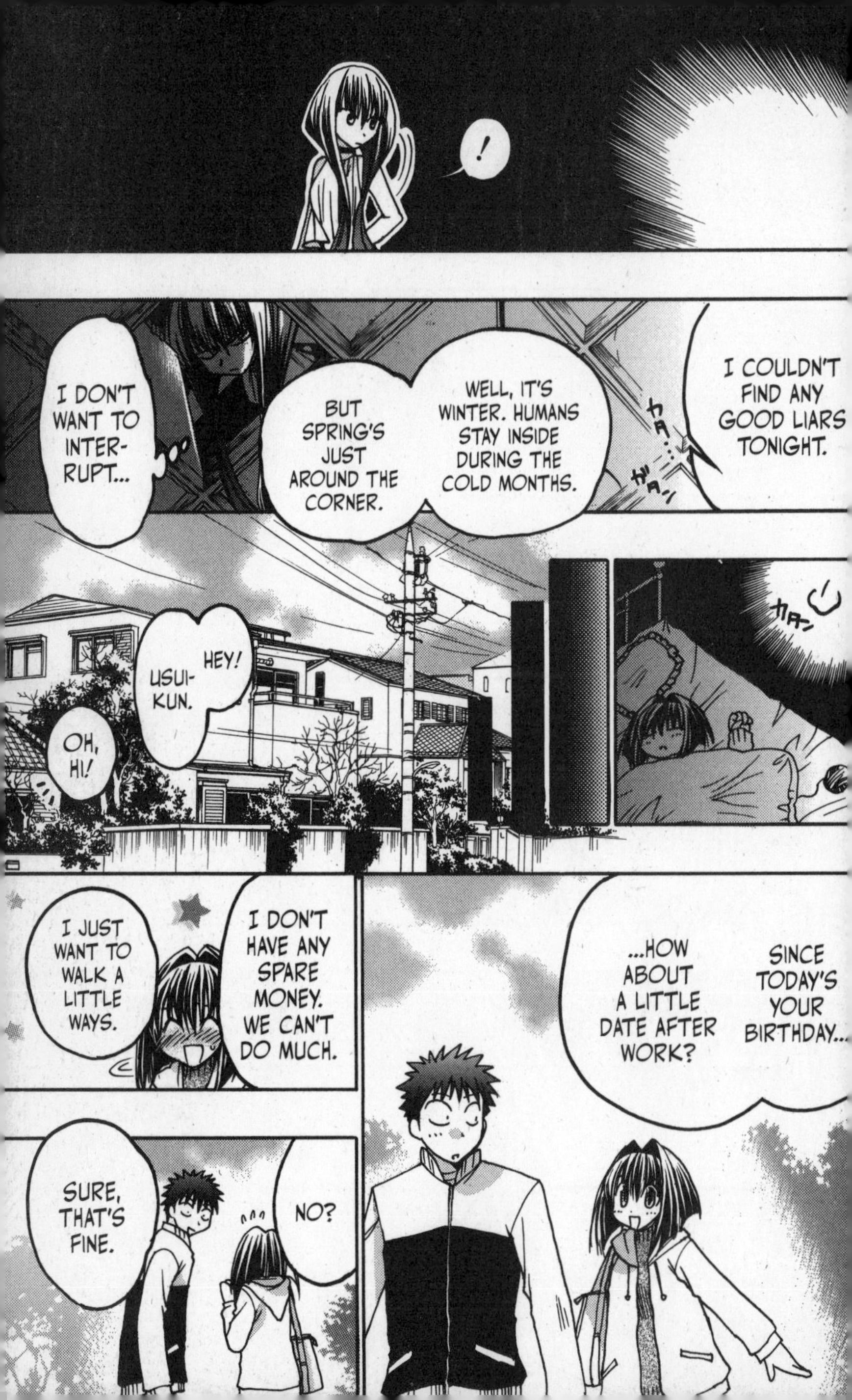
!
I COULDN'T FIND ANY GOOD LIARS TONIGHT.
カタ…
ガタン
WELL, IT'S WINTER. HUMANS STAY INSIDE DURING THE COLD MONTHS.
BUT SPRING'S JUST AROUND THE CORNER.
I DON'T WANT TO INTER-RUPT...
!
カタン
HEY! USUI-KUN.
OH, HI!
SINCE TODAY'S YOUR BIRTHDAY...
...HOW ABOUT A LITTLE DATE AFTER WORK?
I DON'T HAVE ANY SPARE MONEY. WE CAN'T DO MUCH.
I JUST WANT TO WALK A LITTLE WAYS.
NO?
SURE, THAT'S FINE.

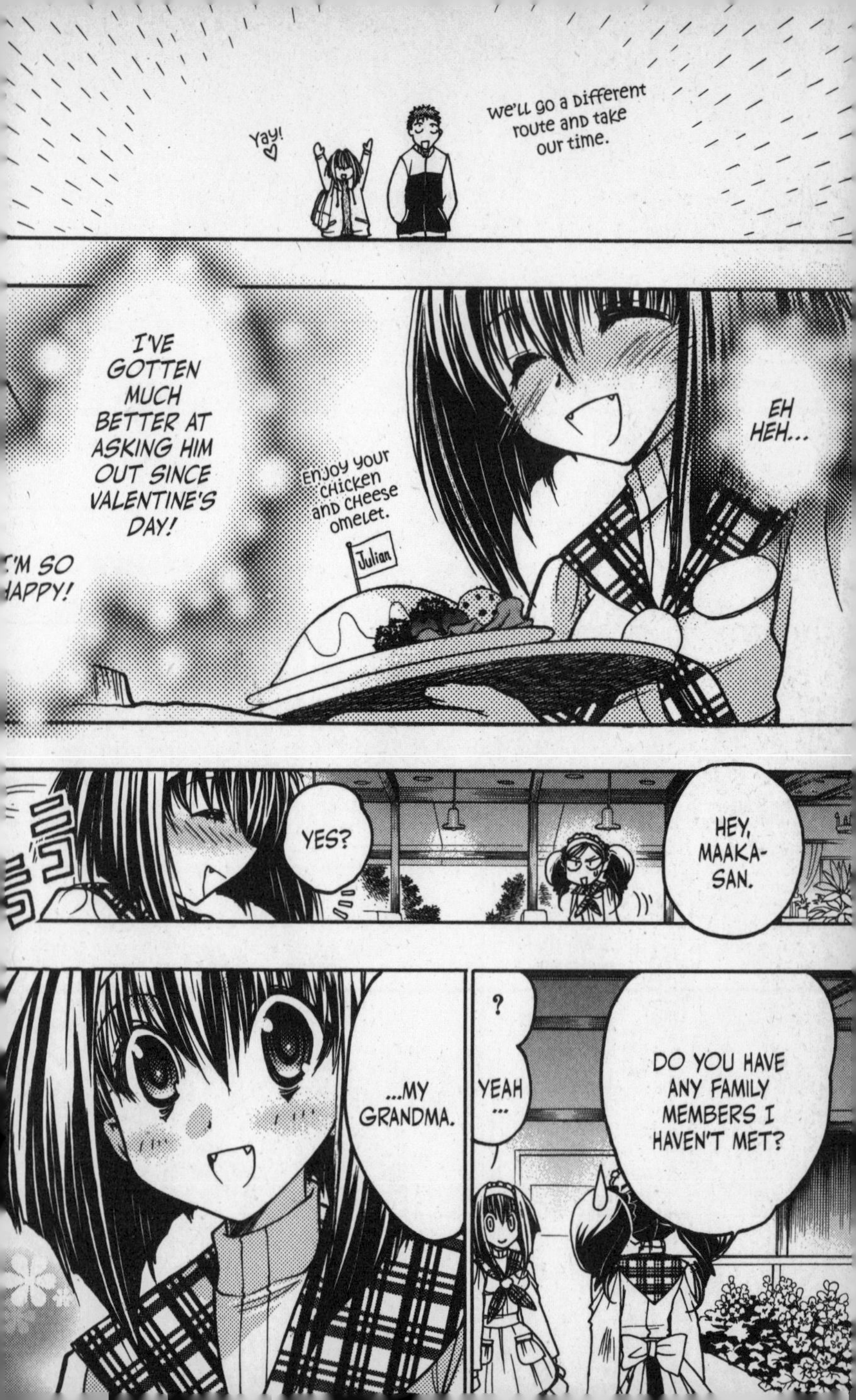
We'll go a different route and take our time.
Yay! ♥
EH HEH...
Enjoy your chicken and cheese omelet.
Julian
I'VE GOTTEN MUCH BETTER AT ASKING HIM OUT SINCE VALENTINE'S DAY!
'M SO APPY!
HEY, MAAKA-SAN.
YES?
DO YOU HAVE ANY FAMILY MEMBERS I HAVEN'T MET?
?
YEAH...
...MY GRANDMA.

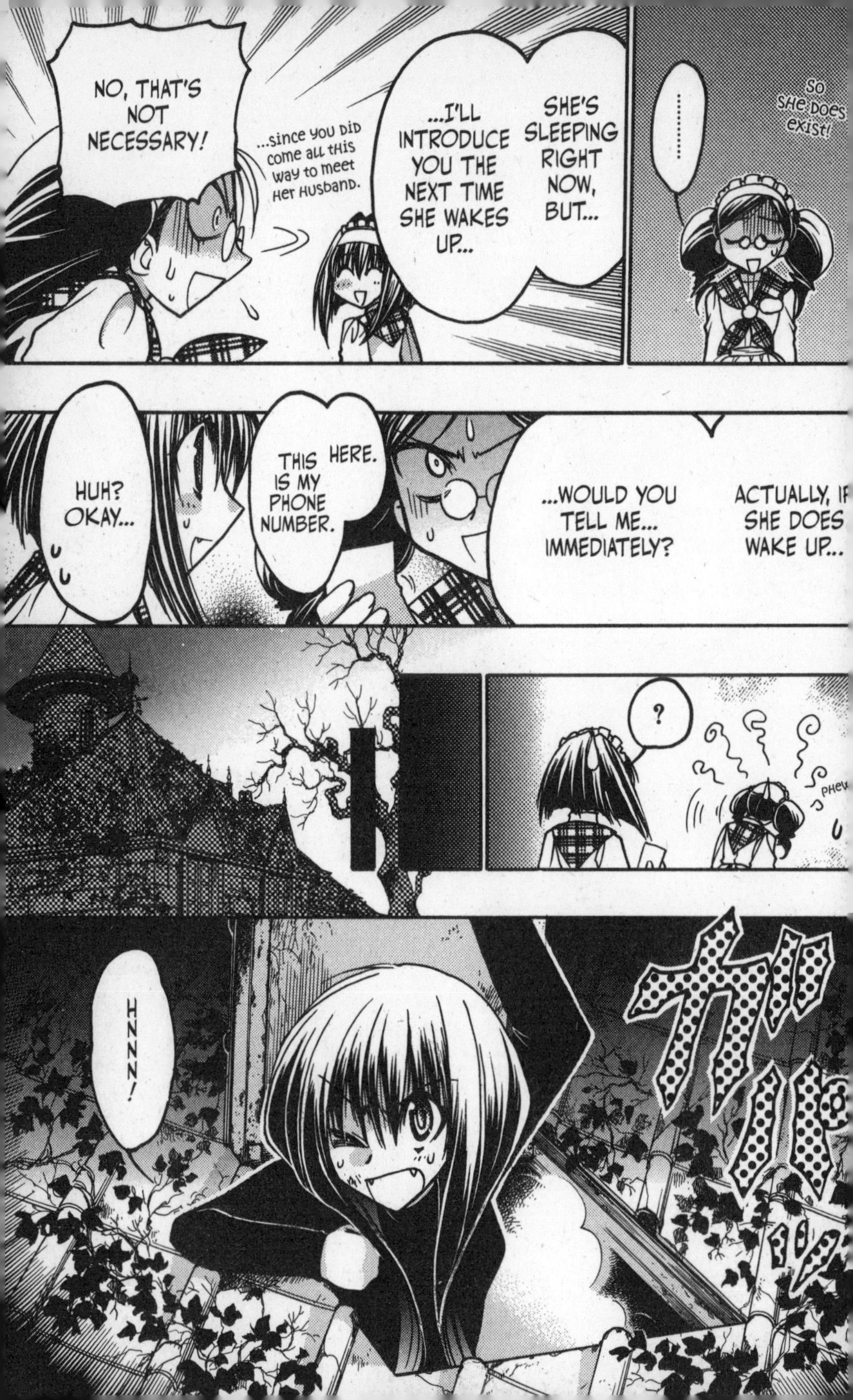
So she does exist!
......
SHE'S SLEEPING RIGHT NOW, BUT...
...I'LL INTRODUCE YOU THE NEXT TIME SHE WAKES UP...
...since you did come all this way to meet her husband.
NO, THAT'S NOT NECESSARY!
ACTUALLY, IF SHE DOES WAKE UP...
...WOULD YOU TELL ME... IMMEDIATELY?
HERE. THIS IS MY PHONE NUMBER.
HUH? OKAY...
?
PHEW
HNNN!

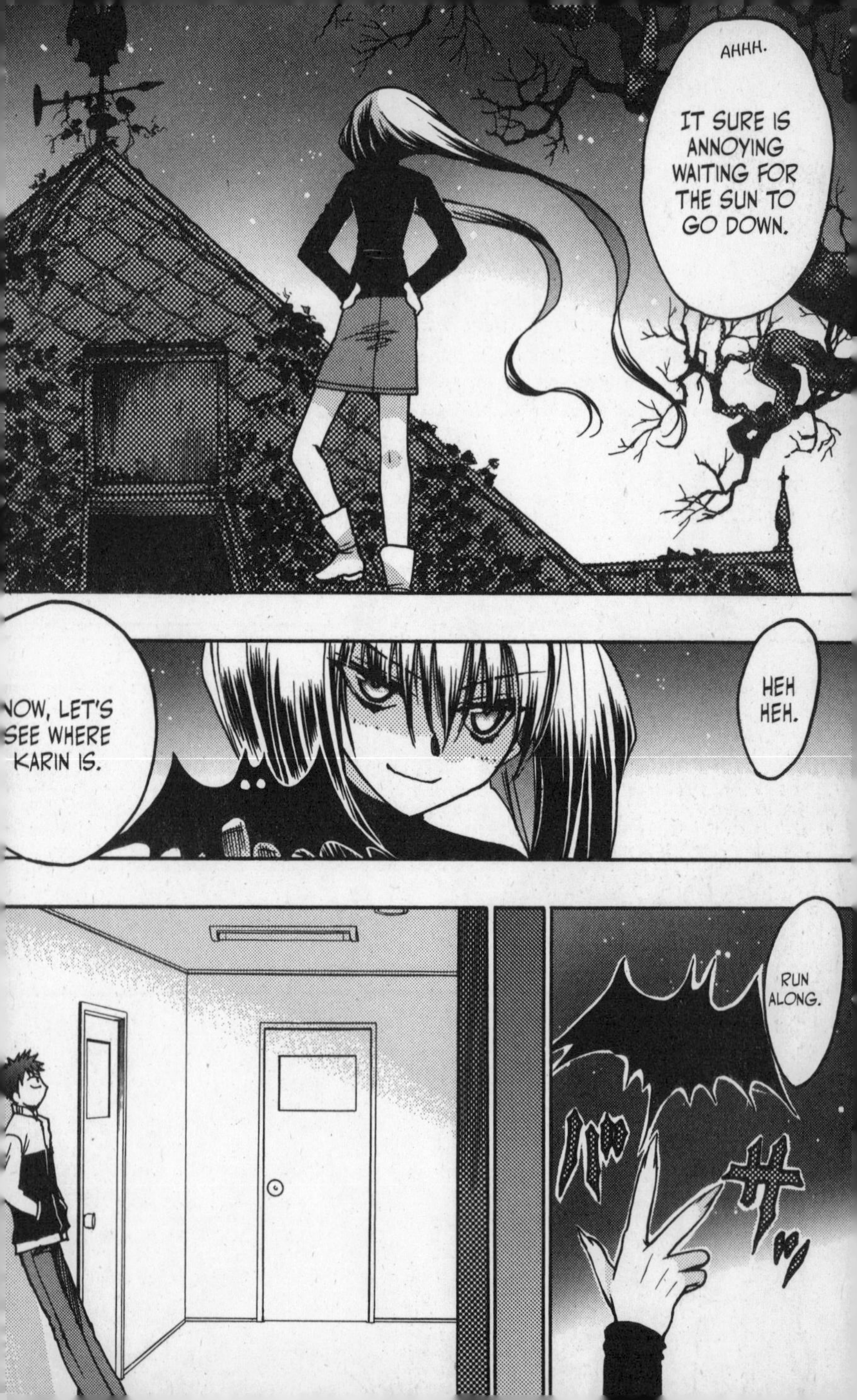
AHHH.
IT SURE IS ANNOYING WAITING FOR THE SUN TO GO DOWN.
HEH HEH.
NOW, LET'S SEE WHERE KARIN IS.
RUN ALONG.
バサッ

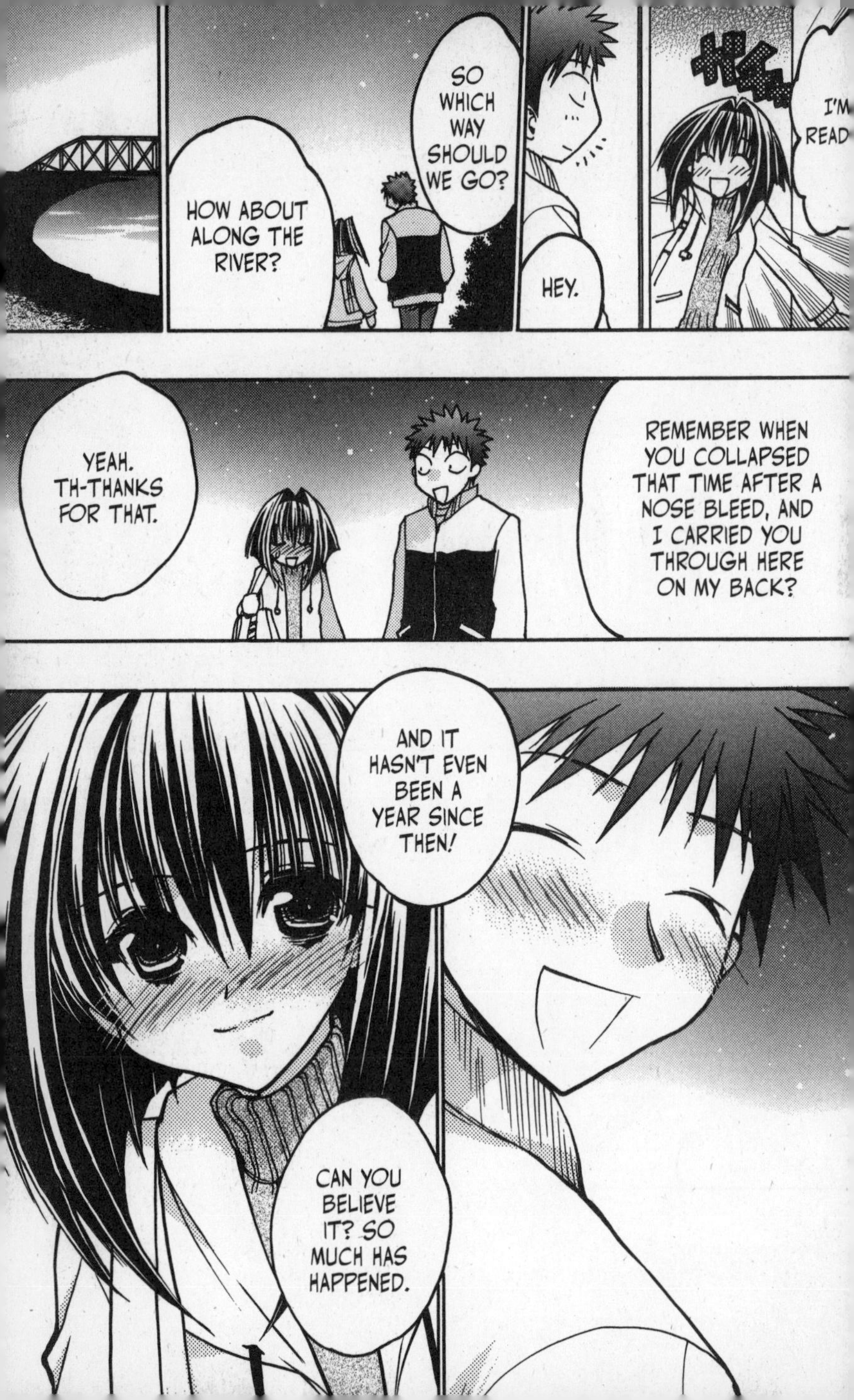
I'M READ
HEY.
SO WHICH WAY SHOULD WE GO?
HOW ABOUT ALONG THE RIVER?
REMEMBER WHEN YOU COLLAPSED THAT TIME AFTER A NOSE BLEED, AND I CARRIED YOU THROUGH HERE ON MY BACK?
YEAH. TH-THANKS FOR THAT.
AND IT HASN'T EVEN BEEN A YEAR SINCE THEN!
CAN YOU BELIEVE IT? SO MUCH HAS HAPPENED.

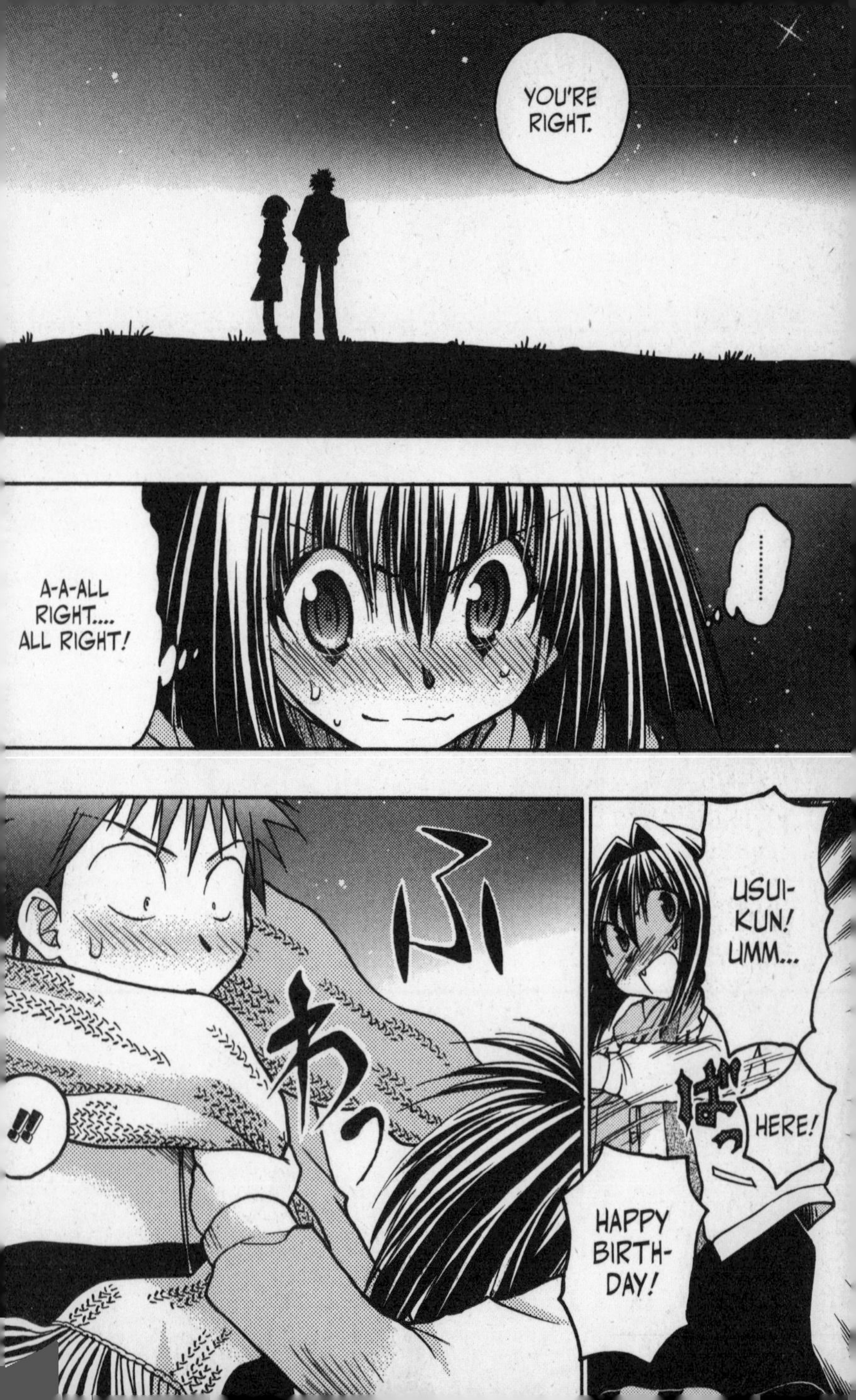

YOU'RE RIGHT.
......
A-A-ALL RIGHT.... ALL RIGHT!
USUI-KUN! UMM...
ぱっ
HERE!
HAPPY BIRTH-DAY!
ふわっ
!!

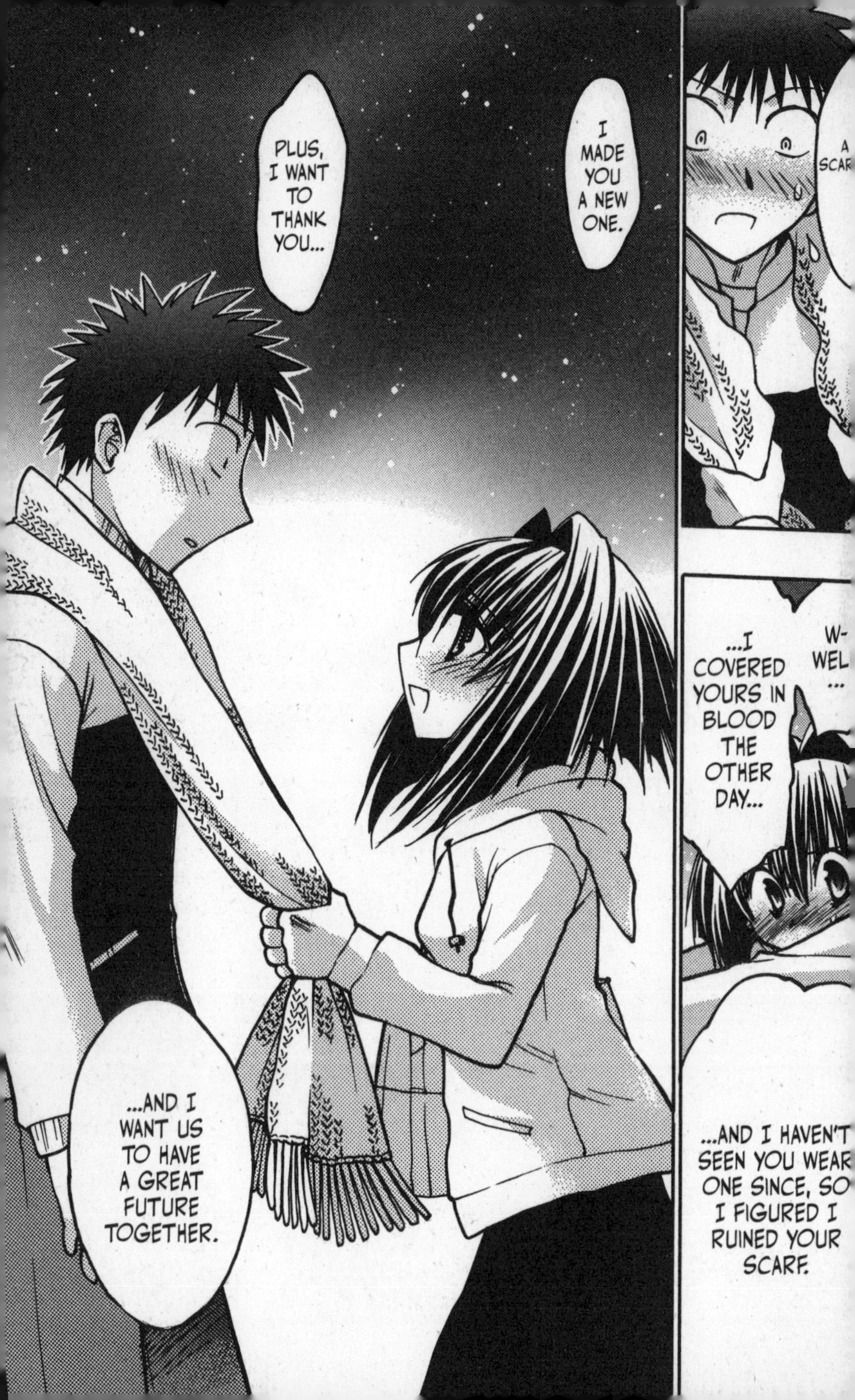
A SCAR
W-WEL...
...I COVERED YOURS IN BLOOD THE OTHER DAY...
...AND I HAVEN'T SEEN YOU WEAR ONE SINCE, SO I FIGURED I RUINED YOUR SCARF.
I MADE YOU A NEW ONE.
PLUS, I WANT TO THANK YOU...
...AND I WANT US TO HAVE A GREAT FUTURE TOGETHER.

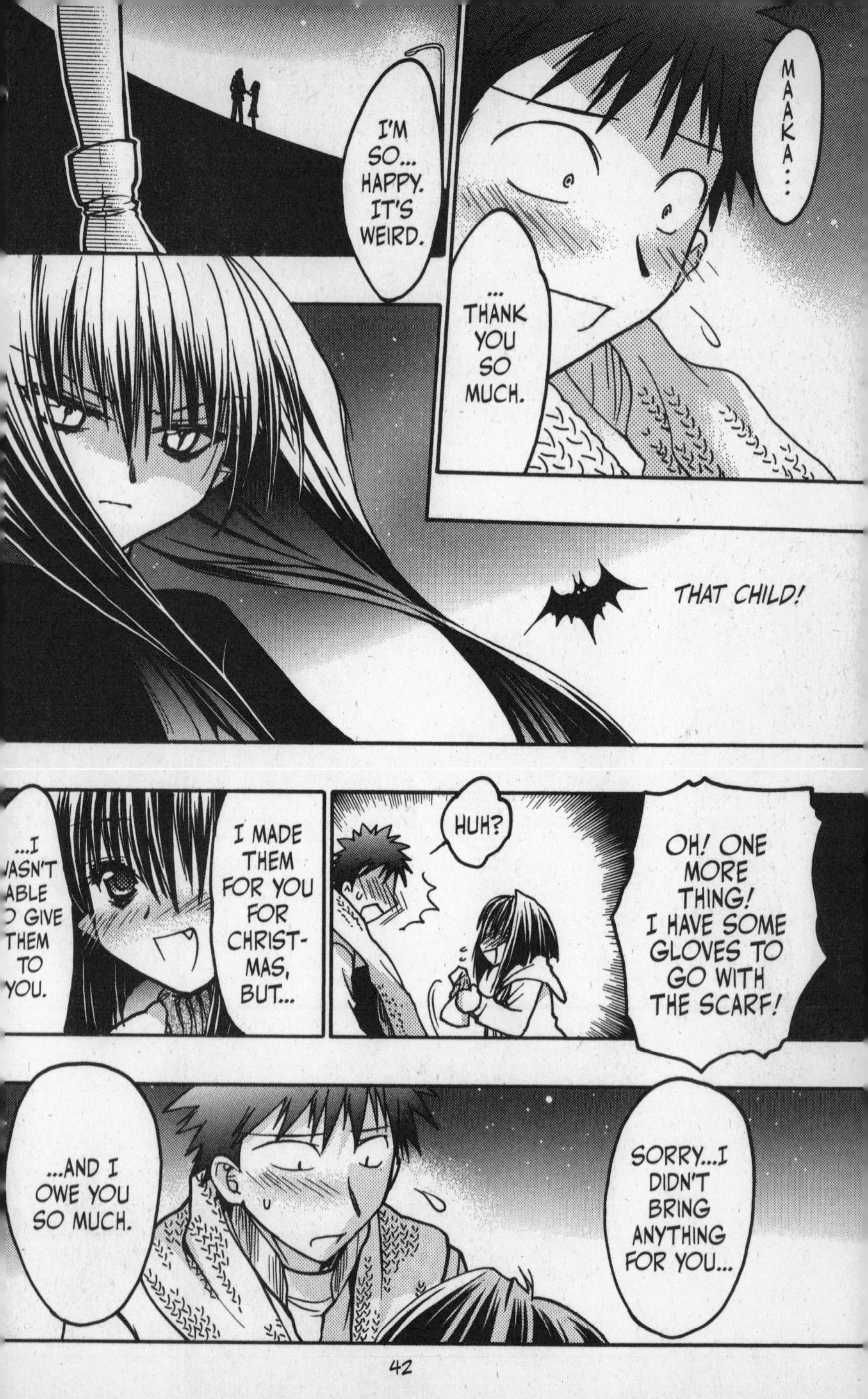
MAAKA...
...THANK YOU SO MUCH.
I'M SO... HAPPY. IT'S WEIRD.
THAT CHILD!
OH! ONE MORE THING! I HAVE SOME GLOVES TO GO WITH THE SCARF!
HUH?
I MADE THEM FOR YOU FOR CHRIST-MAS, BUT...
...I ASN'T ABLE O GIVE THEM TO YOU.
SORRY...I DIDN'T BRING ANYTHING FOR YOU...
...AND I OWE YOU SO MUCH.

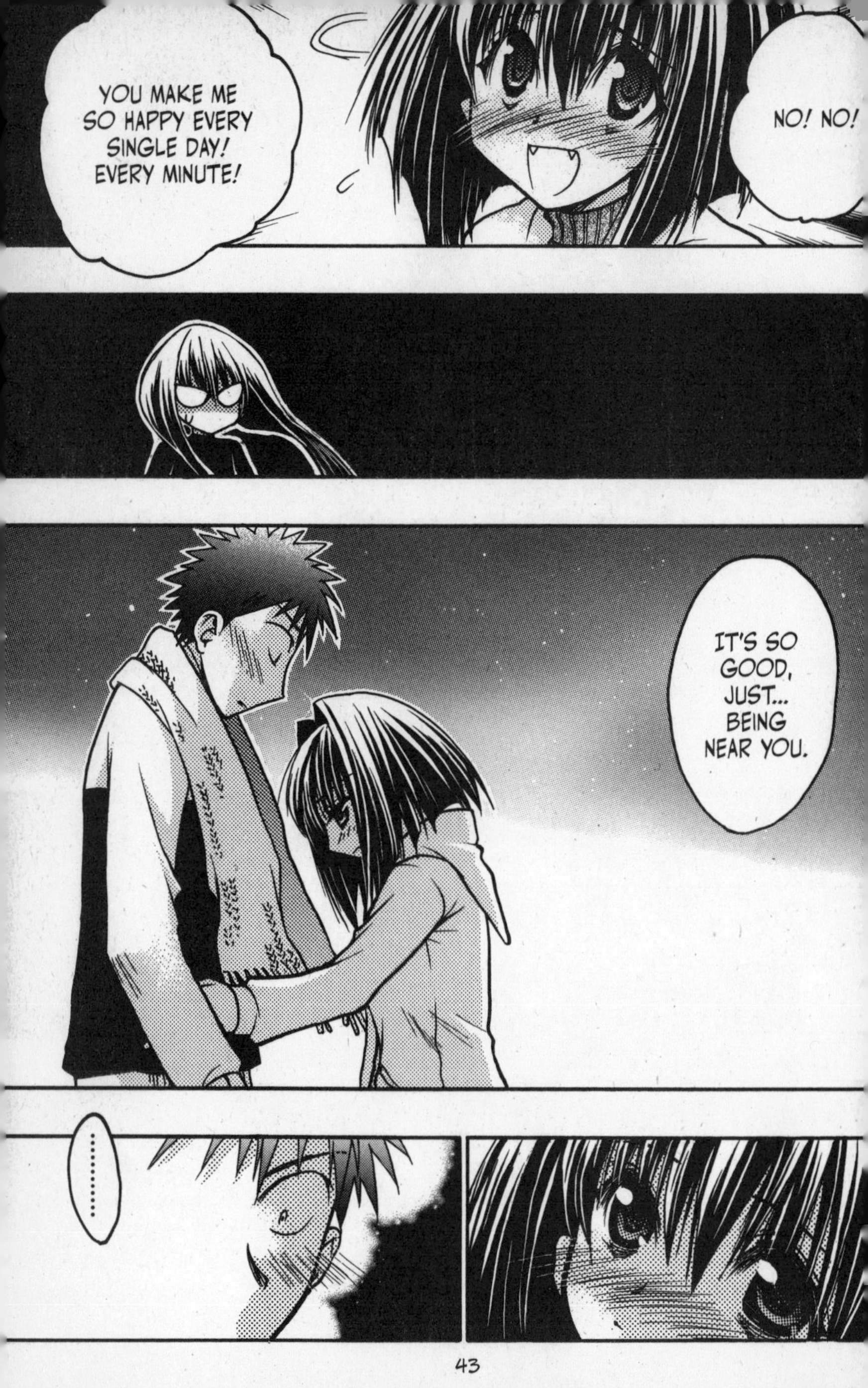
NO! NO!
YOU MAKE ME SO HAPPY EVERY SINGLE DAY! EVERY MINUTE!
IT'S SO GOOD, JUST... BEING NEAR YOU.
......

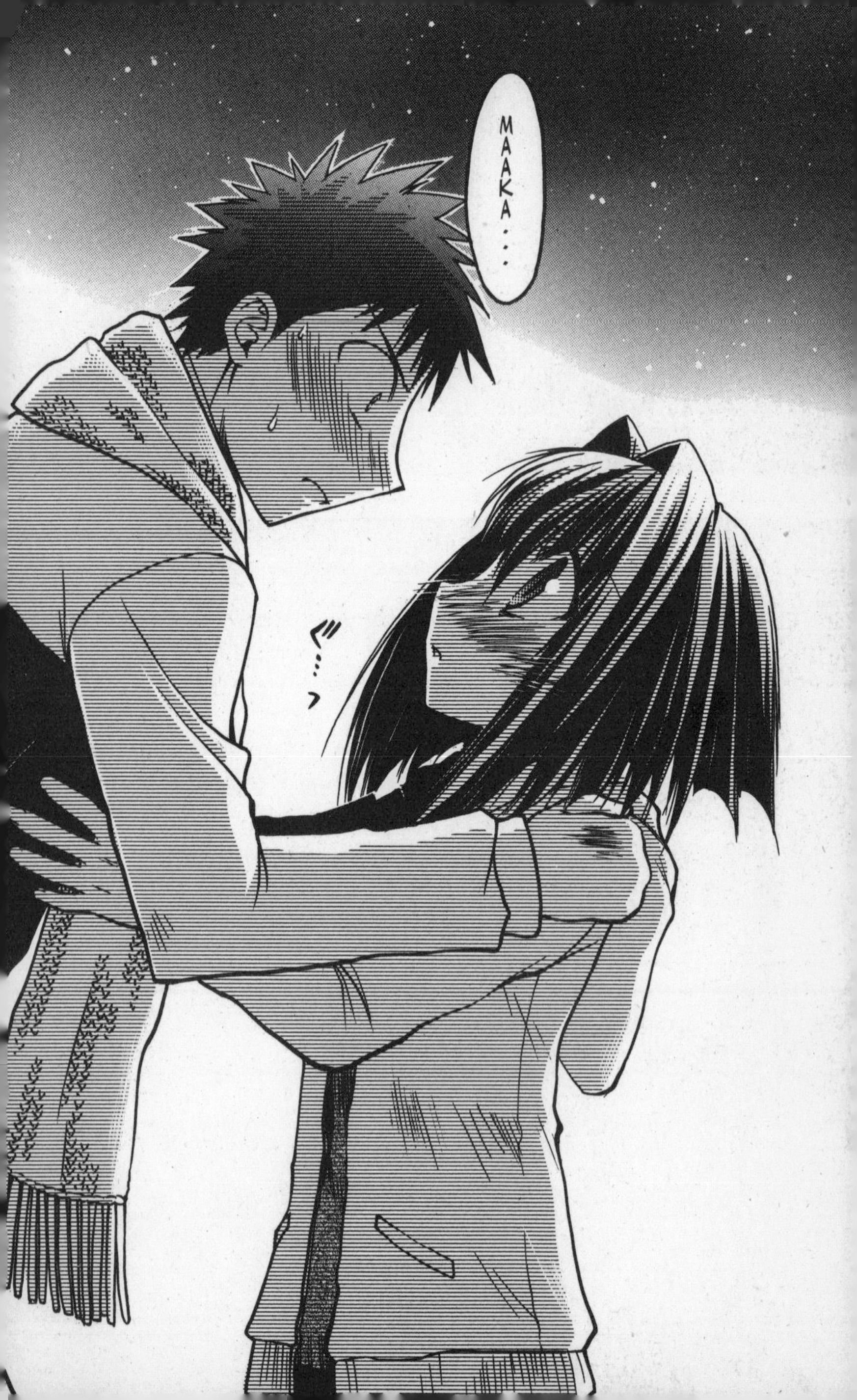
MAAKA...
ぐ…っ

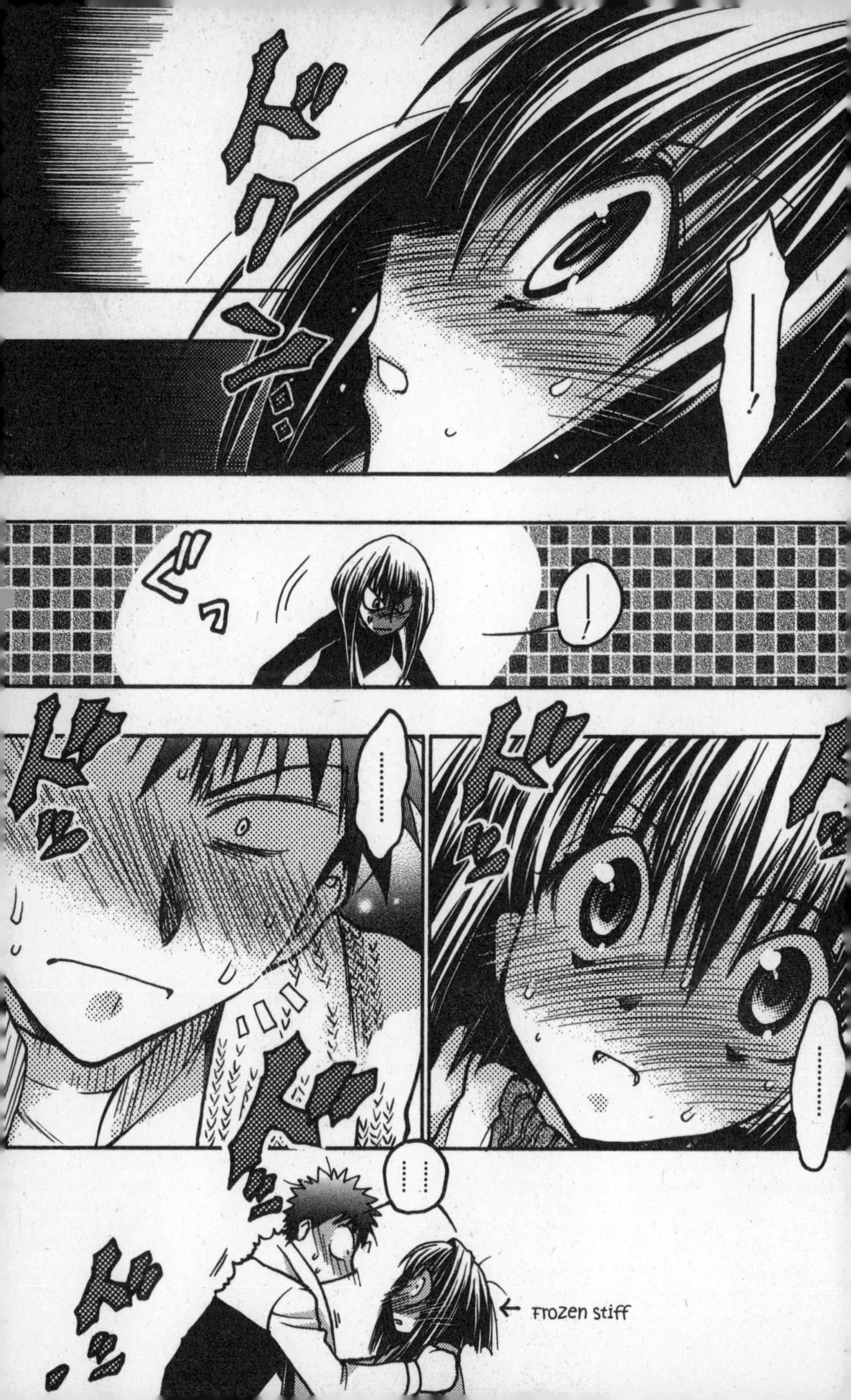

ドクン
!!
!!
ぐっ
ドッ
......
ドッ
......
...
ドッ
ドッ
Frozen stiff

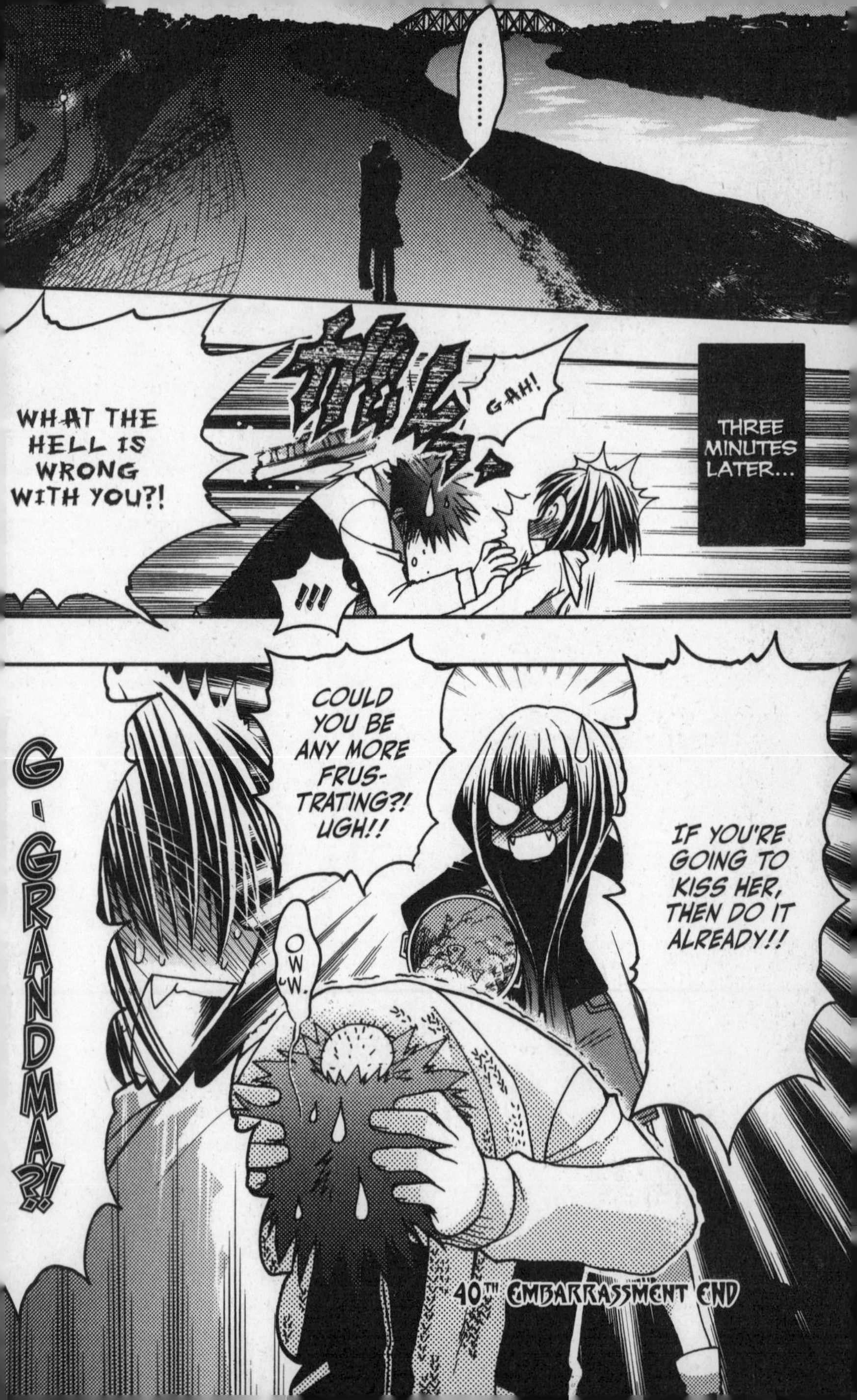
......
THREE MINUTES LATER...
GAH!
!!!
WHAT THE HELL IS WRONG WITH YOU?!
IF YOU'RE GOING TO KISS HER, THEN DO IT ALREADY!!
COULD YOU BE ANY MORE FRUS-TRATING?! UGH!!
OWW.
G-GRANDMA?!
40TH EMBARRASSMENT END

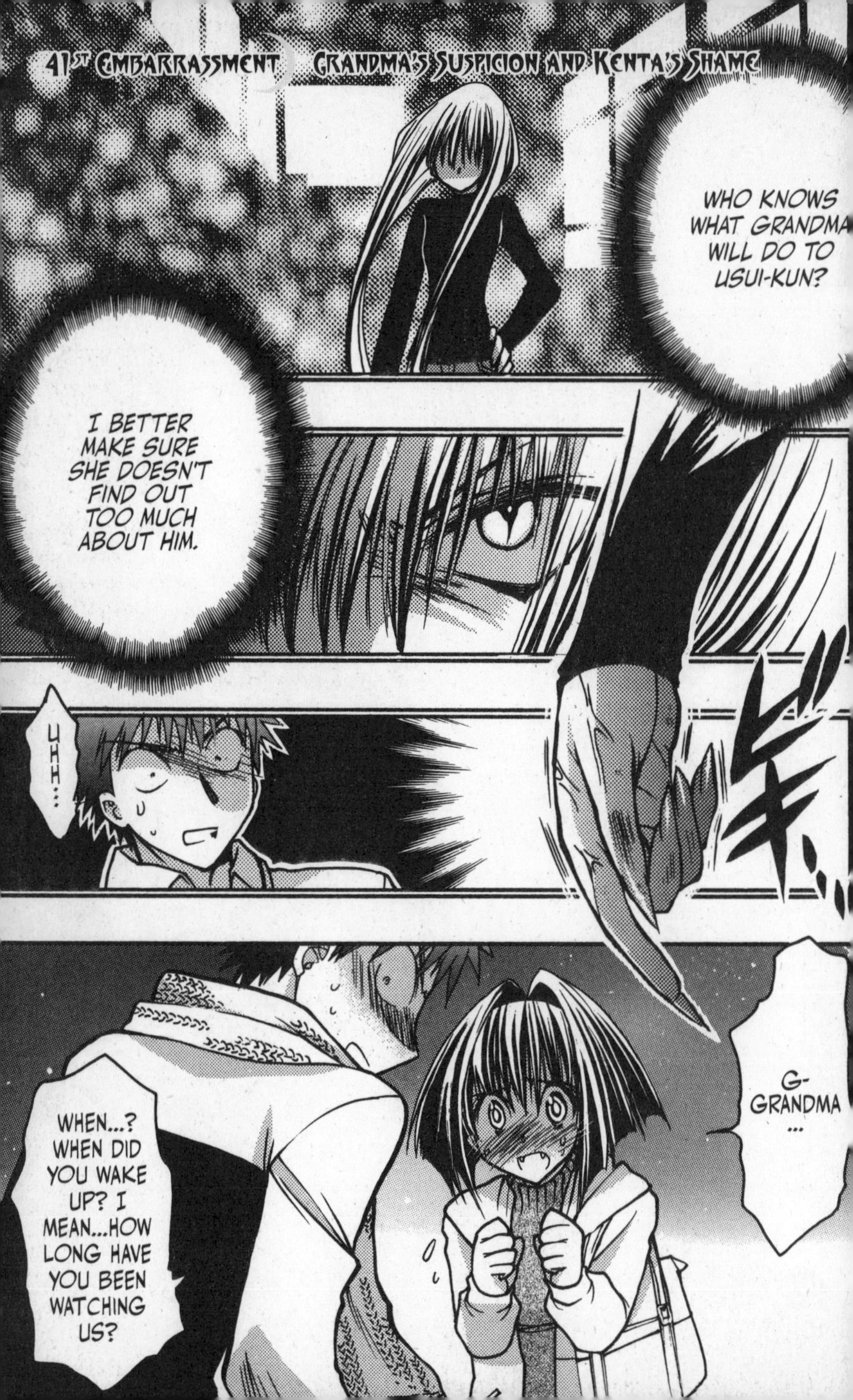
41ST EMBARRASSMENT GRANDMA'S SUSPICION AND KENTA'S SHAME
WHO KNOWS WHAT GRANDMA WILL DO TO USUI-KUN?
I BETTER MAKE SURE SHE DOESN'T FIND OUT TOO MUCH ABOUT HIM.
UHH...
G-GRANDMA...
WHEN...? WHEN DID YOU WAKE UP? I MEAN...HOW LONG HAVE YOU BEEN WATCHING US?

41st Embarrassment (Shame) Grandma's Suspicion and Kenta's Shame

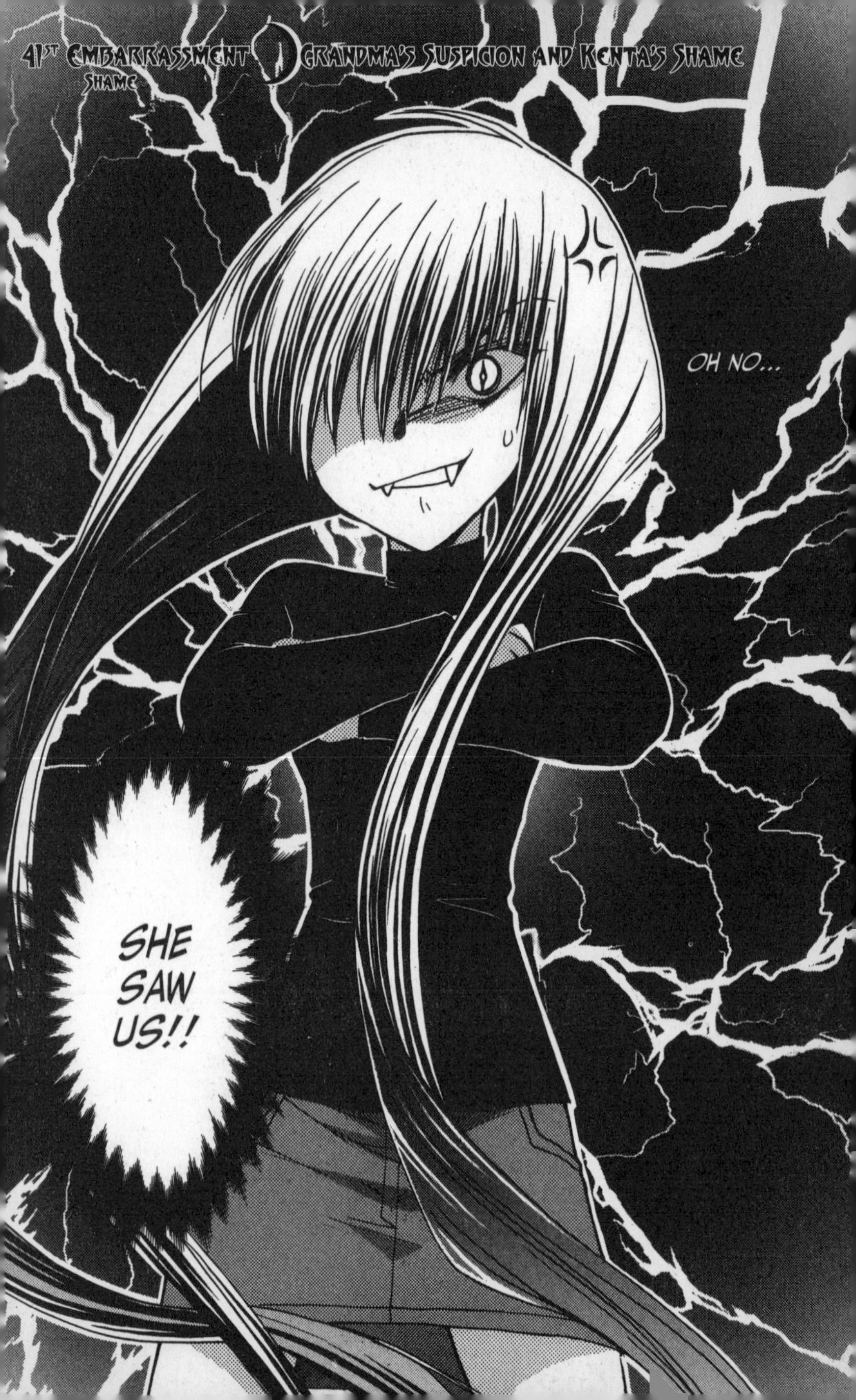
OH NO...
SHE SAW US!!

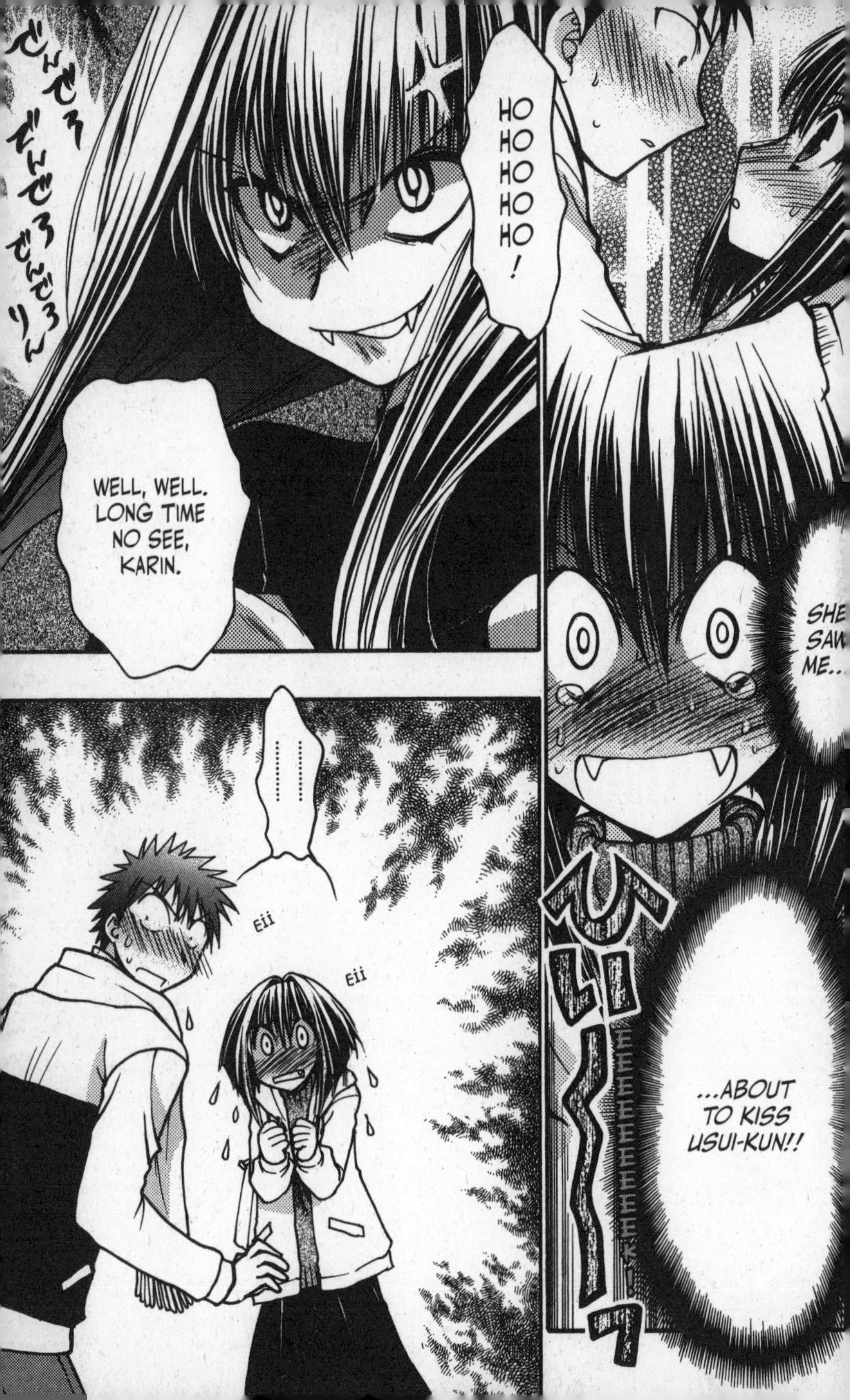
SHE SAW ME...
...ABOUT TO KISS USUI-KUN!!
RULI EEEEEEEEEK!
でんでろ～でんでろでんでろでんでろりん
HO HO HO HO HO!
WELL, WELL. LONG TIME NO SEE, KARIN.
......
Eii
Eii

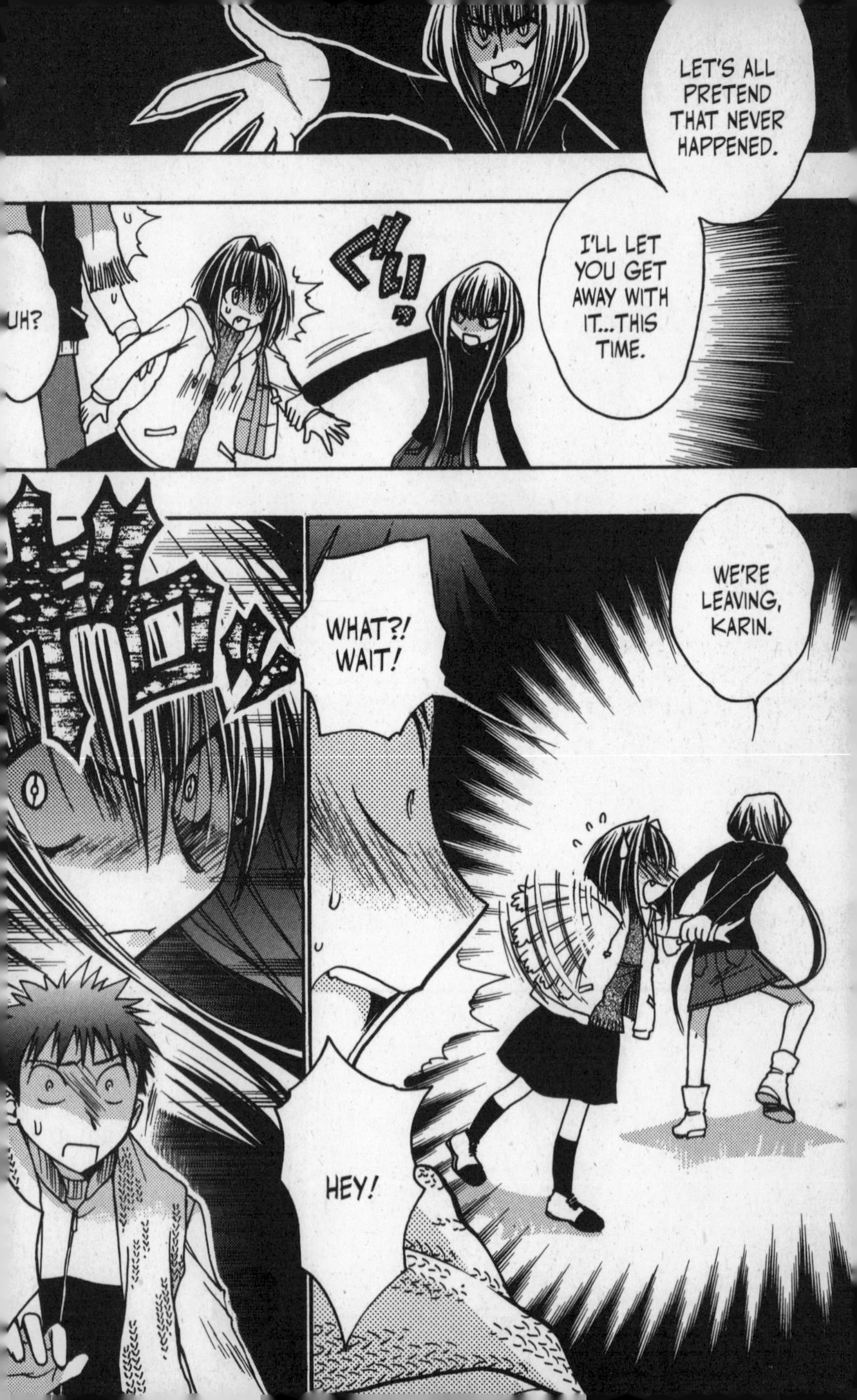
LET'S ALL PRETEND THAT NEVER HAPPENED.
I'LL LET YOU GET AWAY WITH IT...THIS TIME.
UH?
WE'RE LEAVING, KARIN.
WHAT?! WAIT!
HEY!

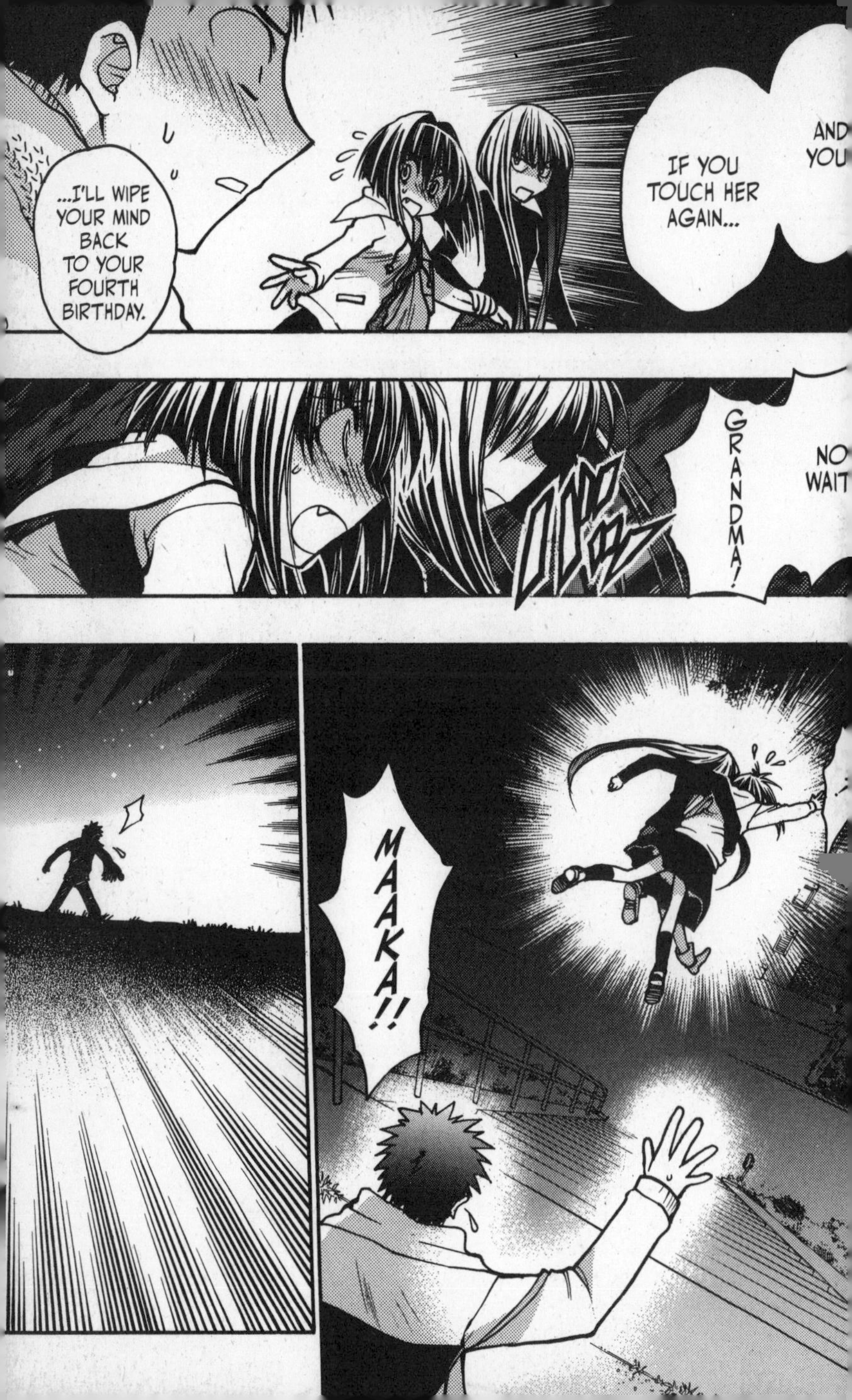
AND YOU
IF YOU TOUCH HER AGAIN...
...I'LL WIPE YOUR MIND BACK TO YOUR FOURTH BIRTHDAY.
NO WAIT
GRANDMA!
MAAKA!!

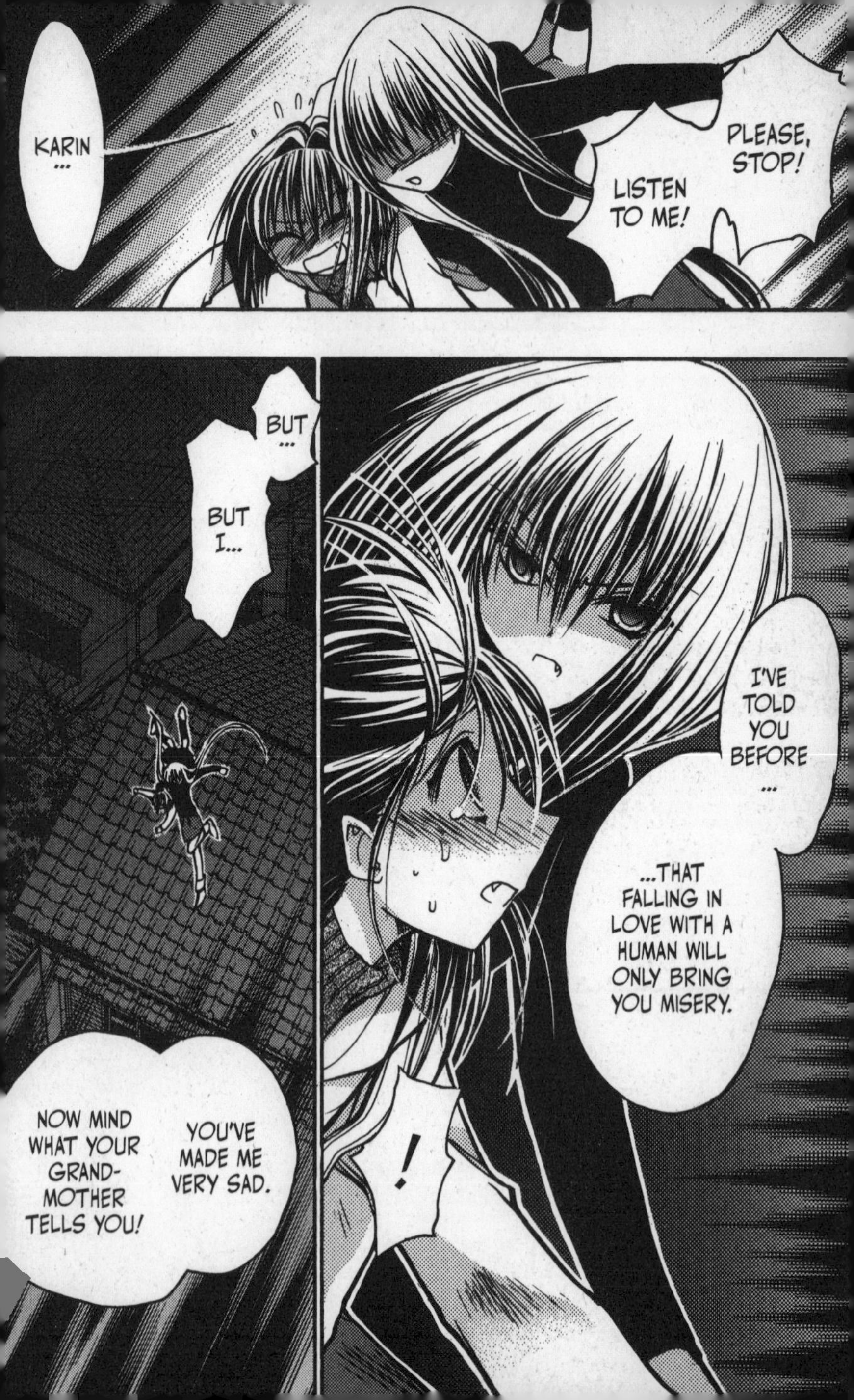
PLEASE, STOP!
LISTEN TO ME!
KARIN ...
I'VE TOLD YOU BEFORE ...
...THAT FALLING IN LOVE WITH A HUMAN WILL ONLY BRING YOU MISERY.
!
YOU'VE MADE ME VERY SAD.
NOW MIND WHAT YOUR GRAND-MOTHER TELLS YOU!
BUT ...
BUT I...

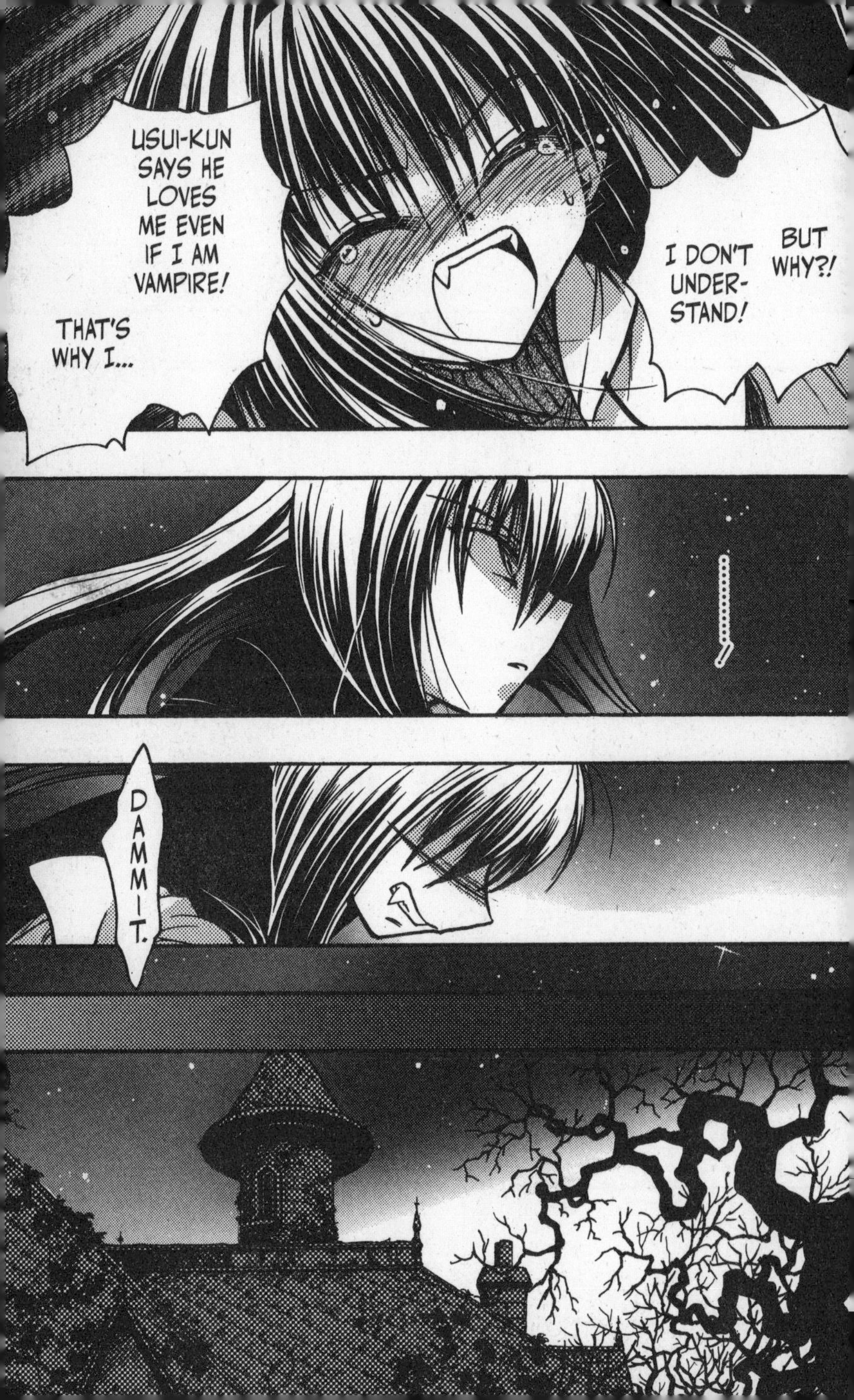
BUT WHY?!
I DON'T UNDER-STAND!
USUI-KUN SAYS HE LOVES ME EVEN IF I AM VAMPIRE!
THAT'S WHY I...
......!
DAMMIT.

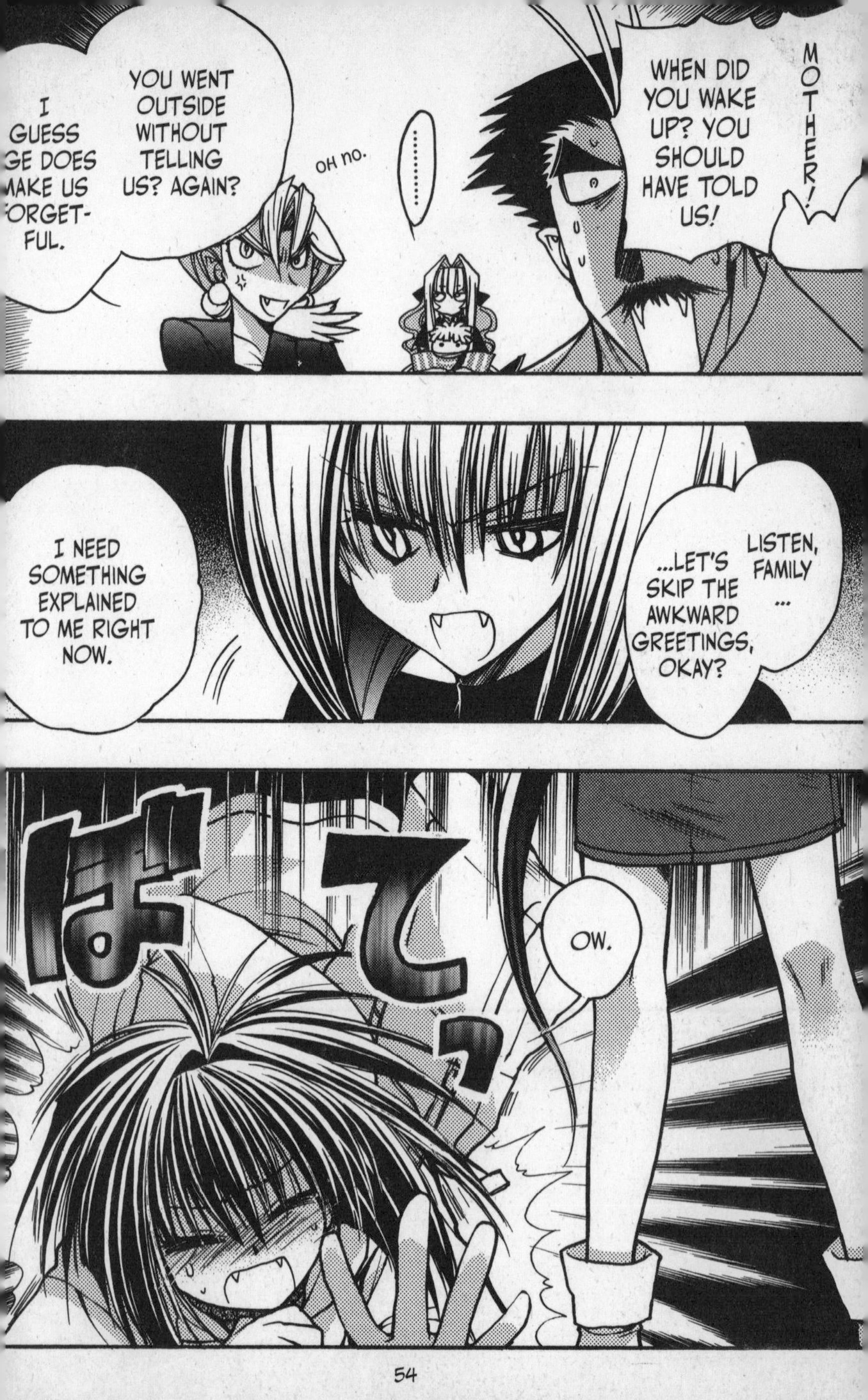
MOTHER!
WHEN DID YOU WAKE UP? YOU SHOULD HAVE TOLD US!
......
OH no.
YOU WENT OUTSIDE WITHOUT TELLING US? AGAIN?
I GUESS GE DOES MAKE US ORGET- FUL.
LISTEN, FAMILY ...
...LET'S SKIP THE AWKWARD GREETINGS, OKAY?
I NEED SOMETHING EXPLAINED TO ME RIGHT NOW.
OW.
はっ

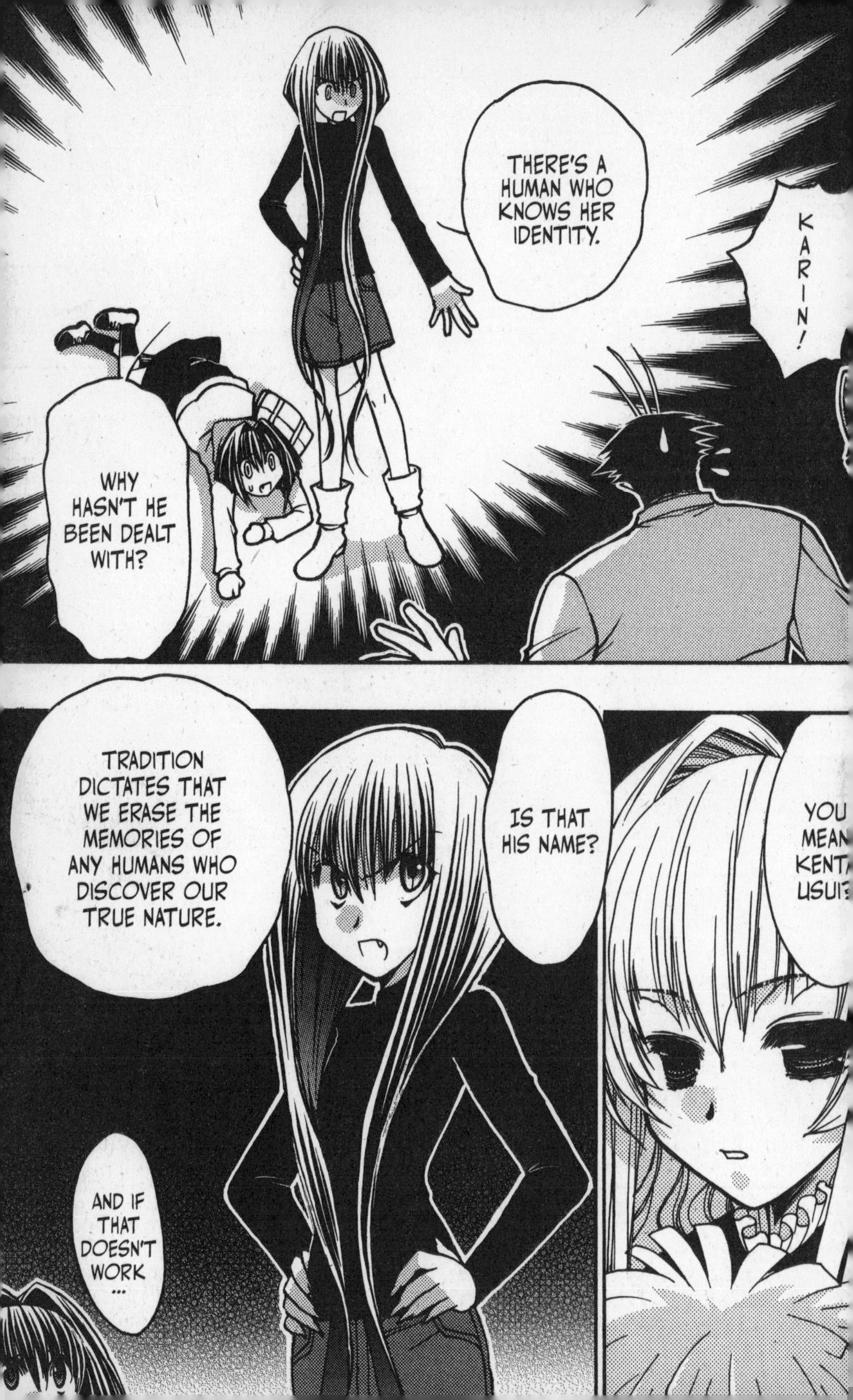
KARIN!
THERE'S A HUMAN WHO KNOWS HER IDENTITY.
WHY HASN'T HE BEEN DEALT WITH?
YOU MEAN KENT USUI?
IS THAT HIS NAME?
TRADITION DICTATES THAT WE ERASE THE MEMORIES OF ANY HUMANS WHO DISCOVER OUR TRUE NATURE.
AND IF THAT DOESN'T WORK...

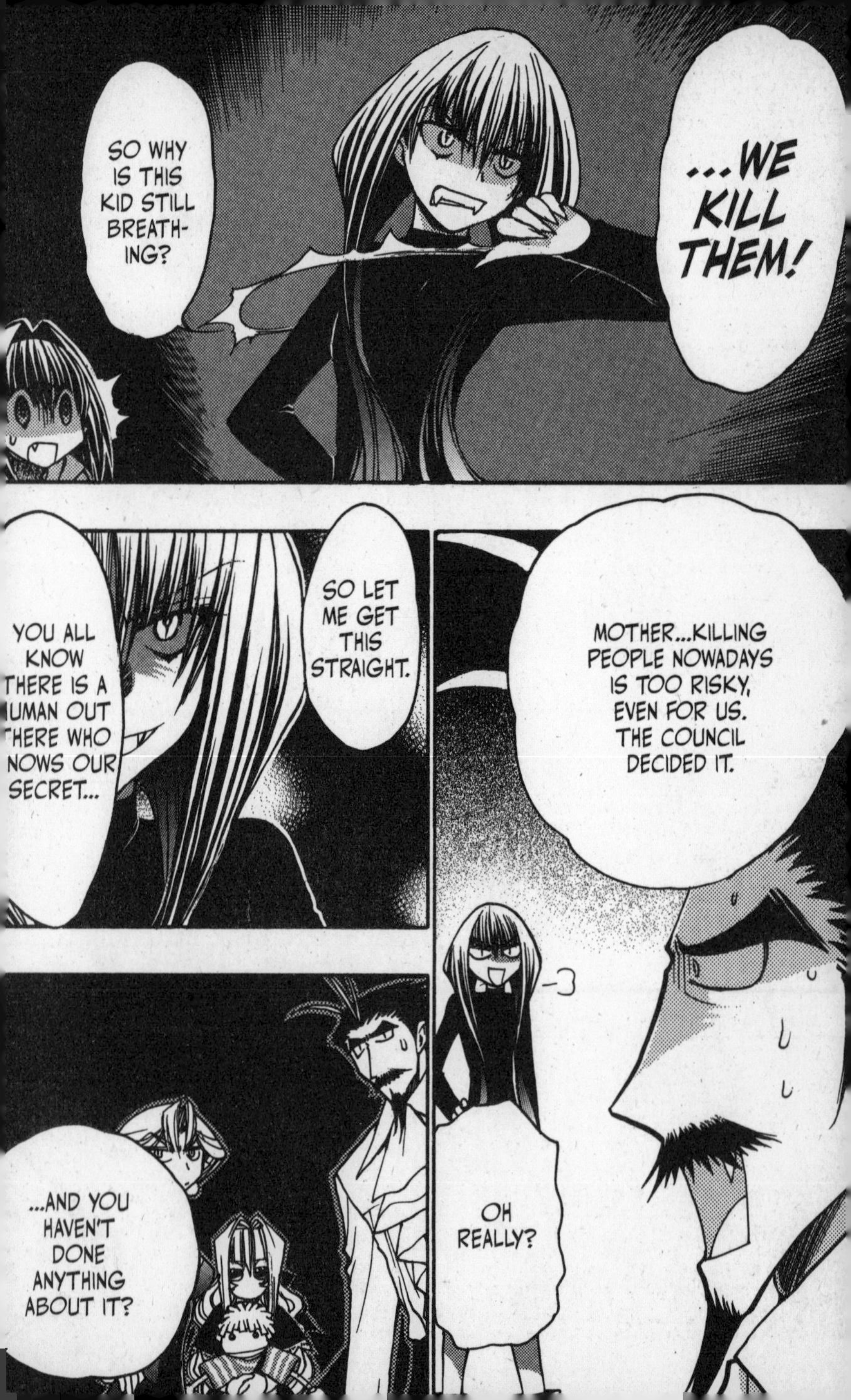
...WE KILL THEM!
SO WHY IS THIS KID STILL BREATH-ING?
MOTHER...KILLING PEOPLE NOWADAYS IS TOO RISKY, EVEN FOR US. THE COUNCIL DECIDED IT.
OH REALLY?
SO LET ME GET THIS STRAIGHT.
YOU ALL KNOW THERE IS A UMAN OUT HERE WHO NOWS OUR SECRET...
...AND YOU HAVEN'T DONE ANYTHING ABOUT IT?

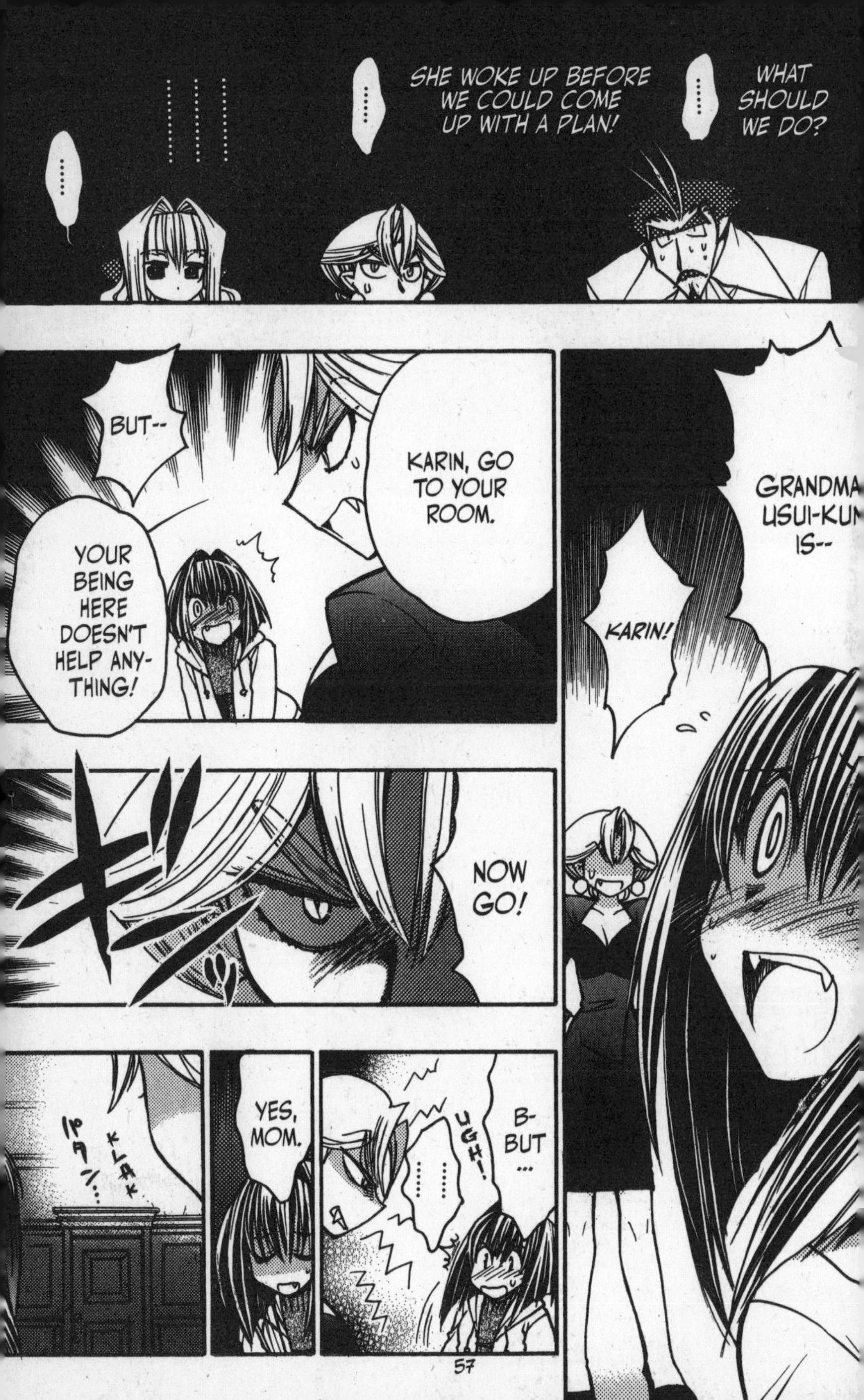

WHAT SHOULD WE DO?
......
SHE WOKE UP BEFORE WE COULD COME UP WITH A PLAN!
......
......
......
......
......
GRANDMA USUI-KUN IS--
KARIN!
KARIN, GO TO YOUR ROOM.
BUT--
YOUR BEING HERE DOESN'T HELP ANY-THING!
NOW GO!
B-BUT ...
UGH!
......
YES, MOM.
KLAK

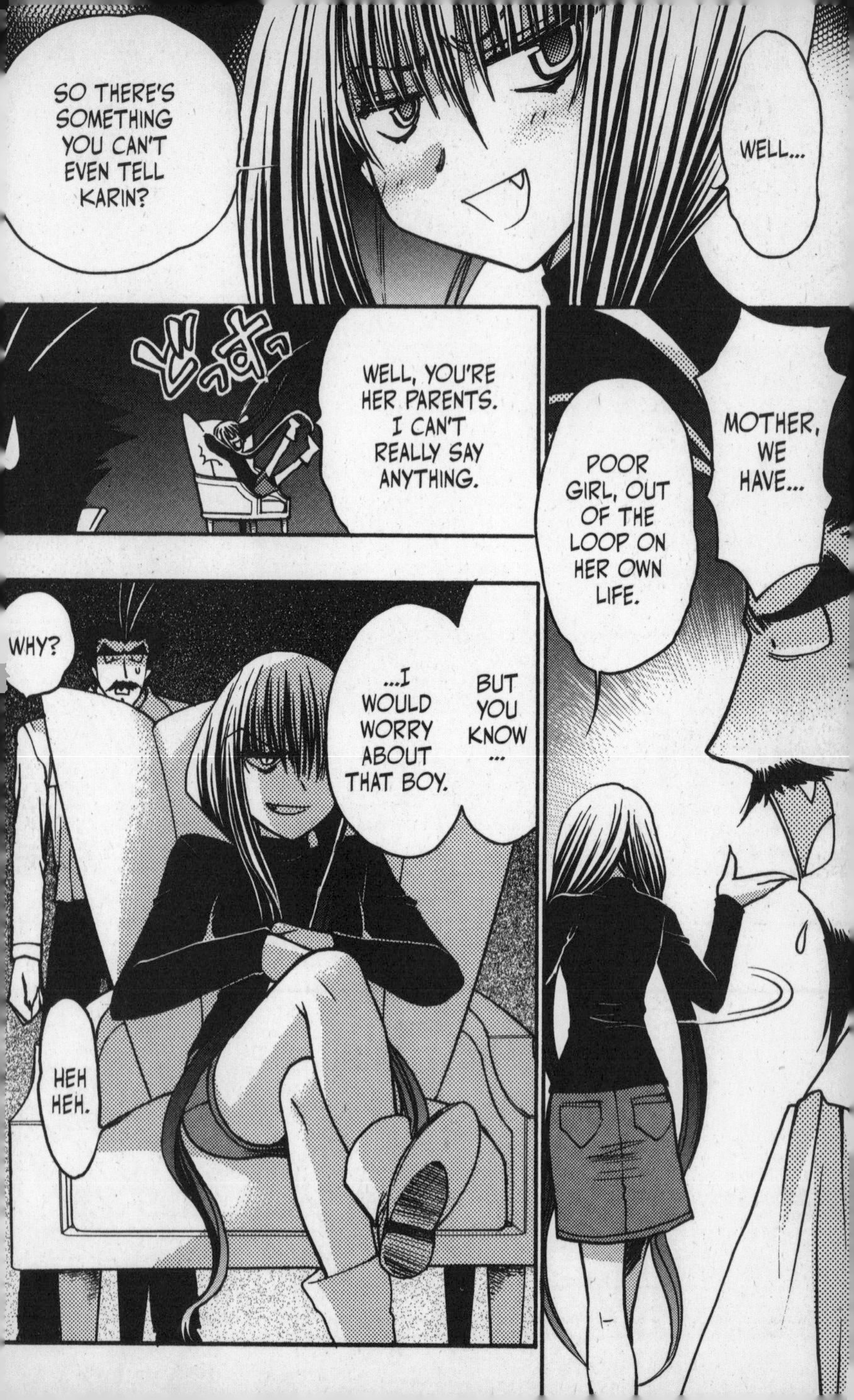
WELL...
SO THERE'S SOMETHING YOU CAN'T EVEN TELL KARIN?
MOTHER, WE HAVE...
POOR GIRL, OUT OF THE LOOP ON HER OWN LIFE.
WELL, YOU'RE HER PARENTS. I CAN'T REALLY SAY ANYTHING.
BUT YOU KNOW...
...I WOULD WORRY ABOUT THAT BOY.
WHY?
HEH HEH.

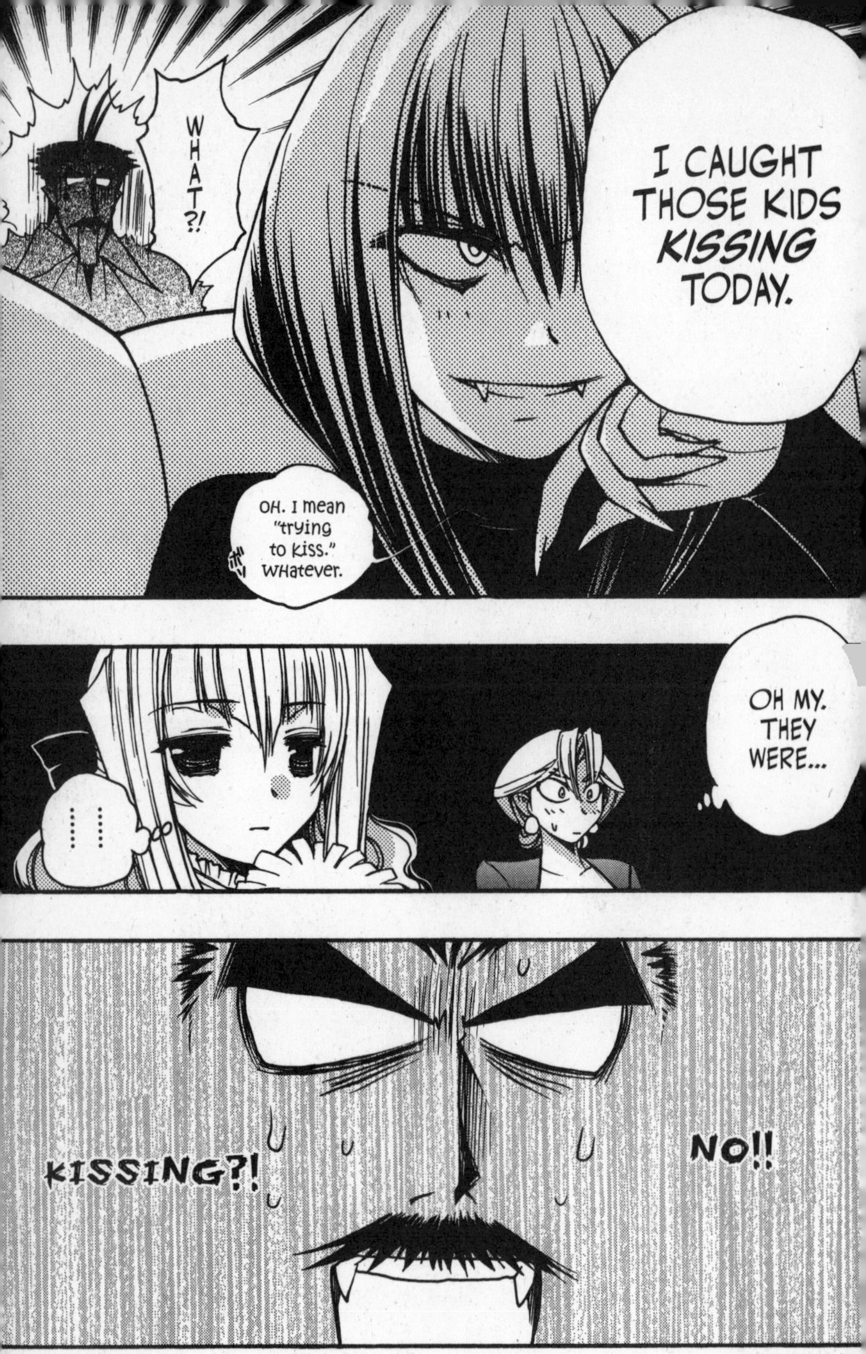
I CAUGHT THOSE KIDS *KISSING* TODAY.
WHAT?!
OH. I mean "trying to kiss." Whatever.
OH MY. THEY WERE...
......
NO!!
KISSING?!

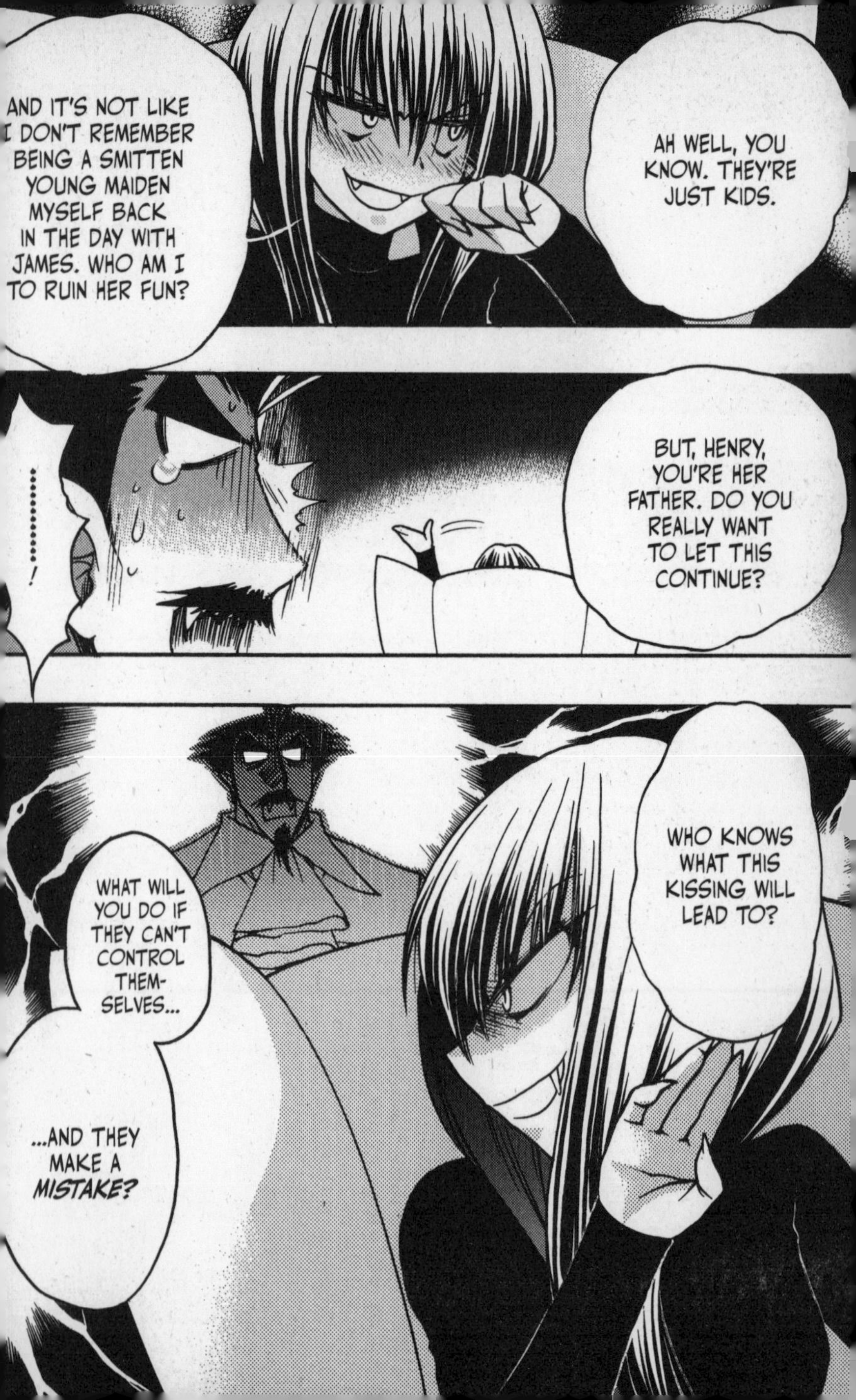
AH WELL, YOU KNOW. THEY'RE JUST KIDS.
AND IT'S NOT LIKE I DON'T REMEMBER BEING A SMITTEN YOUNG MAIDEN MYSELF BACK IN THE DAY WITH JAMES. WHO AM I TO RUIN HER FUN?
BUT, HENRY, YOU'RE HER FATHER. DO YOU REALLY WANT TO LET THIS CONTINUE?
........!
WHO KNOWS WHAT THIS KISSING WILL LEAD TO?
WHAT WILL YOU DO IF THEY CAN'T CONTROL THEM-SELVES...
...AND THEY MAKE A *MISTAKE?*

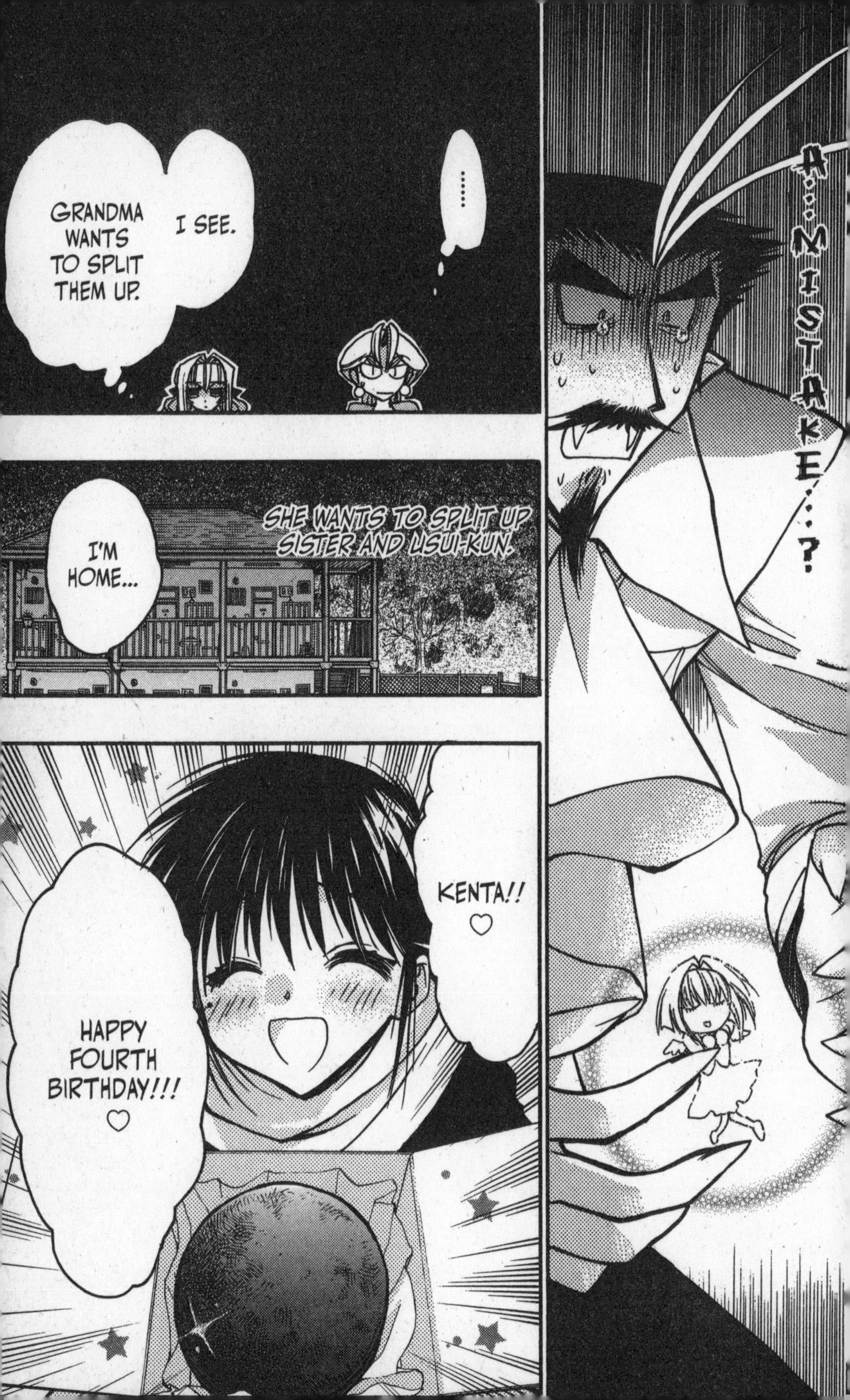
A...MISTAKE...?
......
GRANDMA WANTS TO SPLIT THEM UP.
I SEE.
I'M HOME...
SHE WANTS TO SPLIT UP SISTER AND USUI-KUN.
KENTA!! ♡
HAPPY FOURTH BIRTHDAY!!! ♡

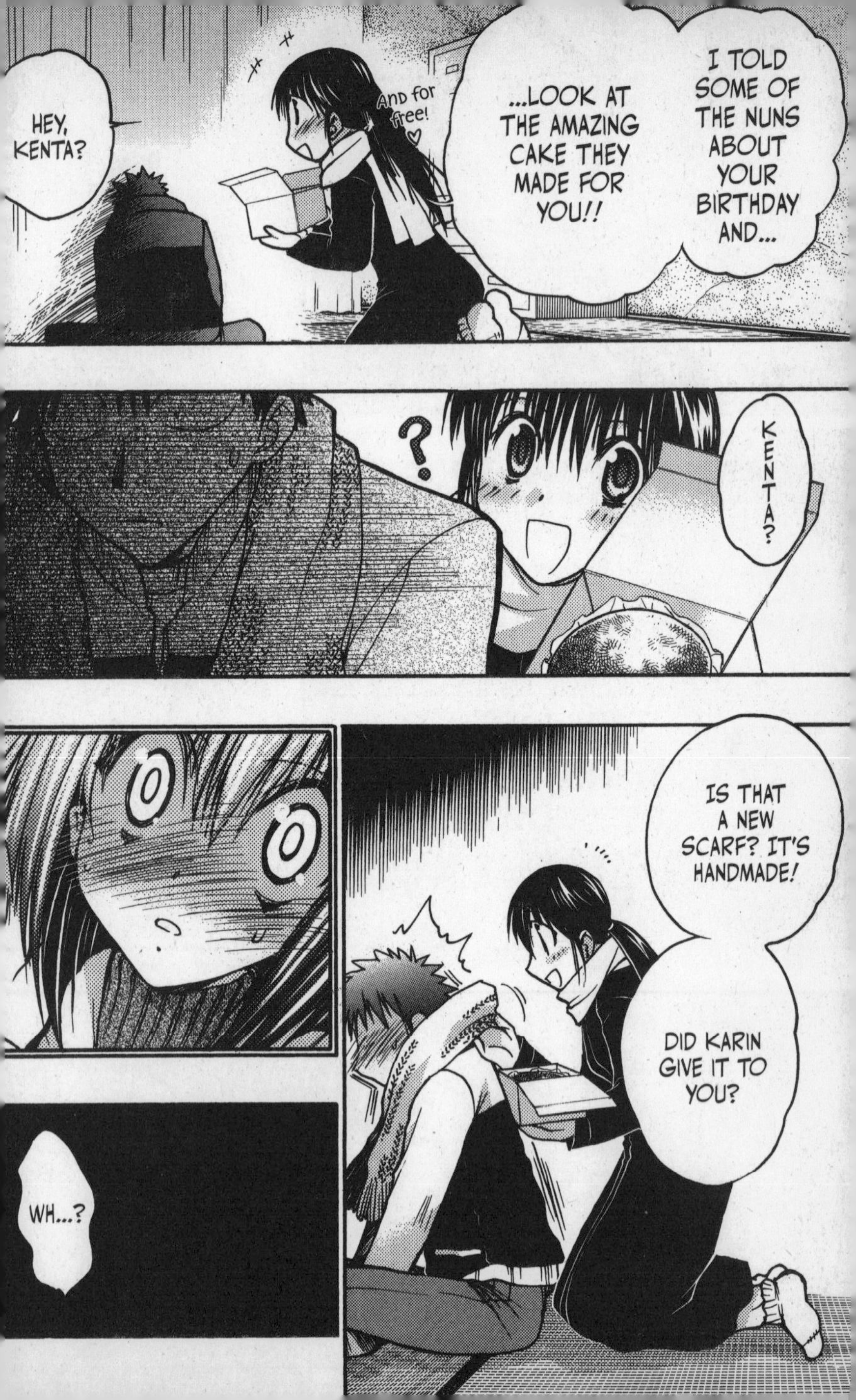
I TOLD SOME OF THE NUNS ABOUT YOUR BIRTHDAY AND...
...LOOK AT THE AMAZING CAKE THEY MADE FOR YOU!!
And for free!
HEY, KENTA?
KENTA?
IS THAT A NEW SCARF? IT'S HANDMADE!
DID KARIN GIVE IT TO YOU?
WH...?

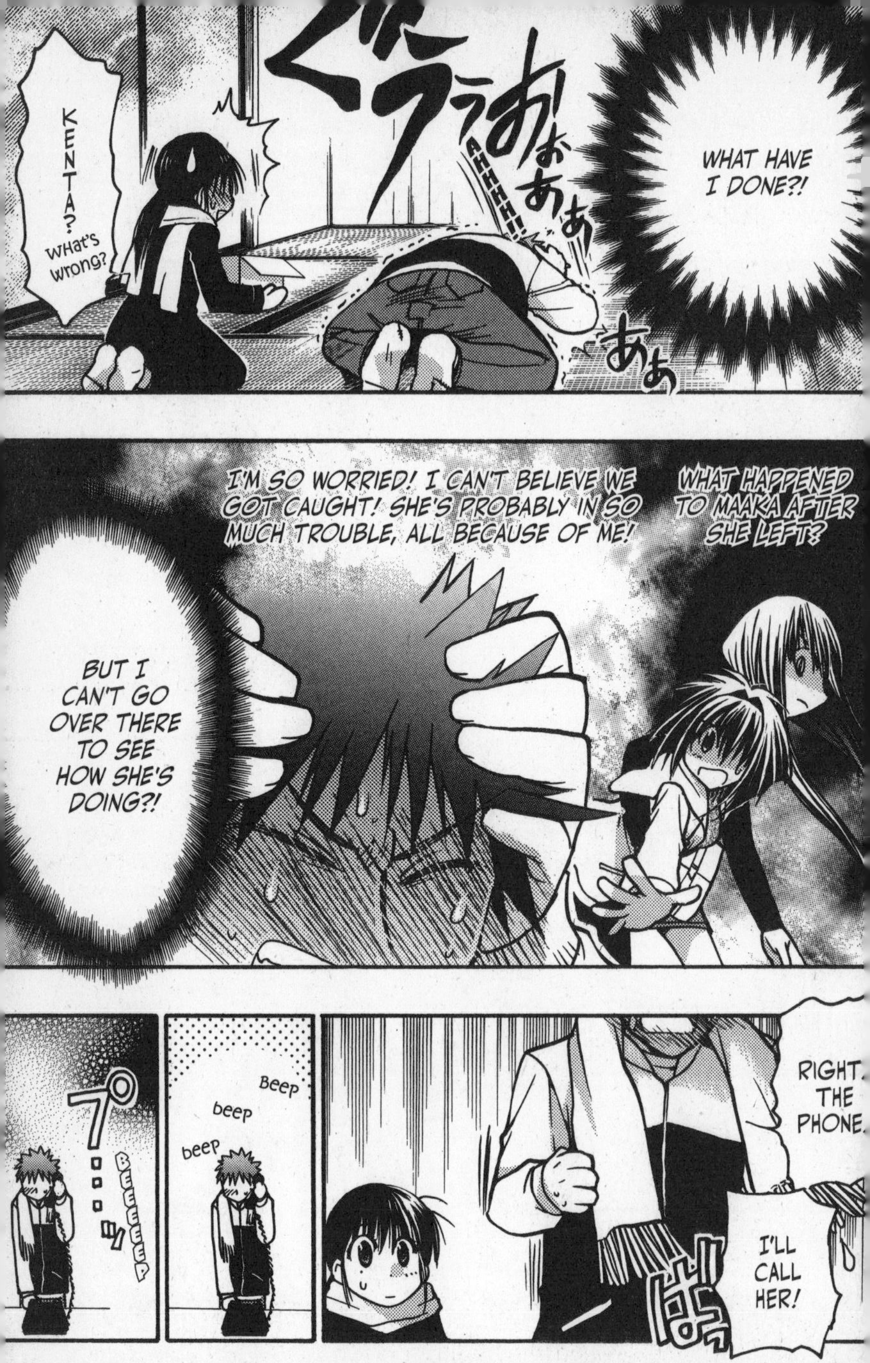
WHAT HAVE I DONE?!
AHHHHH!
KENTA? What's wrong?
WHAT HAPPENED TO MAAKA AFTER SHE LEFT?
I'M SO WORRIED! I CAN'T BELIEVE WE GOT CAUGHT! SHE'S PROBABLY IN SO MUCH TROUBLE, ALL BECAUSE OF ME!
BUT I CAN'T GO OVER THERE TO SEE HOW SHE'S DOING?!
RIGHT. THE PHONE.
I'LL CALL HER!
Beep
beep
beep
BEEEEEP

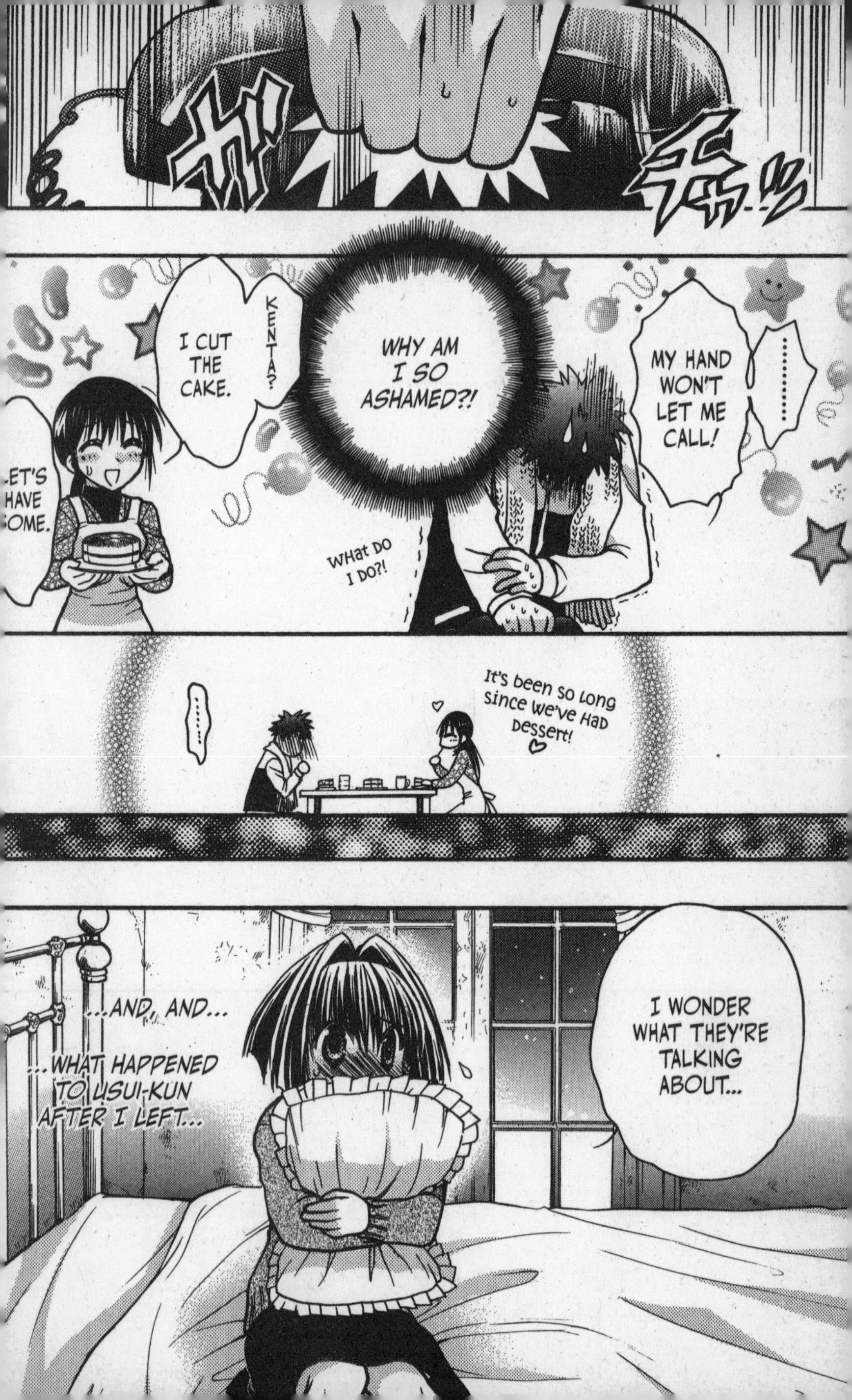
......
MY HAND WON'T LET ME CALL!
WHY AM I SO ASHAMED?!
WHAT DO I DO?!
KENTA?
I CUT THE CAKE.
ET'S HAVE OME.
It's been so long since we've had dessert!
......
I WONDER WHAT THEY'RE TALKING ABOUT...
...AND, AND...
...WHAT HAPPENED TO USUI-KUN AFTER I LEFT...

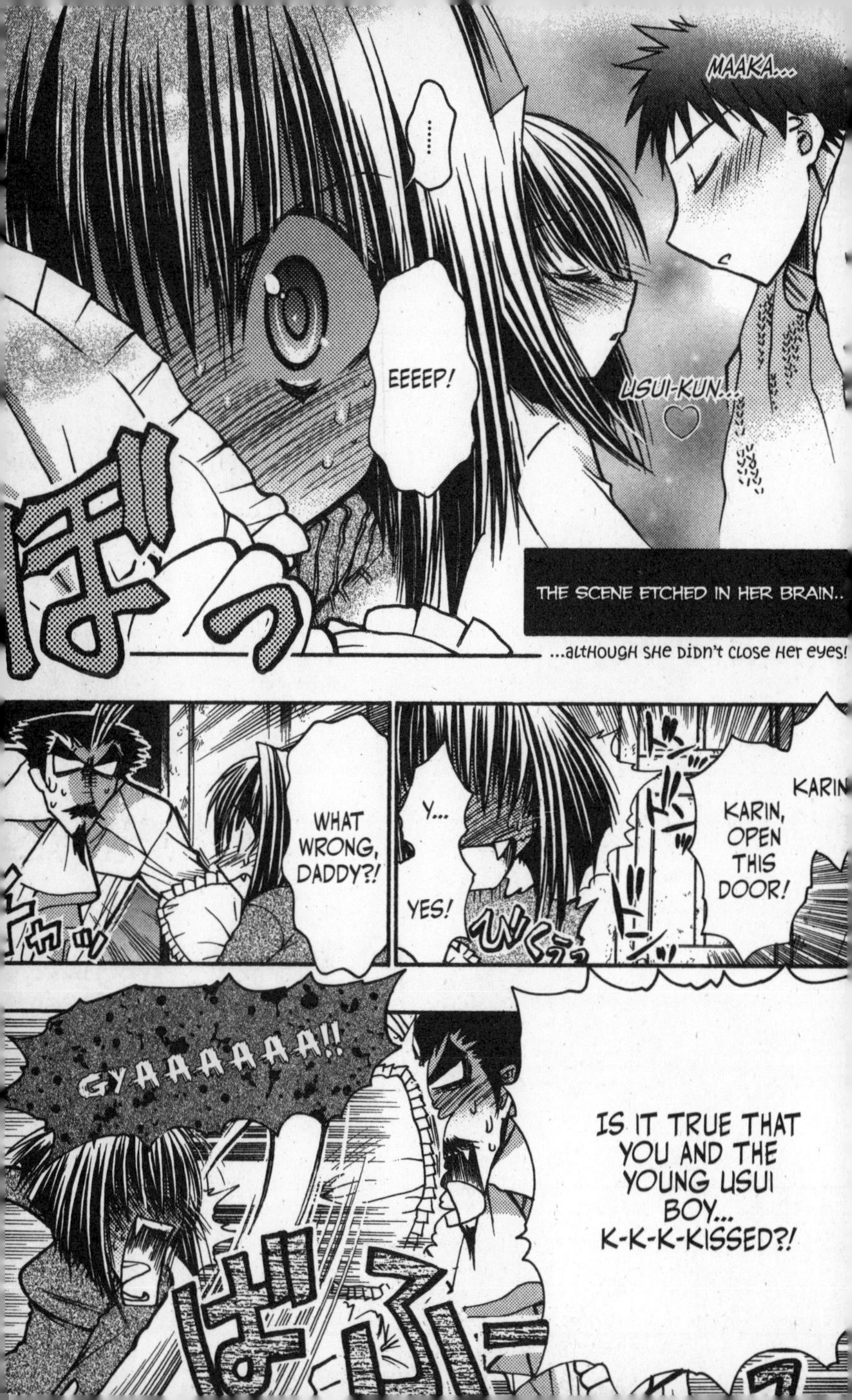
MAAKA...
USUI-KUN...
......
EEEEP!
ぽっ
THE SCENE ETCHED IN HER BRAIN..
...although she didn't close her eyes!
KARIN
KARIN, OPEN THIS DOOR!
Y...
YES!
WHAT WRONG, DADDY?!
IS IT TRUE THAT YOU AND THE YOUNG USUI BOY... K-K-K-KISSED?!
GYAAAAAAA!!

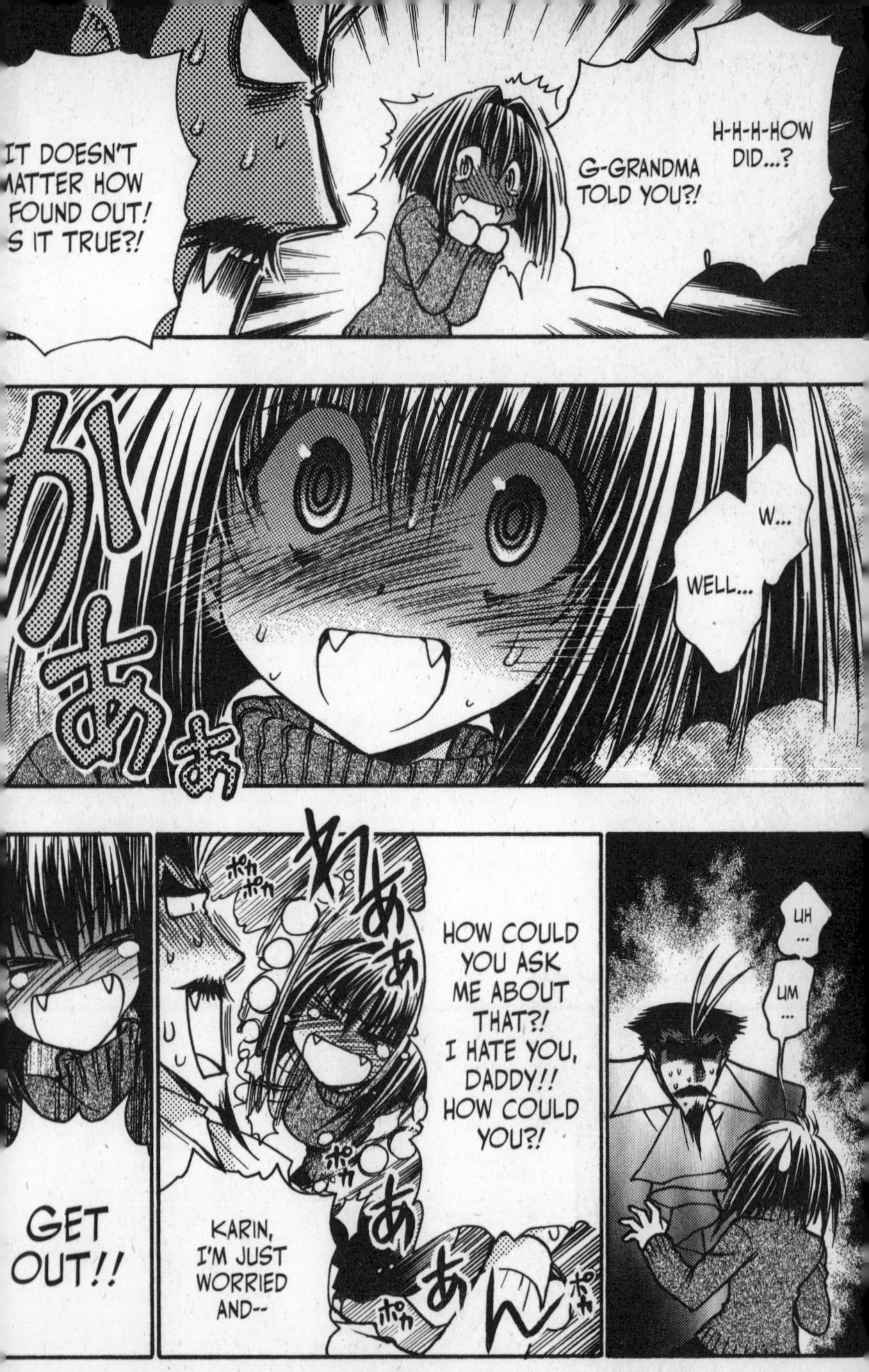

H-H-H-HOW DID...?
G-GRANDMA TOLD YOU?!
IT DOESN'T MATTER HOW FOUND OUT! S IT TRUE?!
W...
WELL...
かあぁ
UH... UM...
HOW COULD YOU ASK ME ABOUT THAT?! I HATE YOU, DADDY!! HOW COULD YOU?!
ポカポカ
わあああん
ポカ
ポカ
ポカ
KARIN, I'M JUST WORRIED AND--
GET OUT!!

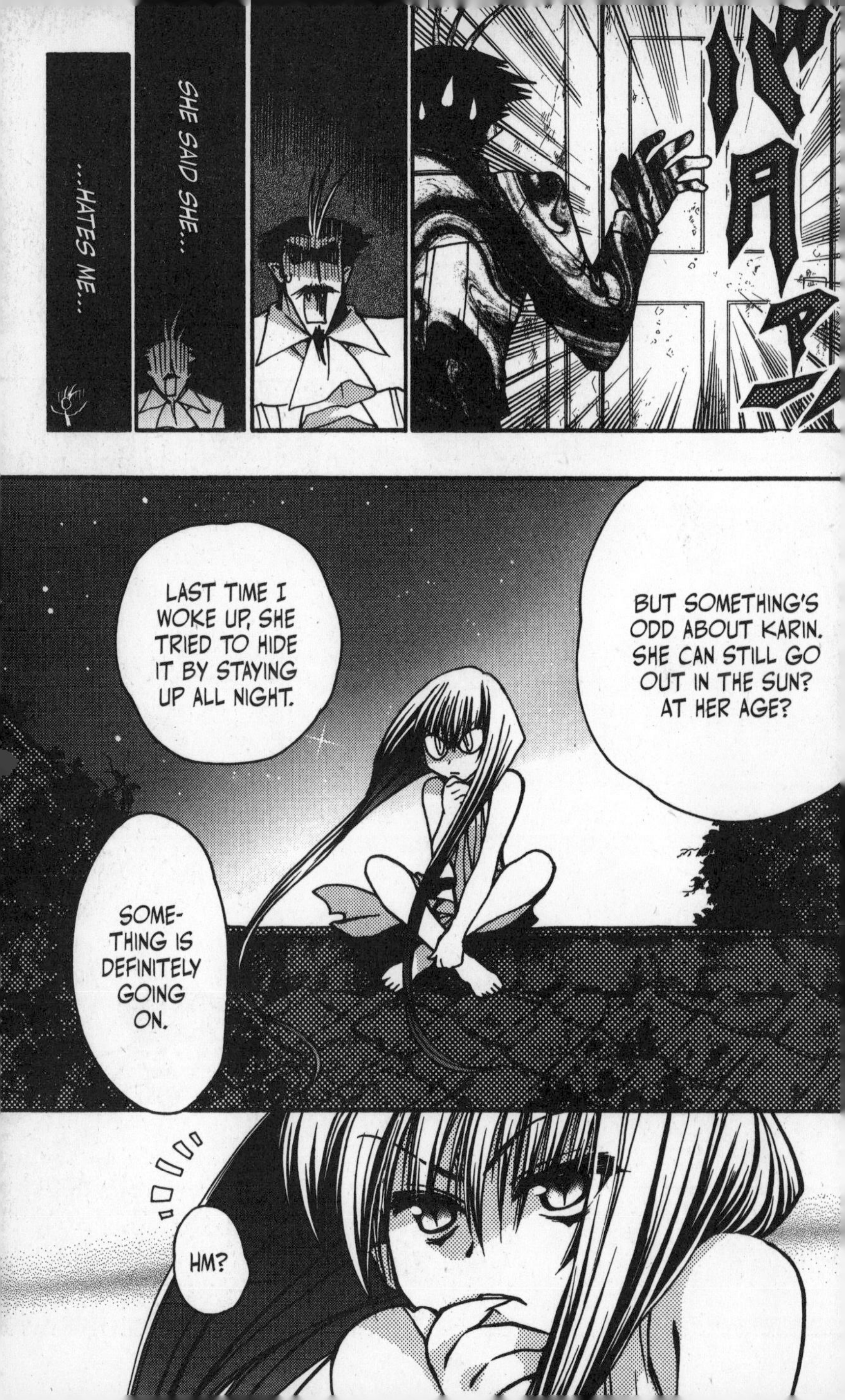
SHE SAID SHE...
...HATES ME...
BUT SOMETHING'S ODD ABOUT KARIN. SHE CAN STILL GO OUT IN THE SUN? AT HER AGE?
LAST TIME I WOKE UP, SHE TRIED TO HIDE IT BY STAYING UP ALL NIGHT.
SOME-THING IS DEFINITELY GOING ON.
HM?

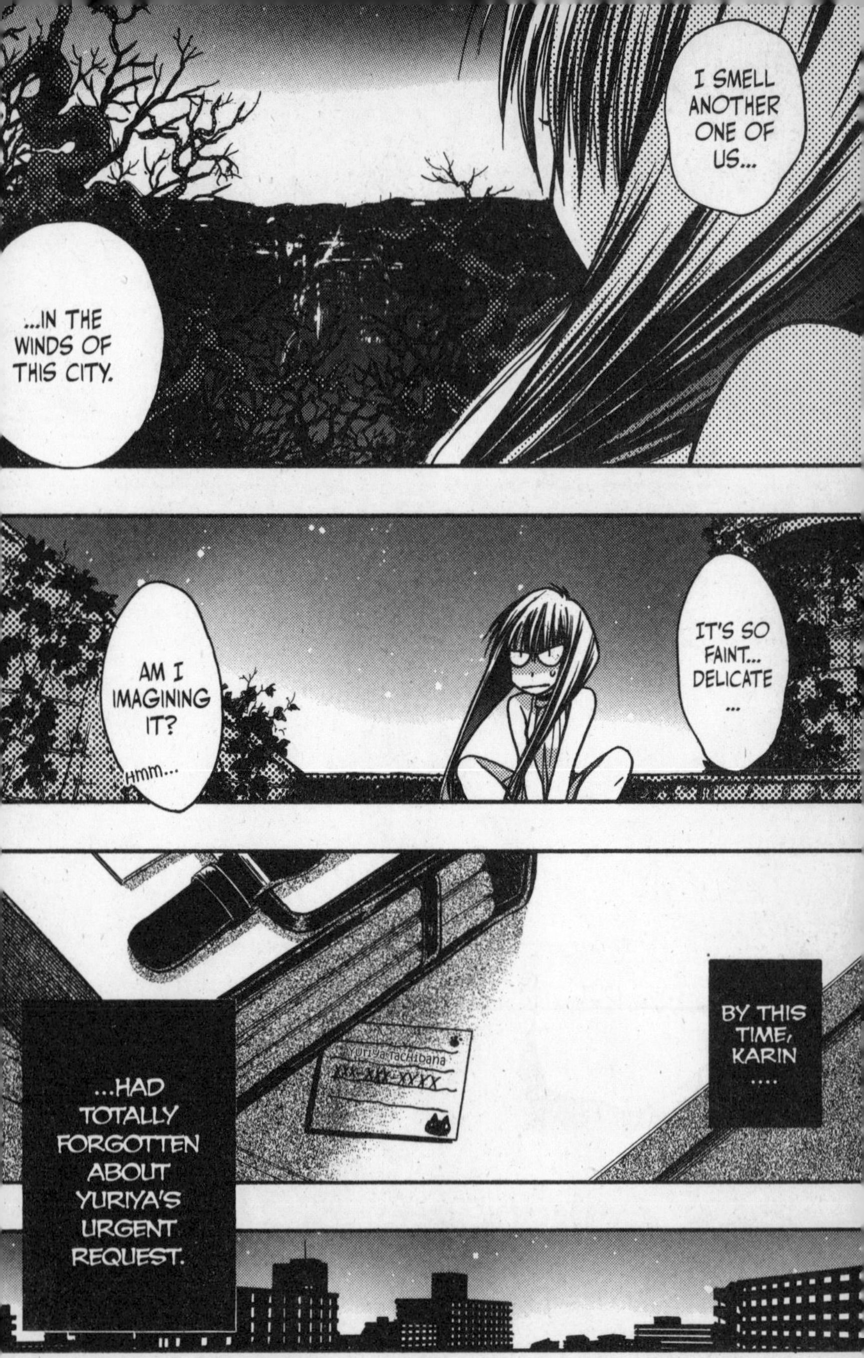
I SMELL ANOTHER ONE OF US...
...IN THE WINDS OF THIS CITY.
IT'S SO FAINT... DELICATE ...
AM I IMAGINING IT?
Hmm...
BY THIS TIME, KARIN ....
Yuriya Tachibana
...HAD TOTALLY FORGOTTEN ABOUT YURIYA'S URGENT REQUEST.

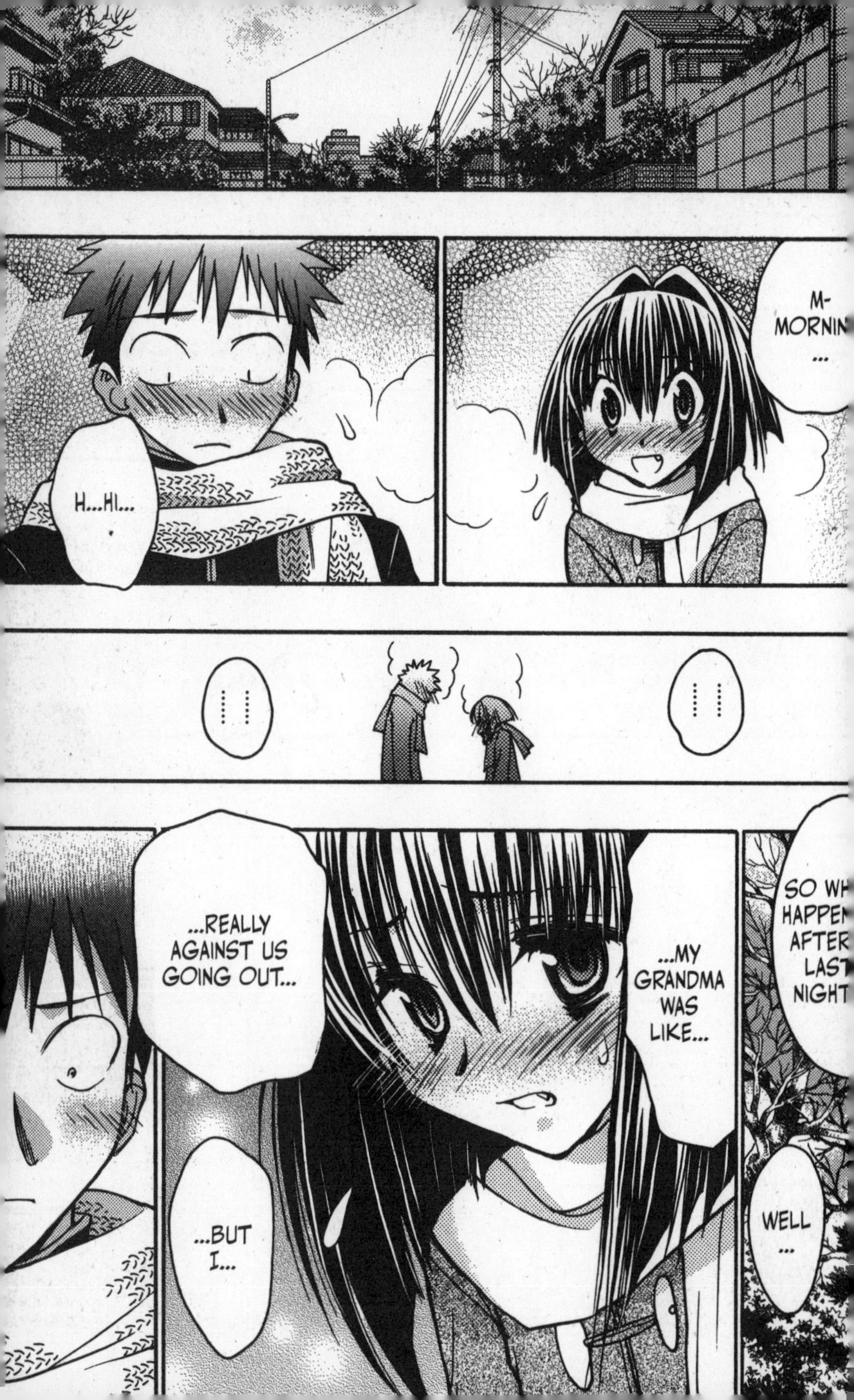
M-MORNIN ...
H...HI...
......
......
SO WH HAPPEN AFTER LAST NIGHT
WELL ...
...MY GRANDMA WAS LIKE...
...REALLY AGAINST US GOING OUT...
...BUT I...

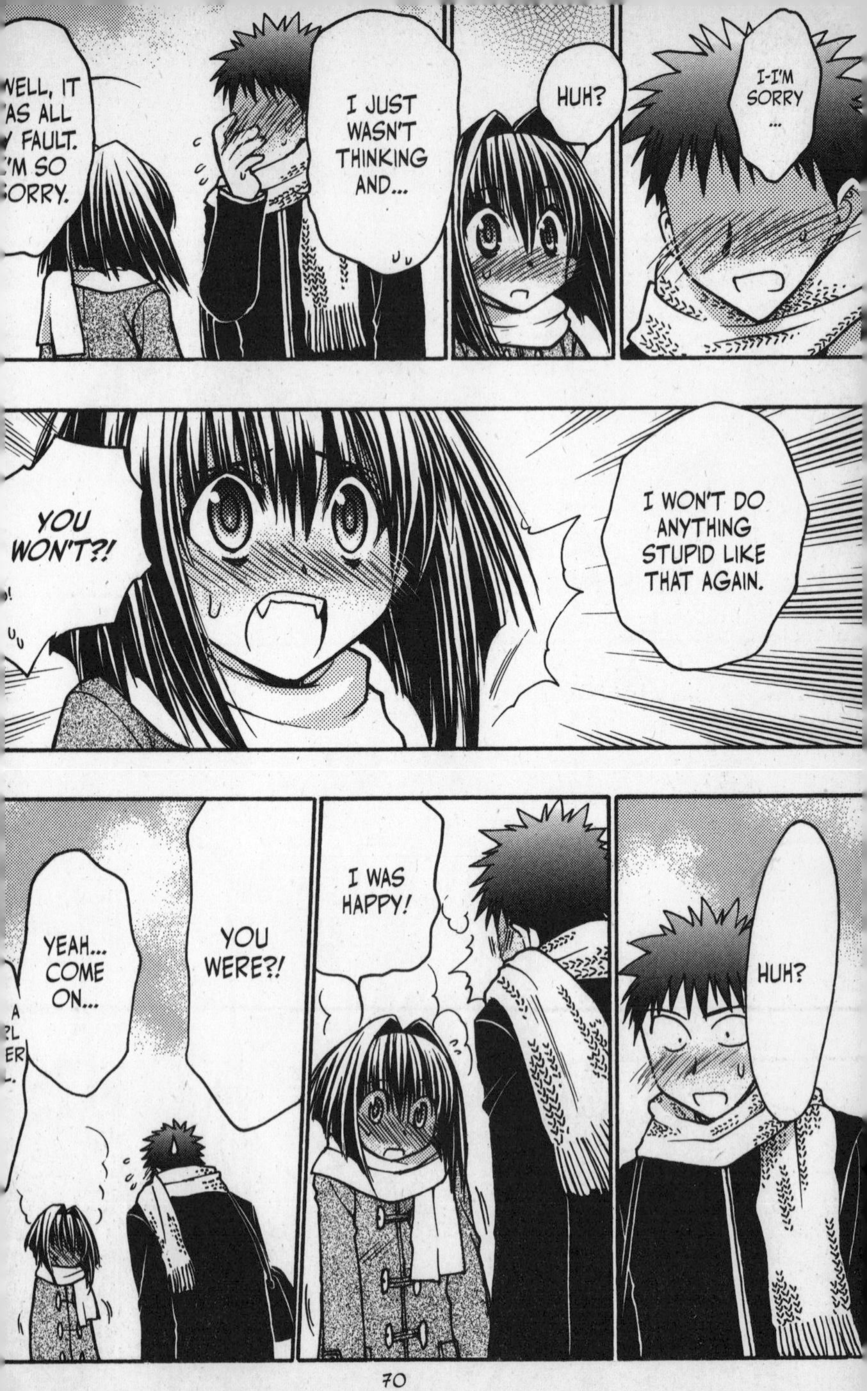
I-I'M SORRY ...
HUH?
I JUST WASN'T THINKING AND...
VELL, IT AS ALL Y FAULT. 'M SO ORRY.
I WON'T DO ANYTHING STUPID LIKE THAT AGAIN.
YOU WON'T?!
HUH?
I WAS HAPPY!
YOU WERE?!
YEAH... COME ON...

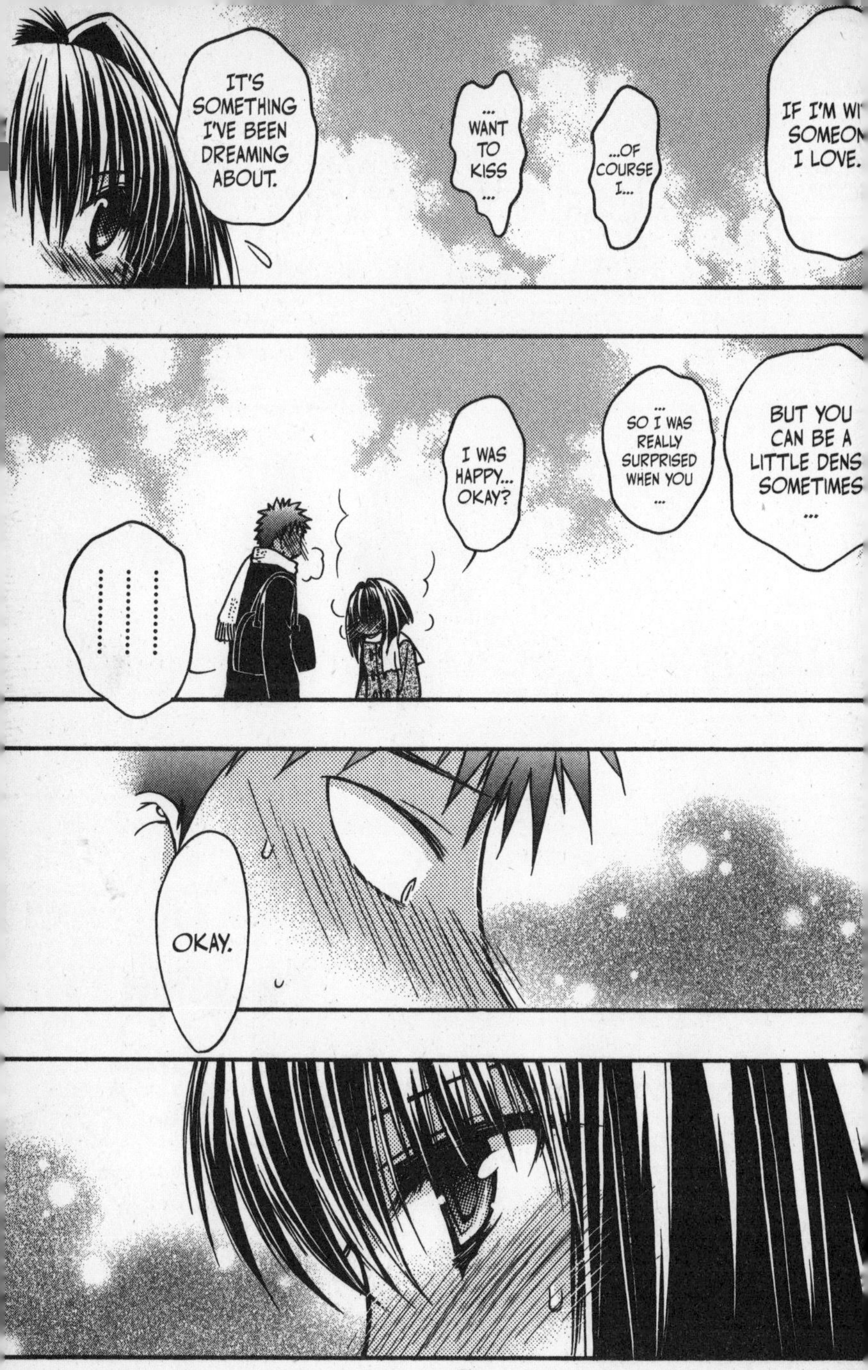
IF I'M WI SOMEON I LOVE.
...OF COURSE I...
... WANT TO KISS ...
IT'S SOMETHING I'VE BEEN DREAMING ABOUT.
BUT YOU CAN BE A LITTLE DENS SOMETIMES ...
... SO I WAS REALLY SURPRISED WHEN YOU ...
I WAS HAPPY... OKAY?
......
OKAY.

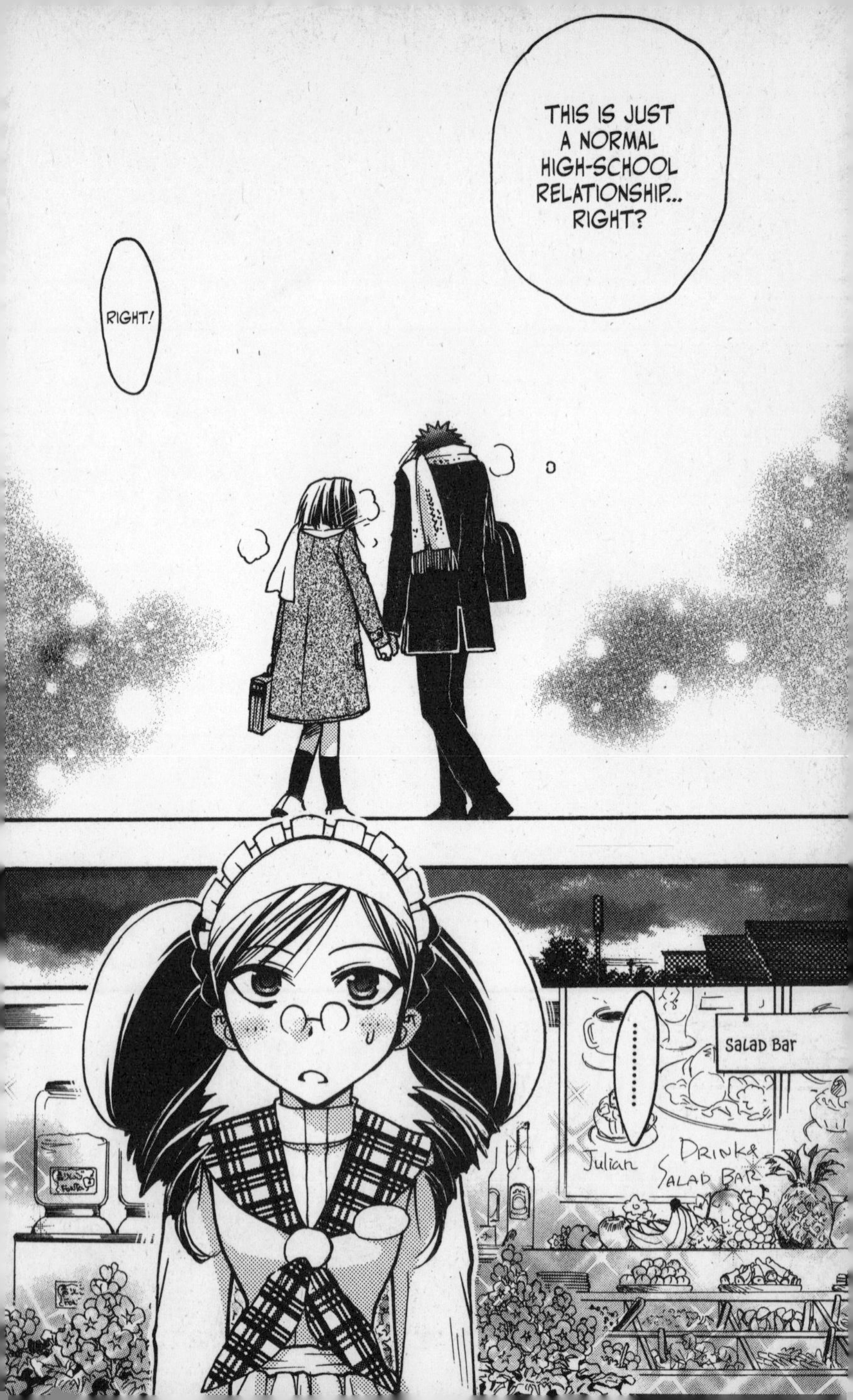
THIS IS JUST A NORMAL HIGH-SCHOOL RELATIONSHIP... RIGHT?
RIGHT!
......
Salad Bar
Julian
DRINK& SALAD BAR

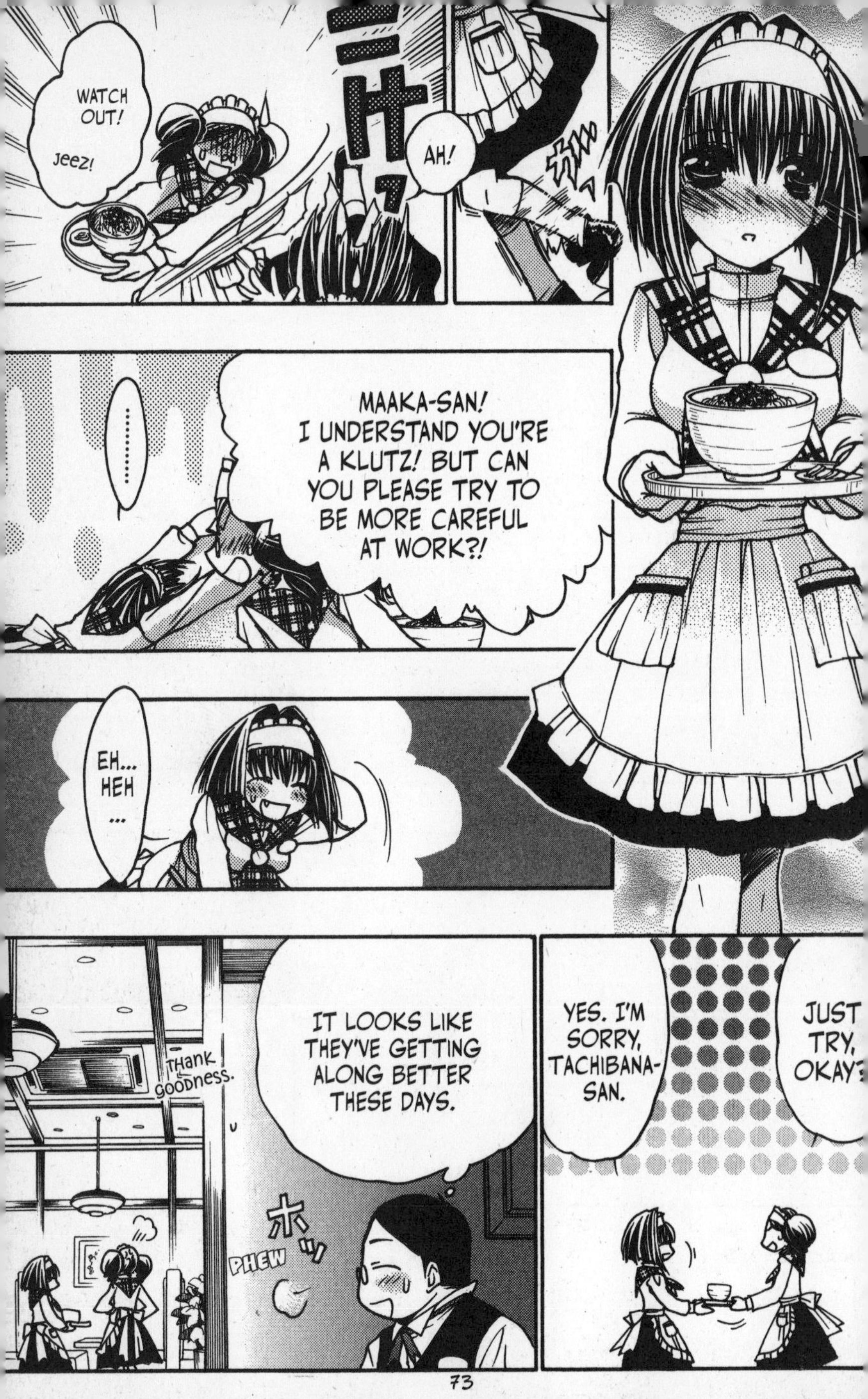
AH!
WATCH OUT!
JEEZ!
MAAKA-SAN! I UNDERSTAND YOU'RE A KLUTZ! BUT CAN YOU PLEASE TRY TO BE MORE CAREFUL AT WORK?!
......
EH... HEH ...
JUST TRY, OKAY?
YES. I'M SORRY, TACHIBANA-SAN.
IT LOOKS LIKE THEY'VE GETTING ALONG BETTER THESE DAYS.
Thank goodness.
PHEW

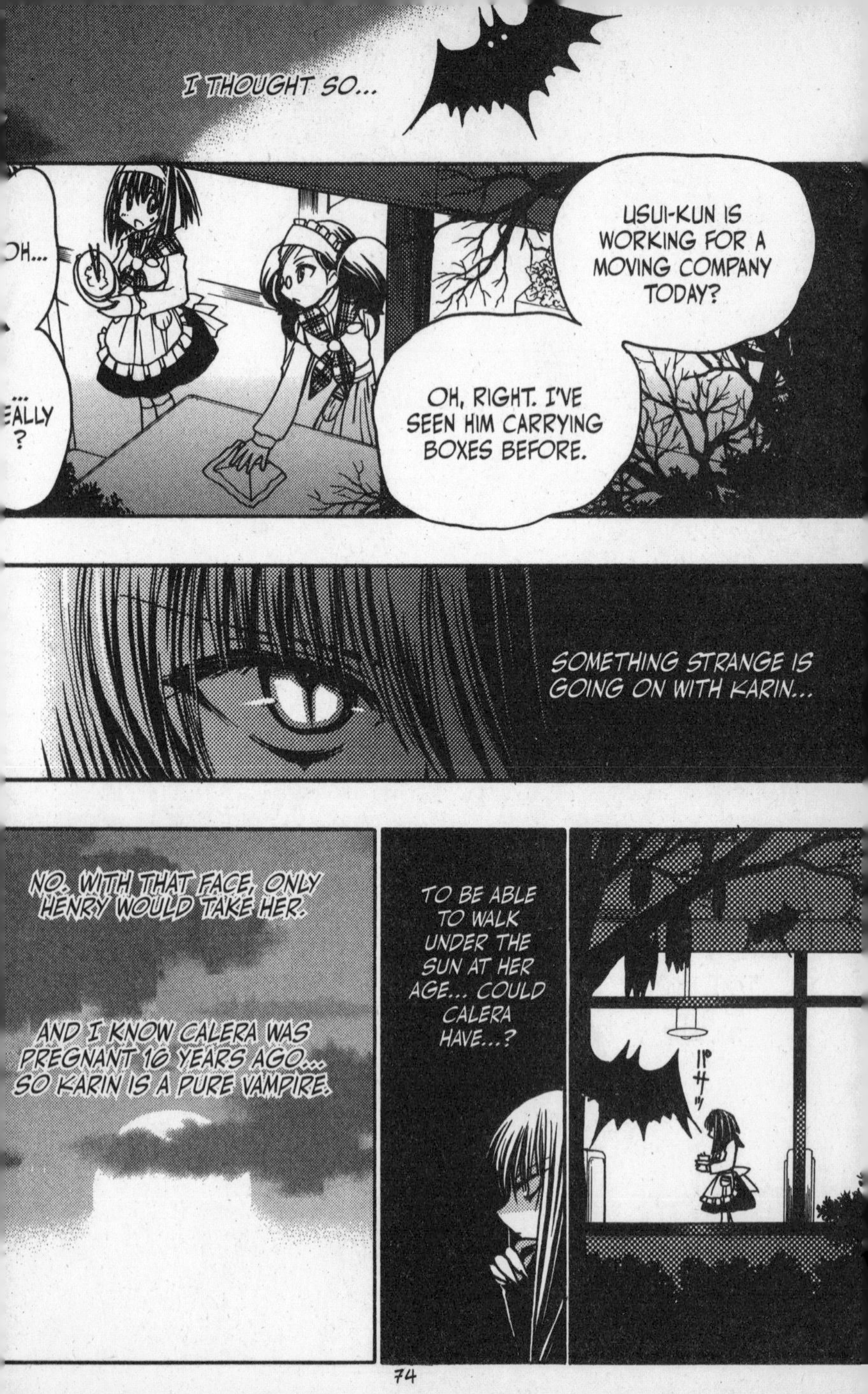
I THOUGHT SO...
USUI-KUN IS WORKING FOR A MOVING COMPANY TODAY?
OH, RIGHT. I'VE SEEN HIM CARRYING BOXES BEFORE.
H...
... EALLY ?
SOMETHING STRANGE IS GOING ON WITH KARIN...
パサッ
TO BE ABLE TO WALK UNDER THE SUN AT HER AGE... COULD CALERA HAVE...?
NO. WITH THAT FACE, ONLY HENRY WOULD TAKE HER.
AND I KNOW CALERA WAS PREGNANT 16 YEARS AGO... SO KARIN IS A PURE VAMPIRE.

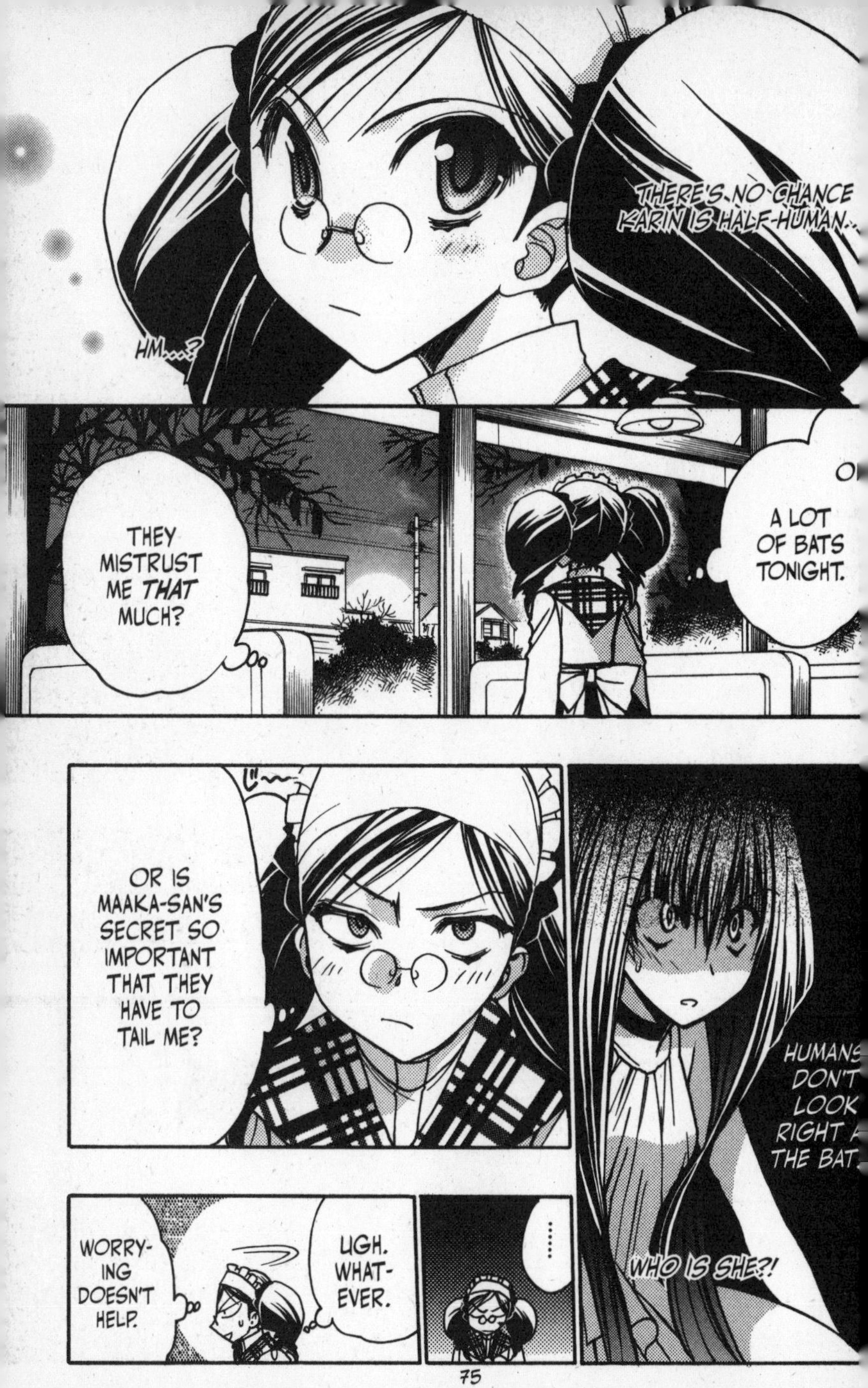
THERE'S NO CHANCE KARIN IS HALF-HUMAN...
HM...?
A LOT OF BATS TONIGHT.
THEY MISTRUST ME *THAT* MUCH?
HUMANS DON'T LOOK RIGHT A THE BAT
WHO IS SHE?!
OR IS MAAKA-SAN'S SECRET SO IMPORTANT THAT THEY HAVE TO TAIL ME?
......
UGH. WHATEVER.
WORRYING DOESN'T HELP.

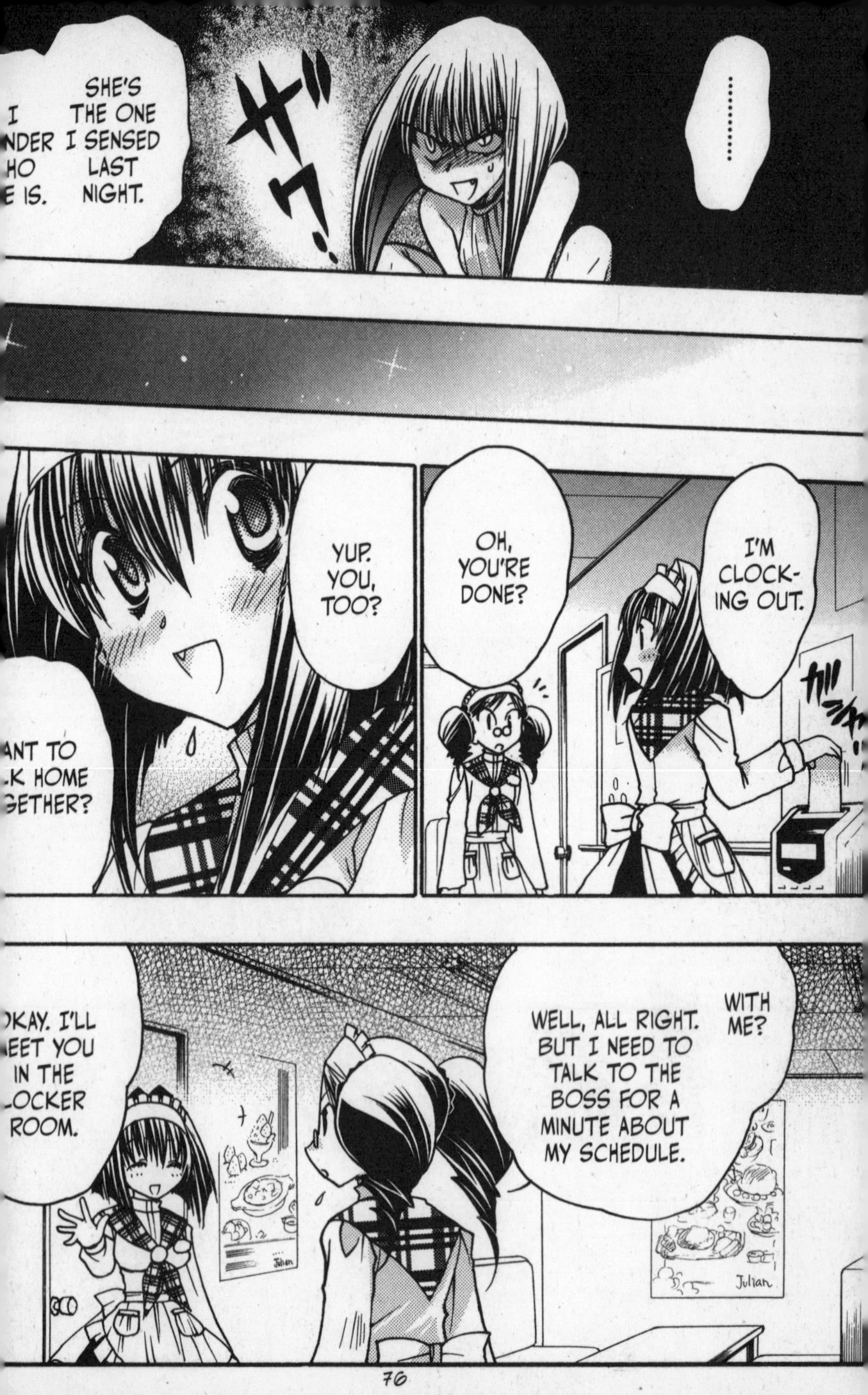
……
SHE'S THE ONE I SENSED LAST NIGHT.
I NDER HO E IS.
I'M CLOCK-ING OUT.
OH, YOU'RE DONE?
YUP. YOU, TOO?
ANT TO K HOME GETHER?
WITH ME?
WELL, ALL RIGHT. BUT I NEED TO TALK TO THE BOSS FOR A MINUTE ABOUT MY SCHEDULE.
KAY. I'LL EET YOU IN THE OCKER ROOM.
Julian
Julian

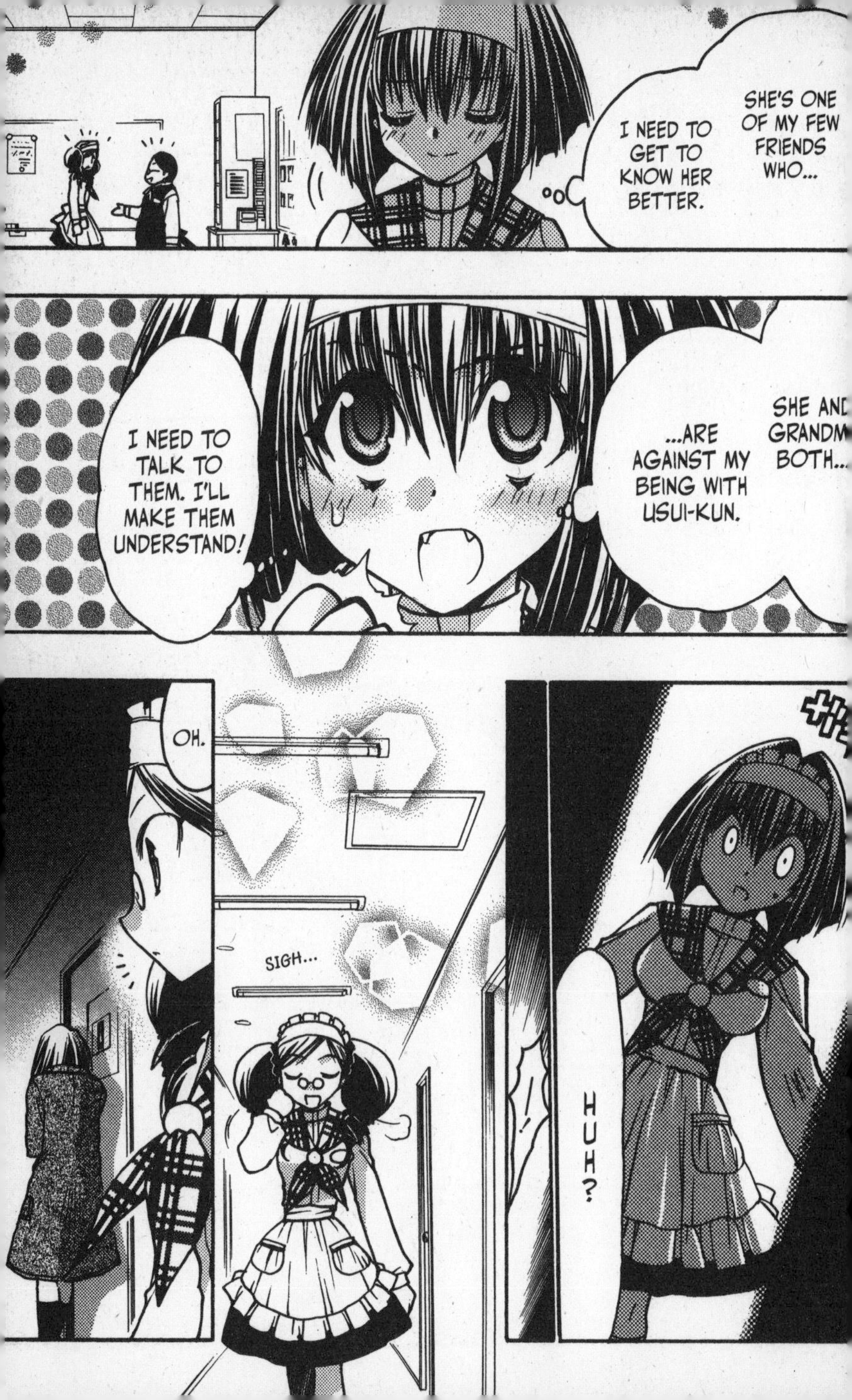
SHE'S ONE OF MY FEW FRIENDS WHO...
I NEED TO GET TO KNOW HER BETTER.
SHE AND GRANDM BOTH...
...ARE AGAINST MY BEING WITH USUI-KUN.
I NEED TO TALK TO THEM. I'LL MAKE THEM UNDERSTAND!
HUH?
SIGH...
OH.

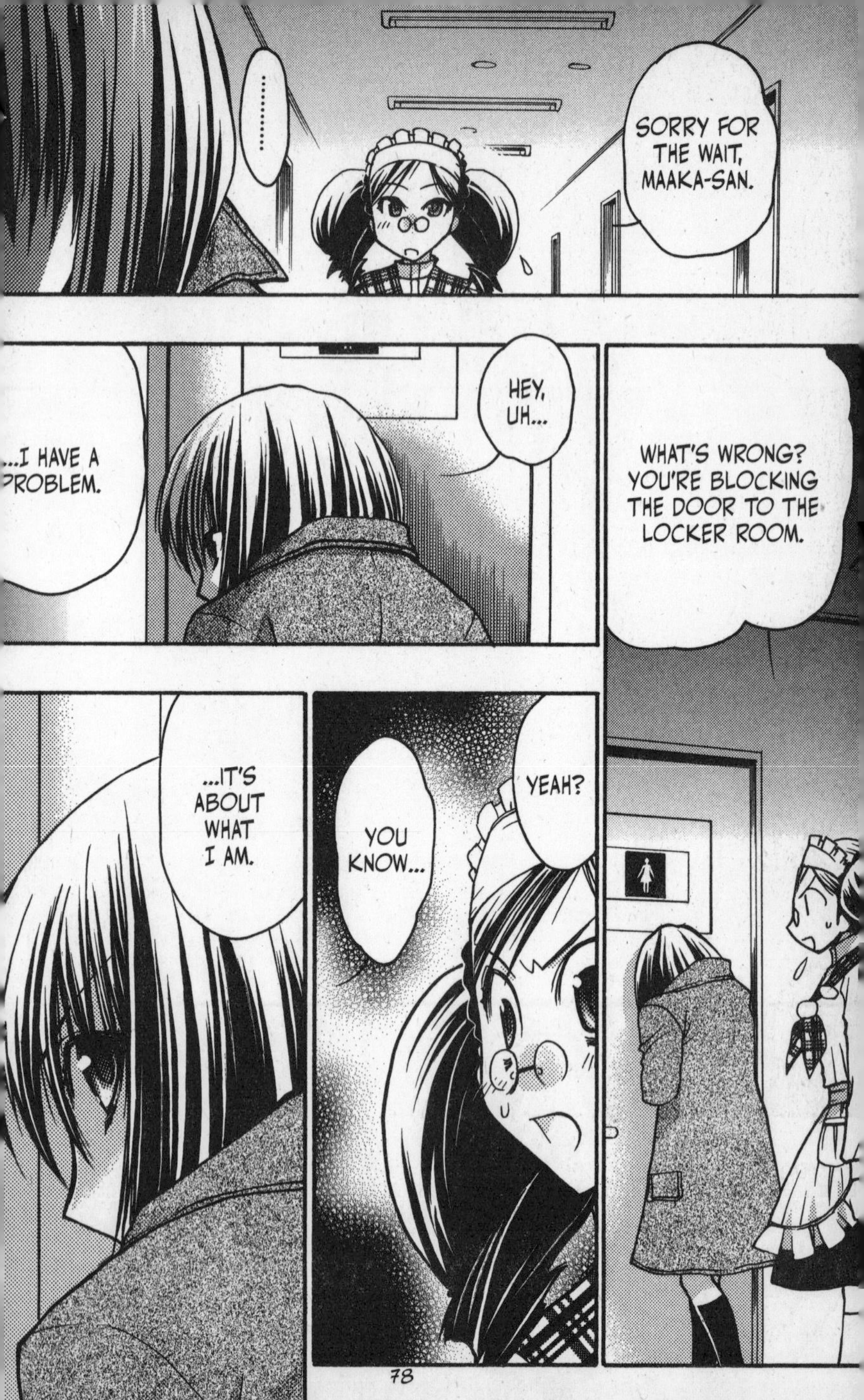
SORRY FOR THE WAIT, MAAKA-SAN.
......
WHAT'S WRONG? YOU'RE BLOCKING THE DOOR TO THE LOCKER ROOM.
HEY, UH...
...I HAVE A PROBLEM.
YEAH?
YOU KNOW...
...IT'S ABOUT WHAT I AM.

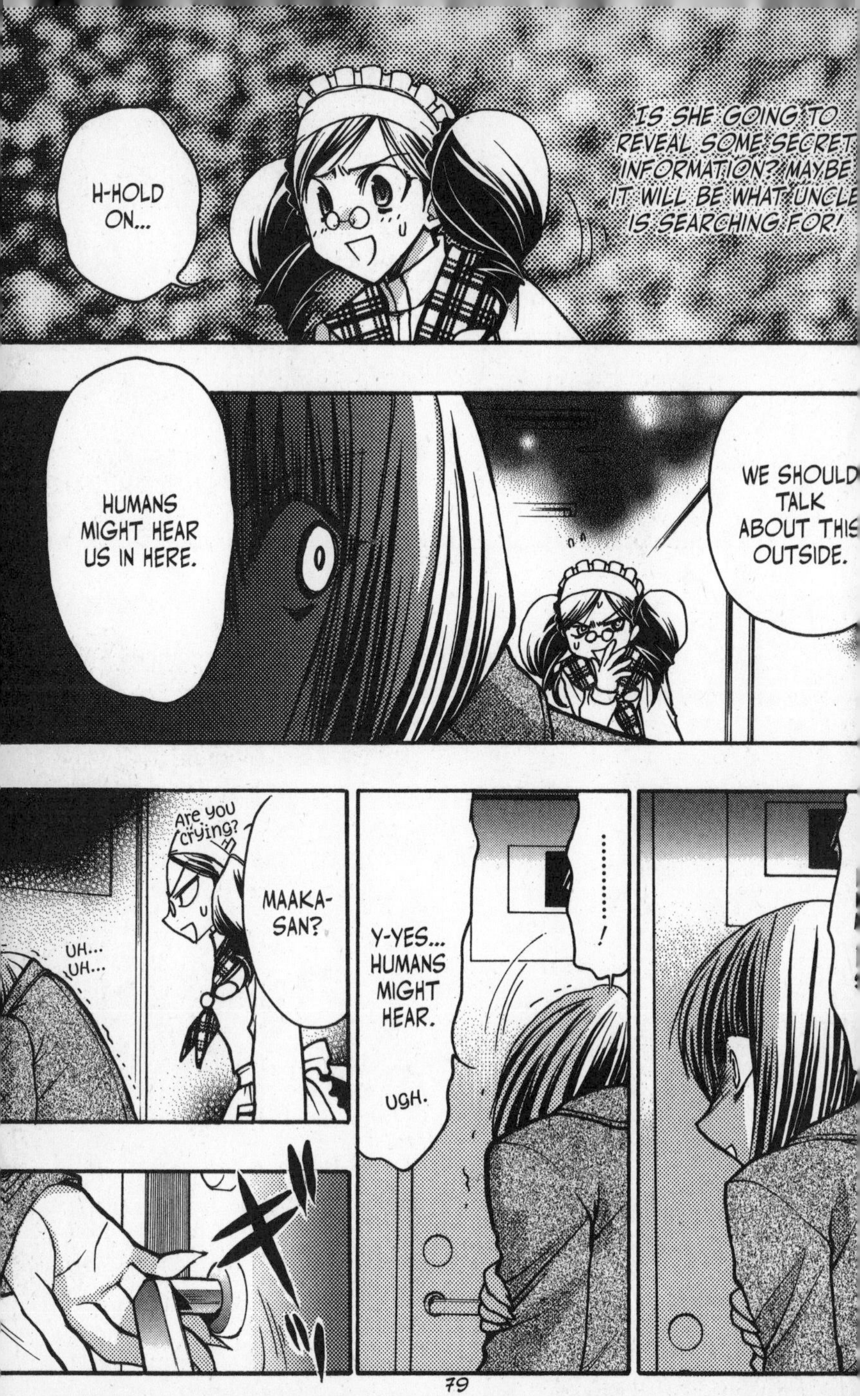
IS SHE GOING TO REVEAL SOME SECRET INFORMATION? MAYBE IT WILL BE WHAT UNCLE IS SEARCHING FOR!
H-HOLD ON...
WE SHOULD TALK ABOUT THIS OUTSIDE.
HUMANS MIGHT HEAR US IN HERE.
......!
Y-YES... HUMANS MIGHT HEAR.
UGH.
Are you crying?
MAAKA-SAN?
UH... UH...

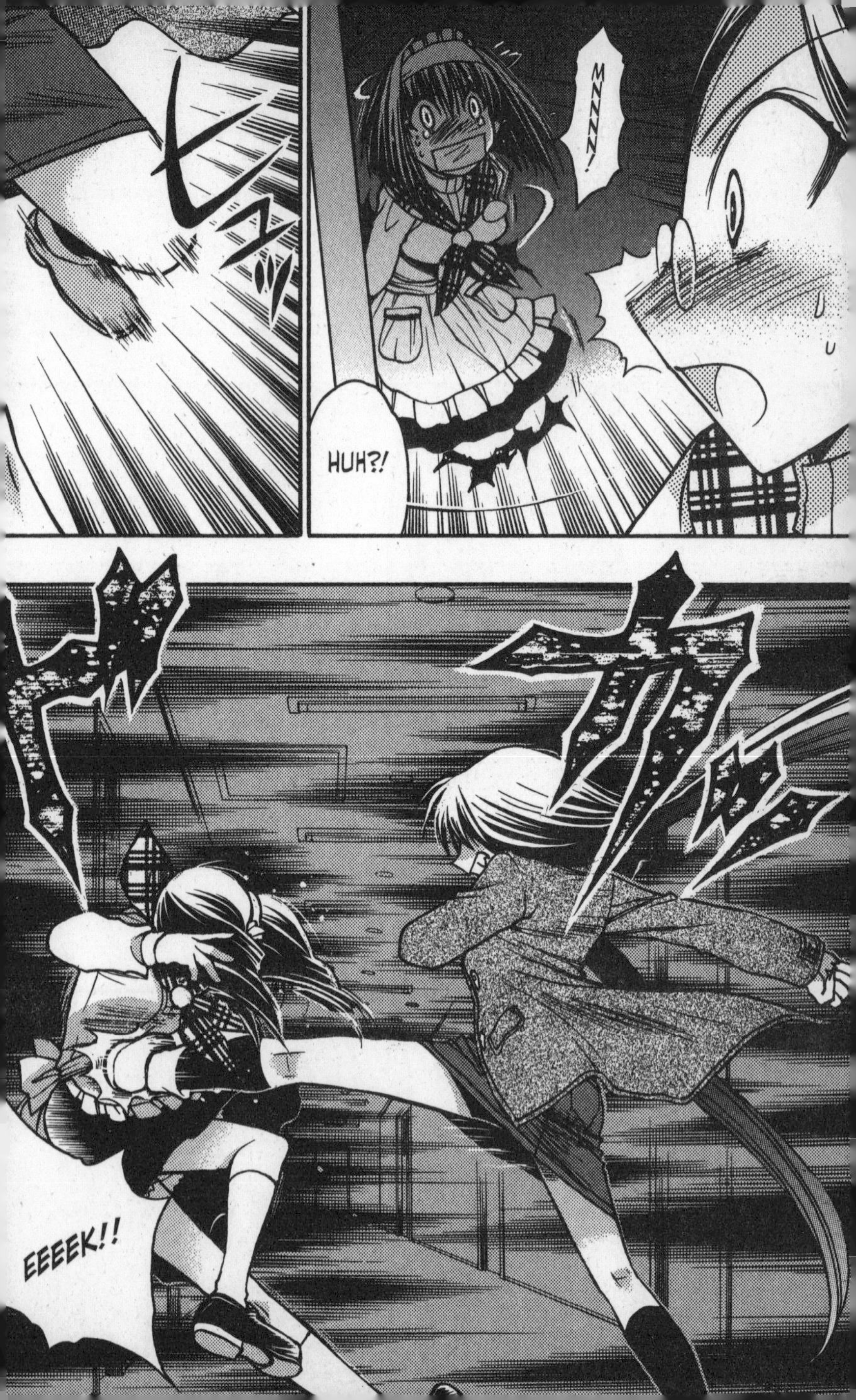
MNNNN!
HUH?!
EEEEK!!

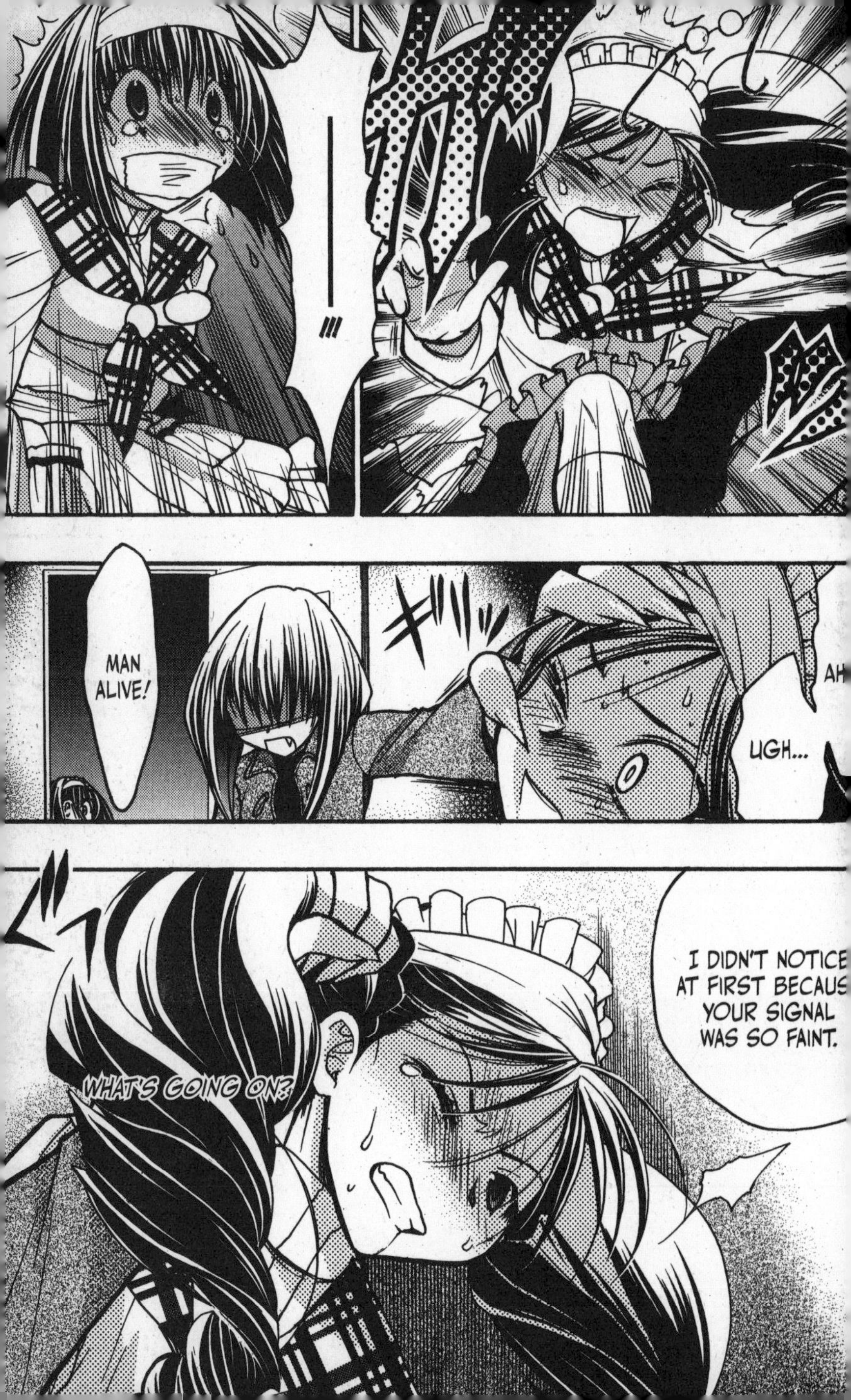
AH
UGH...
MAN ALIVE!
I DIDN'T NOTICE AT FIRST BECAUS YOUR SIGNAL WAS SO FAINT.
WHAT'S GOING ON?

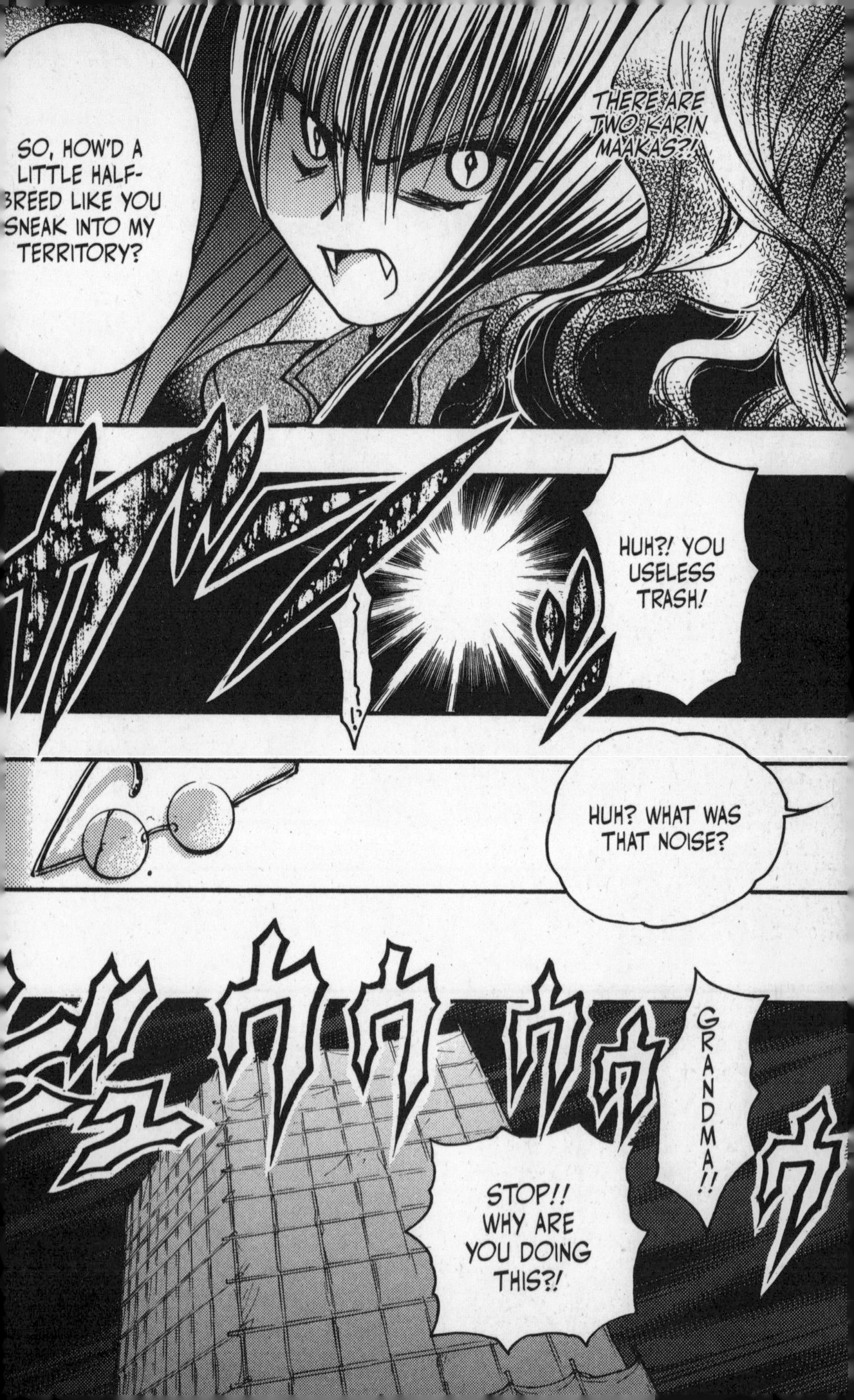
THERE ARE TWO KARIN MAAKAS?!
SO, HOW'D A LITTLE HALF-BREED LIKE YOU SNEAK INTO MY TERRITORY?
HUH?! YOU USELESS TRASH!
HUH? WHAT WAS THAT NOISE?
GRANDMA!!
STOP!! WHY ARE YOU DOING THIS?!

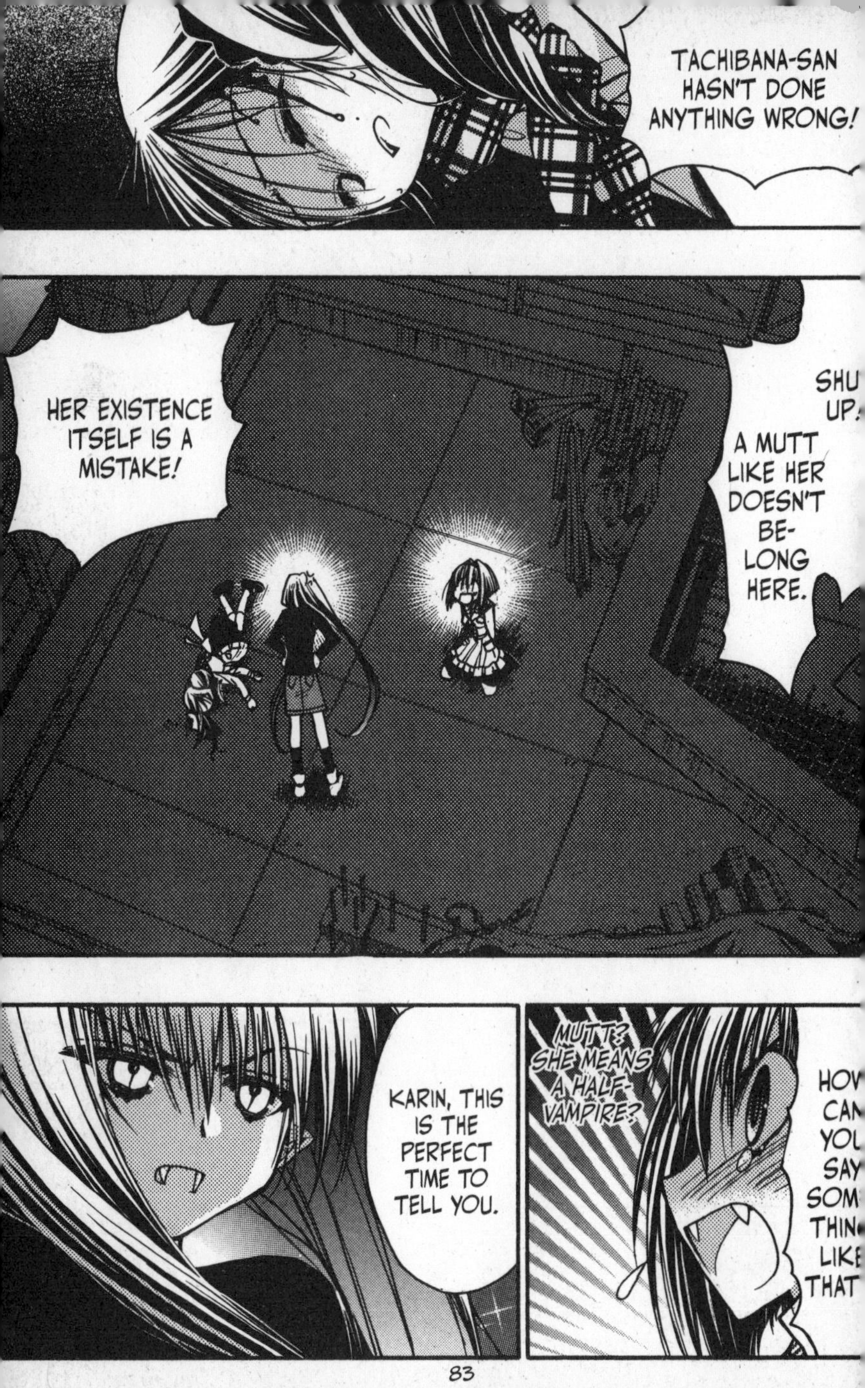
TACHIBANA-SAN HASN'T DONE ANYTHING WRONG!
SHU UP.
A MUTT LIKE HER DOESN'T BE-LONG HERE.
HER EXISTENCE ITSELF IS A MISTAKE!
HOW CAN YOU SAY SOMETHING LIKE THAT
MUTT? SHE MEANS A HALF-VAMPIRE?
KARIN, THIS IS THE PERFECT TIME TO TELL YOU.

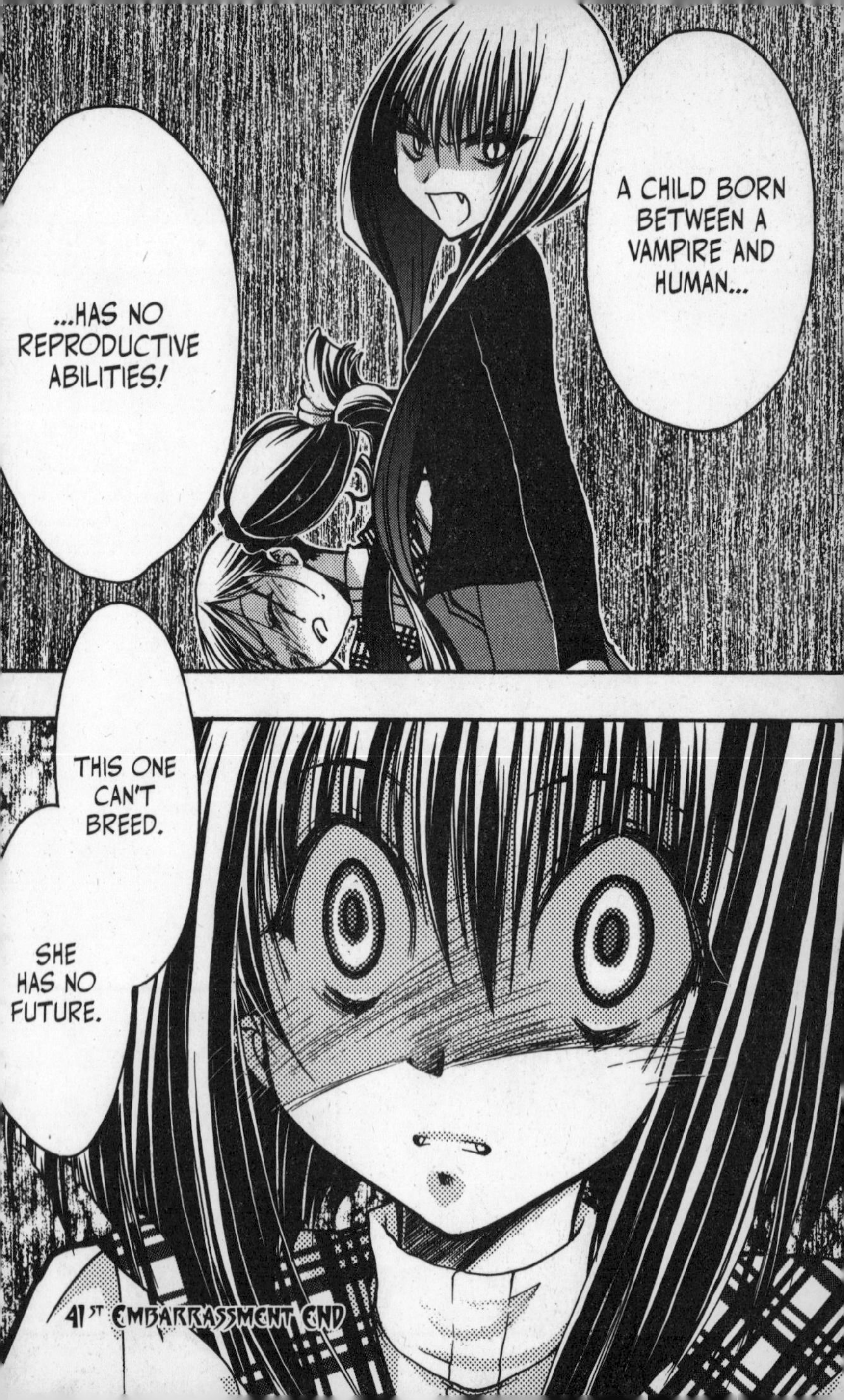
A CHILD BORN BETWEEN A VAMPIRE AND HUMAN...
...HAS NO REPRODUCTIVE ABILITIES!
THIS ONE CAN'T BREED.
SHE HAS NO FUTURE.
41ST EMBARRASSMENT END

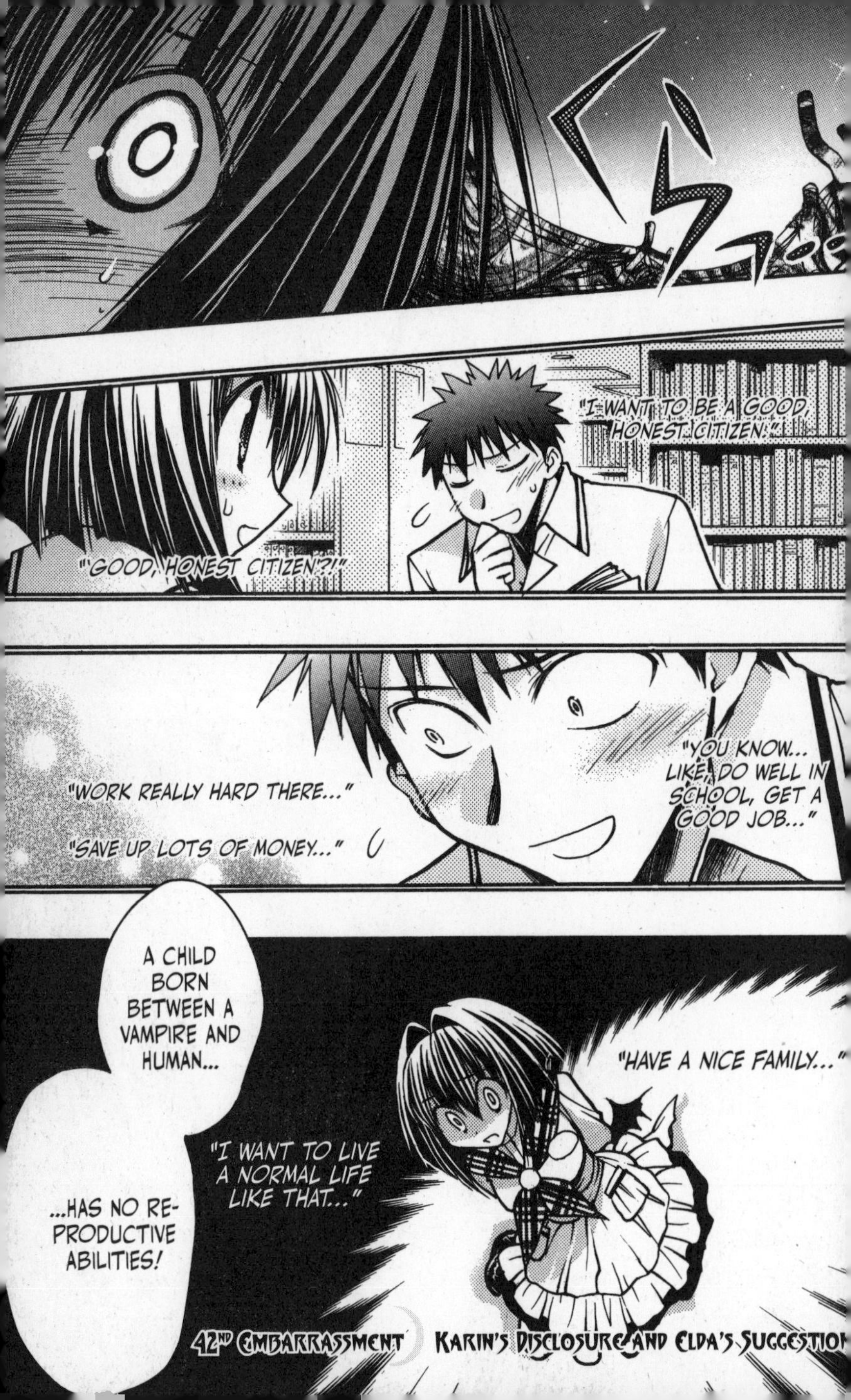
"I WANT TO BE A GOOD, HONEST CITIZEN."
"GOOD, HONEST CITIZEN?!"
"YOU KNOW... LIKE, DO WELL IN SCHOOL, GET A GOOD JOB..."
"WORK REALLY HARD THERE..."
"SAVE UP LOTS OF MONEY..."
"HAVE A NICE FAMILY..."
"I WANT TO LIVE A NORMAL LIFE LIKE THAT..."
A CHILD BORN BETWEEN A VAMPIRE AND HUMAN...
...HAS NO RE-PRODUCTIVE ABILITIES!
42ND EMBARRASSMENT KARIN'S DISCLOSURE AND ELDA'S SUGGESTION

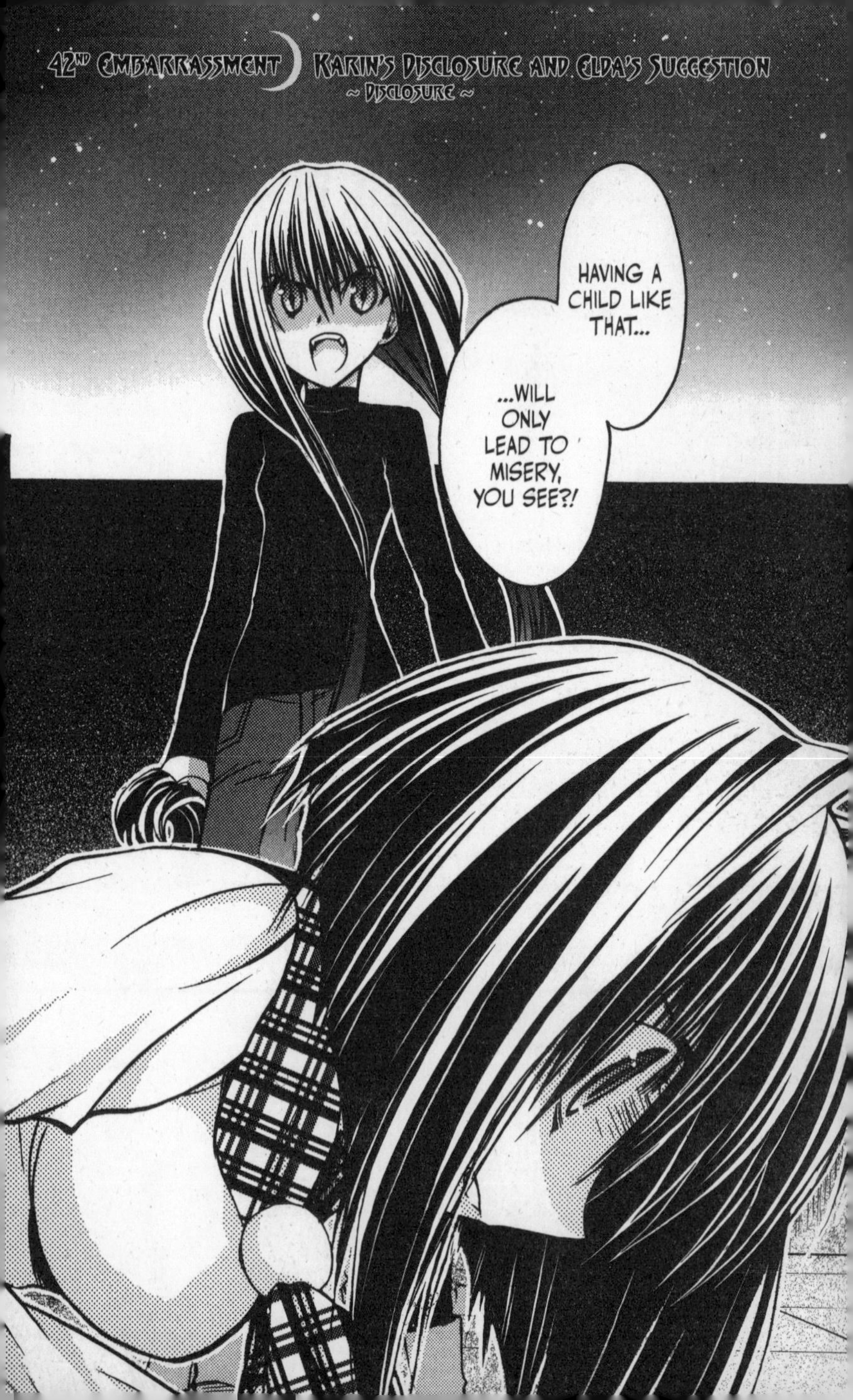
42ND EMBARRASSMENT KARIN'S DISCLOSURE AND ELDA'S SUGGESTION
~ DISCLOSURE ~
HAVING A CHILD LIKE THAT...
...WILL ONLY LEAD TO MISERY, YOU SEE?!

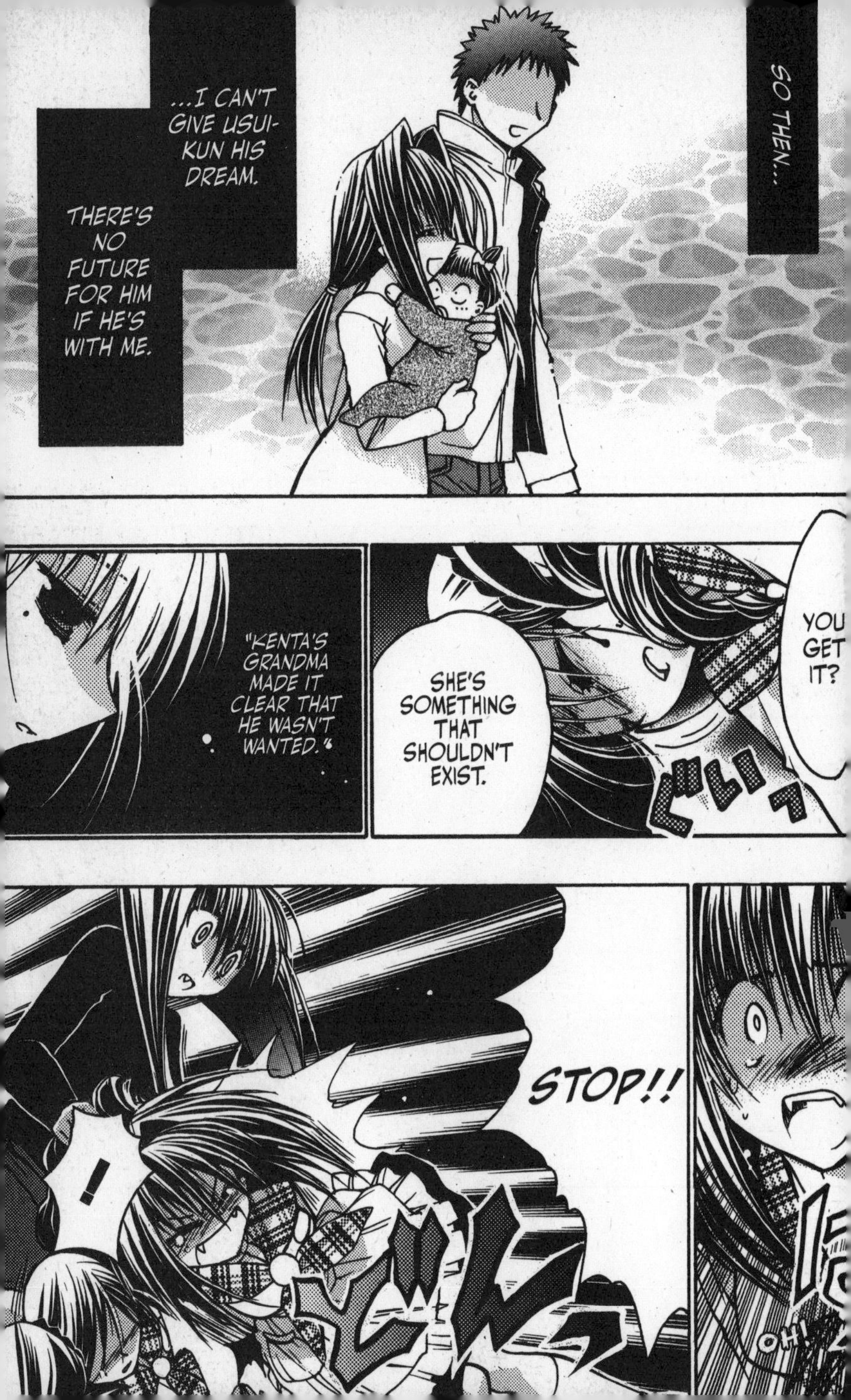
SO THEN...
...I CAN'T GIVE USUI-KUN HIS DREAM.
THERE'S NO FUTURE FOR HIM IF HE'S WITH ME.
YOU GET IT?
SHE'S SOMETHING THAT SHOULDN'T EXIST.
"KENTA'S GRANDMA MADE IT CLEAR THAT HE WASN'T WANTED."
OH...
STOP!!
!

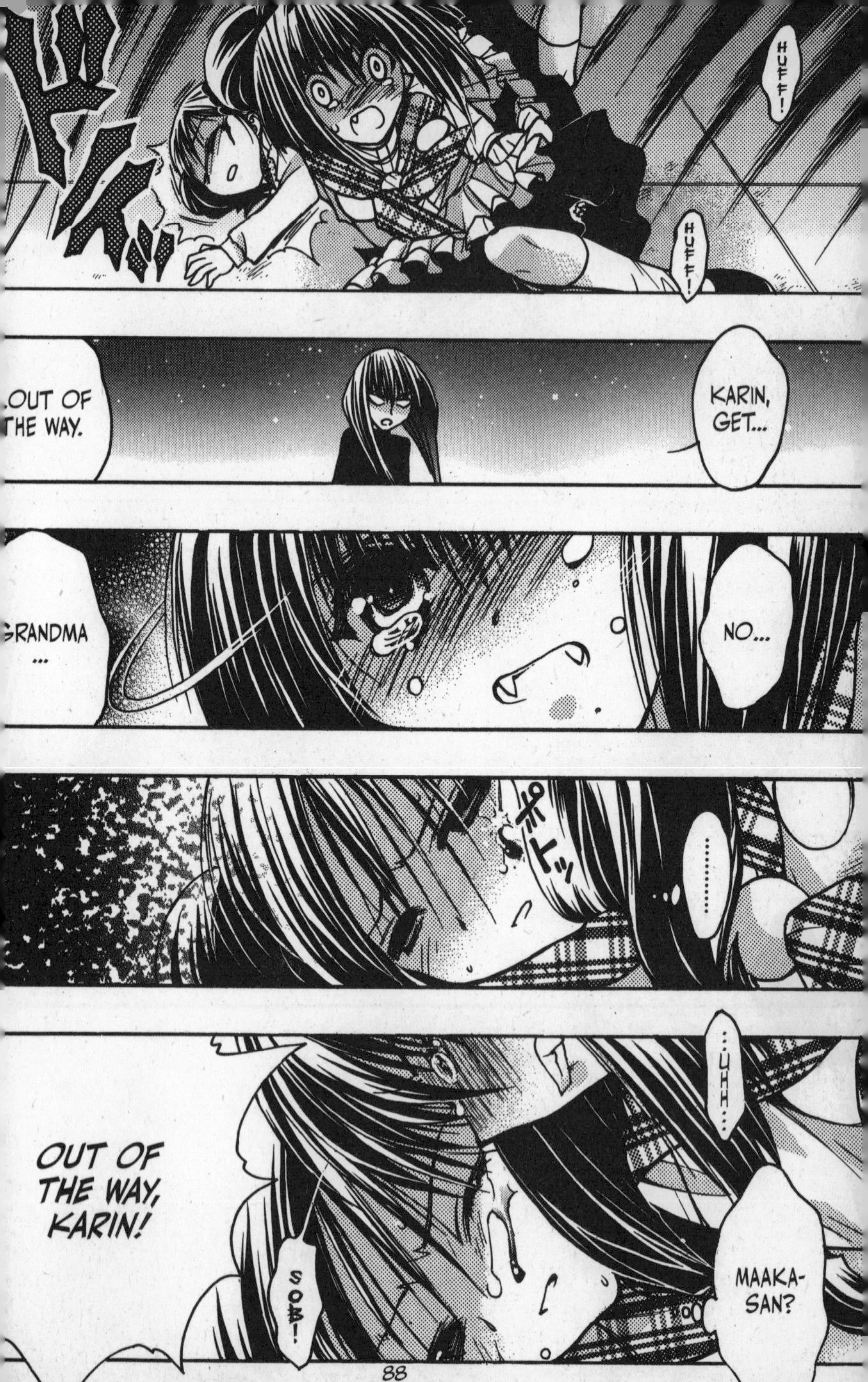
HUFF!
HUFF!
KARIN, GET...
.OUT OF THE WAY.
NO...
GRANDMA ...
......
ポトッ
...UHH...
MAAKA-SAN?
SOB!
OUT OF THE WAY, KARIN!

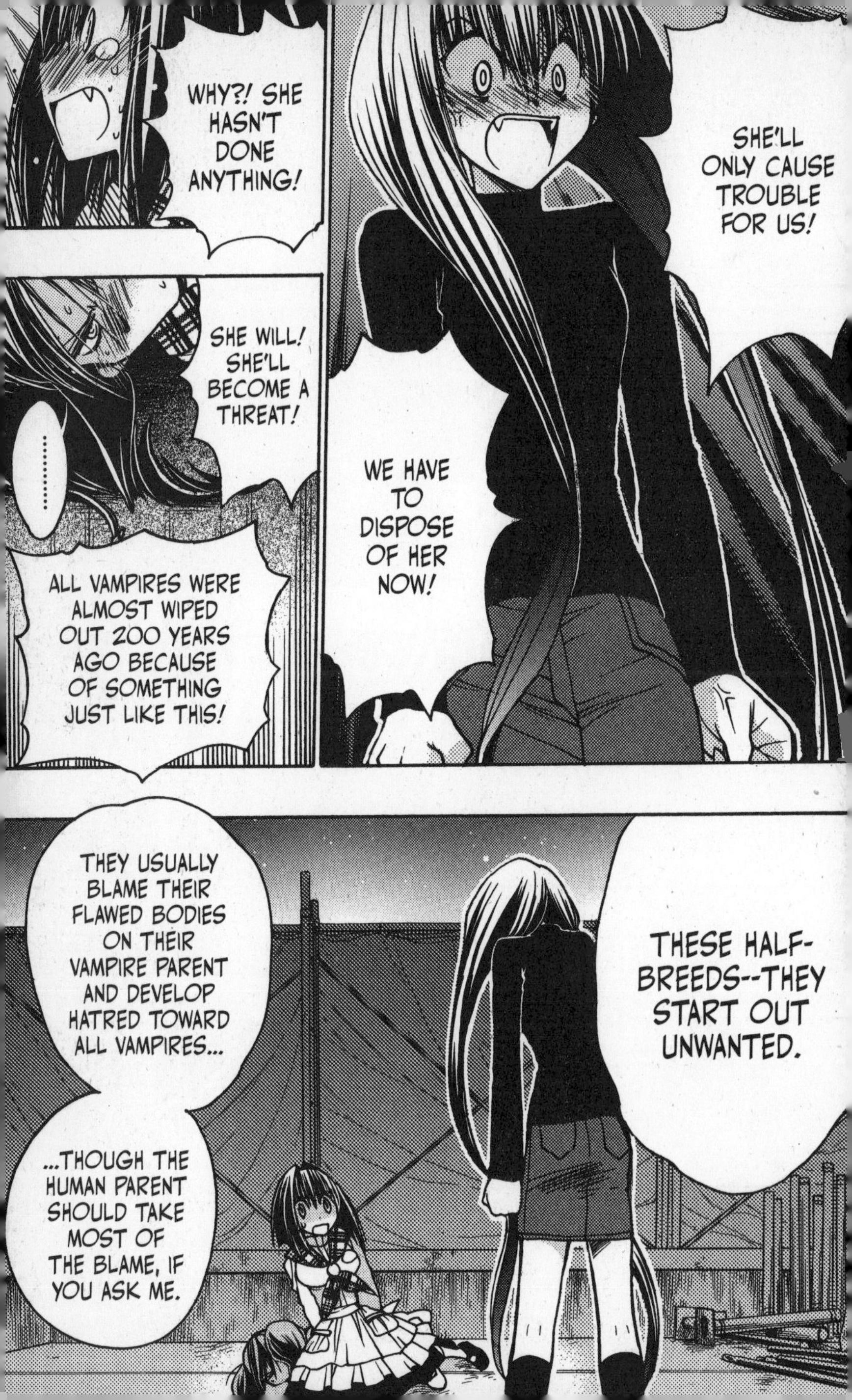
SHE'LL ONLY CAUSE TROUBLE FOR US!
WE HAVE TO DISPOSE OF HER NOW!
WHY?! SHE HASN'T DONE ANYTHING!
SHE WILL! SHE'LL BECOME A THREAT!
......
ALL VAMPIRES WERE ALMOST WIPED OUT 200 YEARS AGO BECAUSE OF SOMETHING JUST LIKE THIS!
THESE HALF-BREEDS--THEY START OUT UNWANTED.
THEY USUALLY BLAME THEIR FLAWED BODIES ON THEIR VAMPIRE PARENT AND DEVELOP HATRED TOWARD ALL VAMPIRES...
...THOUGH THE HUMAN PARENT SHOULD TAKE MOST OF THE BLAME, IF YOU ASK ME.

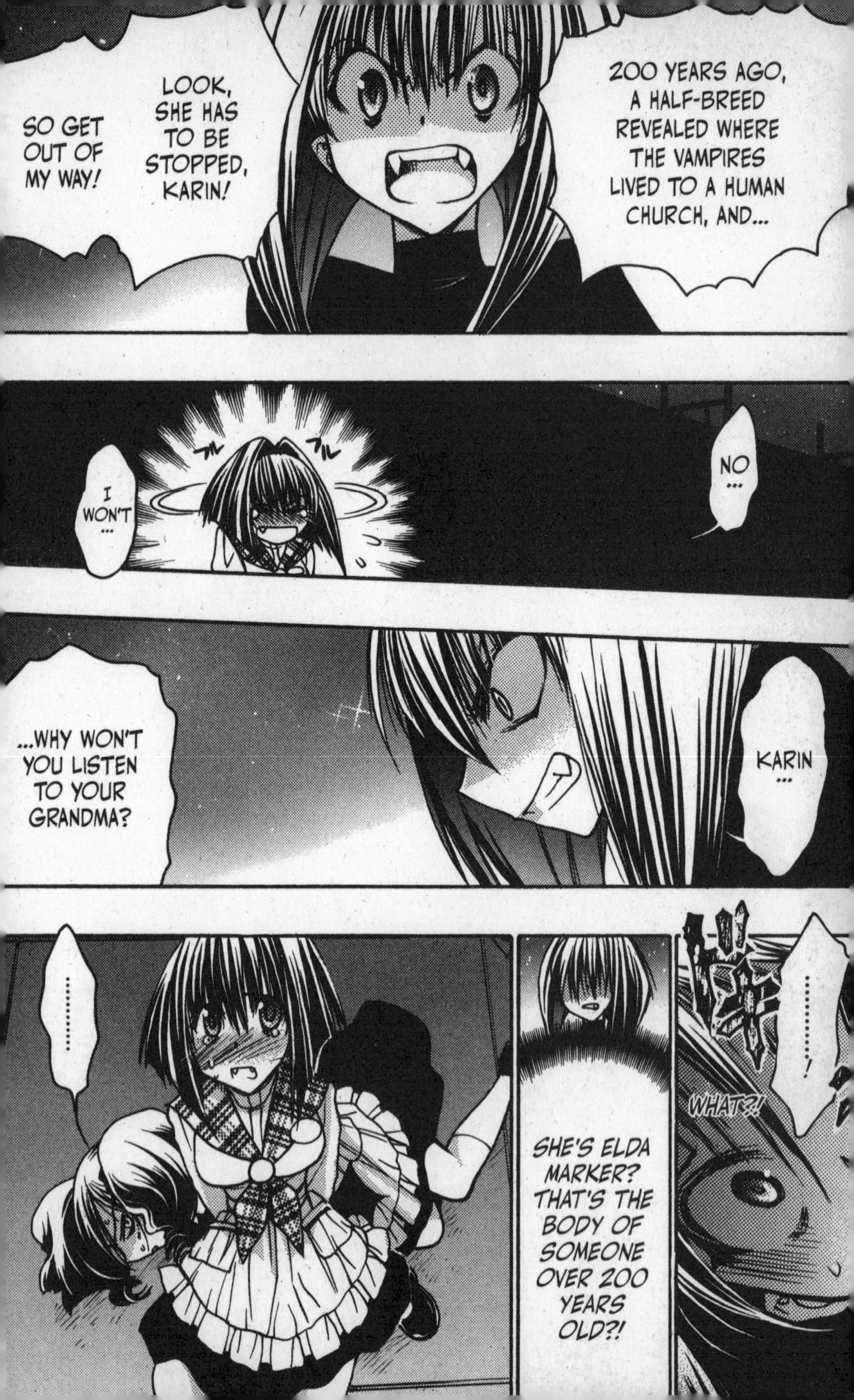
200 YEARS AGO, A HALF-BREED REVEALED WHERE THE VAMPIRES LIVED TO A HUMAN CHURCH, AND...
LOOK, SHE HAS TO BE STOPPED, KARIN!
SO GET OUT OF MY WAY!
NO...
I WON'T...
KARIN...
...WHY WON'T YOU LISTEN TO YOUR GRANDMA?
......!
WHAT?!
SHE'S ELDA MARKER? THAT'S THE BODY OF SOMEONE OVER 200 YEARS OLD?!
....

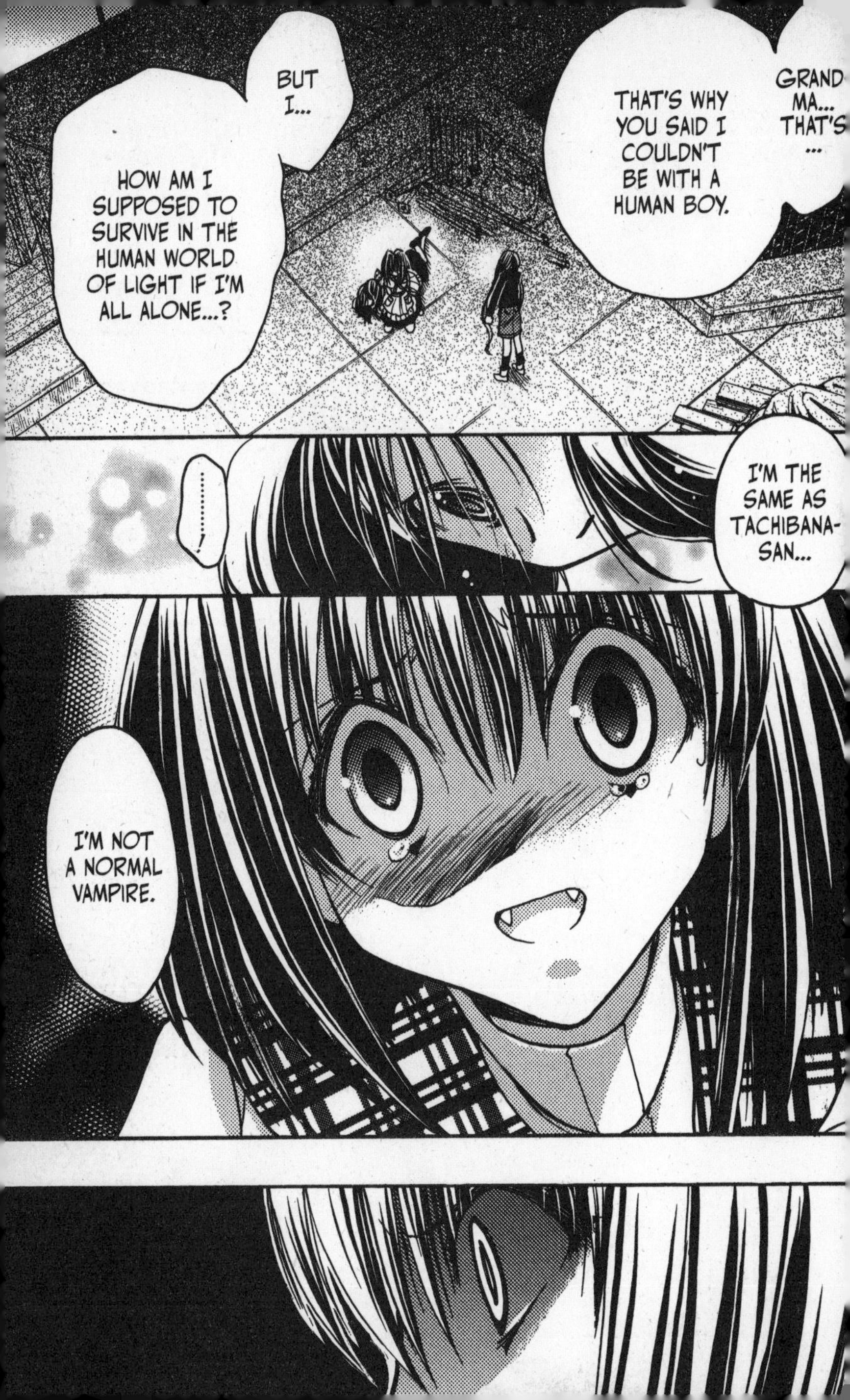
GRANDMA... THAT'S ...
THAT'S WHY YOU SAID I COULDN'T BE WITH A HUMAN BOY.
BUT I...
HOW AM I SUPPOSED TO SURVIVE IN THE HUMAN WORLD OF LIGHT IF I'M ALL ALONE...?
I'M THE SAME AS TACHIBANA-SAN...
......!
I'M NOT A NORMAL VAMPIRE.

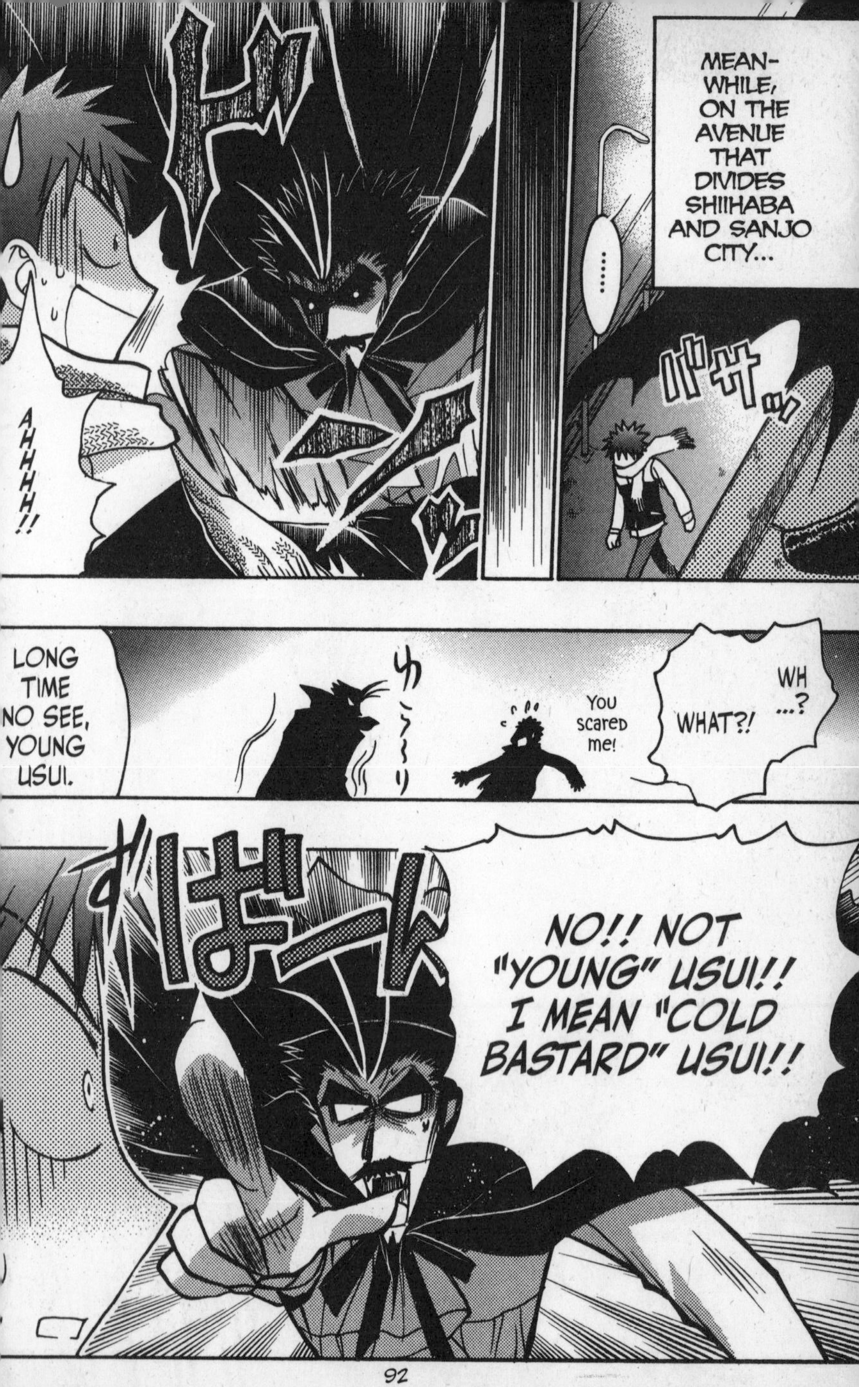
MEAN-WHILE, ON THE AVENUE THAT DIVIDES SHIIHABA AND SANJO CITY...
......
AHHHHH!!
WH...?
WHAT?!
You scared me!
LONG TIME NO SEE, YOUNG USUI.
NO!! NOT "YOUNG" USUI!! I MEAN "COLD BASTARD" USUI!!

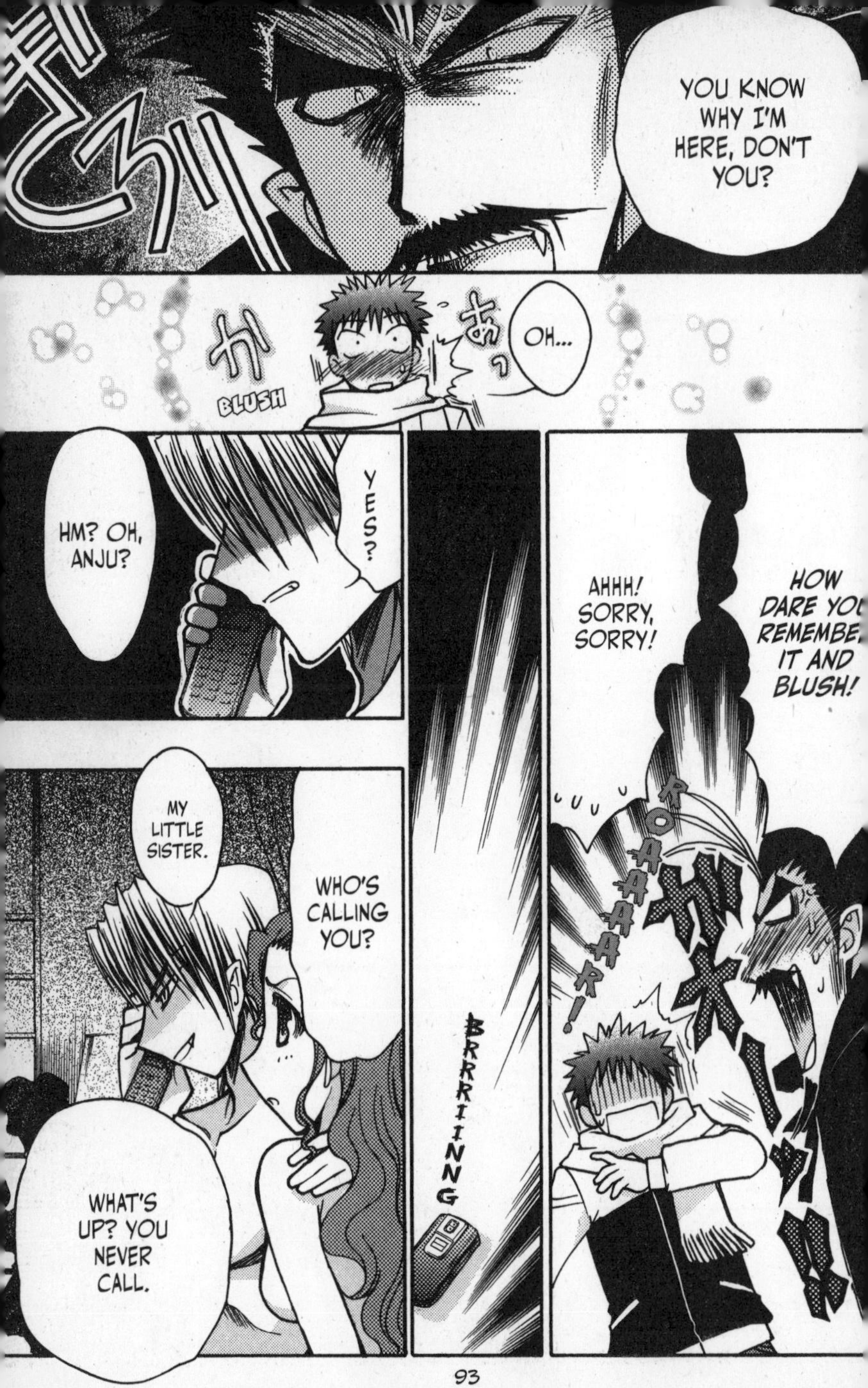
YOU KNOW WHY I'M HERE, DON'T YOU?
OH...
BLUSH
HOW DARE YO REMEMBE IT AND BLUSH!
AHHH! SORRY, SORRY!
ROAAAAR!
BRRRIINNG
YES?
HM? OH, ANJU?
WHO'S CALLING YOU?
MY LITTLE SISTER.
WHAT'S UP? YOU NEVER CALL.

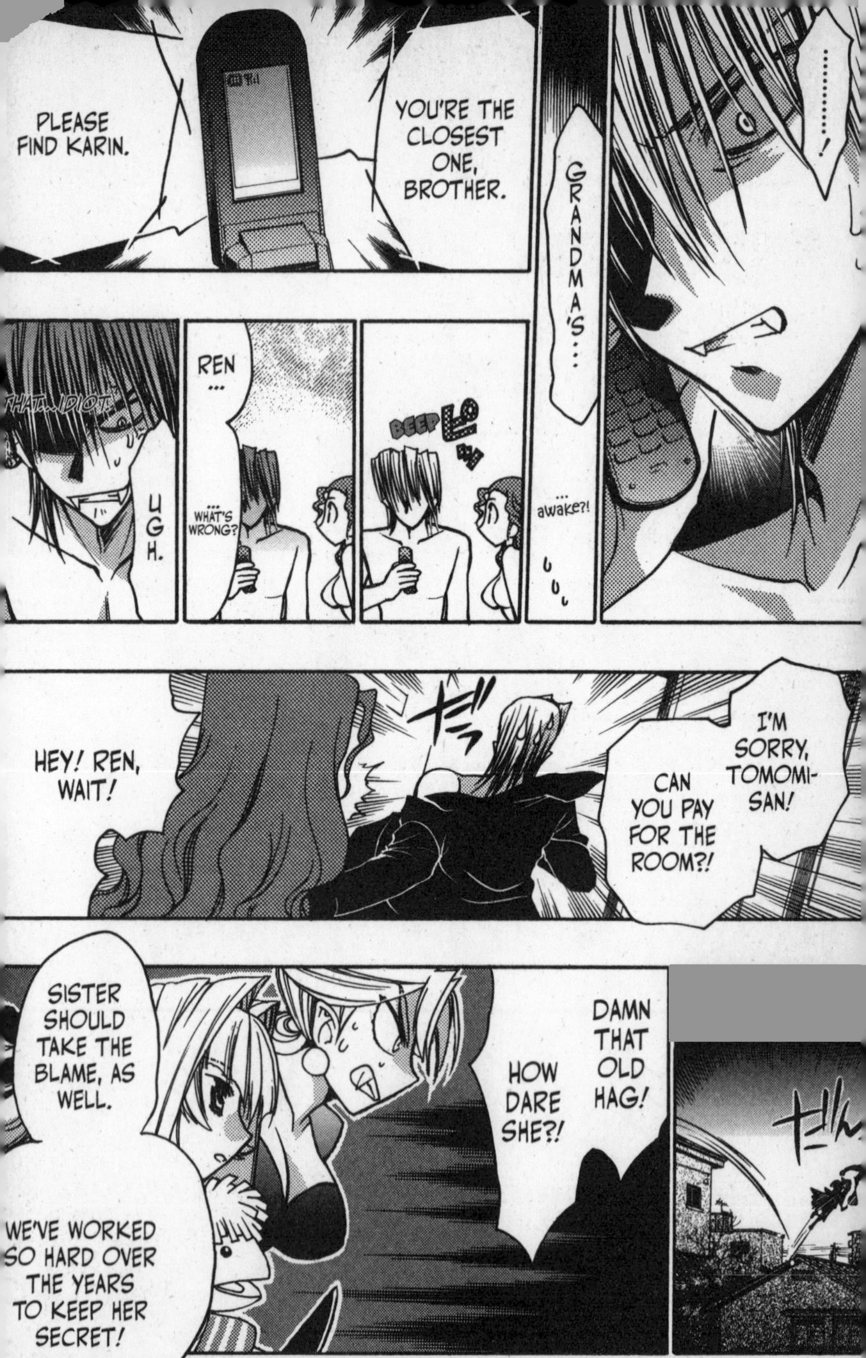
......!
GRANDMA'S...
... awake?!
YOU'RE THE CLOSEST ONE, BROTHER.
PLEASE FIND KARIN.
BEEP
REN ...
... WHAT'S WRONG?
UGH.
THAT... IDIOT.
I'M SORRY, TOMOMI-SAN!
CAN YOU PAY FOR THE ROOM?!
HEY! REN, WAIT!
DAMN THAT OLD HAG!
HOW DARE SHE?!
SISTER SHOULD TAKE THE BLAME, AS WELL.
WE'VE WORKED SO HARD OVER THE YEARS TO KEEP HER SECRET!

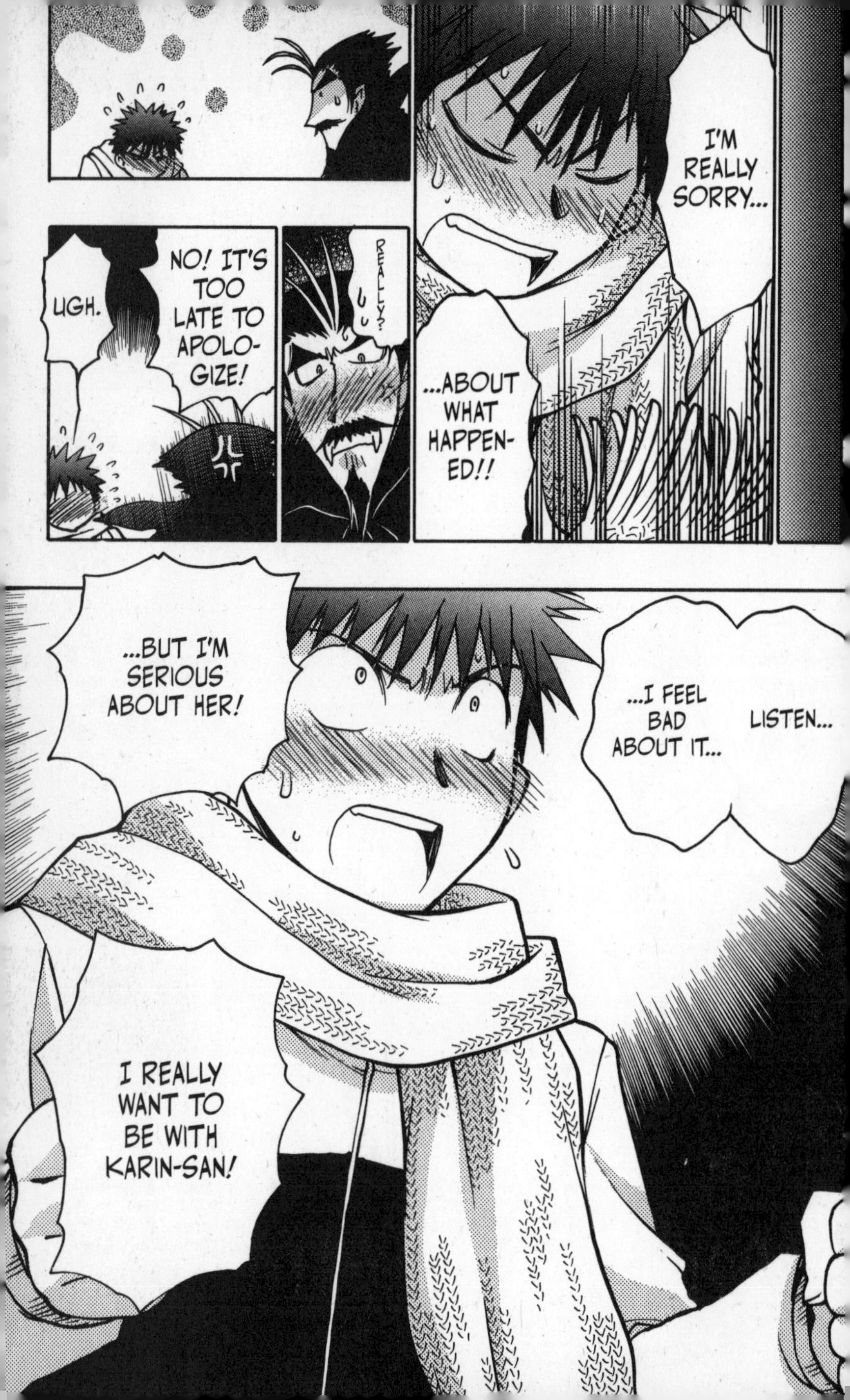
I'M REALLY SORRY...
...ABOUT WHAT HAPPEN-ED!!
REALLY?
NO! IT'S TOO LATE TO APOLO-GIZE!
UGH.
LISTEN...
...I FEEL BAD ABOUT IT...
...BUT I'M SERIOUS ABOUT HER!
I REALLY WANT TO BE WITH KARIN-SAN!

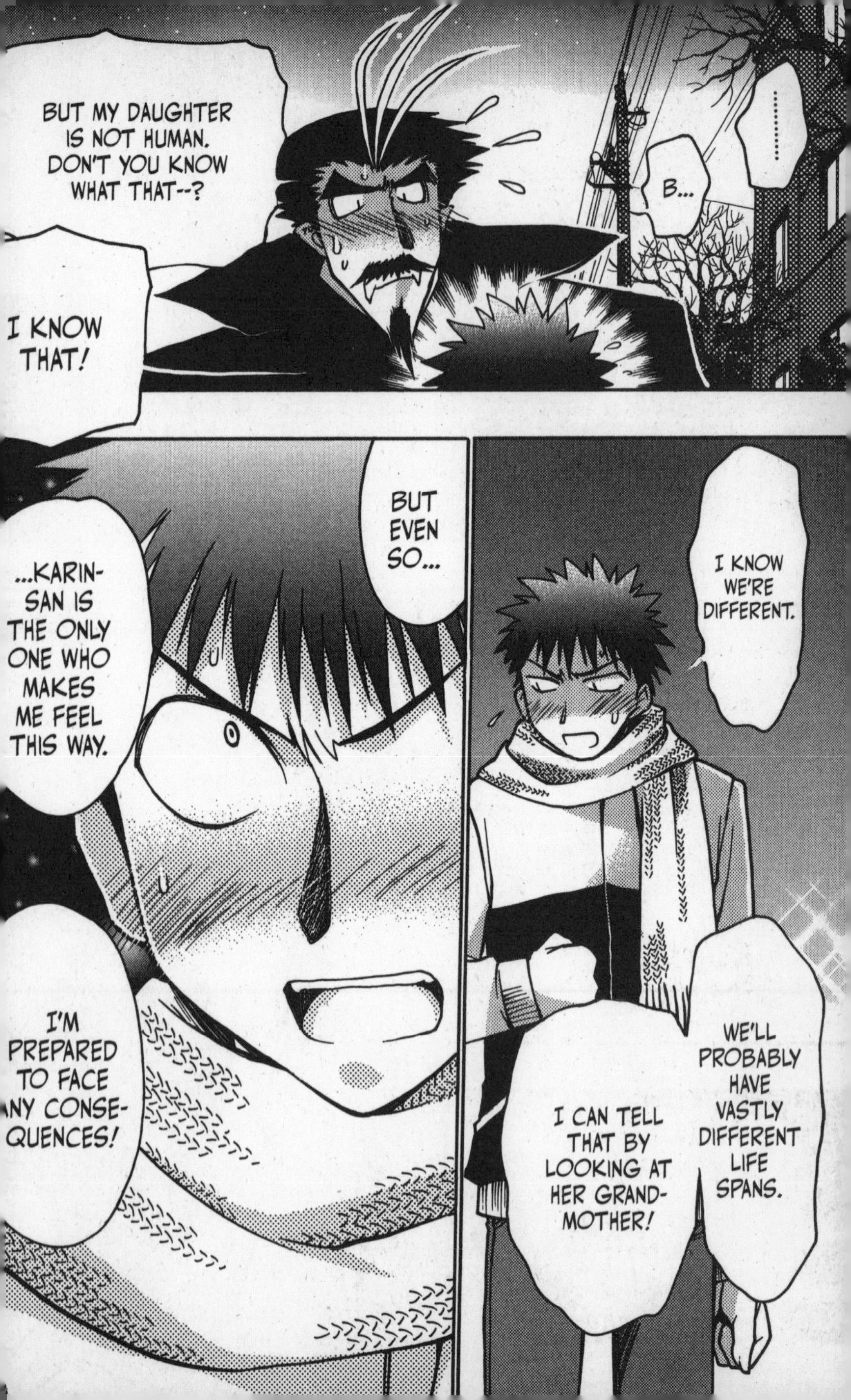
......
B...
BUT MY DAUGHTER IS NOT HUMAN. DON'T YOU KNOW WHAT THAT--?
I KNOW THAT!
I KNOW WE'RE DIFFERENT.
WE'LL PROBABLY HAVE VASTLY DIFFERENT LIFE SPANS.
I CAN TELL THAT BY LOOKING AT HER GRAND-MOTHER!
BUT EVEN SO...
...KARIN-SAN IS THE ONLY ONE WHO MAKES ME FEEL THIS WAY.
I'M PREPARED TO FACE NY CONSE-QUENCES!

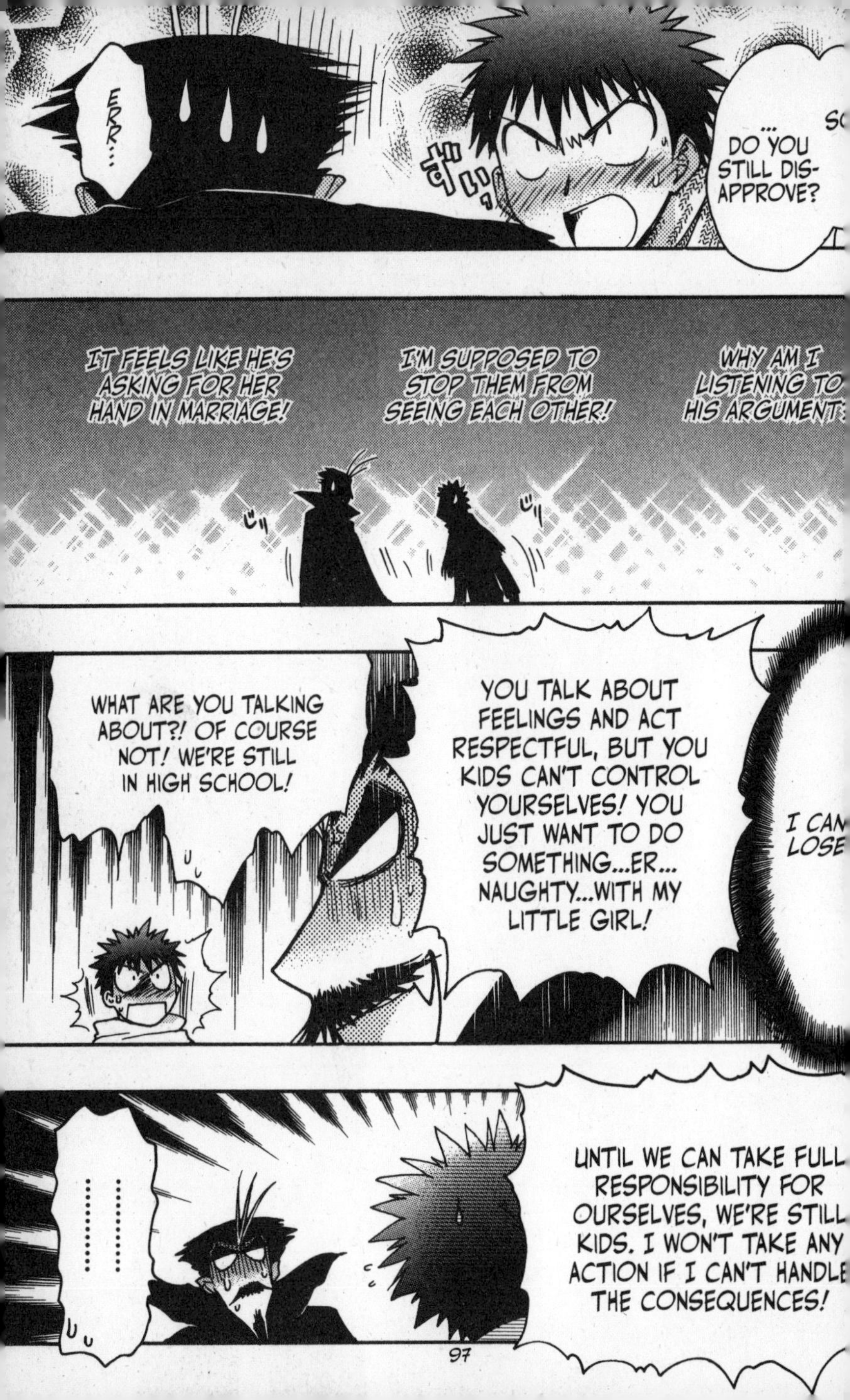

... DO YOU STILL DIS- APPROVE?
ERR...
WHY AM I LISTENING TO HIS ARGUMENT
I'M SUPPOSED TO STOP THEM FROM SEEING EACH OTHER!
IT FEELS LIKE HE'S ASKING FOR HER HAND IN MARRIAGE!
I CAN LOSE
YOU TALK ABOUT FEELINGS AND ACT RESPECTFUL, BUT YOU KIDS CAN'T CONTROL YOURSELVES! YOU JUST WANT TO DO SOMETHING...ER... NAUGHTY...WITH MY LITTLE GIRL!
WHAT ARE YOU TALKING ABOUT?! OF COURSE NOT! WE'RE STILL IN HIGH SCHOOL!
UNTIL WE CAN TAKE FULL RESPONSIBILITY FOR OURSELVES, WE'RE STILL KIDS. I WON'T TAKE ANY ACTION IF I CAN'T HANDLE THE CONSEQUENCES!
....

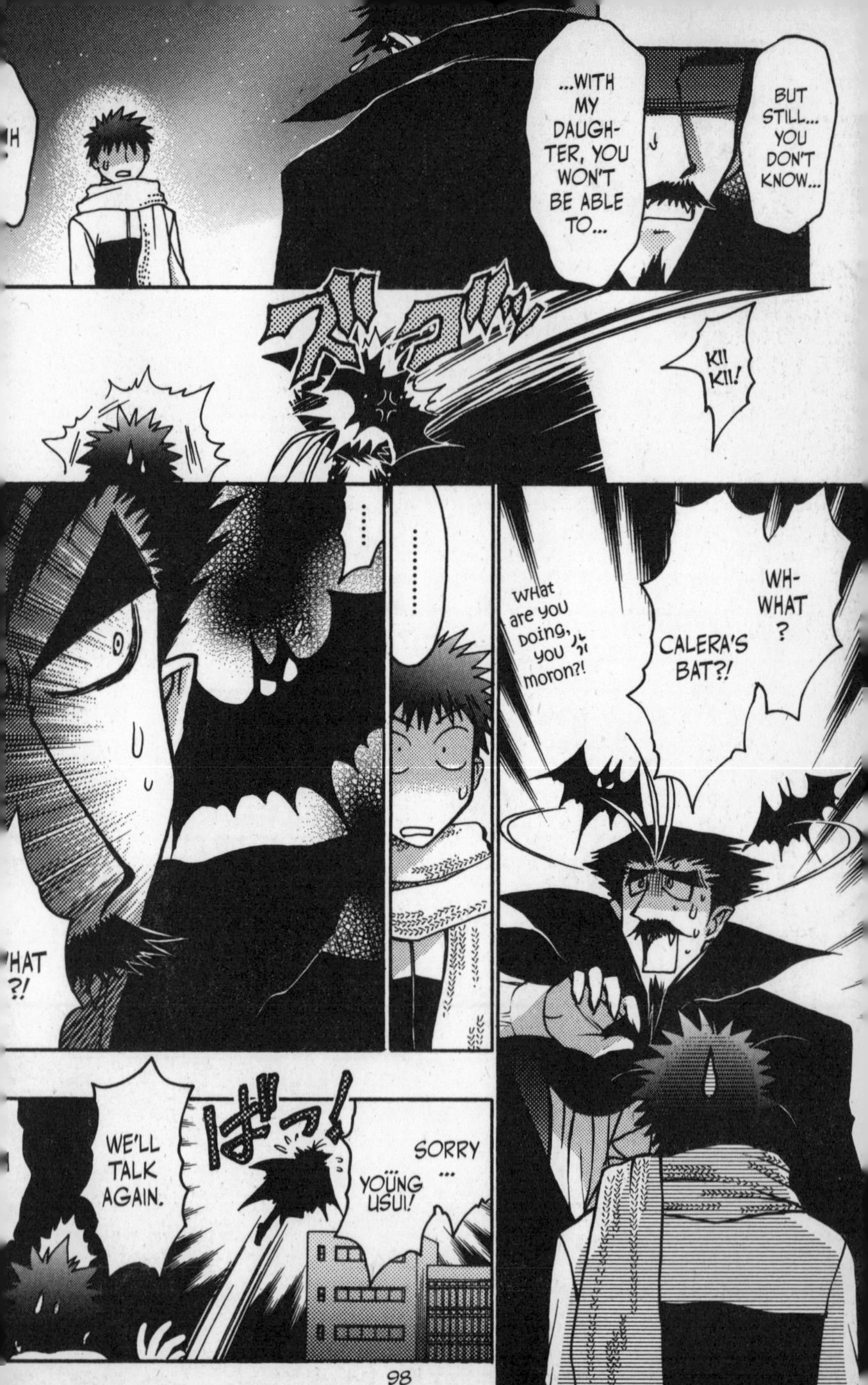
BUT STILL... YOU DON'T KNOW...
...WITH MY DAUGHTER, YOU WON'T BE ABLE TO...
H
KII KII!
WH- WHAT?
CALERA'S BAT?!
What are you doing, you moron?!
......
......
HAT ?!
SORRY... YOUNG USUI!
ばっ!
WE'LL TALK AGAIN.

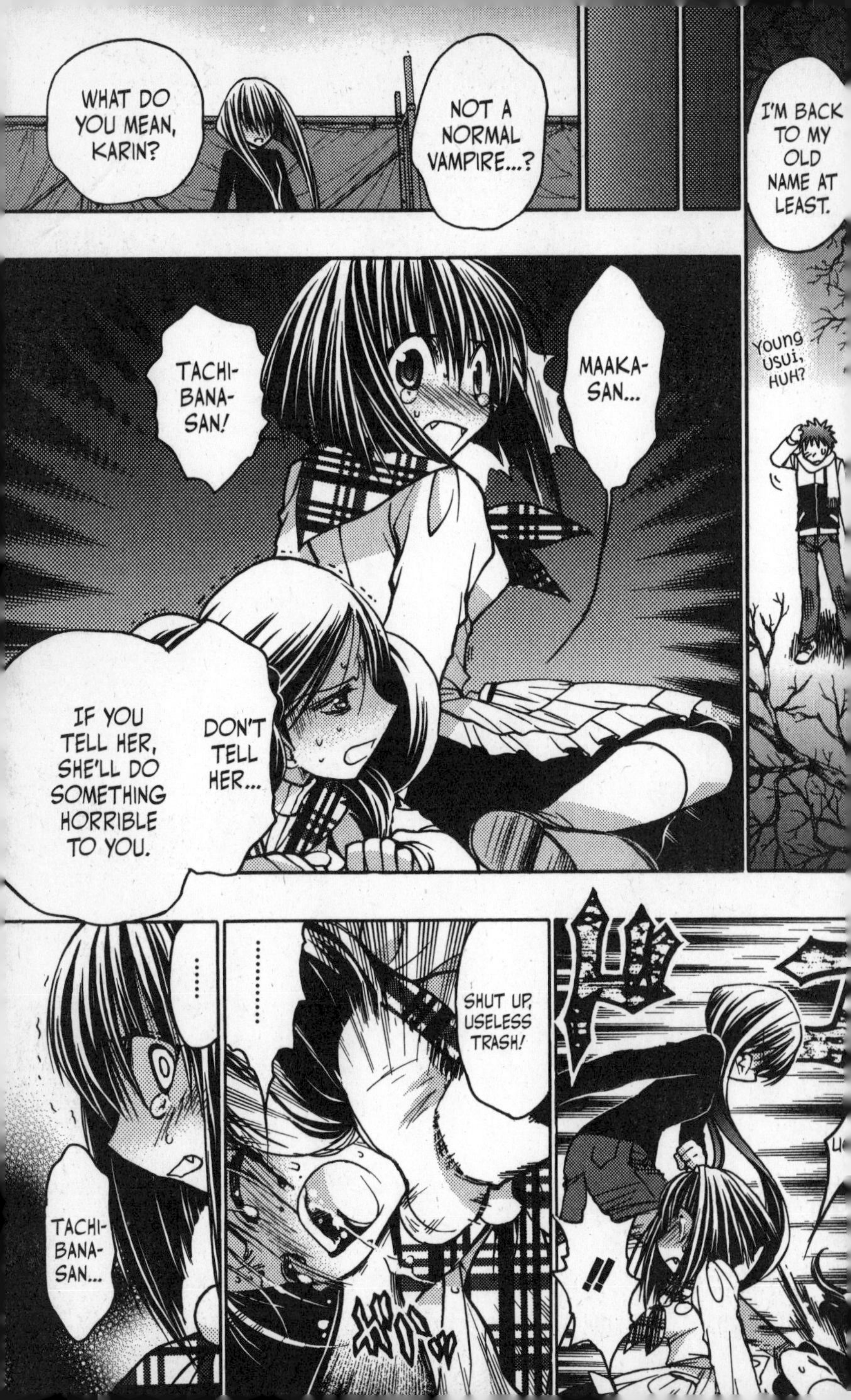

I'M BACK TO MY OLD NAME AT LEAST.
Young USUi, HUH?
NOT A NORMAL VAMPIRE...?
WHAT DO YOU MEAN, KARIN?
MAAKA-SAN...
TACHI-BANA-SAN!
DON'T TELL HER...
IF YOU TELL HER, SHE'LL DO SOMETHING HORRIBLE TO YOU.
!!
SHUT UP, USELESS TRASH!
......
......
TACHI-BANA-SAN...

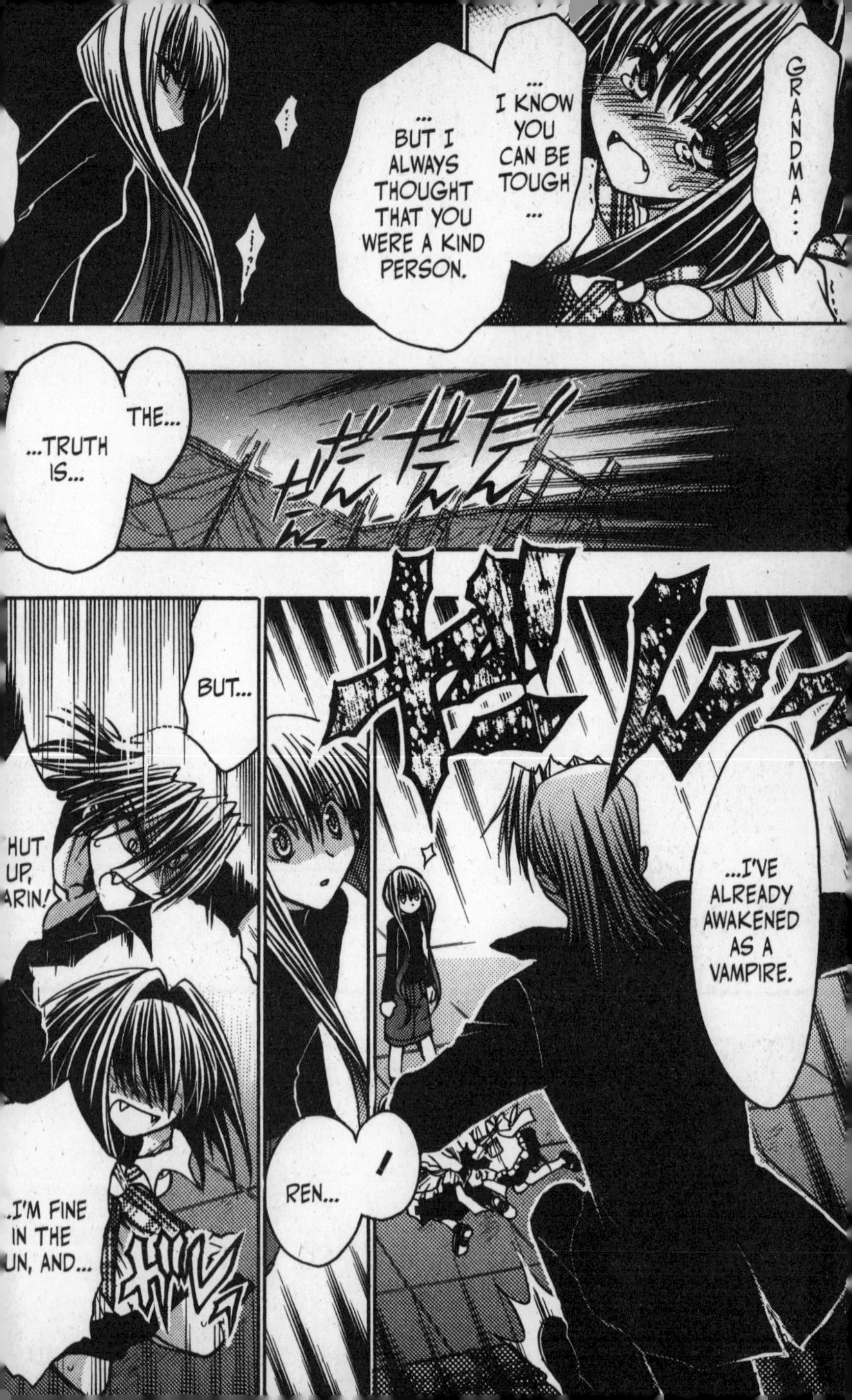
GRANDMA...
...I KNOW YOU CAN BE TOUGH...
...BUT I ALWAYS THOUGHT THAT YOU WERE A KIND PERSON.
THE...
...TRUTH IS...
...I'VE ALREADY AWAKENED AS A VAMPIRE.
!
REN...
BUT...
HUT UP, ARIN!
.I'M FINE IN THE UN, AND...

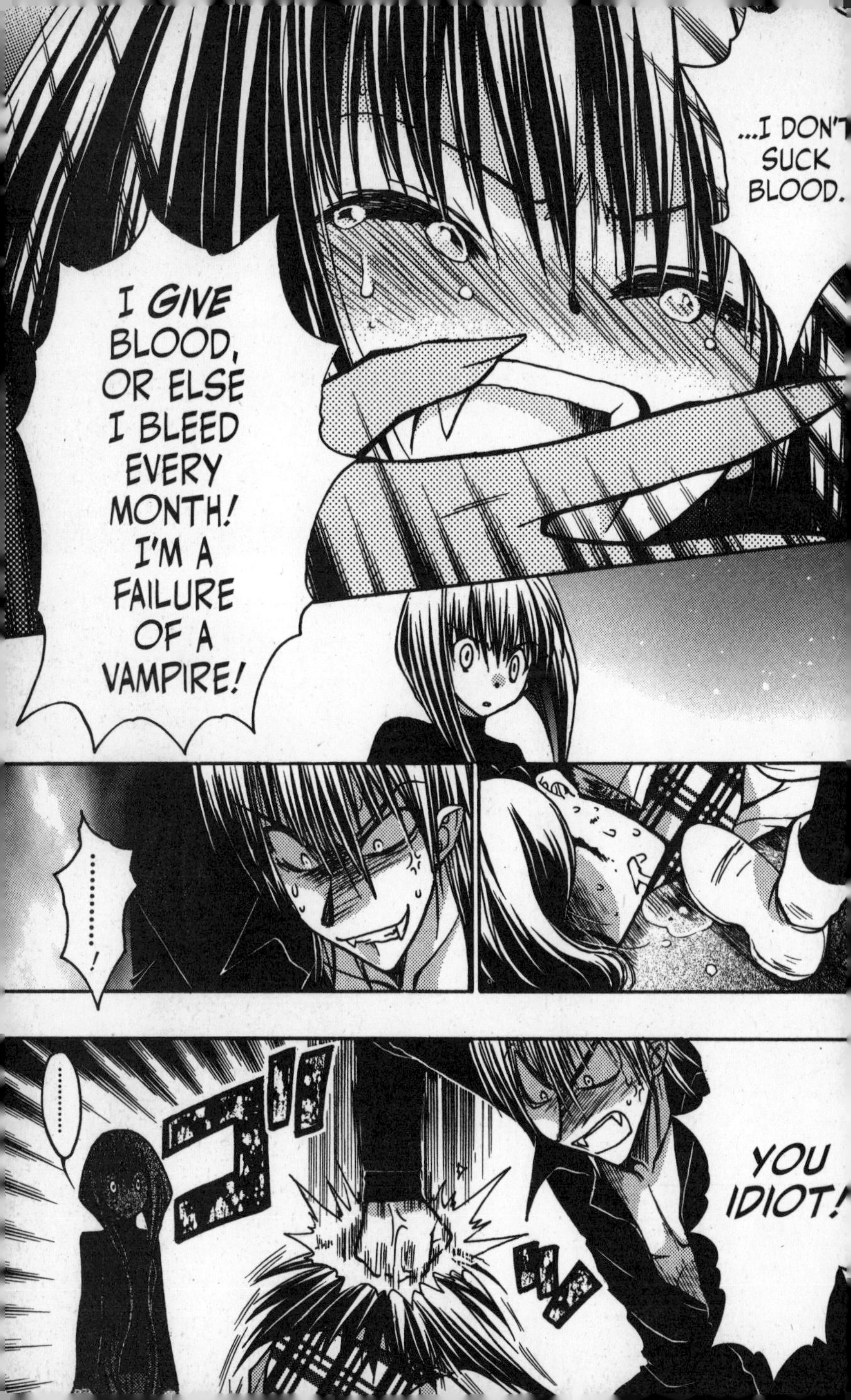
...I DON'T SUCK BLOOD.
I GIVE BLOOD, OR ELSE I BLEED EVERY MONTH! I'M A FAILURE OF A VAMPIRE!
......!
YOU IDIOT!
......

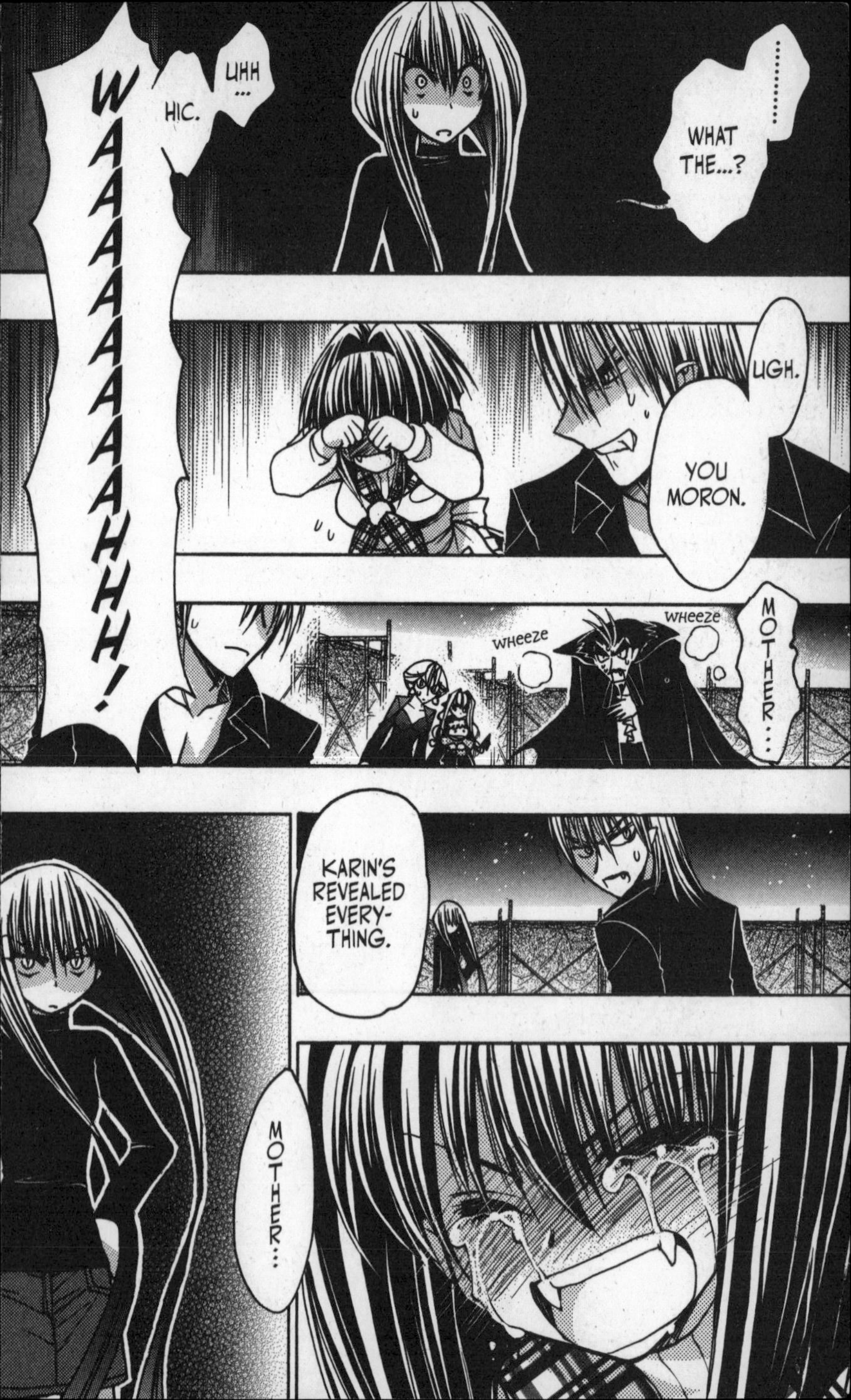
......
WHAT THE...?
UHH...
HIC.
WAAAAAAAAAAAHHH!
UGH.
YOU MORON.
MOTHER...
wheeze
wheeze
KARIN'S REVEALED EVERY-THING.
MOTHER...

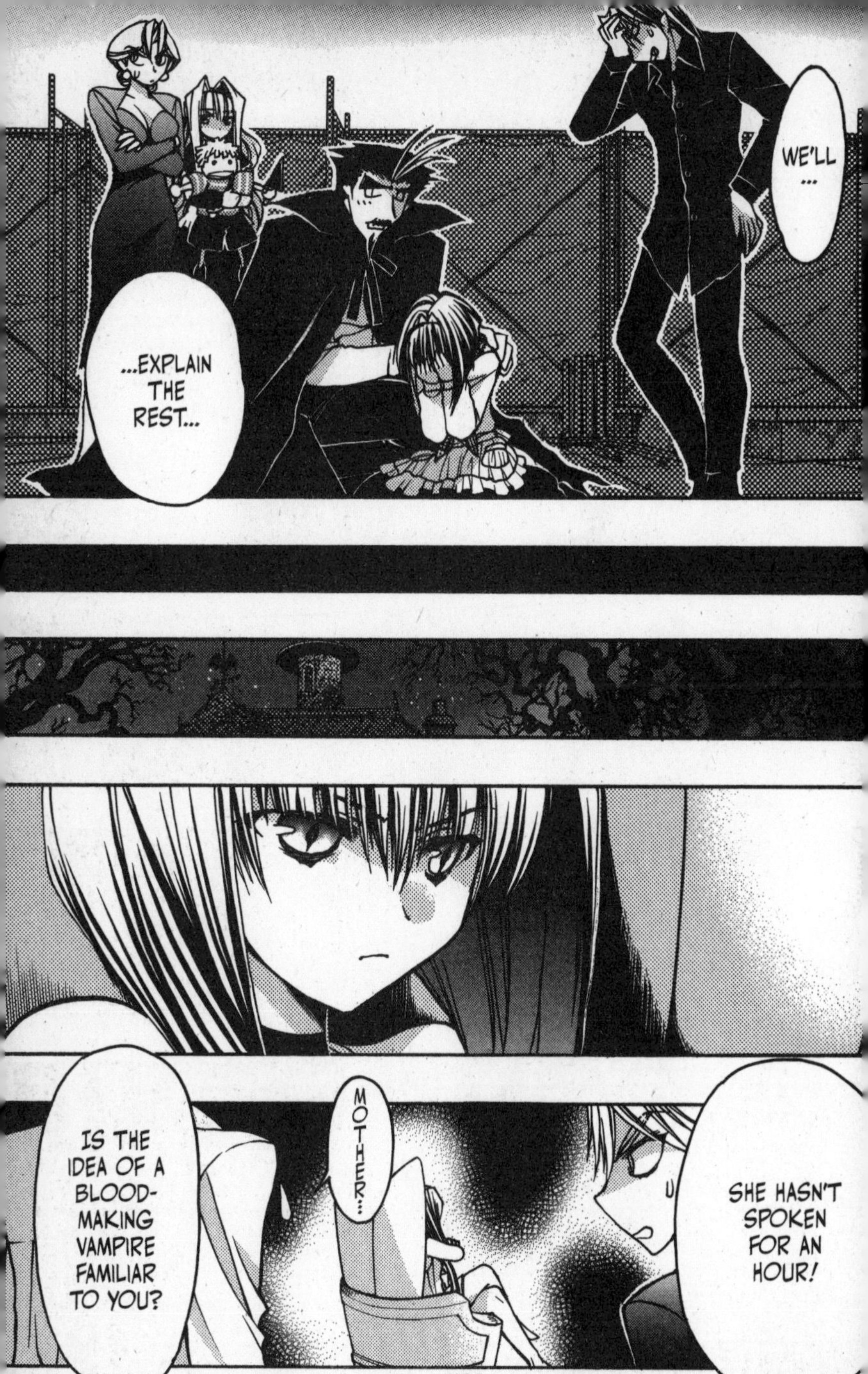
WE'LL ...
...EXPLAIN THE REST...
SHE HASN'T SPOKEN FOR AN HOUR!
MOTHER...
IS THE IDEA OF A BLOOD-MAKING VAMPIRE FAMILIAR TO YOU?

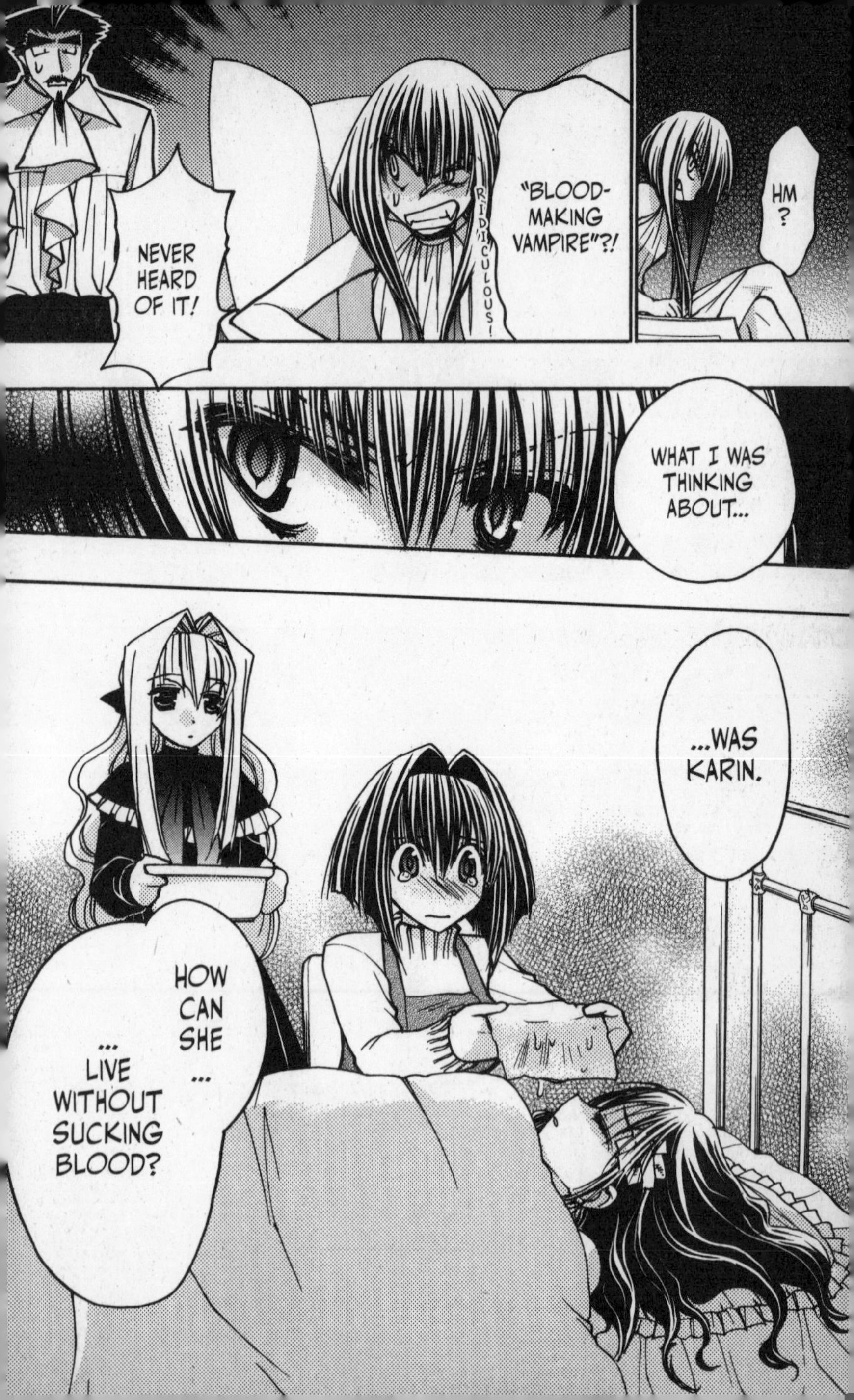
HM ?
"BLOOD-MAKING VAMPIRE"?!
RIDICULOUS!
NEVER HEARD OF IT!
WHAT I WAS THINKING ABOUT...
...WAS KARIN.
HOW CAN SHE... ...LIVE WITHOUT SUCKING BLOOD?

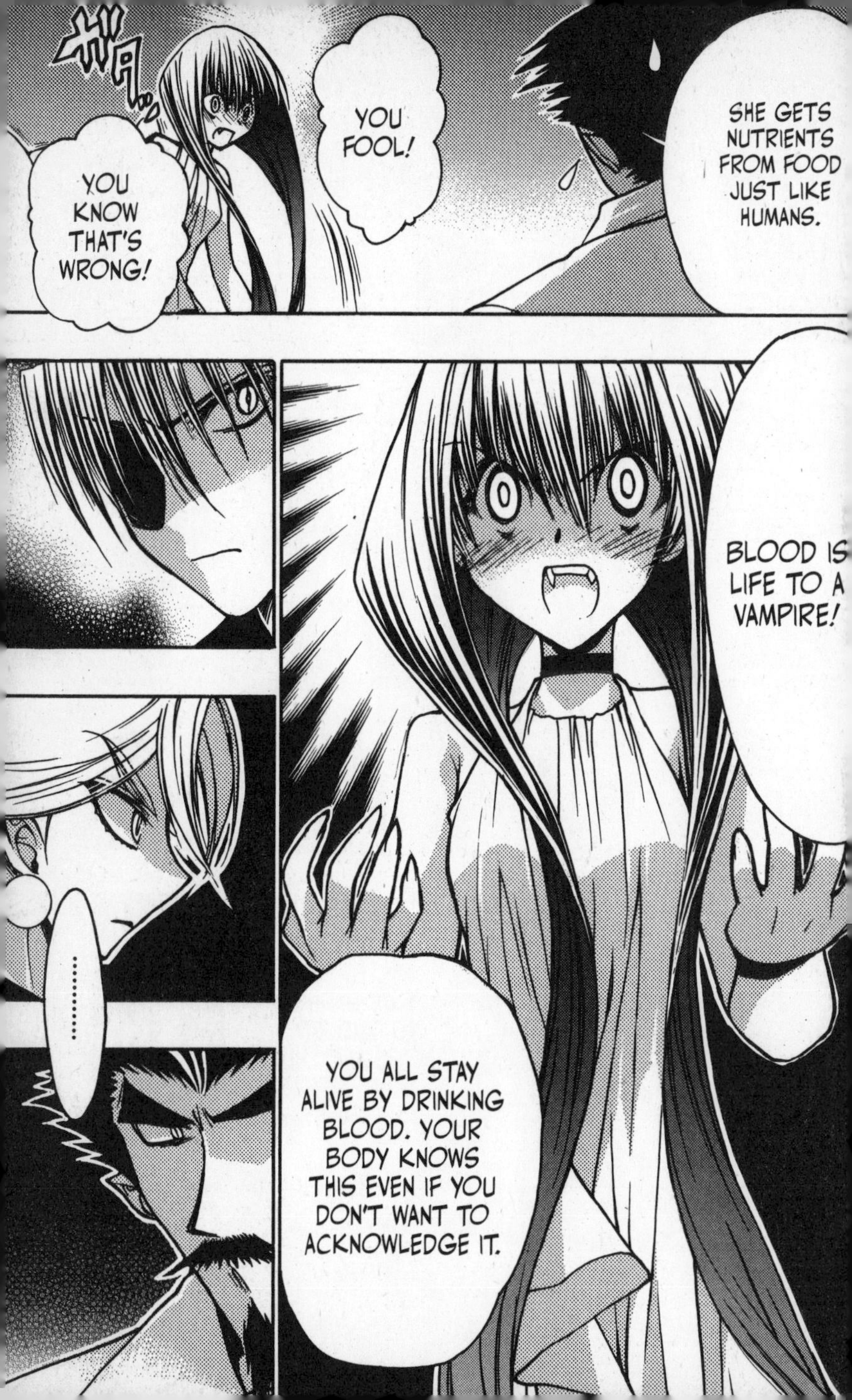
SHE GETS NUTRIENTS FROM FOOD JUST LIKE HUMANS.
YOU FOOL!
YOU KNOW THAT'S WRONG!
BLOOD IS LIFE TO A VAMPIRE!
YOU ALL STAY ALIVE BY DRINKING BLOOD. YOUR BODY KNOWS THIS EVEN IF YOU DON'T WANT TO ACKNOWLEDGE IT.
......

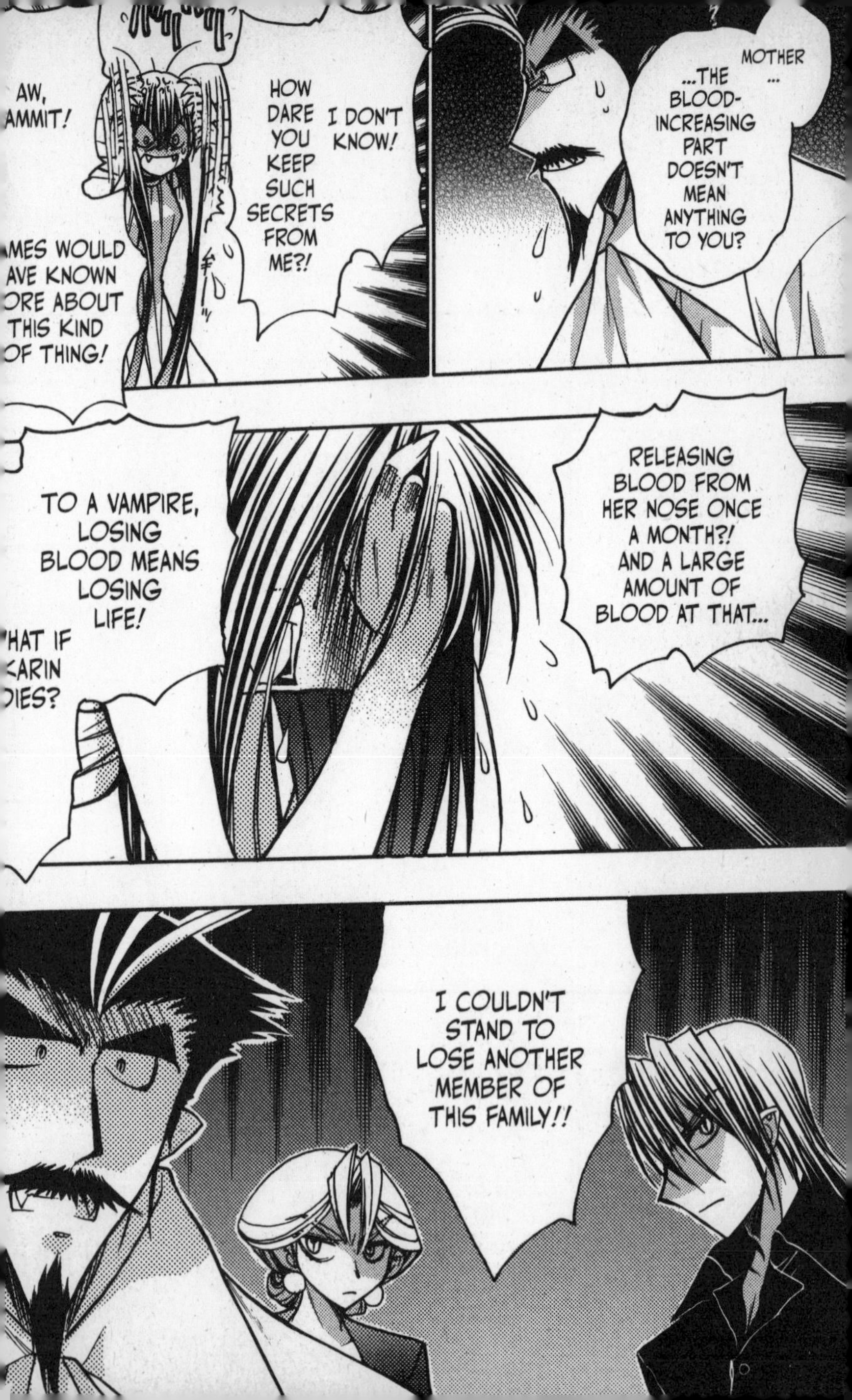
MOTHER ...
...THE BLOOD-INCREASING PART DOESN'T MEAN ANYTHING TO YOU?
I DON'T KNOW!
HOW DARE YOU KEEP SUCH SECRETS FROM ME?!
AW, AMMIT!
AMES WOULD AVE KNOWN ORE ABOUT THIS KIND OF THING!
RELEASING BLOOD FROM HER NOSE ONCE A MONTH?! AND A LARGE AMOUNT OF BLOOD AT THAT...
TO A VAMPIRE, LOSING BLOOD MEANS LOSING LIFE!
HAT IF ARIN DIES?
I COULDN'T STAND TO LOSE ANOTHER MEMBER OF THIS FAMILY!!

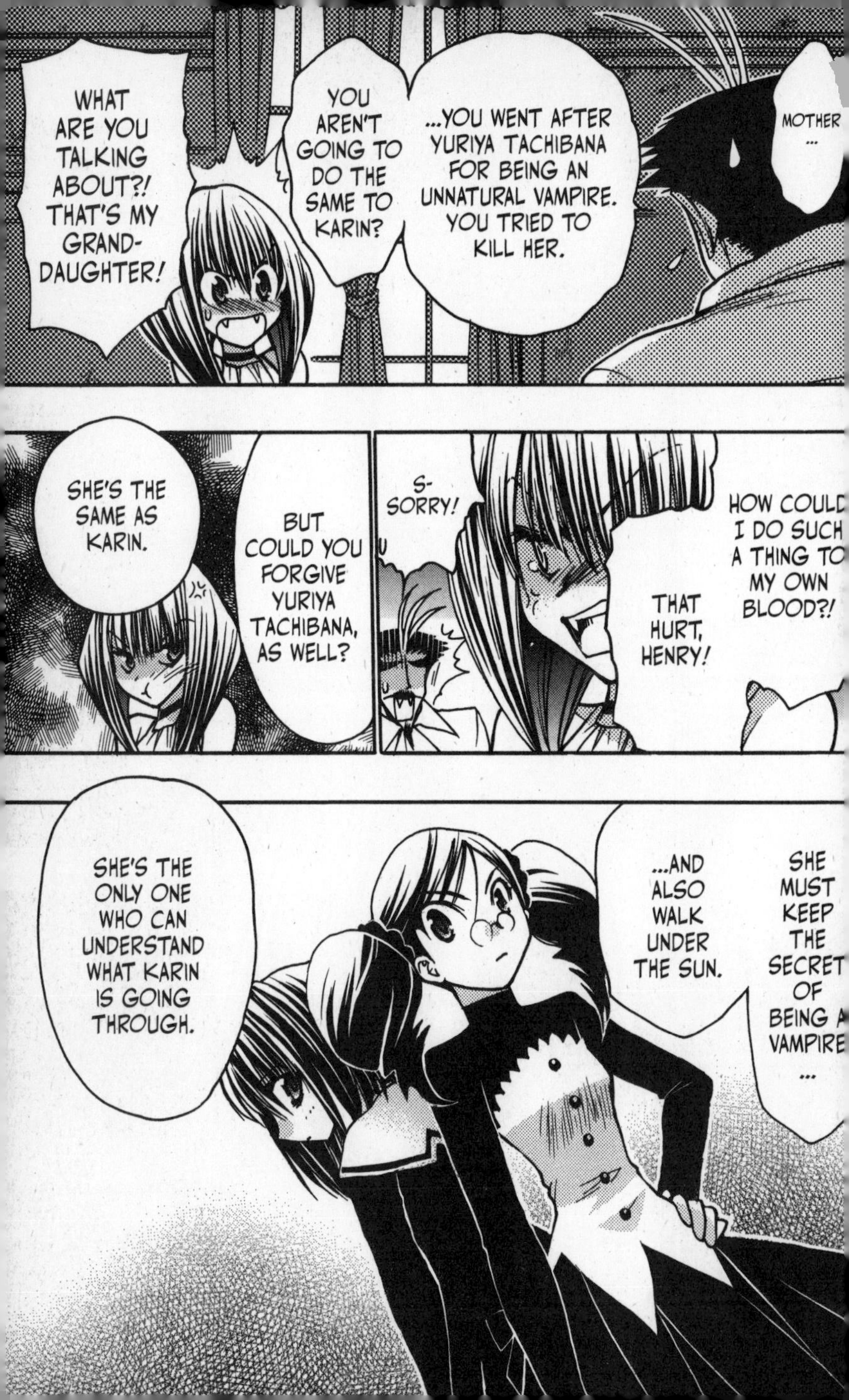
MOTHER ...
...YOU WENT AFTER YURIYA TACHIBANA FOR BEING AN UNNATURAL VAMPIRE. YOU TRIED TO KILL HER.
YOU AREN'T GOING TO DO THE SAME TO KARIN?
WHAT ARE YOU TALKING ABOUT?! THAT'S MY GRAND-DAUGHTER!
HOW COULD I DO SUCH A THING TO MY OWN BLOOD?!
THAT HURT, HENRY!
S-SORRY!
BUT COULD YOU FORGIVE YURIYA TACHIBANA, AS WELL?
SHE'S THE SAME AS KARIN.
SHE MUST KEEP THE SECRET OF BEING A VAMPIRE ...
...AND ALSO WALK UNDER THE SUN.
SHE'S THE ONLY ONE WHO CAN UNDERSTAND WHAT KARIN IS GOING THROUGH.

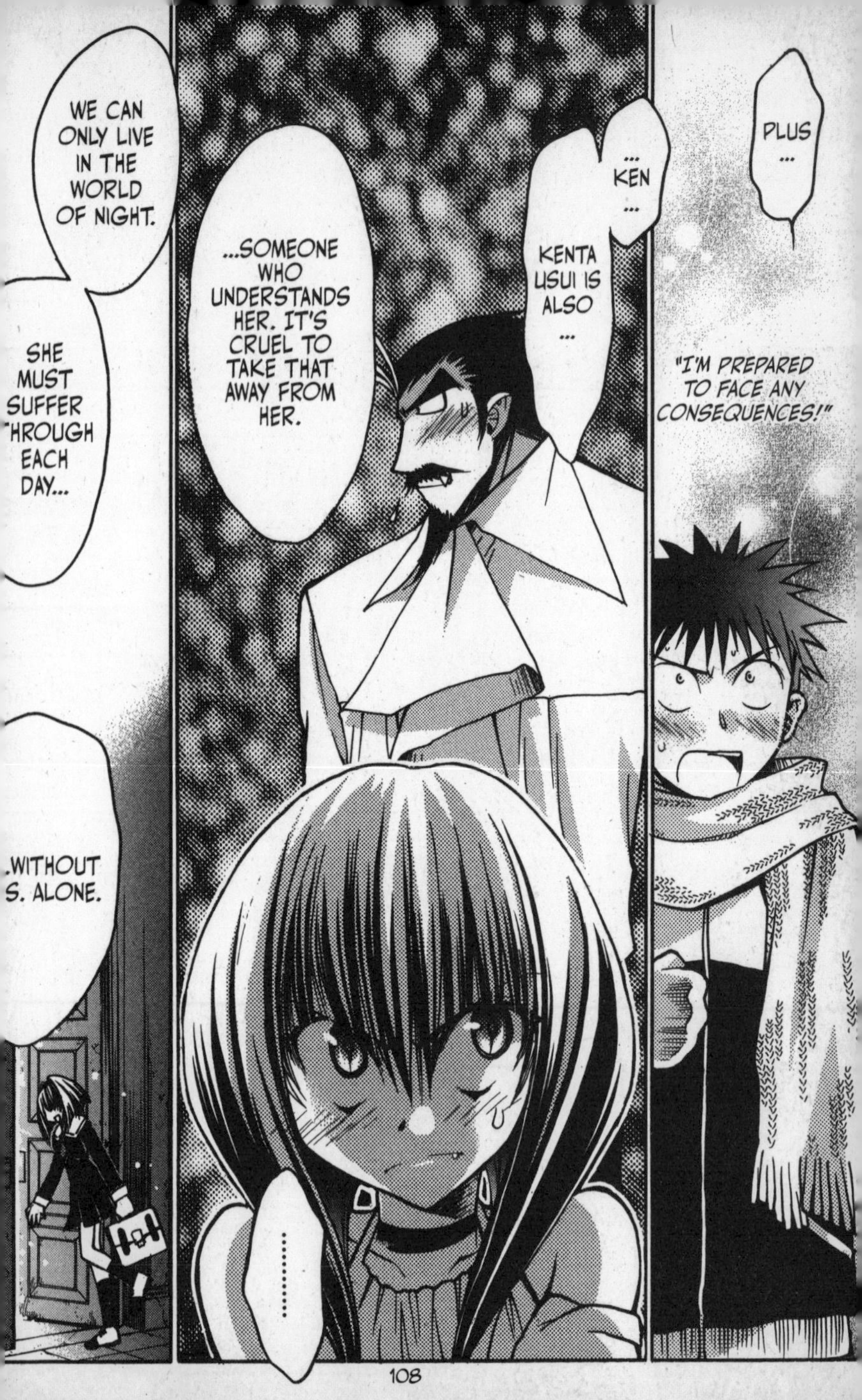
PLUS ...
"I'M PREPARED TO FACE ANY CONSEQUENCES!"
... KEN ...
KENTA USUI IS ALSO ...
...SOMEONE WHO UNDERSTANDS HER. IT'S CRUEL TO TAKE THAT AWAY FROM HER.
....
WE CAN ONLY LIVE IN THE WORLD OF NIGHT.
SHE MUST SUFFER HROUGH EACH DAY...
.WITHOUT S. ALONE.

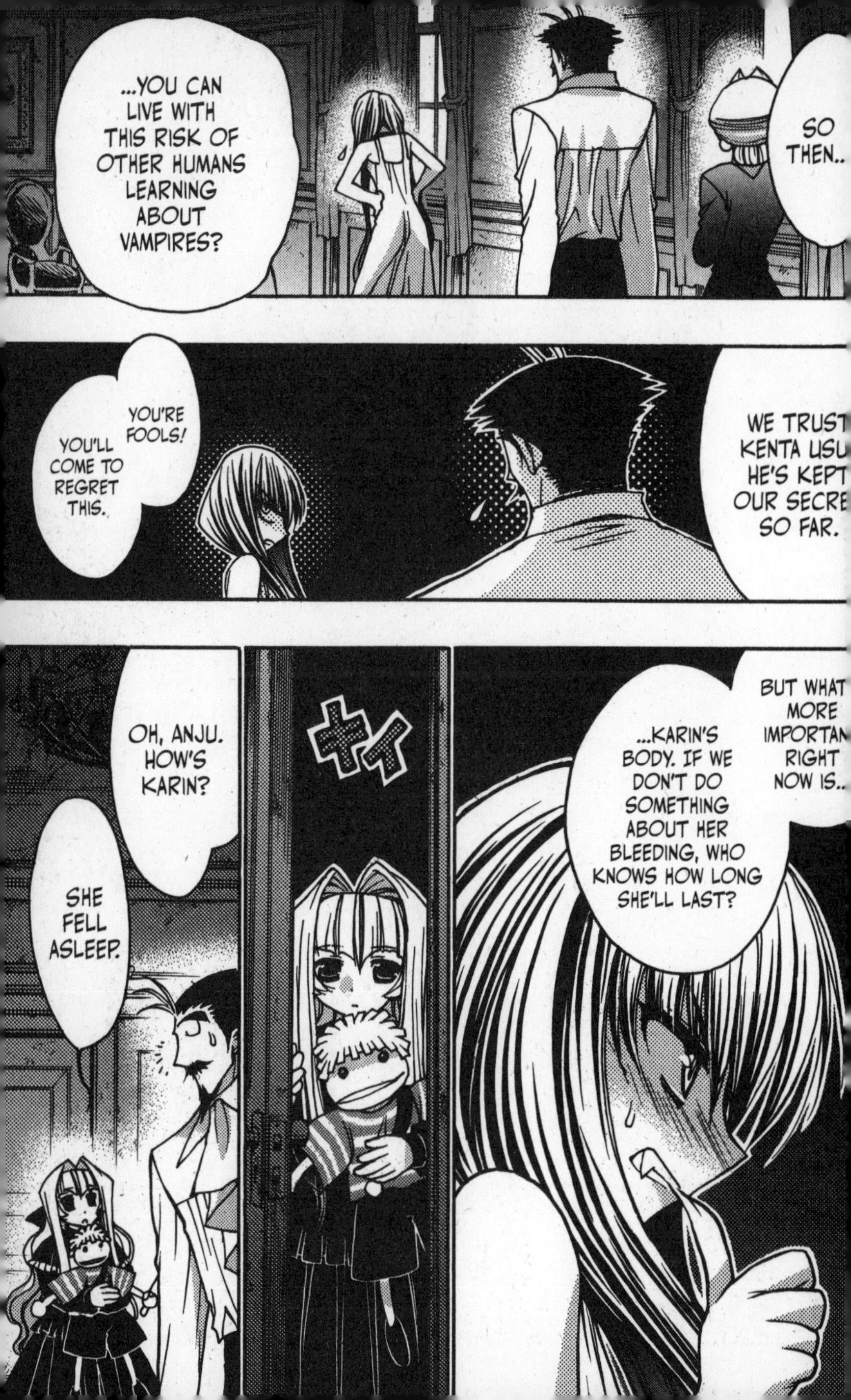
SO THEN..
...YOU CAN LIVE WITH THIS RISK OF OTHER HUMANS LEARNING ABOUT VAMPIRES?
WE TRUST KENTA USU HE'S KEPT OUR SECRE SO FAR.
YOU'RE FOOLS!
YOU'LL COME TO REGRET THIS.
BUT WHAT MORE IMPORTAN RIGHT NOW IS..
...KARIN'S BODY. IF WE DON'T DO SOMETHING ABOUT HER BLEEDING, WHO KNOWS HOW LONG SHE'LL LAST?
OH, ANJU. HOW'S KARIN?
SHE FELL ASLEEP.

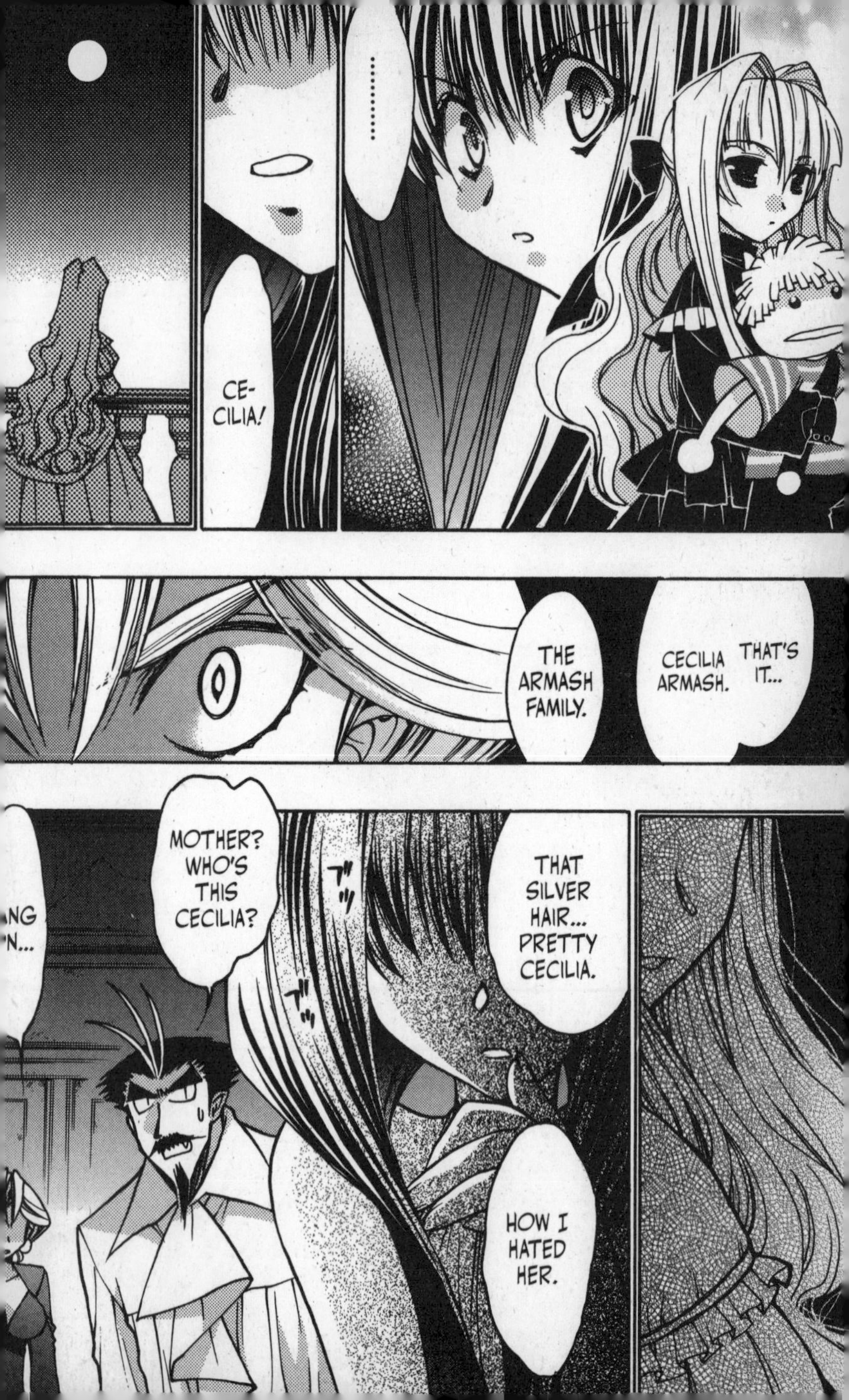
......
CE-CILIA!
THAT'S IT... CECILIA ARMASH.
THE ARMASH FAMILY.
THAT SILVER HAIR... PRETTY CECILIA.
HOW I HATED HER.
MOTHER? WHO'S THIS CECILIA?

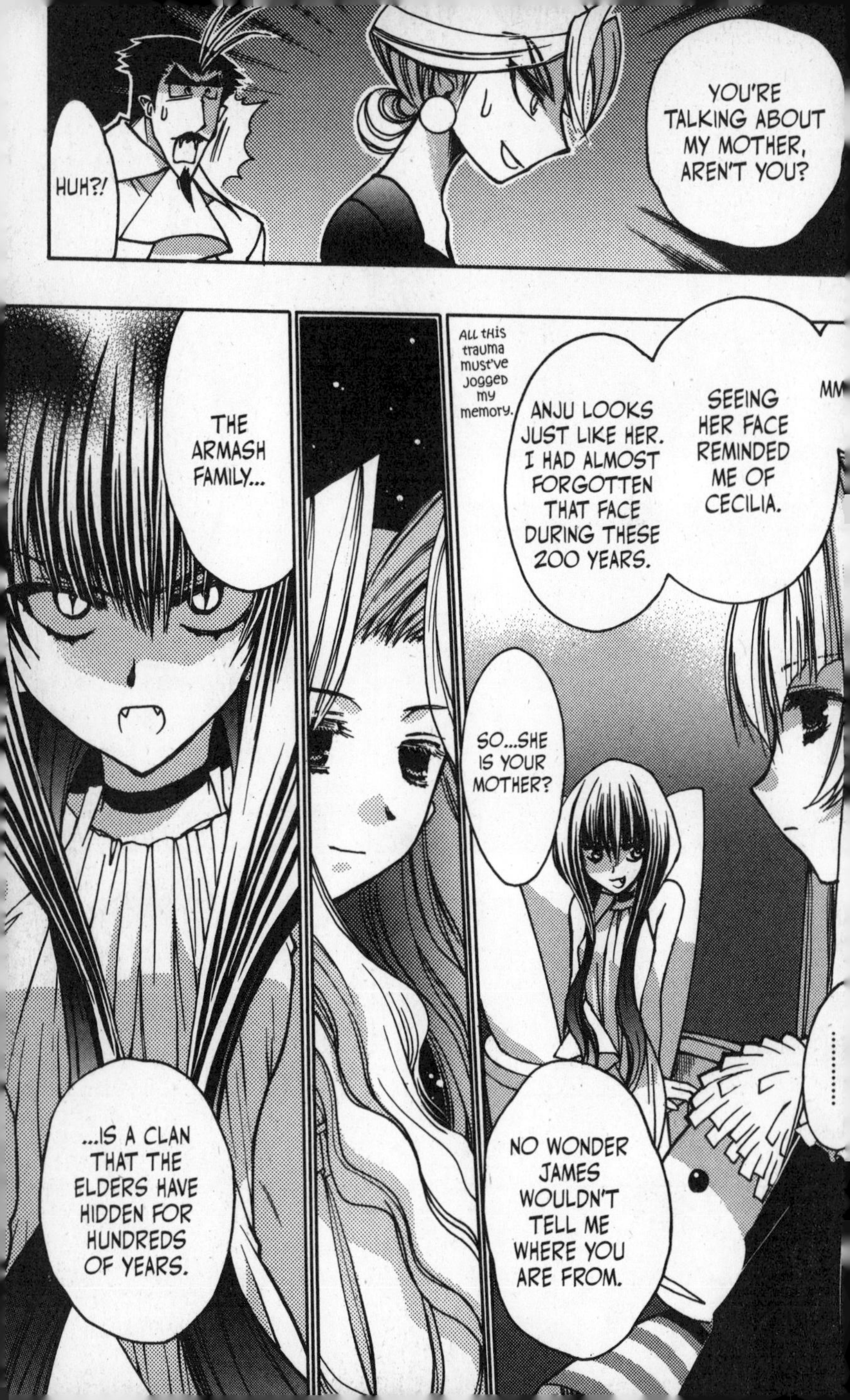
YOU'RE TALKING ABOUT MY MOTHER, AREN'T YOU?
HUH?!
MM
SEEING HER FACE REMINDED ME OF CECILIA.
ANJU LOOKS JUST LIKE HER. I HAD ALMOST FORGOTTEN THAT FACE DURING THESE 200 YEARS.
All this trauma must've jogged my memory.
SO...SHE IS YOUR MOTHER?
......
NO WONDER JAMES WOULDN'T TELL ME WHERE YOU ARE FROM.
THE ARMASH FAMILY...
...IS A CLAN THAT THE ELDERS HAVE HIDDEN FOR HUNDREDS OF YEARS.

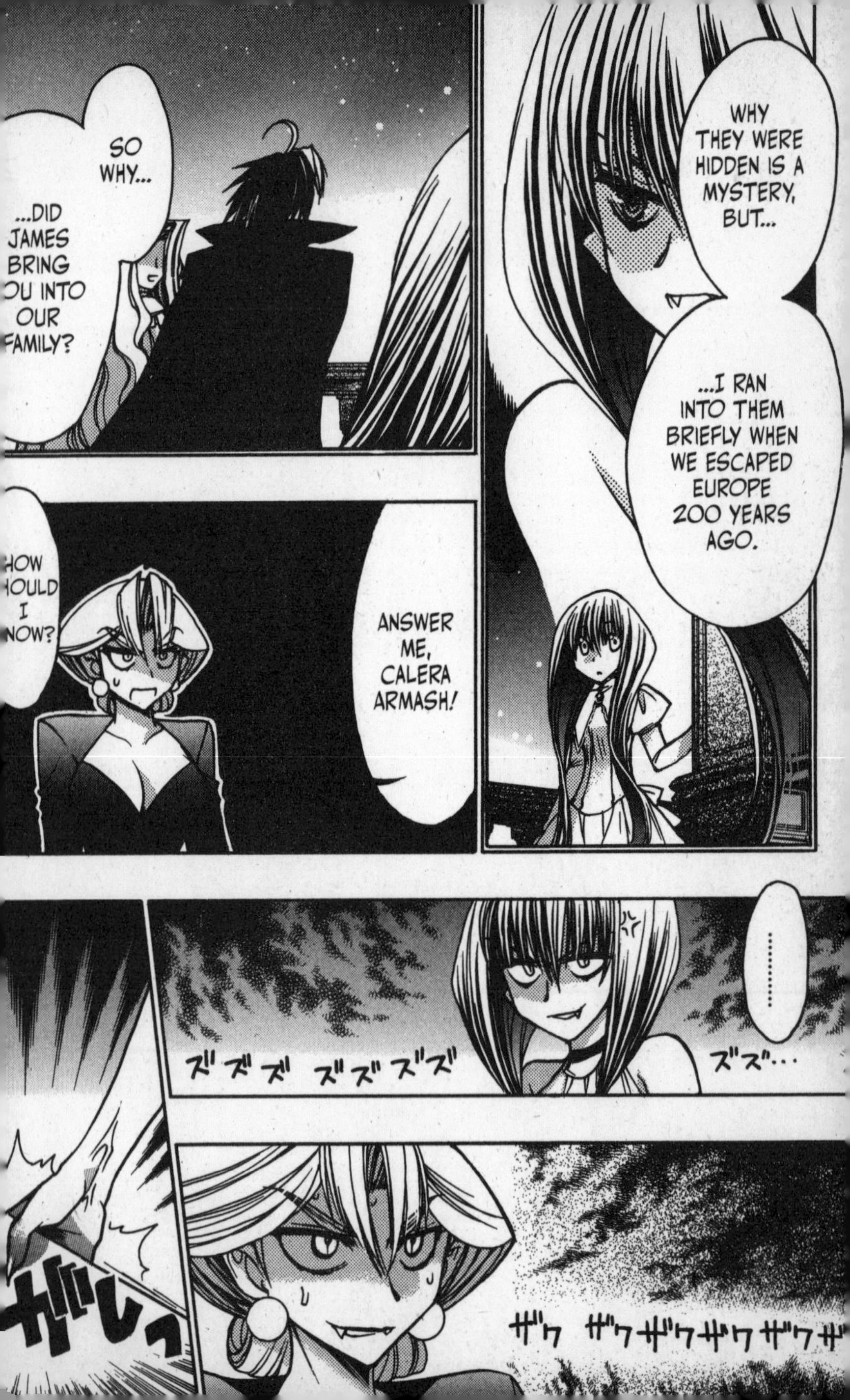
WHY THEY WERE HIDDEN IS A MYSTERY, BUT...
...I RAN INTO THEM BRIEFLY WHEN WE ESCAPED EUROPE 200 YEARS AGO.
SO WHY...
...DID JAMES BRING OU INTO OUR FAMILY?
ANSWER ME, CALERA ARMASH!
HOW HOULD I NOW?
......
ズズ…
ズズズ ズズズズ
ガシッ
ザク ザクザクザクザクザ

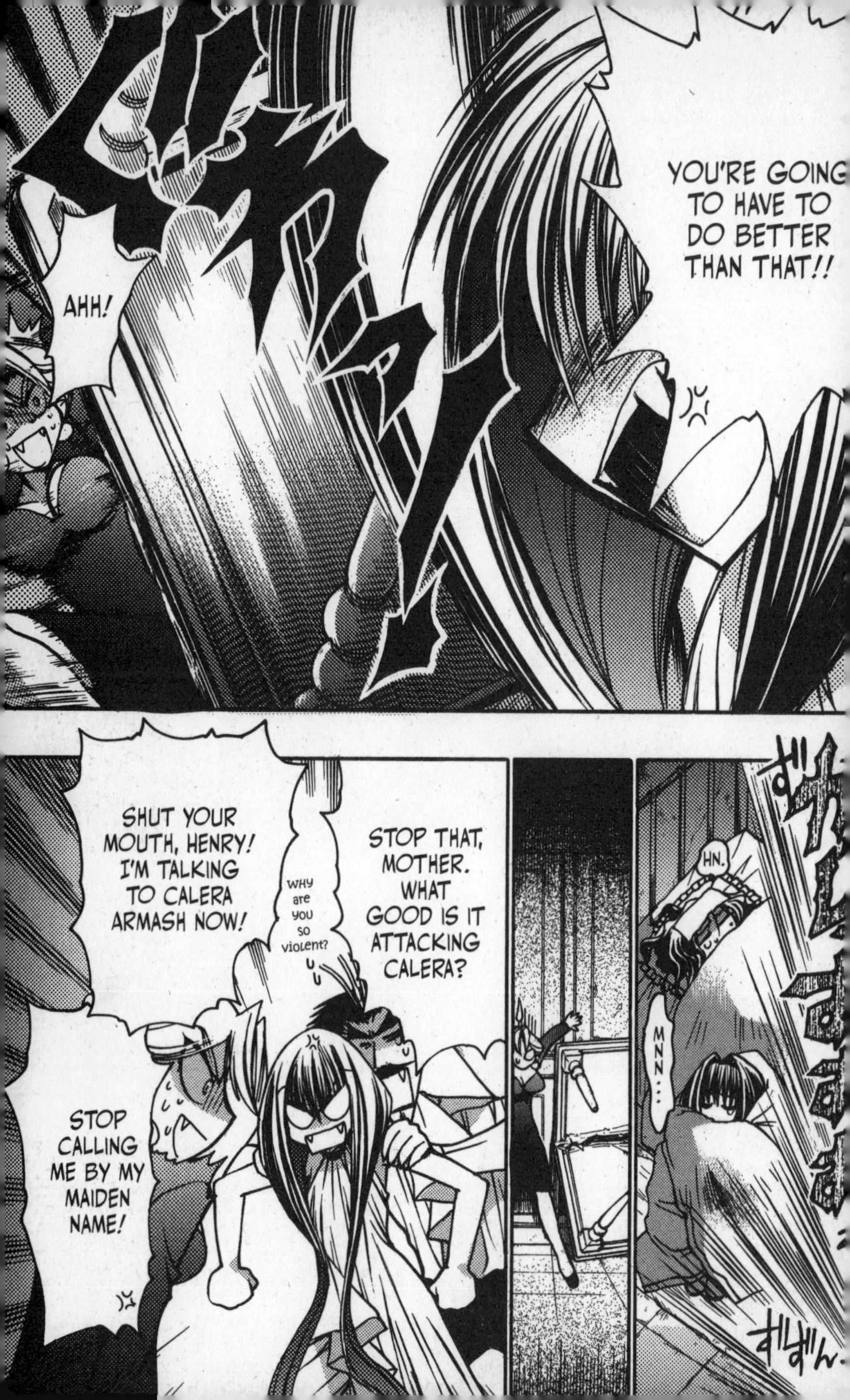
YOU'RE GOING TO HAVE TO DO BETTER THAN THAT!!
AHH!
HN.
MNN...
ずしずん
STOP THAT, MOTHER. WHAT GOOD IS IT ATTACKING CALERA?
WHY are you so violent?
SHUT YOUR MOUTH, HENRY! I'M TALKING TO CALERA ARMASH NOW!
STOP CALLING ME BY MY MAIDEN NAME!

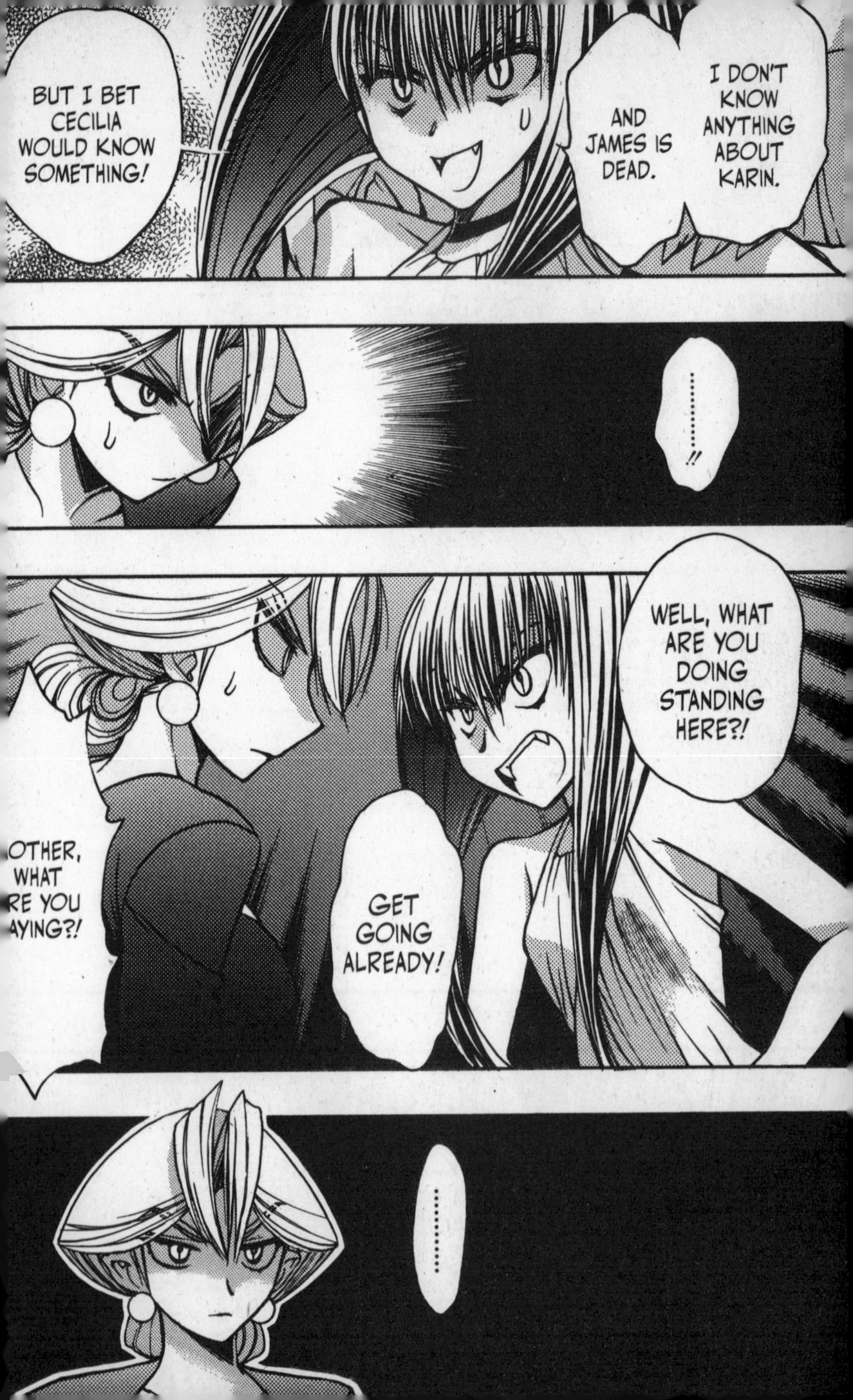
I DON'T KNOW ANYTHING ABOUT KARIN.
AND JAMES IS DEAD.
BUT I BET CECILIA WOULD KNOW SOMETHING!
......!!
WELL, WHAT ARE YOU DOING STANDING HERE?!
GET GOING ALREADY!
OTHER, WHAT RE YOU AYING?!
......

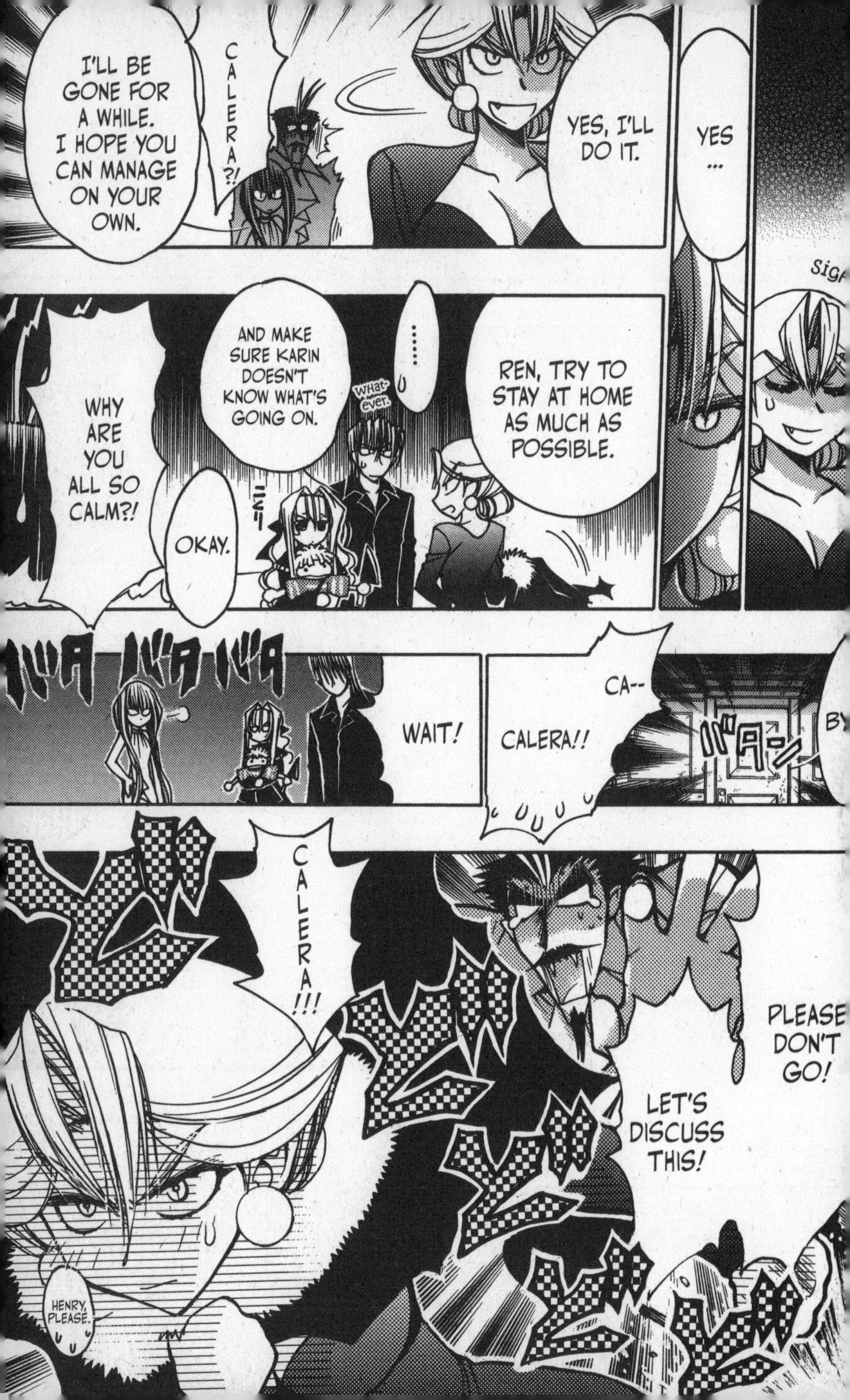
YES ...
SIG
YES, I'LL DO IT.
I'LL BE GONE FOR A WHILE. I HOPE YOU CAN MANAGE ON YOUR OWN.
CALERA?!
REN, TRY TO STAY AT HOME AS MUCH AS POSSIBLE.
......
WHATEVER.
AND MAKE SURE KARIN DOESN'T KNOW WHAT'S GOING ON.
OKAY.
WHY ARE YOU ALL SO CALM?!
BY
CA--
CALERA!!
WAIT!
PLEASE DON'T GO!
LET'S DISCUSS THIS!
CALERA!!!
HENRY, PLEASE.

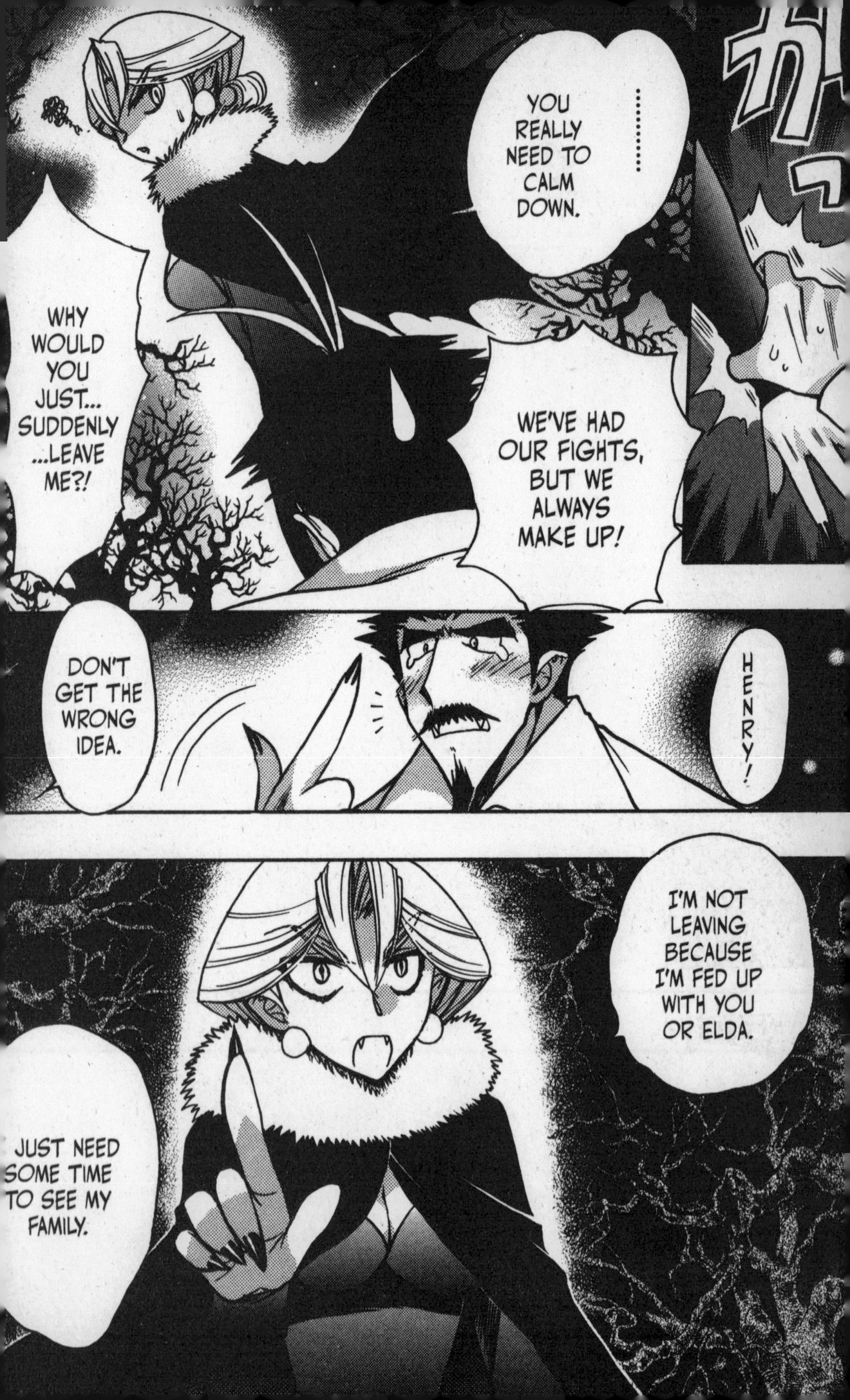

......
YOU REALLY NEED TO CALM DOWN.
WE'VE HAD OUR FIGHTS, BUT WE ALWAYS MAKE UP!
WHY WOULD YOU JUST... SUDDENLY ...LEAVE ME?!
HENRY!
DON'T GET THE WRONG IDEA.
I'M NOT LEAVING BECAUSE I'M FED UP WITH YOU OR ELDA.
JUST NEED SOME TIME TO SEE MY FAMILY.

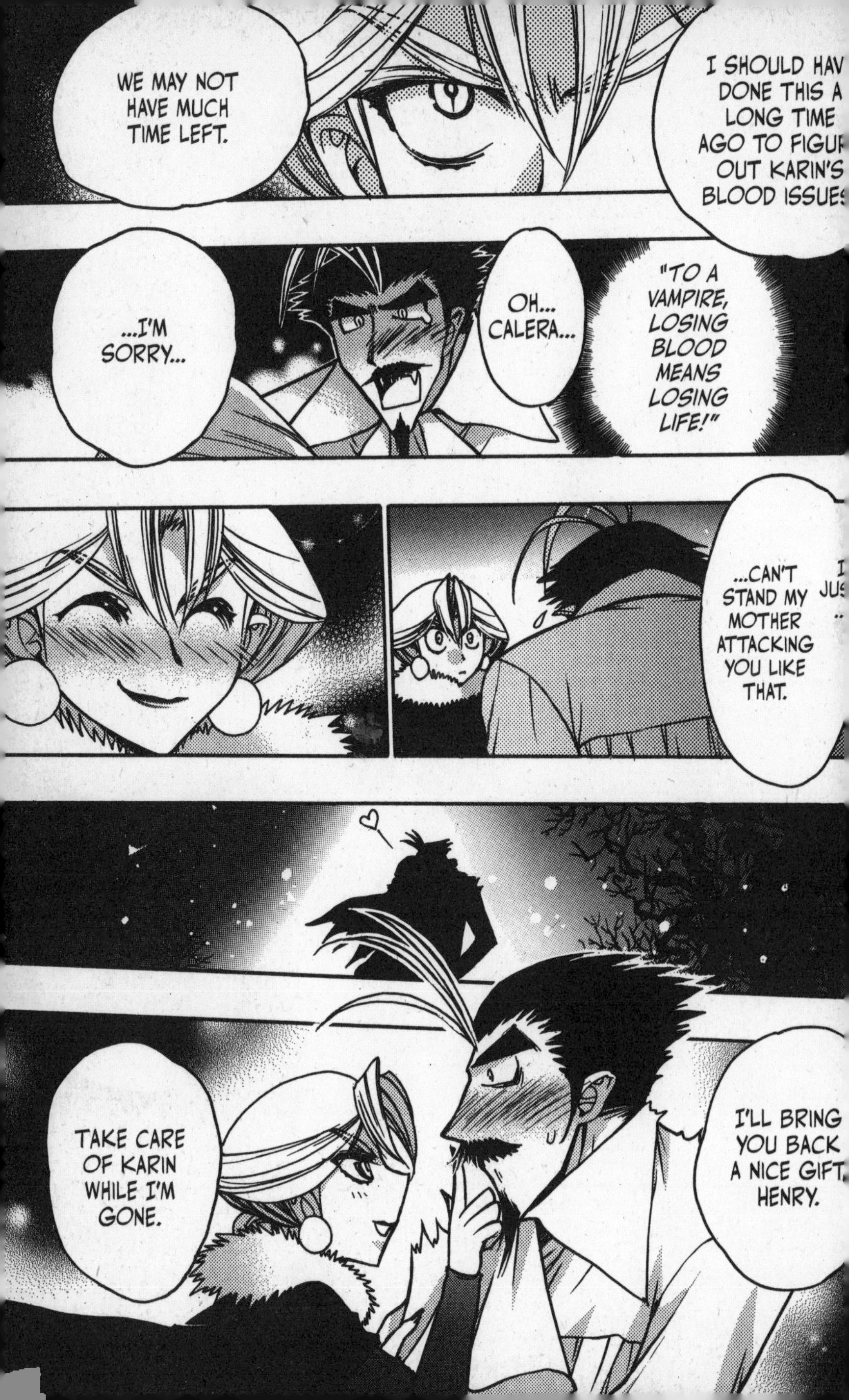
I SHOULD HAV DONE THIS A LONG TIME AGO TO FIGUR OUT KARIN'S BLOOD ISSUE
WE MAY NOT HAVE MUCH TIME LEFT.
"TO A VAMPIRE, LOSING BLOOD MEANS LOSING LIFE!"
OH... CALERA...
...I'M SORRY...
I JUS
...CAN'T STAND MY MOTHER ATTACKING YOU LIKE THAT.
I'LL BRING YOU BACK A NICE GIFT, HENRY.
TAKE CARE OF KARIN WHILE I'M GONE.

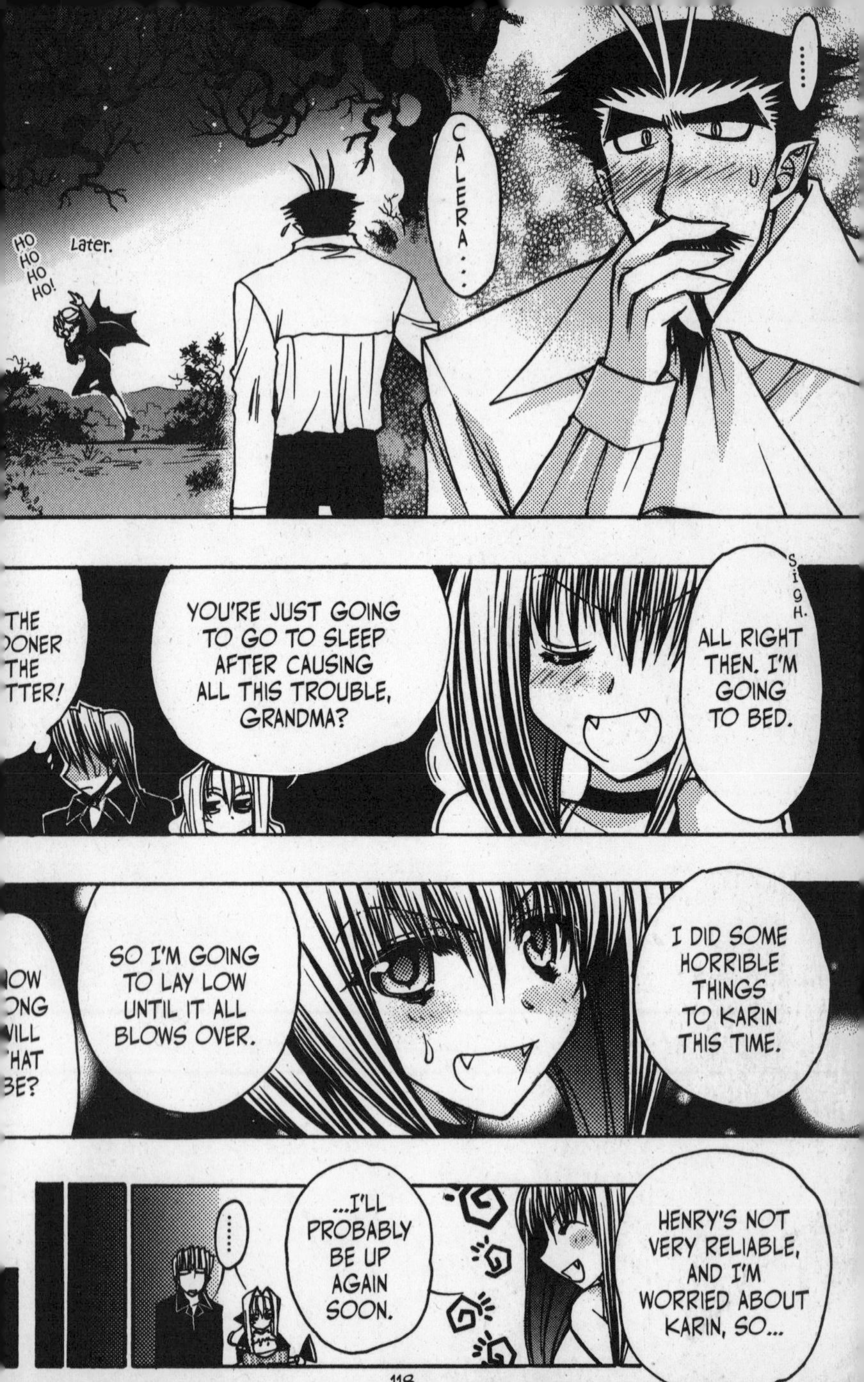
......
CALERA...
Later.
HO HO HO HO!
SIGH.
ALL RIGHT THEN. I'M GOING TO BED.
YOU'RE JUST GOING TO GO TO SLEEP AFTER CAUSING ALL THIS TROUBLE, GRANDMA?
I DID SOME HORRIBLE THINGS TO KARIN THIS TIME.
SO I'M GOING TO LAY LOW UNTIL IT ALL BLOWS OVER.
HENRY'S NOT VERY RELIABLE, AND I'M WORRIED ABOUT KARIN, SO...
...I'LL PROBABLY BE UP AGAIN SOON.
......

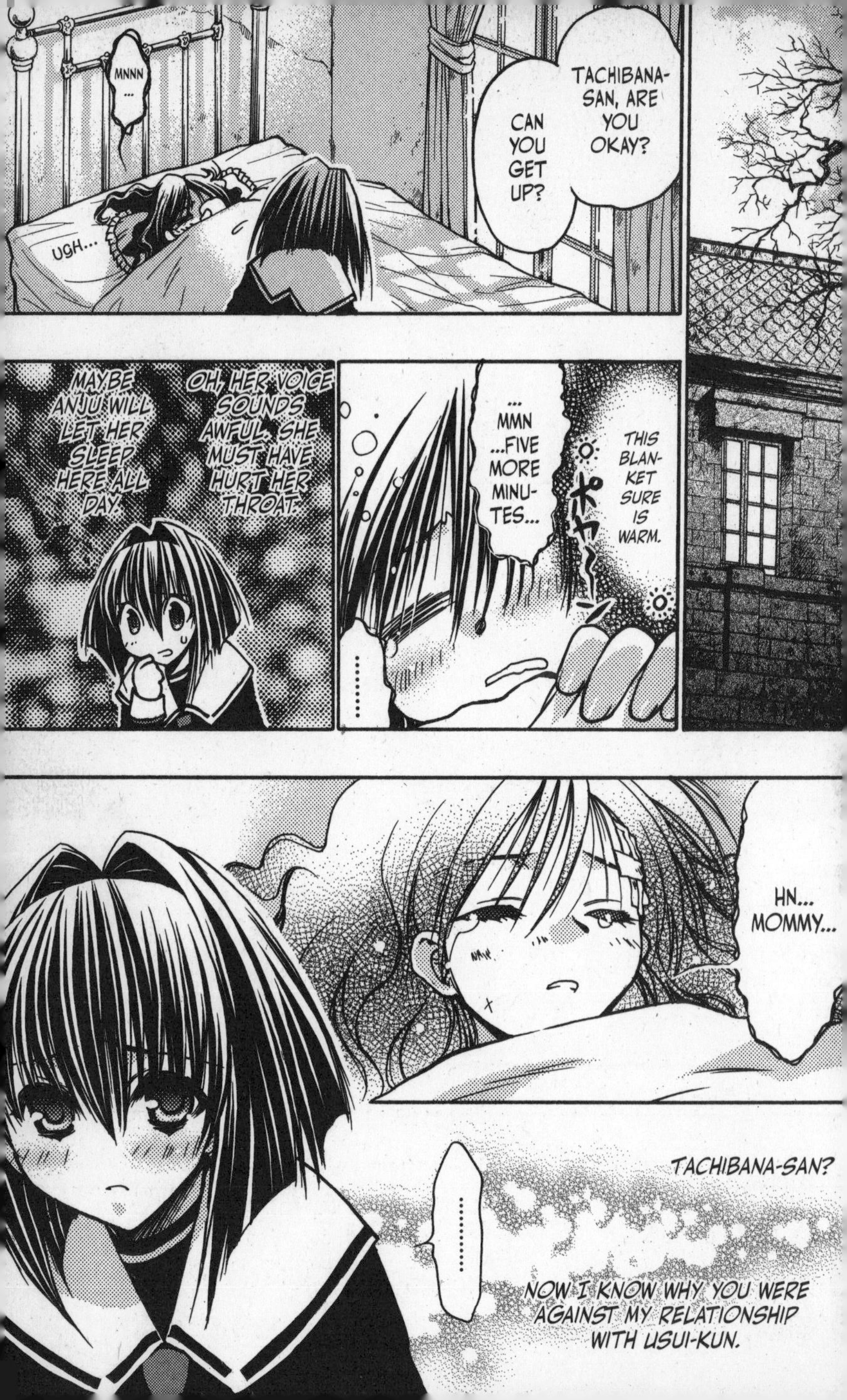
TACHIBANA-SAN, ARE YOU OKAY? CAN YOU GET UP?
MNNN...
UGH...
THIS BLANKET SURE IS WARM.
ポヤ～
...MMN ...FIVE MORE MINUTES...
......
OH, HER VOICE SOUNDS AWFUL. SHE MUST HAVE HURT HER THROAT.
MAYBE ANJU WILL LET HER SLEEP HERE ALL DAY.
HN... MOMMY...
TACHIBANA-SAN?
......
NOW I KNOW WHY YOU WERE AGAINST MY RELATIONSHIP WITH USUI-KUN.

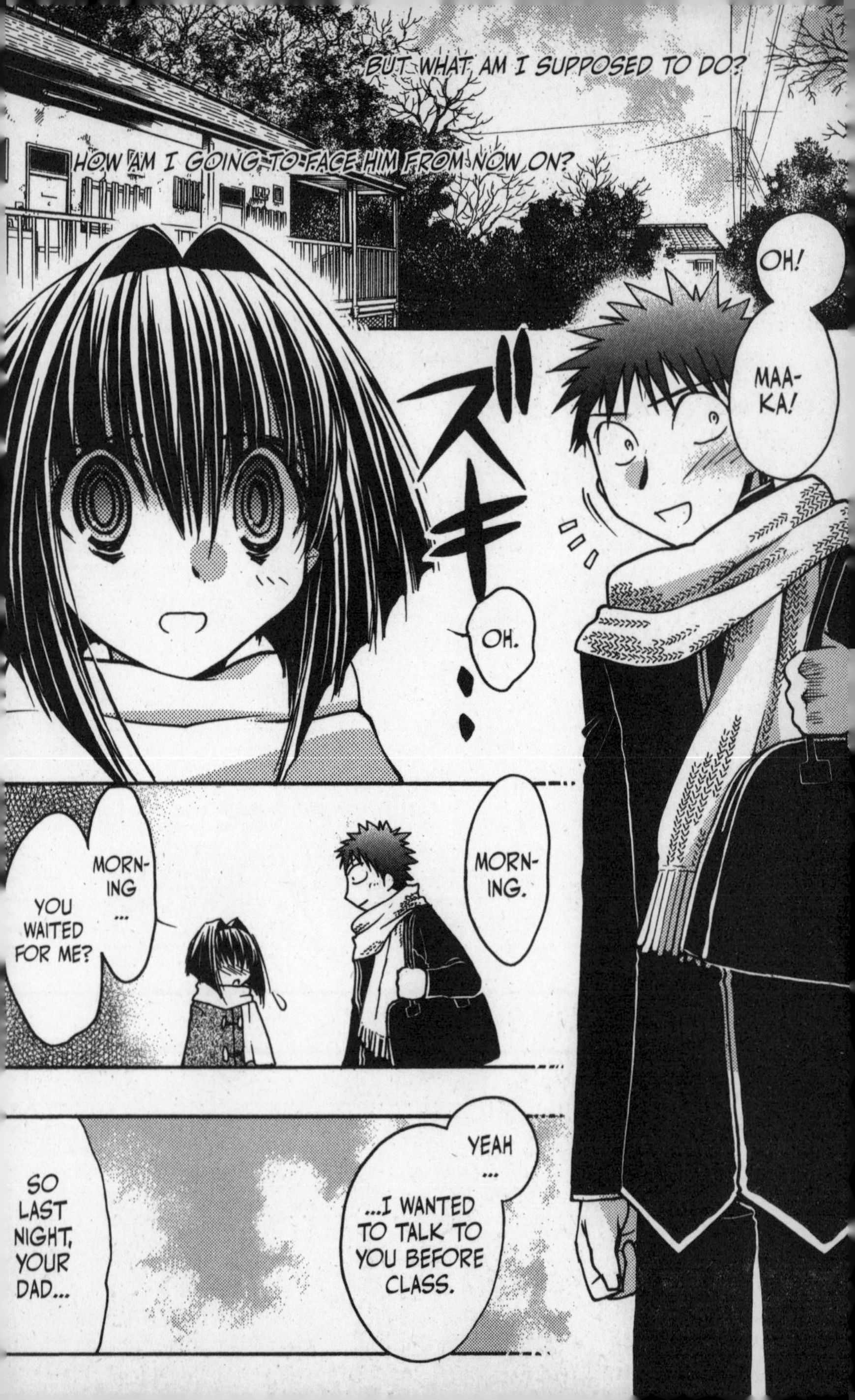
BUT WHAT AM I SUPPOSED TO DO?
HOW AM I GOING TO FACE HIM FROM NOW ON?
OH! MAA-KA!
ズキ
OH.
MORN-ING.
MORN-ING ... YOU WAITED FOR ME?
YEAH ... ...I WANTED TO TALK TO YOU BEFORE CLASS.
SO LAST NIGHT, YOUR DAD...

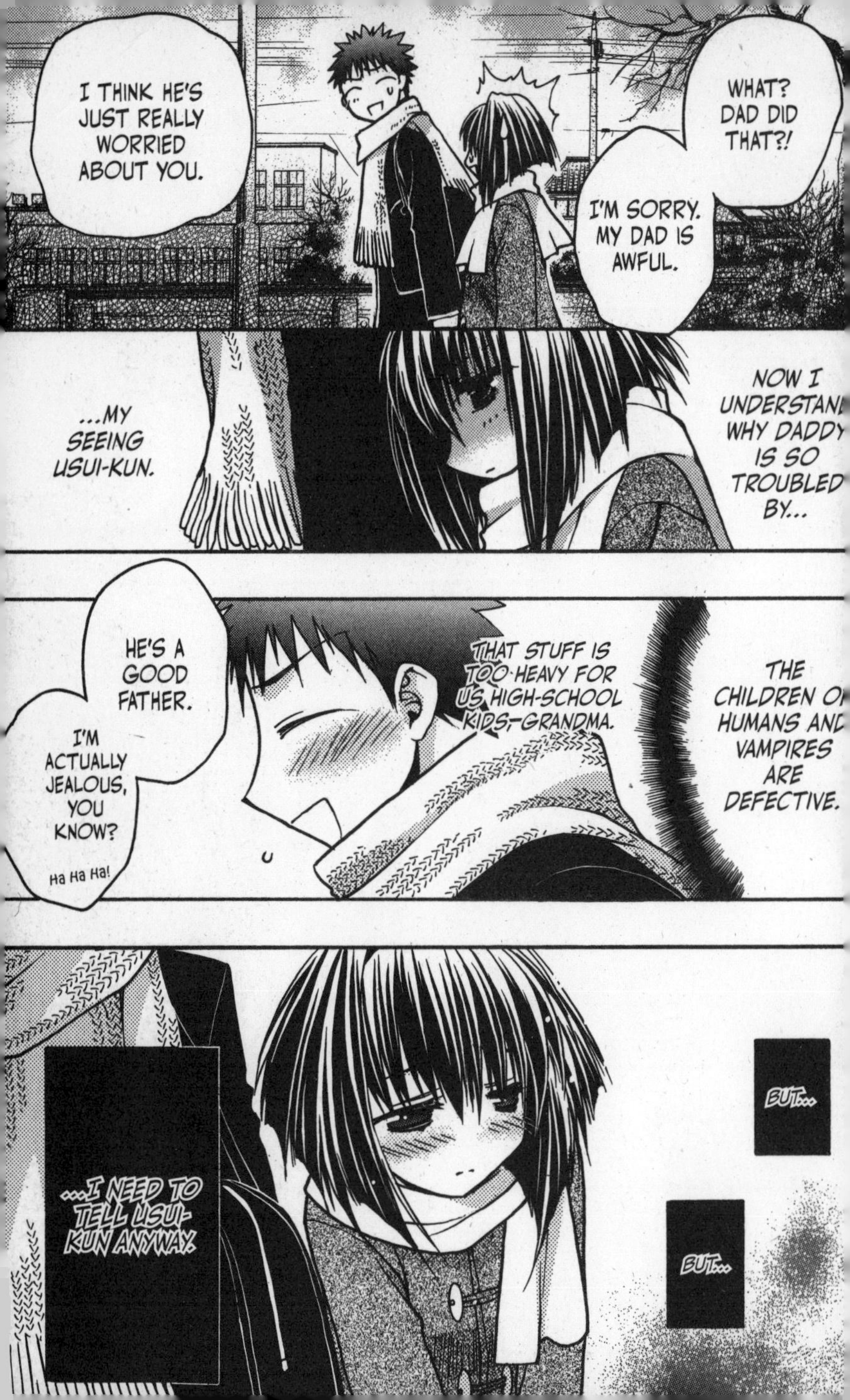
WHAT? DAD DID THAT?!
I'M SORRY. MY DAD IS AWFUL.
I THINK HE'S JUST REALLY WORRIED ABOUT YOU.
NOW I UNDERSTAND WHY DADDY IS SO TROUBLED BY...
...MY SEEING USUI-KUN.
THE CHILDREN OF HUMANS AND VAMPIRES ARE DEFECTIVE.
THAT STUFF IS TOO HEAVY FOR US HIGH-SCHOOL KIDS—GRANDMA.
HE'S A GOOD FATHER.
I'M ACTUALLY JEALOUS, YOU KNOW?
Ha Ha Ha!
BUT...
BUT...
...I NEED TO TELL USUI-KUN ANYWAY.

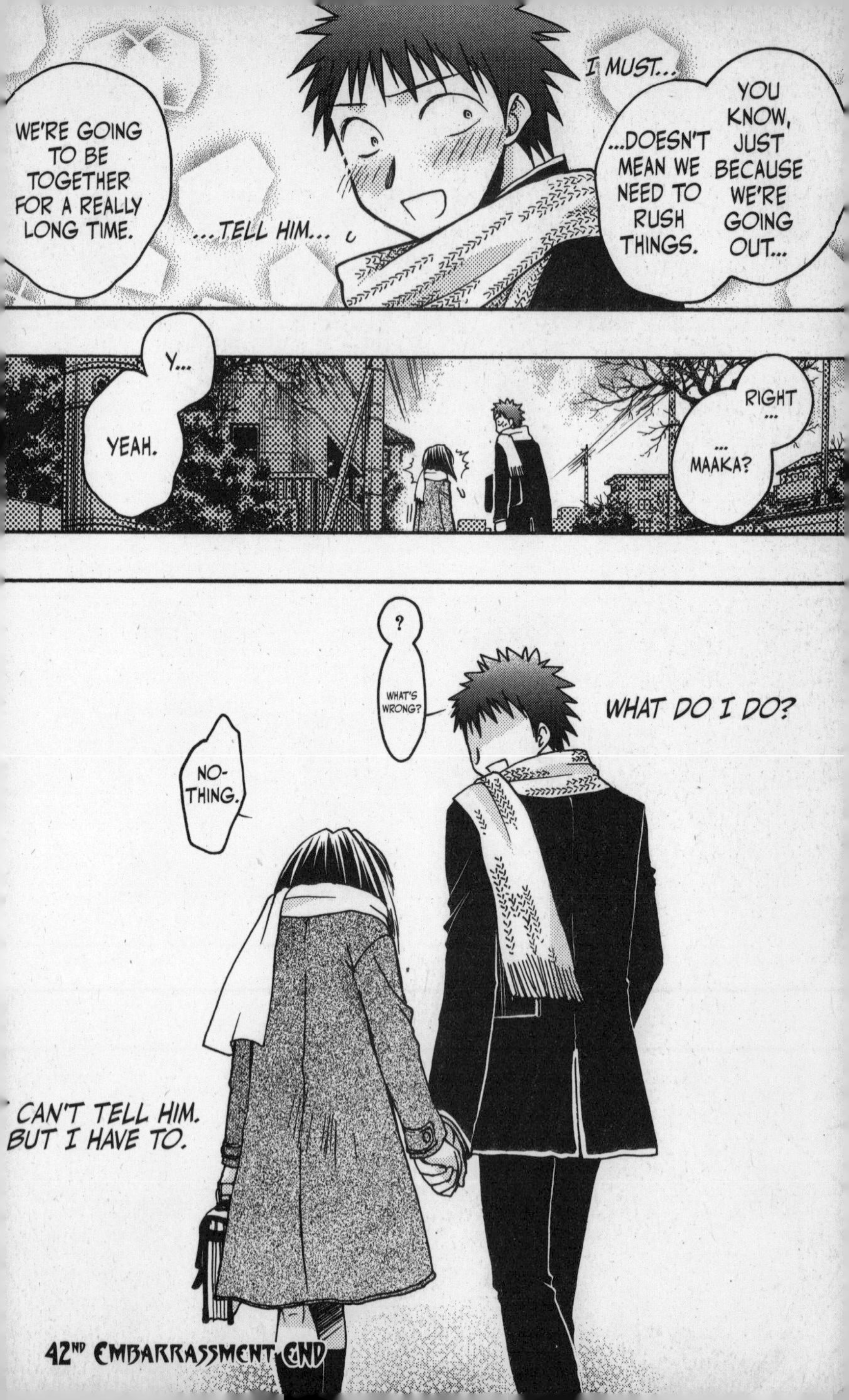
YOU KNOW, JUST BECAUSE WE'RE GOING OUT...
...DOESN'T MEAN WE NEED TO RUSH THINGS.
I MUST...
...TELL HIM...
WE'RE GOING TO BE TOGETHER FOR A REALLY LONG TIME.
RIGHT... ...MAAKA?
Y... YEAH.
WHAT DO I DO?
?
WHAT'S WRONG?
NO-THING.
CAN'T TELL HIM. BUT I HAVE TO.
42ND EMBARRASSMENT END

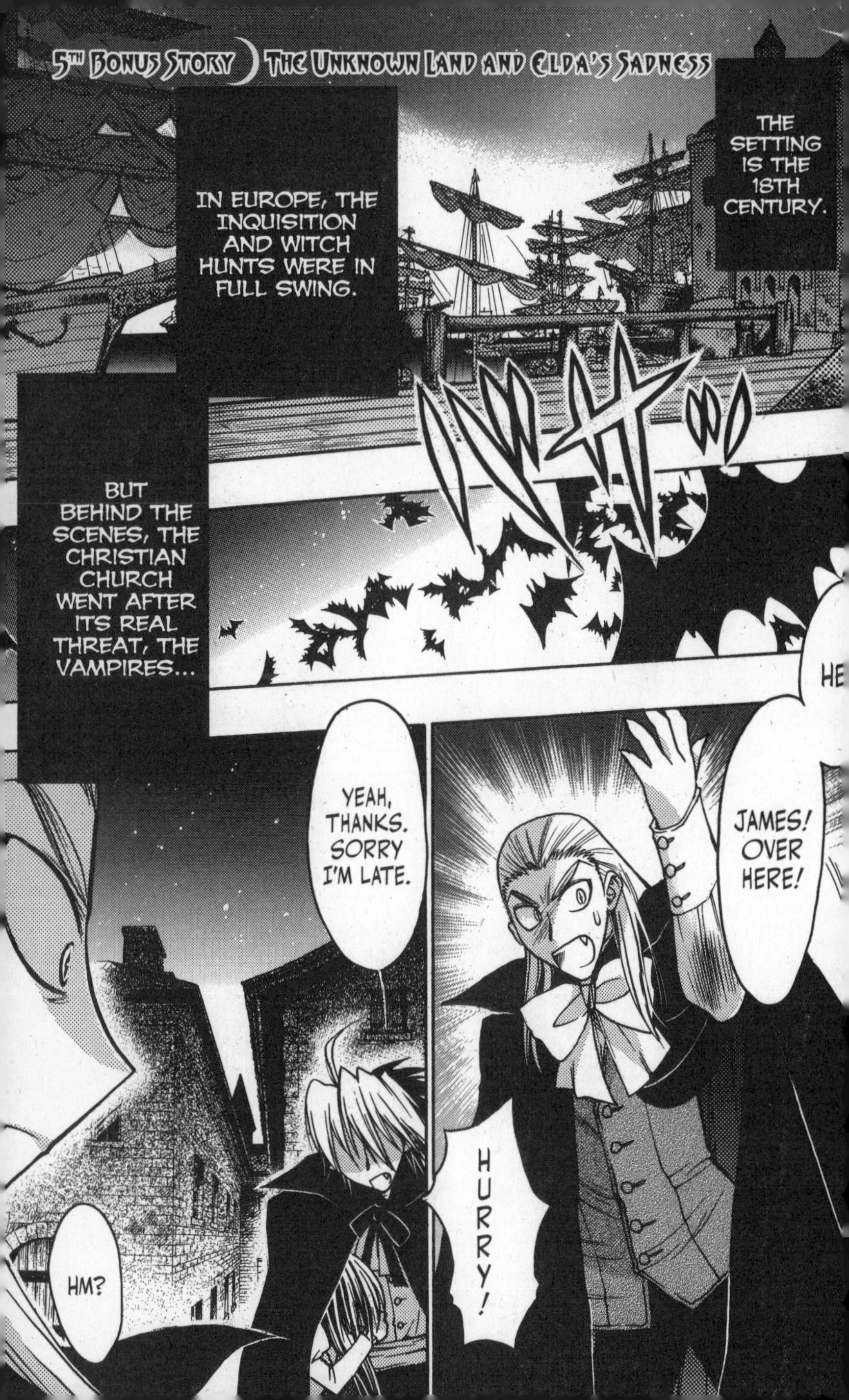
5TH BONUS STORY THE UNKNOWN LAND AND ELDA'S SADNESS
THE SETTING IS THE 18TH CENTURY.
IN EUROPE, THE INQUISITION AND WITCH HUNTS WERE IN FULL SWING.
BUT BEHIND THE SCENES, THE CHRISTIAN CHURCH WENT AFTER ITS REAL THREAT, THE VAMPIRES...
HE
JAMES! OVER HERE!
HURRY!
YEAH, THANKS. SORRY I'M LATE.
HM?

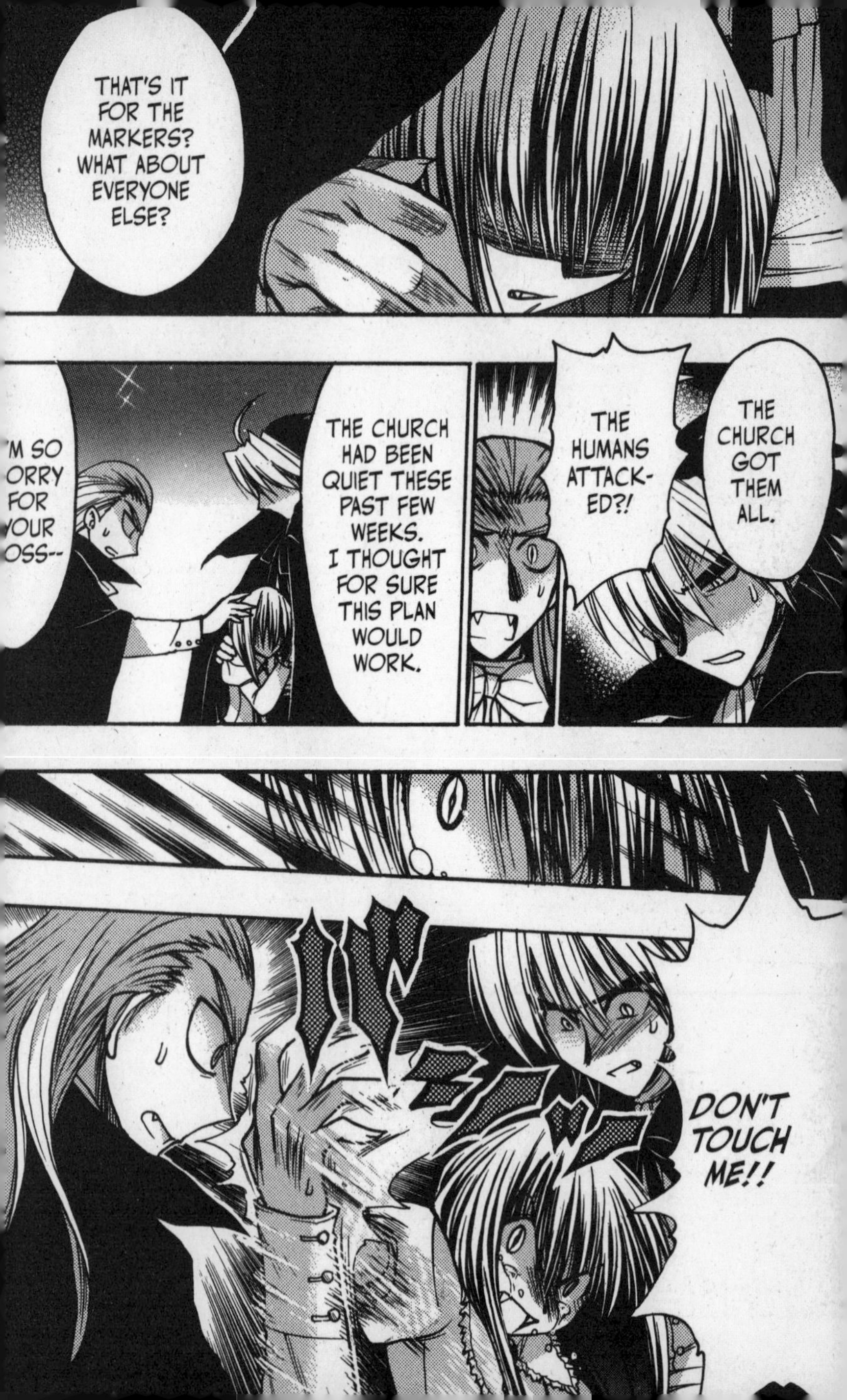
THAT'S IT FOR THE MARKERS? WHAT ABOUT EVERYONE ELSE?
THE CHURCH GOT THEM ALL.
THE HUMANS ATTACK-ED?!
THE CHURCH HAD BEEN QUIET THESE PAST FEW WEEKS. I THOUGHT FOR SURE THIS PLAN WOULD WORK.
'M SO ORRY FOR YOUR OSS--
DON'T TOUCH ME!!

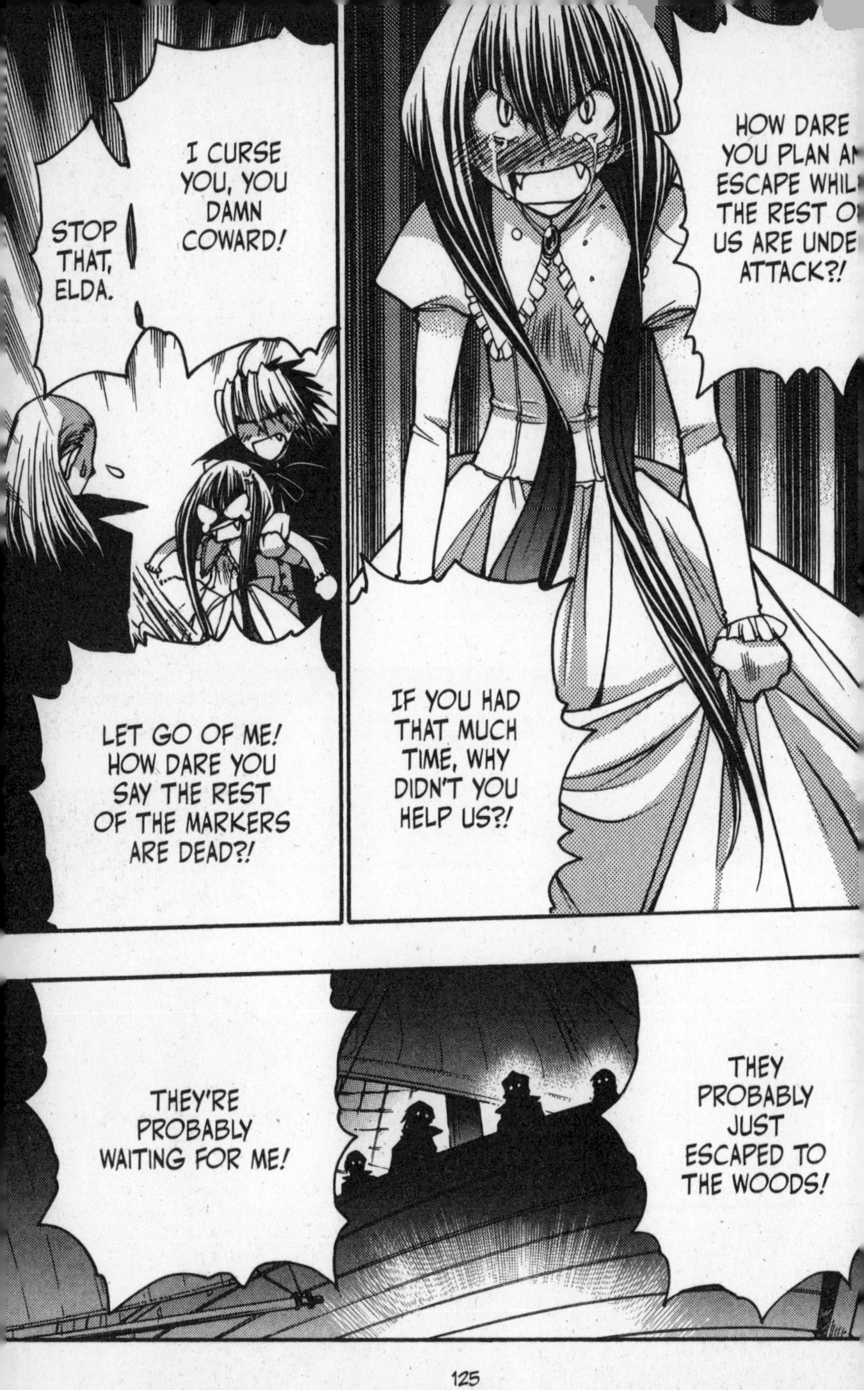
HOW DARE YOU PLAN AN ESCAPE WHIL THE REST O US ARE UNDE ATTACK?!
IF YOU HAD THAT MUCH TIME, WHY DIDN'T YOU HELP US?!
I CURSE YOU, YOU DAMN COWARD!
STOP THAT, ELDA.
LET GO OF ME! HOW DARE YOU SAY THE REST OF THE MARKERS ARE DEAD?!
THEY PROBABLY JUST ESCAPED TO THE WOODS!
THEY'RE PROBABLY WAITING FOR ME!

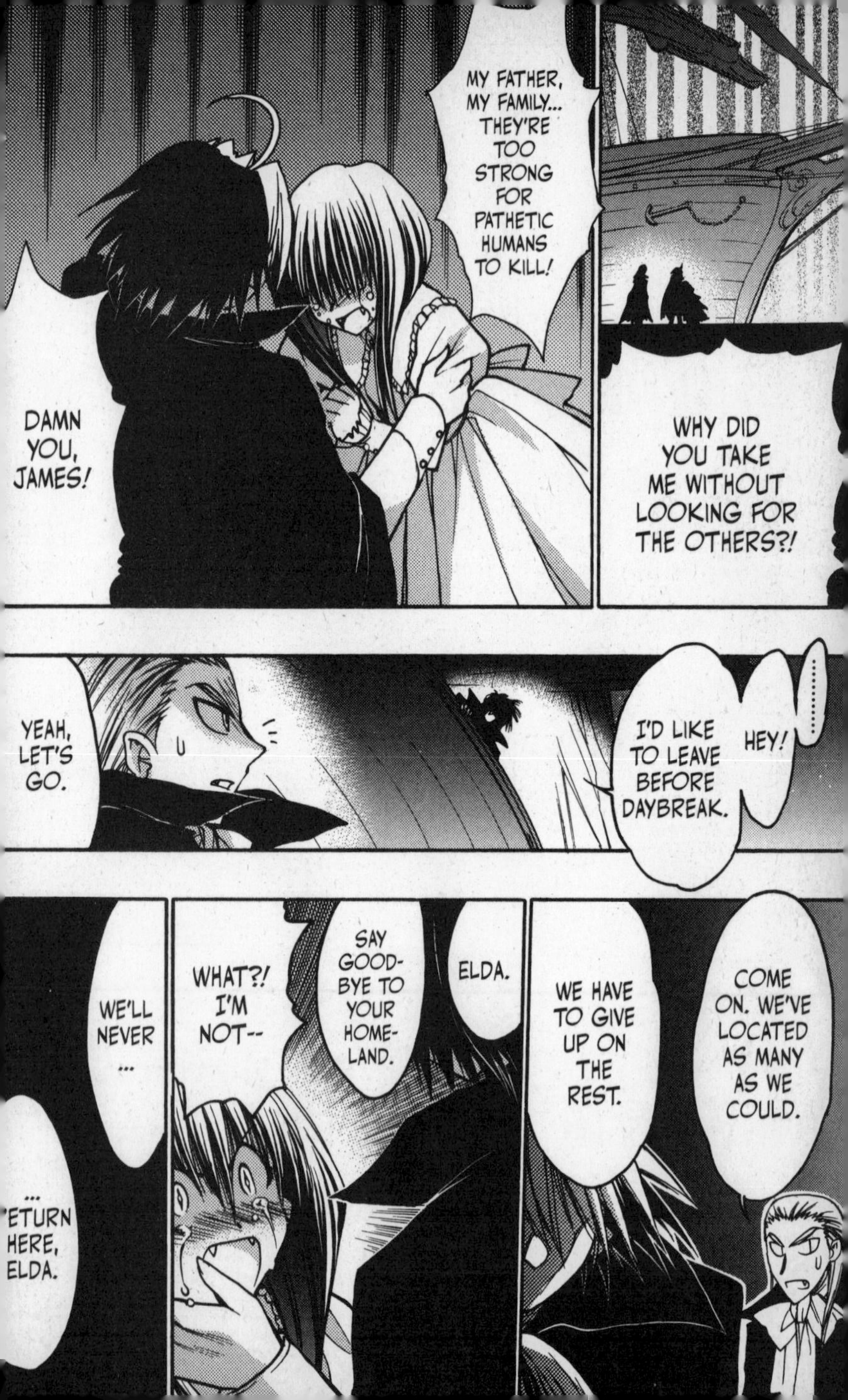
WHY DID YOU TAKE ME WITHOUT LOOKING FOR THE OTHERS?!
MY FATHER, MY FAMILY... THEY'RE TOO STRONG FOR PATHETIC HUMANS TO KILL!
DAMN YOU, JAMES!
......
HEY!
I'D LIKE TO LEAVE BEFORE DAYBREAK.
YEAH, LET'S GO.
COME ON. WE'VE LOCATED AS MANY AS WE COULD.
WE HAVE TO GIVE UP ON THE REST.
ELDA.
SAY GOOD-BYE TO YOUR HOME-LAND.
WHAT?! I'M NOT--
WE'LL NEVER ...
... 'ETURN HERE, ELDA.

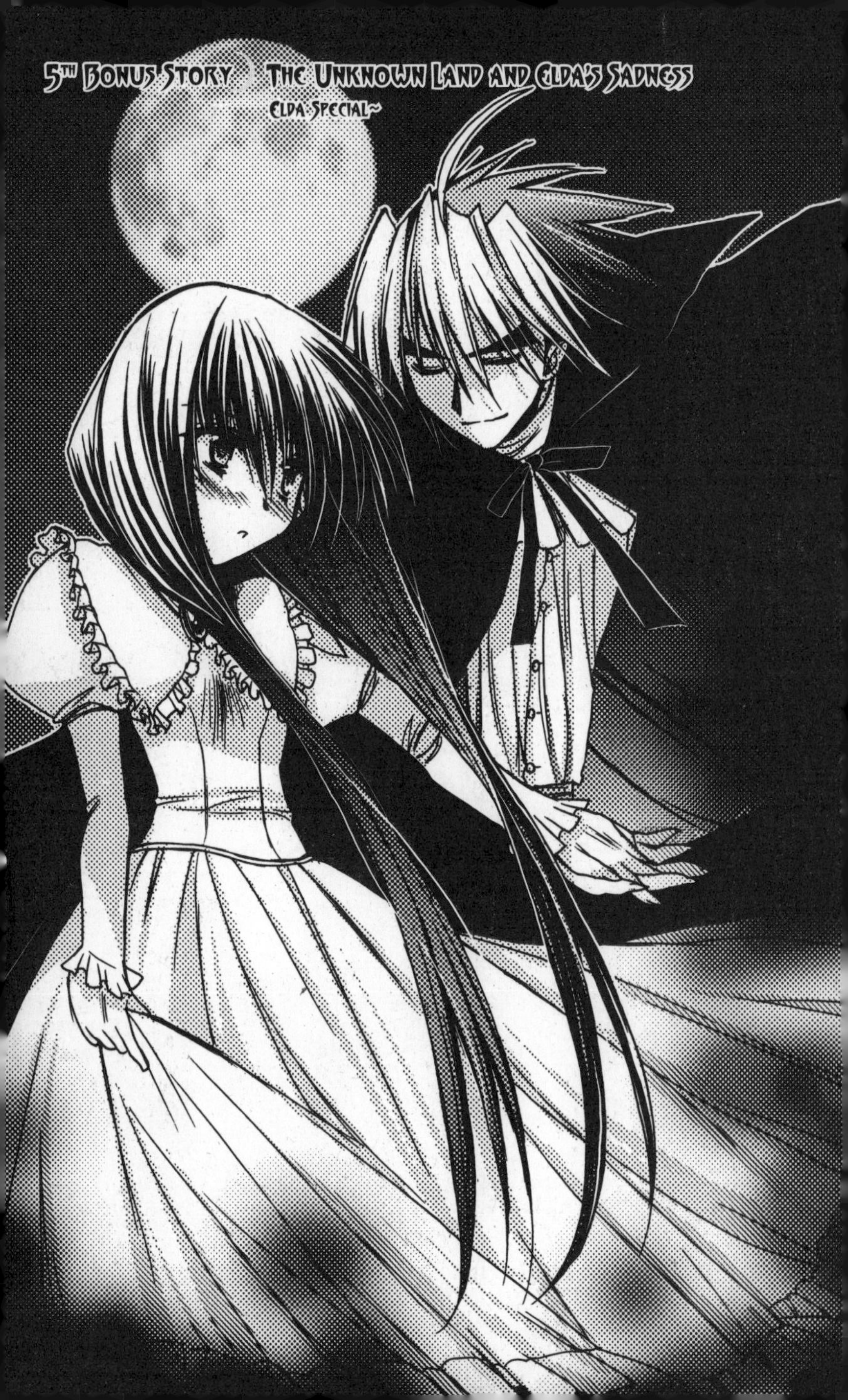
5TH Bonus Story The Unknown Land and Elda's Sadness
~Elda Special~

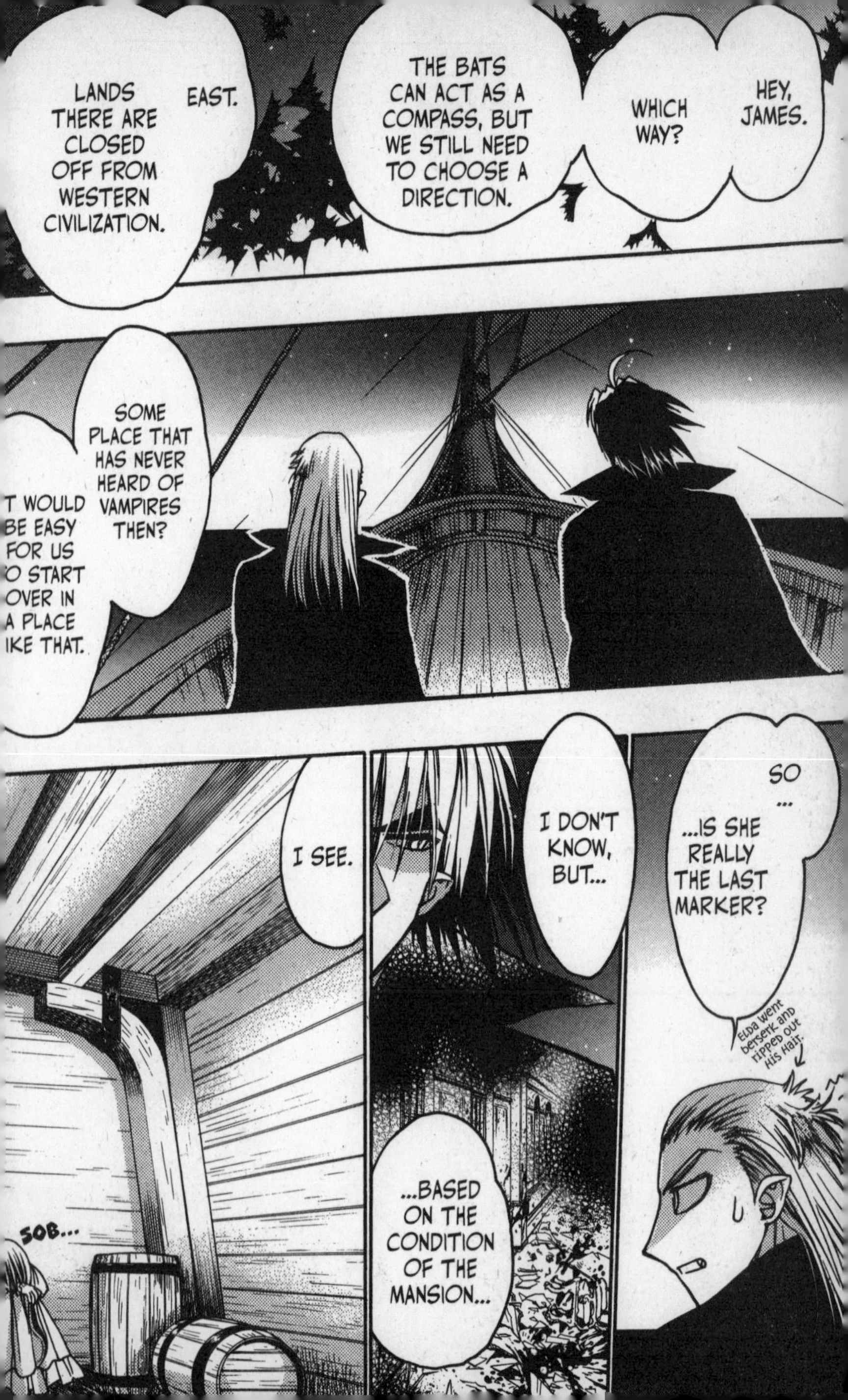
HEY, JAMES.
WHICH WAY?
THE BATS CAN ACT AS A COMPASS, BUT WE STILL NEED TO CHOOSE A DIRECTION.
EAST.
LANDS THERE ARE CLOSED OFF FROM WESTERN CIVILIZATION.
SOME PLACE THAT HAS NEVER HEARD OF VAMPIRES THEN?
T WOULD BE EASY FOR US O START OVER IN A PLACE IKE THAT.
SO...
...IS SHE REALLY THE LAST MARKER?
Elda went berserk and ripped out his hair.
I DON'T KNOW, BUT...
...BASED ON THE CONDITION OF THE MANSION...
I SEE.
SOB...

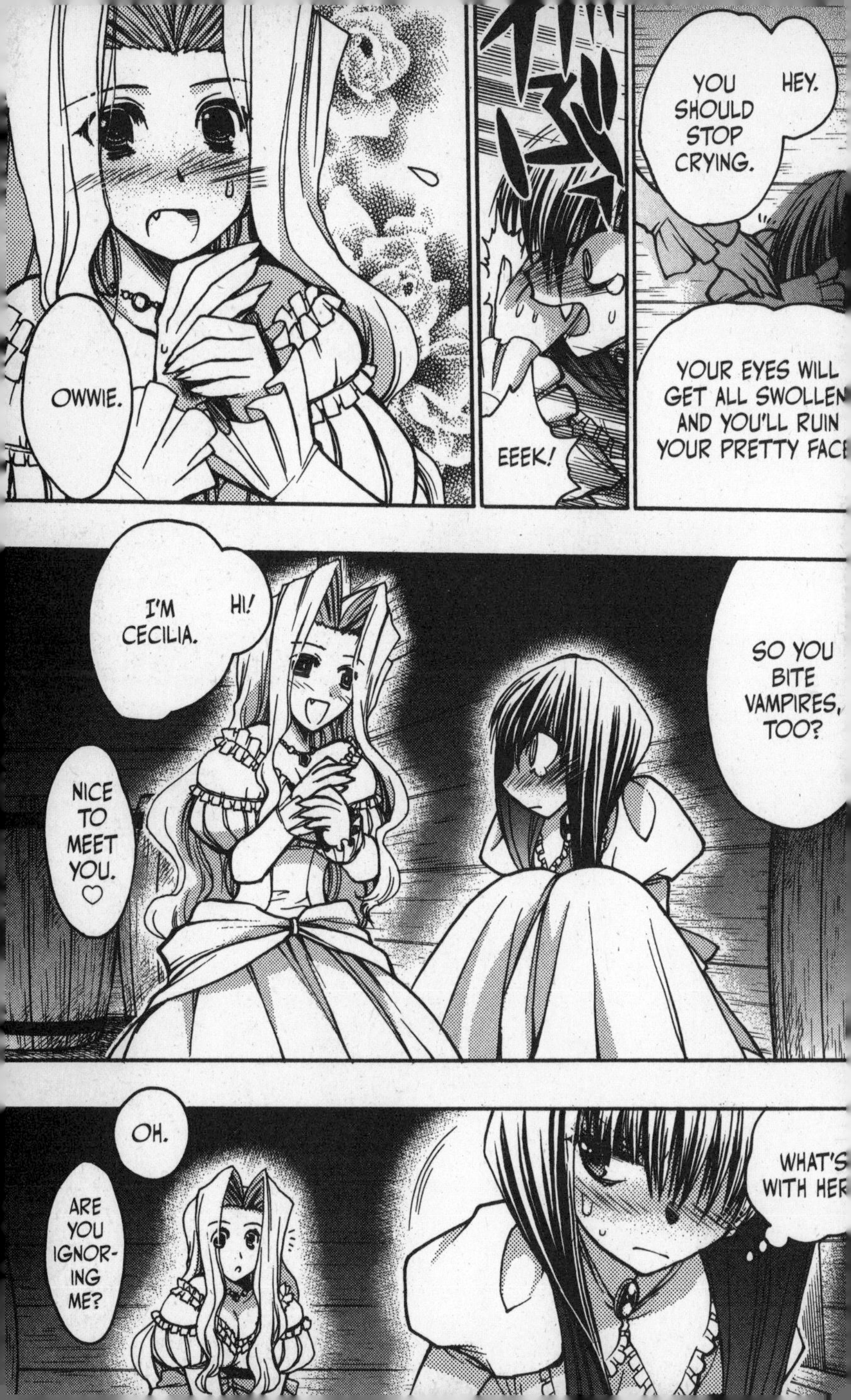
HEY.
YOU SHOULD STOP CRYING.
YOUR EYES WILL GET ALL SWOLLEN AND YOU'LL RUIN YOUR PRETTY FAC
EEEK!
OWWIE.
SO YOU BITE VAMPIRES, TOO?
HI!
I'M CECILIA.
NICE TO MEET YOU. ♡
WHAT'S WITH HER
OH.
ARE YOU IGNOR-ING ME?

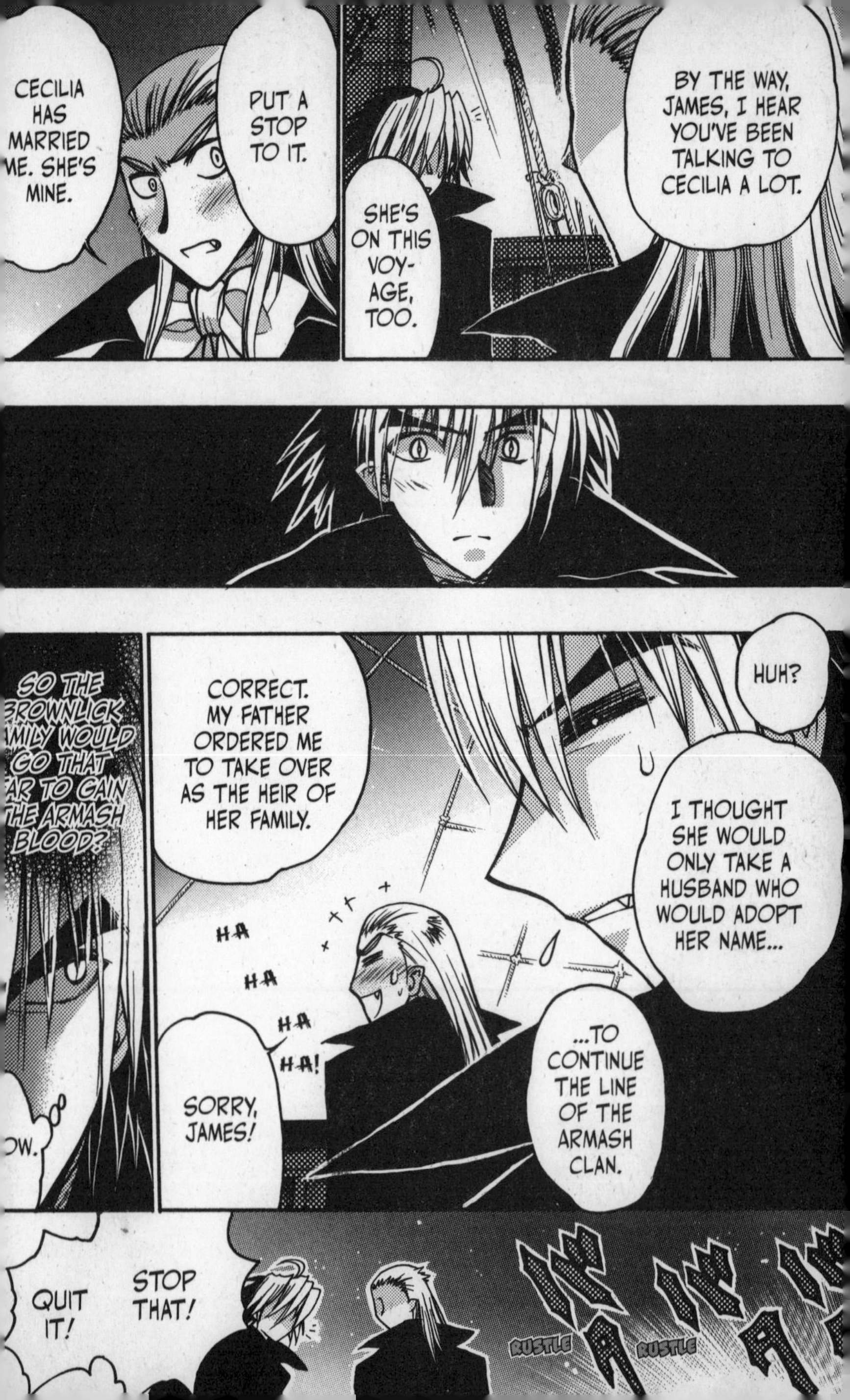
BY THE WAY, JAMES, I HEAR YOU'VE BEEN TALKING TO CECILIA A LOT.
SHE'S ON THIS VOY-AGE, TOO.
PUT A STOP TO IT.
CECILIA HAS MARRIED ME. SHE'S MINE.
HUH?
I THOUGHT SHE WOULD ONLY TAKE A HUSBAND WHO WOULD ADOPT HER NAME...
...TO CONTINUE THE LINE OF THE ARMASH CLAN.
CORRECT. MY FATHER ORDERED ME TO TAKE OVER AS THE HEIR OF HER FAMILY.
HA HA HA HA!
SORRY, JAMES!
SO THE BROWNLICK AMILY WOULD GO THAT AR TO GAIN THE ARMASH BLOOD?
OW.
RUSTLE RUSTLE
STOP THAT!
QUIT IT!

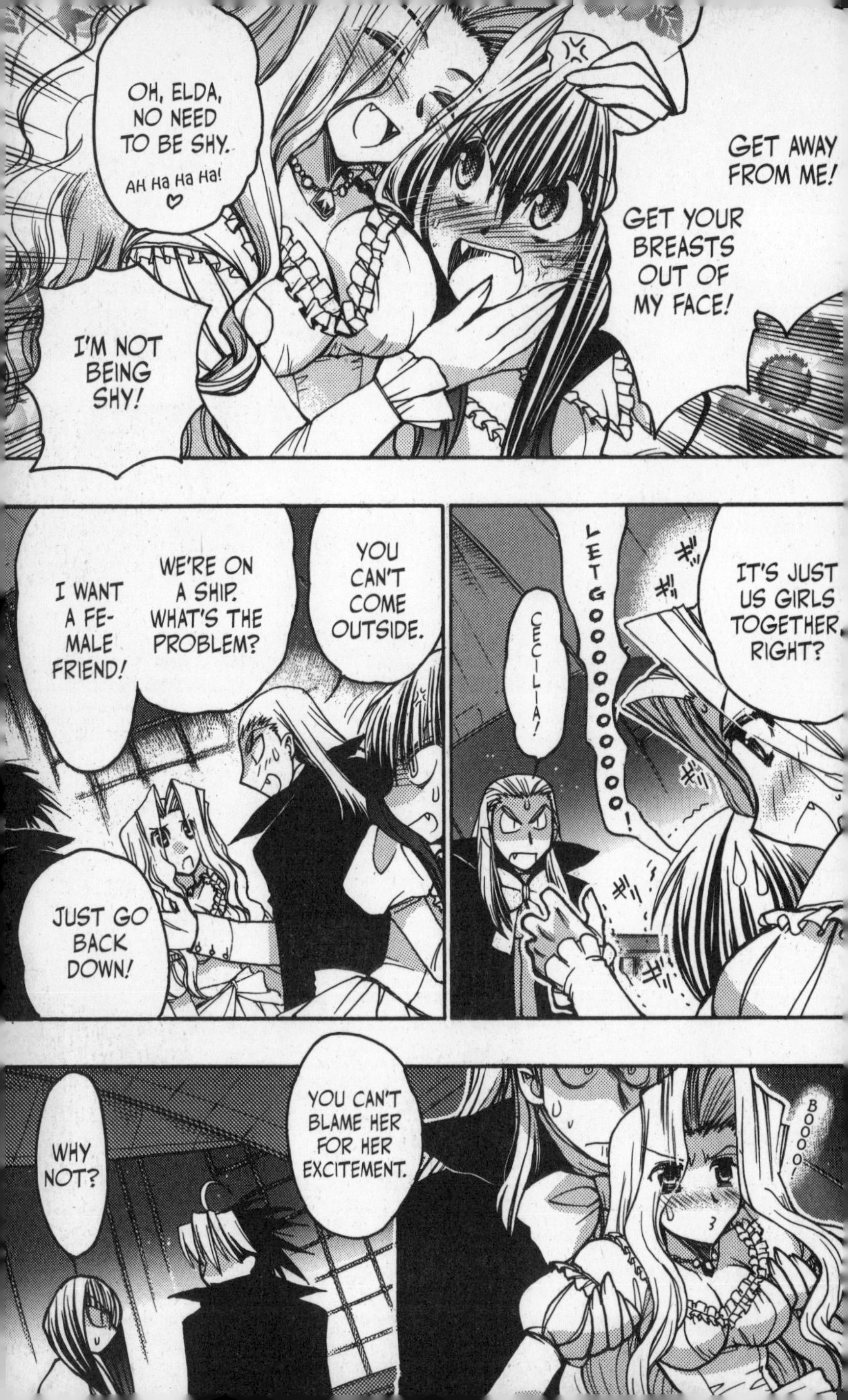
GET AWAY FROM ME!
GET YOUR BREASTS OUT OF MY FACE!
OH, ELDA, NO NEED TO BE SHY. AH HA HA HA! ♡
I'M NOT BEING SHY!
IT'S JUST US GIRLS TOGETHER, RIGHT?
LET GOOOOOOOOOO!
CECILIA!
YOU CAN'T COME OUTSIDE.
WE'RE ON A SHIP. WHAT'S THE PROBLEM?
I WANT A FE-MALE FRIEND!
JUST GO BACK DOWN!
BOOOOO!
YOU CAN'T BLAME HER FOR HER EXCITEMENT.
WHY NOT?

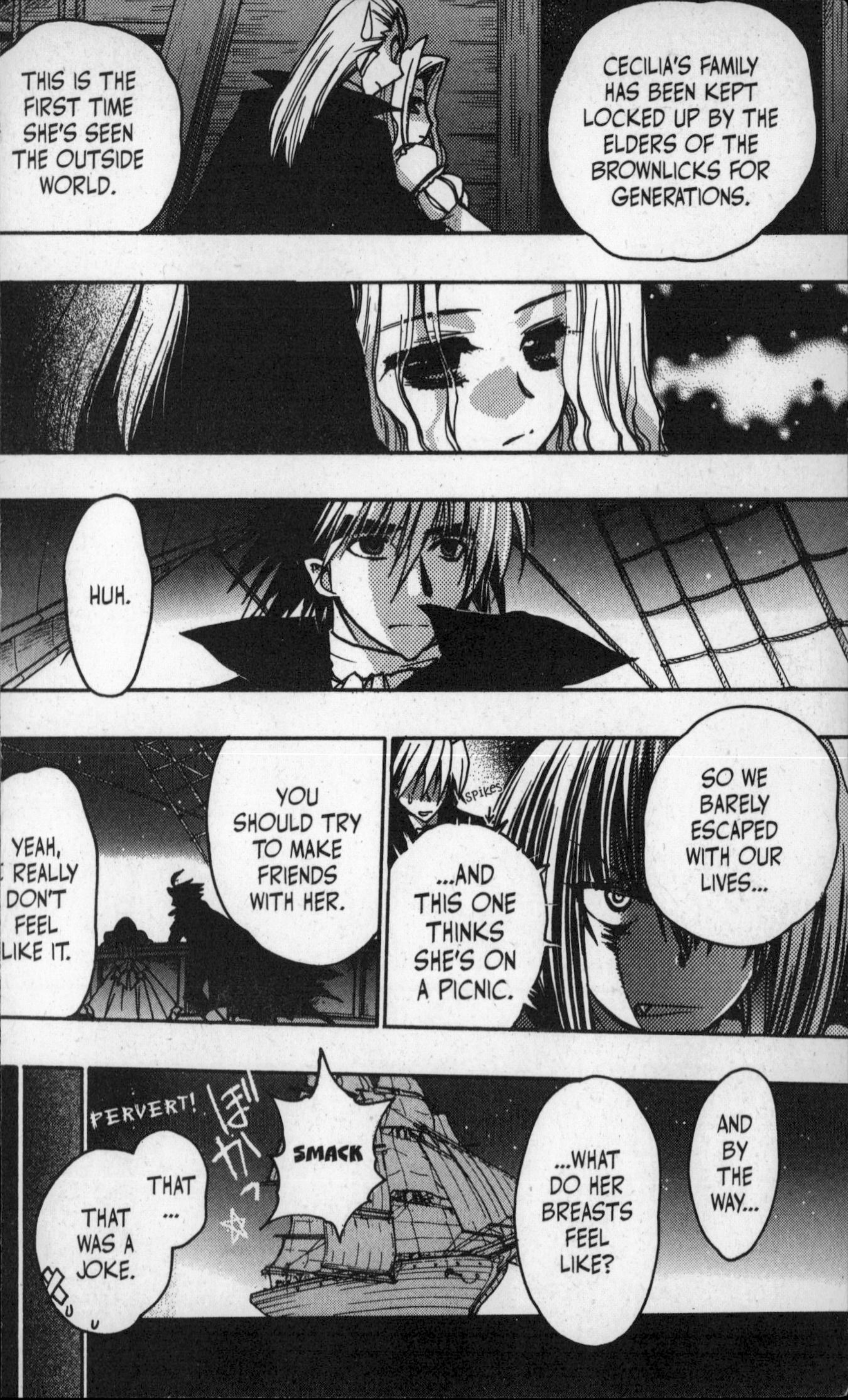
CECILIA'S FAMILY HAS BEEN KEPT LOCKED UP BY THE ELDERS OF THE BROWNLICKS FOR GENERATIONS.
THIS IS THE FIRST TIME SHE'S SEEN THE OUTSIDE WORLD.
HUH.
SO WE BARELY ESCAPED WITH OUR LIVES...
SPIKES
...AND THIS ONE THINKS SHE'S ON A PICNIC.
YOU SHOULD TRY TO MAKE FRIENDS WITH HER.
YEAH, REALLY DON'T FEEL LIKE IT.
AND BY THE WAY...
...WHAT DO HER BREASTS FEEL LIKE?
SMACK
PERVERT!
THAT ...
THAT WAS A JOKE.

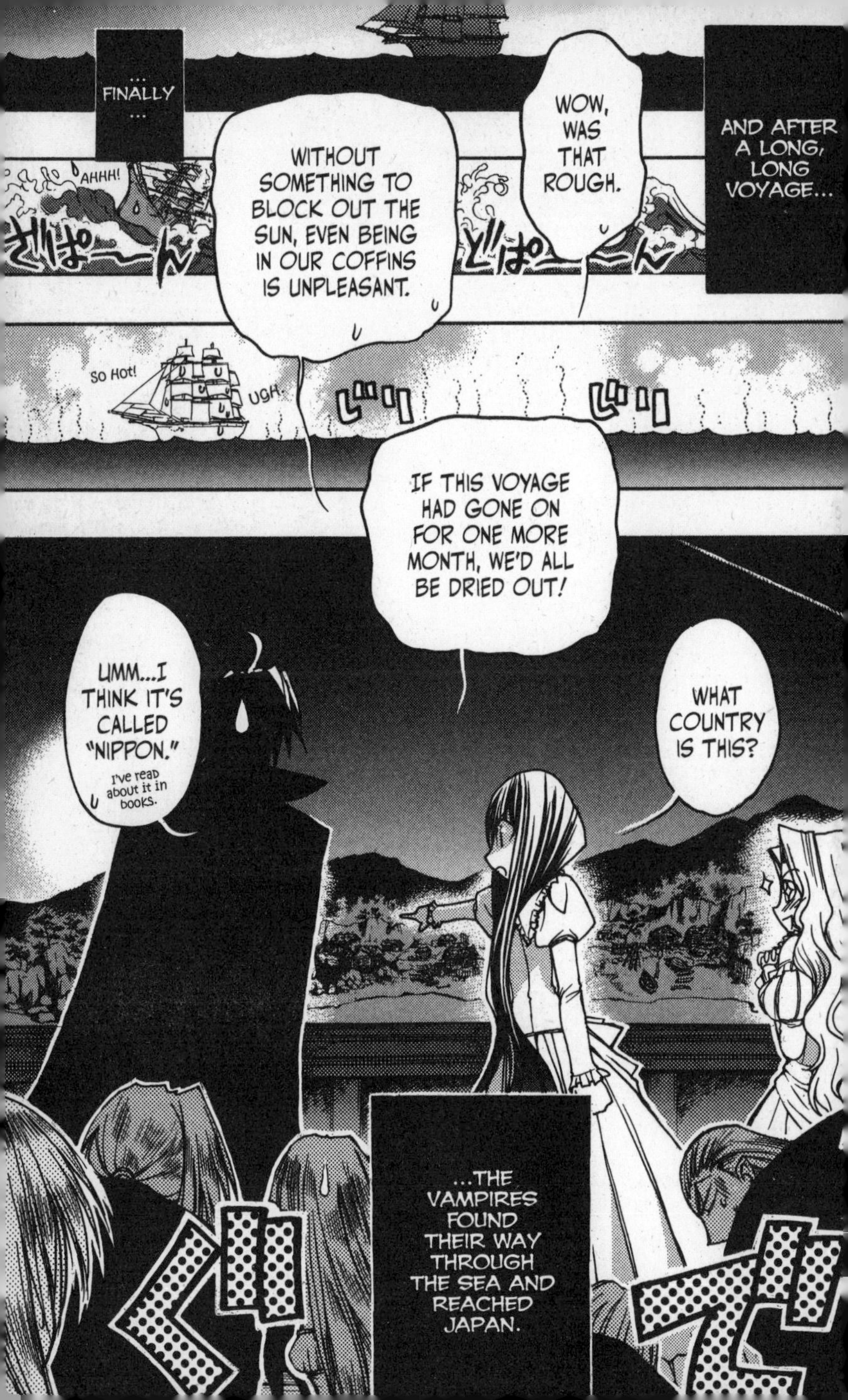

AND AFTER A LONG, LONG VOYAGE...
...FINALLY...
WOW, WAS THAT ROUGH.
どぱ〜ん
WITHOUT SOMETHING TO BLOCK OUT THE SUN, EVEN BEING IN OUR COFFINS IS UNPLEASANT.
AHHH!
ざぱ〜ん
UGH.
SO HOT!
IF THIS VOYAGE HAD GONE ON FOR ONE MORE MONTH, WE'D ALL BE DRIED OUT!
WHAT COUNTRY IS THIS?
UMM...I THINK IT'S CALLED "NIPPON."
I've read about it in books.
...THE VAMPIRES FOUND THEIR WAY THROUGH THE SEA AND REACHED JAPAN.

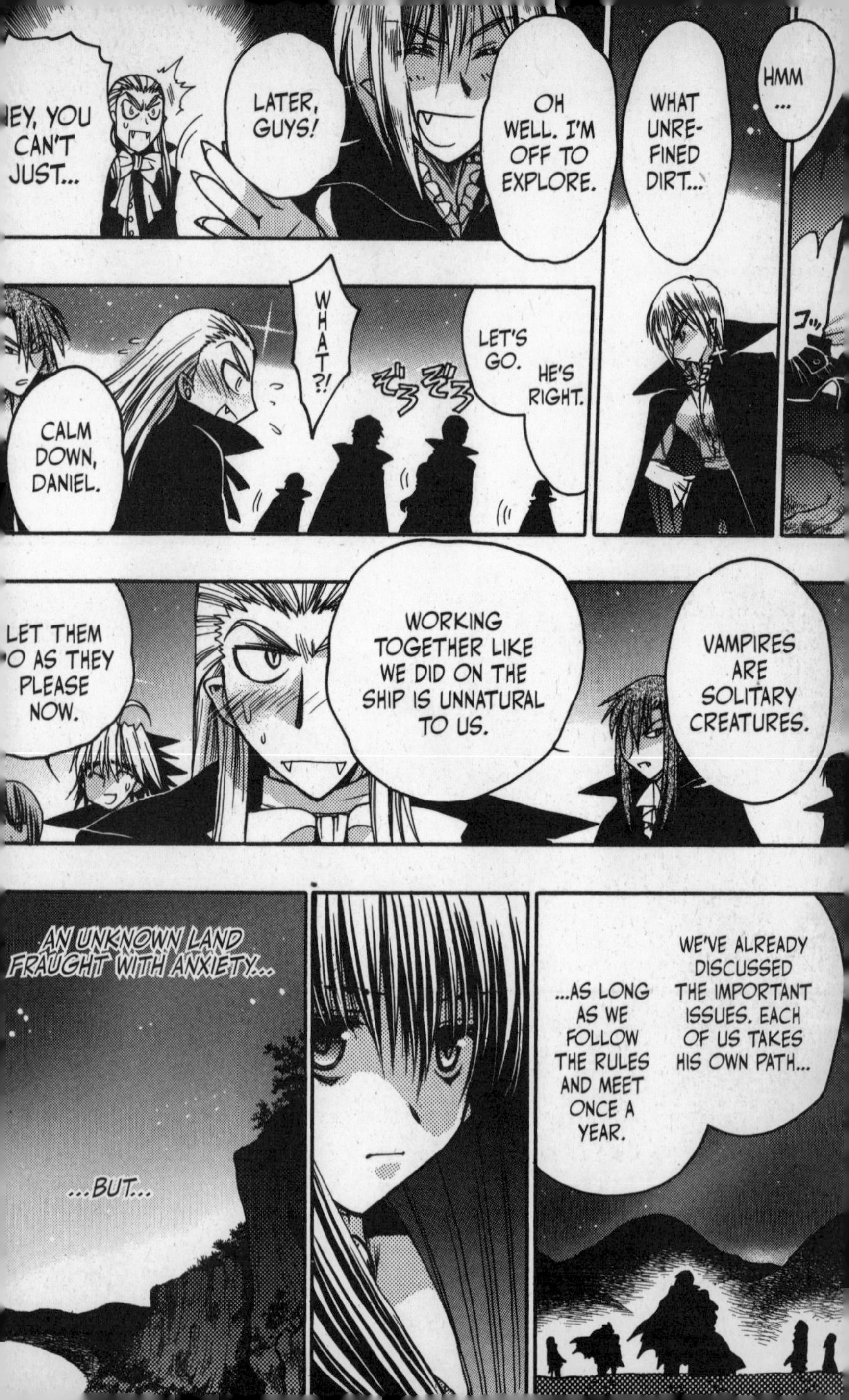
HMM ...
WHAT UNRE-FINED DIRT...
ゴッ
OH WELL. I'M OFF TO EXPLORE.
LATER, GUYS!
EY, YOU CAN'T JUST...
HE'S RIGHT.
LET'S GO.
WHAT?!
ぞろぞろ
CALM DOWN, DANIEL.
VAMPIRES ARE SOLITARY CREATURES.
WORKING TOGETHER LIKE WE DID ON THE SHIP IS UNNATURAL TO US.
LET THEM O AS THEY PLEASE NOW.
WE'VE ALREADY DISCUSSED THE IMPORTANT ISSUES. EACH OF US TAKES HIS OWN PATH...
...AS LONG AS WE FOLLOW THE RULES AND MEET ONCE A YEAR.
AN UNKNOWN LAND FRAUGHT WITH ANXIETY...
...BUT...

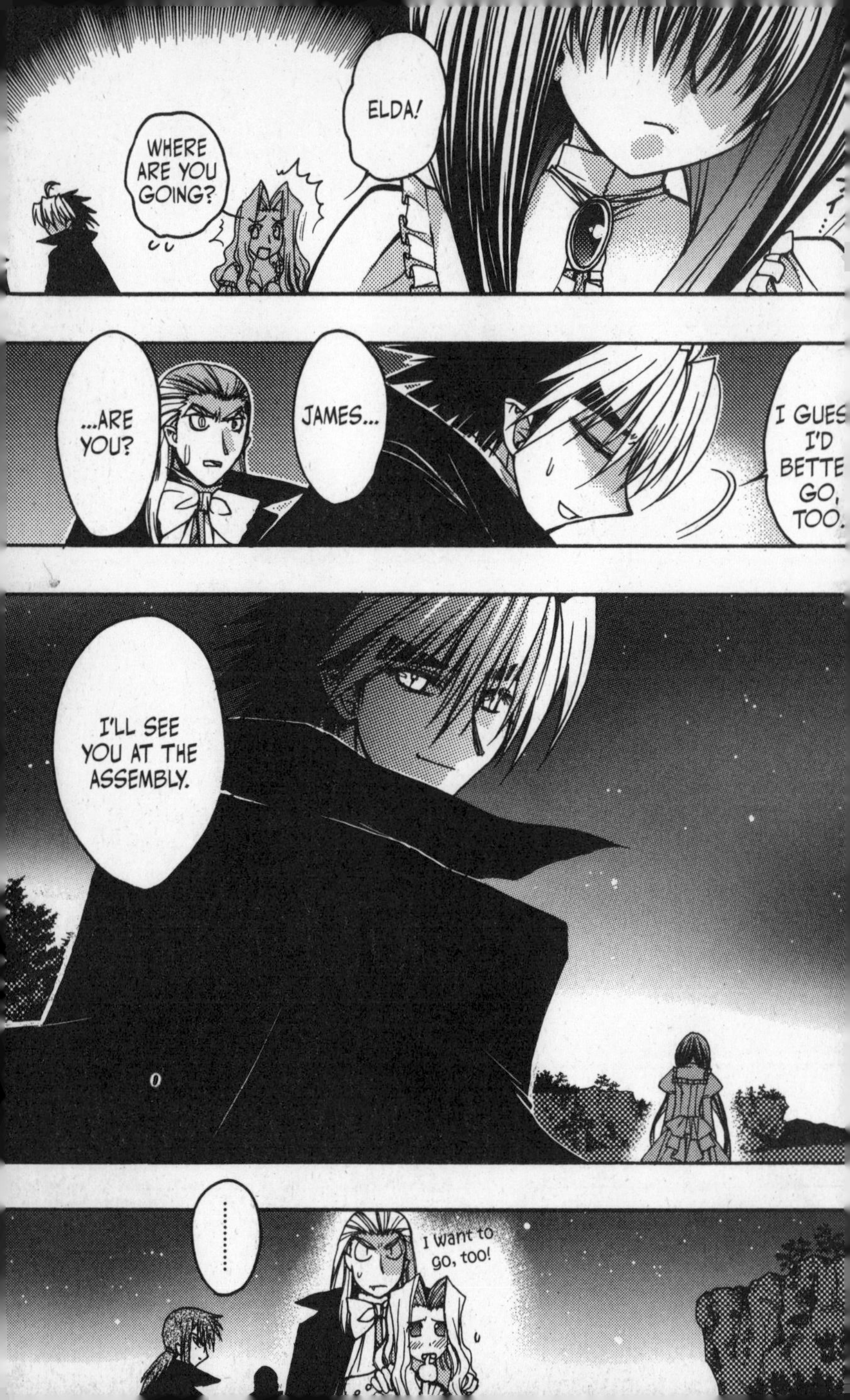
ELDA!
WHERE ARE YOU GOING?
I GUES I'D BETTE GO, TOO.
JAMES...
...ARE YOU?
I'LL SEE YOU AT THE ASSEMBLY.
I want to go, too!
....

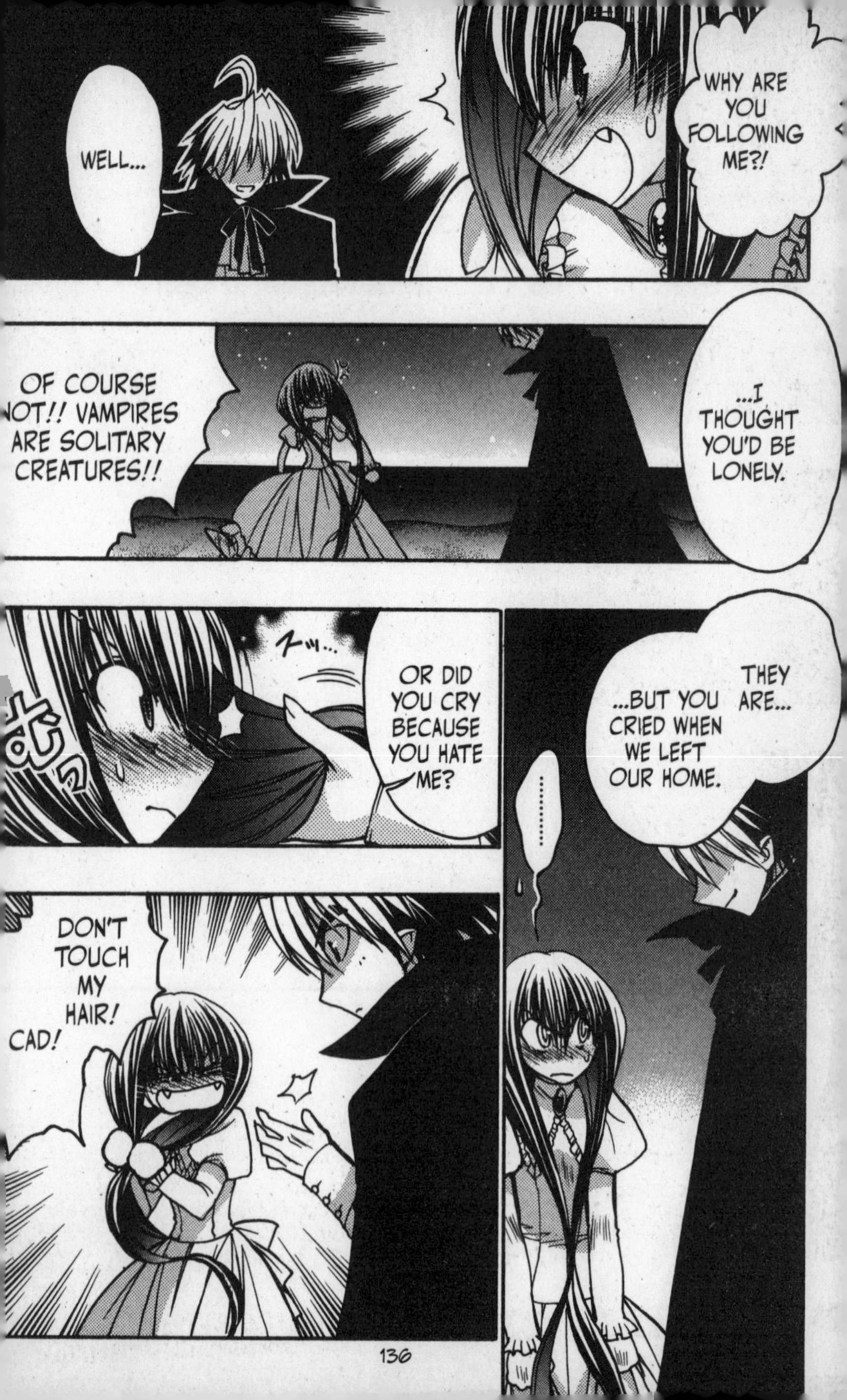
WHY ARE YOU FOLLOWING ME?!
WELL...
...I THOUGHT YOU'D BE LONELY.
OF COURSE NOT!! VAMPIRES ARE SOLITARY CREATURES!!
THEY ARE...
...BUT YOU CRIED WHEN WE LEFT OUR HOME.
....
OR DID YOU CRY BECAUSE YOU HATE ME?
DON'T TOUCH MY HAIR!
CAD!

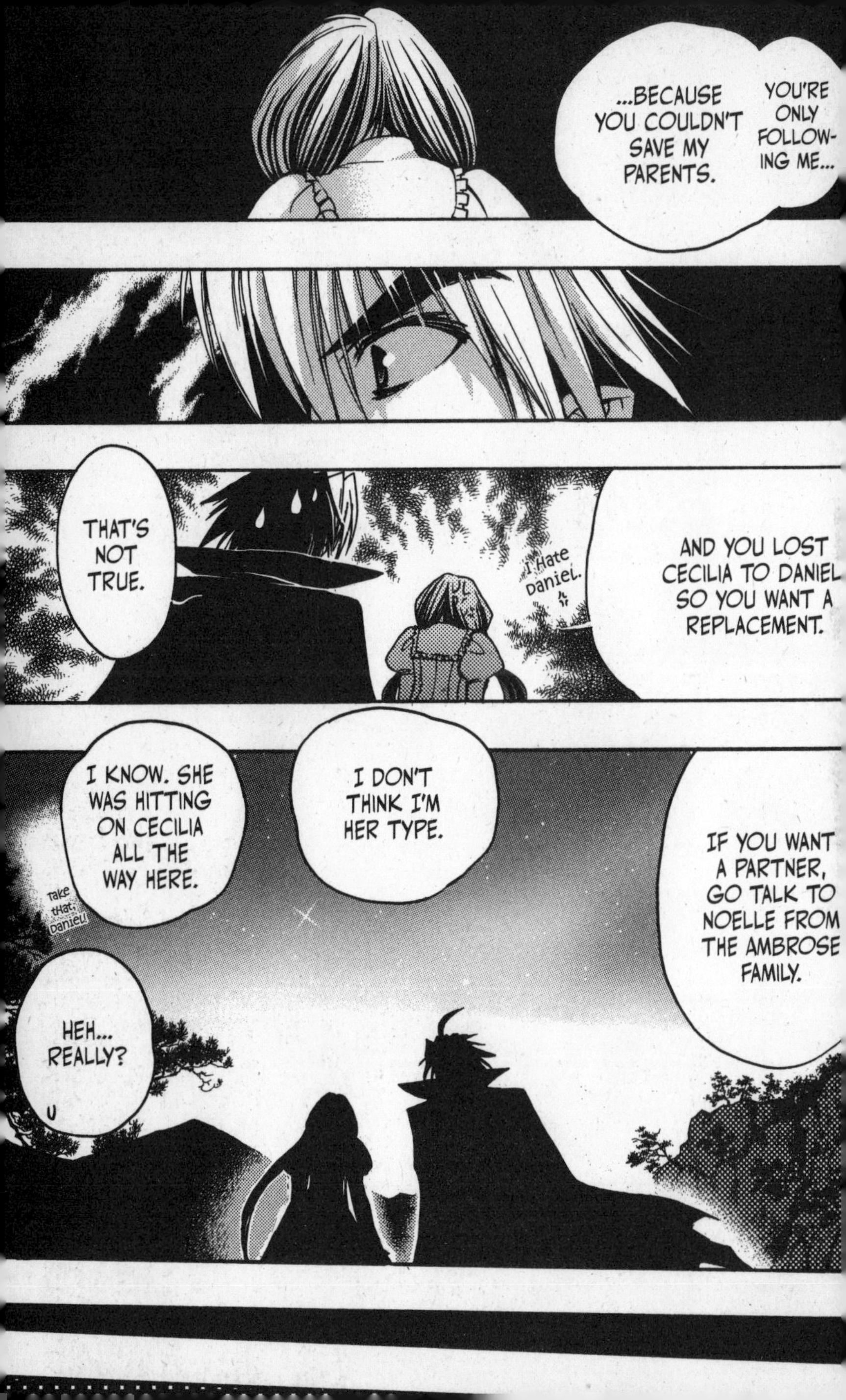
YOU'RE ONLY FOLLOW- ING ME...
...BECAUSE YOU COULDN'T SAVE MY PARENTS.
AND YOU LOST CECILIA TO DANIEL SO YOU WANT A REPLACEMENT.
I Hate Daniel.
THAT'S NOT TRUE.
IF YOU WANT A PARTNER, GO TALK TO NOELLE FROM THE AMBROSE FAMILY.
I DON'T THINK I'M HER TYPE.
I KNOW. SHE WAS HITTING ON CECILIA ALL THE WAY HERE.
Take tHat, Daniel!
HEH... REALLY?

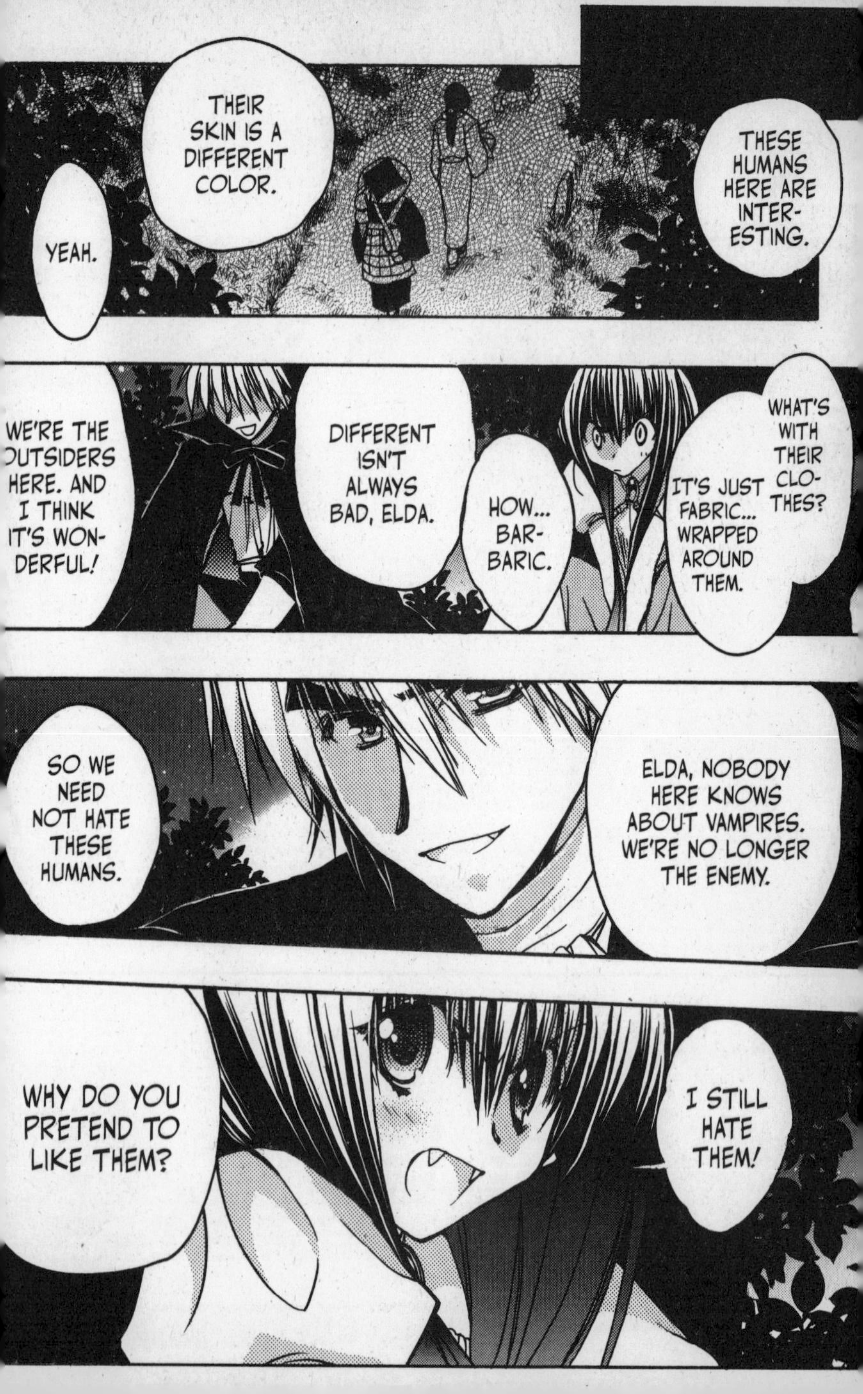
THESE HUMANS HERE ARE INTERESTING.
THEIR SKIN IS A DIFFERENT COLOR.
YEAH.
WHAT'S WITH THEIR CLOTHES?
IT'S JUST FABRIC... WRAPPED AROUND THEM.
HOW... BARBARIC.
DIFFERENT ISN'T ALWAYS BAD, ELDA.
WE'RE THE OUTSIDERS HERE. AND I THINK IT'S WONDERFUL!
ELDA, NOBODY HERE KNOWS ABOUT VAMPIRES. WE'RE NO LONGER THE ENEMY.
SO WE NEED NOT HATE THESE HUMANS.
I STILL HATE THEM!
WHY DO YOU PRETEND TO LIKE THEM?

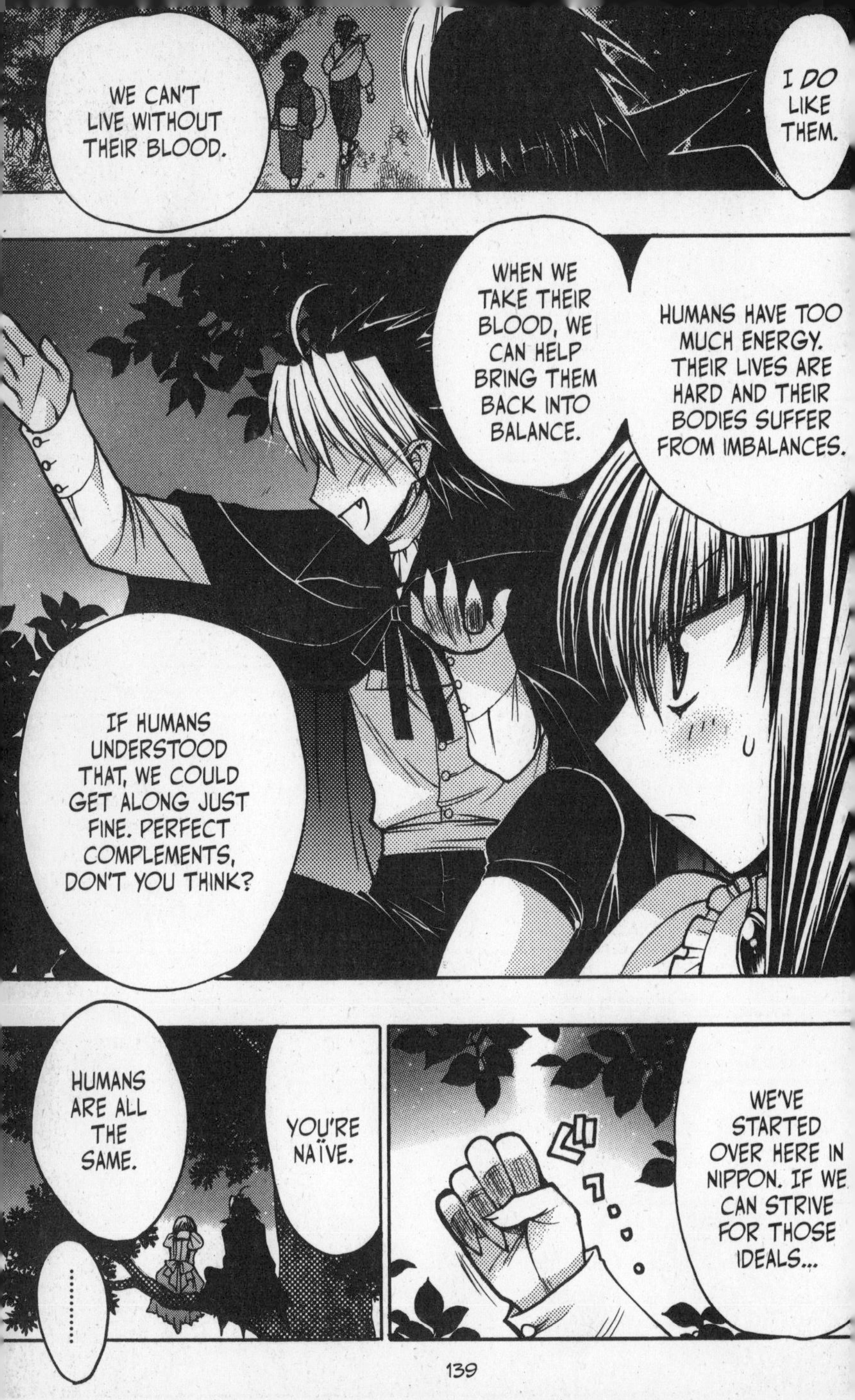
I DO LIKE THEM.
WE CAN'T LIVE WITHOUT THEIR BLOOD.
HUMANS HAVE TOO MUCH ENERGY. THEIR LIVES ARE HARD AND THEIR BODIES SUFFER FROM IMBALANCES.
WHEN WE TAKE THEIR BLOOD, WE CAN HELP BRING THEM BACK INTO BALANCE.
IF HUMANS UNDERSTOOD THAT, WE COULD GET ALONG JUST FINE. PERFECT COMPLEMENTS, DON'T YOU THINK?
WE'VE STARTED OVER HERE IN NIPPON. IF WE CAN STRIVE FOR THOSE IDEALS...
YOU'RE NAÏVE.
HUMANS ARE ALL THE SAME.
....

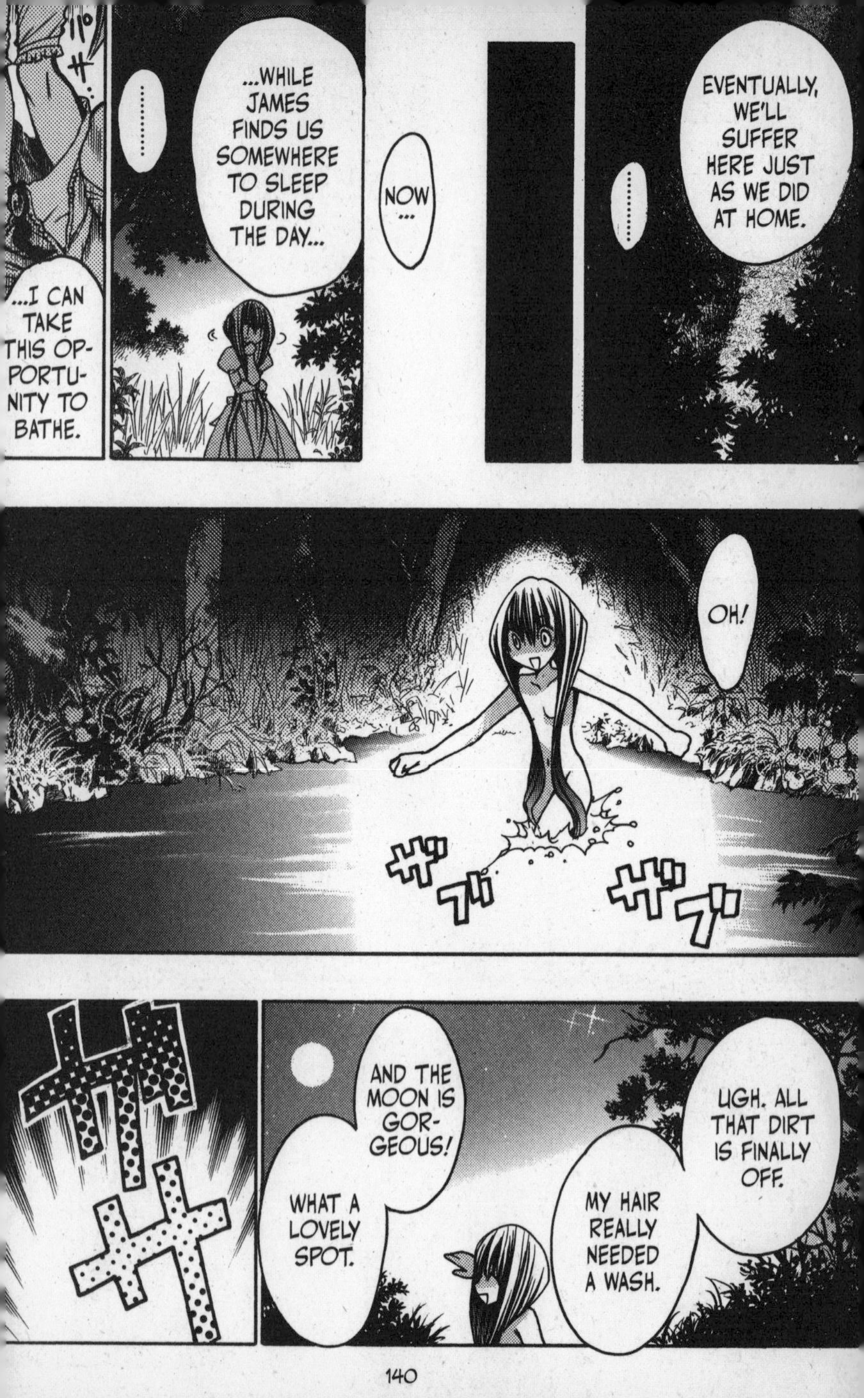
EVENTUALLY, WE'LL SUFFER HERE JUST AS WE DID AT HOME.
......
NOW...
...WHILE JAMES FINDS US SOMEWHERE TO SLEEP DURING THE DAY...
......
...I CAN TAKE THIS OP-PORTU-NITY TO BATHE.
OH!
ザブ ザブ
UGH. ALL THAT DIRT IS FINALLY OFF.
MY HAIR REALLY NEEDED A WASH.
AND THE MOON IS GOR-GEOUS!
WHAT A LOVELY SPOT.

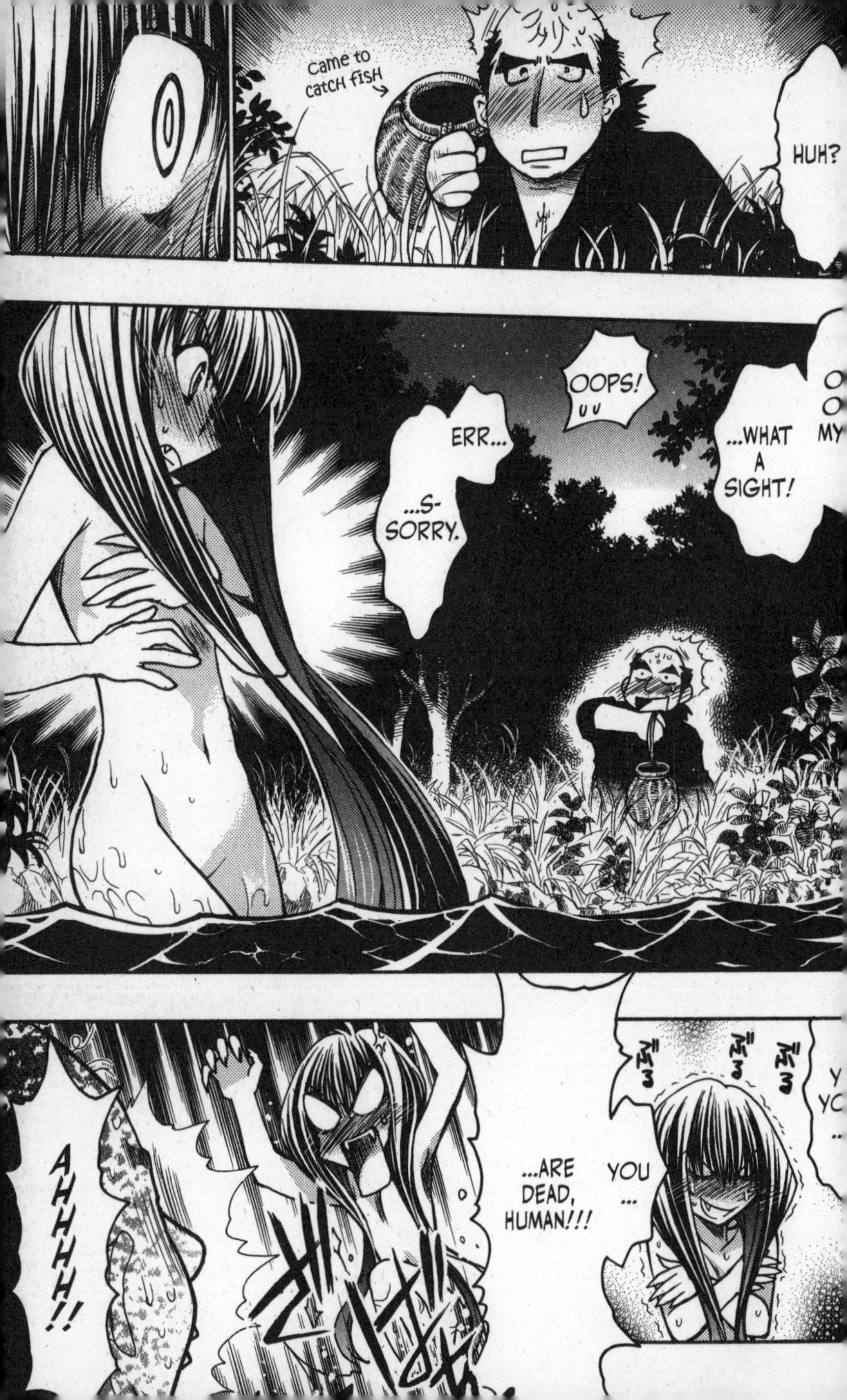
HUH?
Came to catch fish
O O MY
...WHAT A SIGHT!
OOPS!
ERR...
...S-SORRY.
Y YC ...
YOU ...
...ARE DEAD, HUMAN!!!
AHHHHH!!

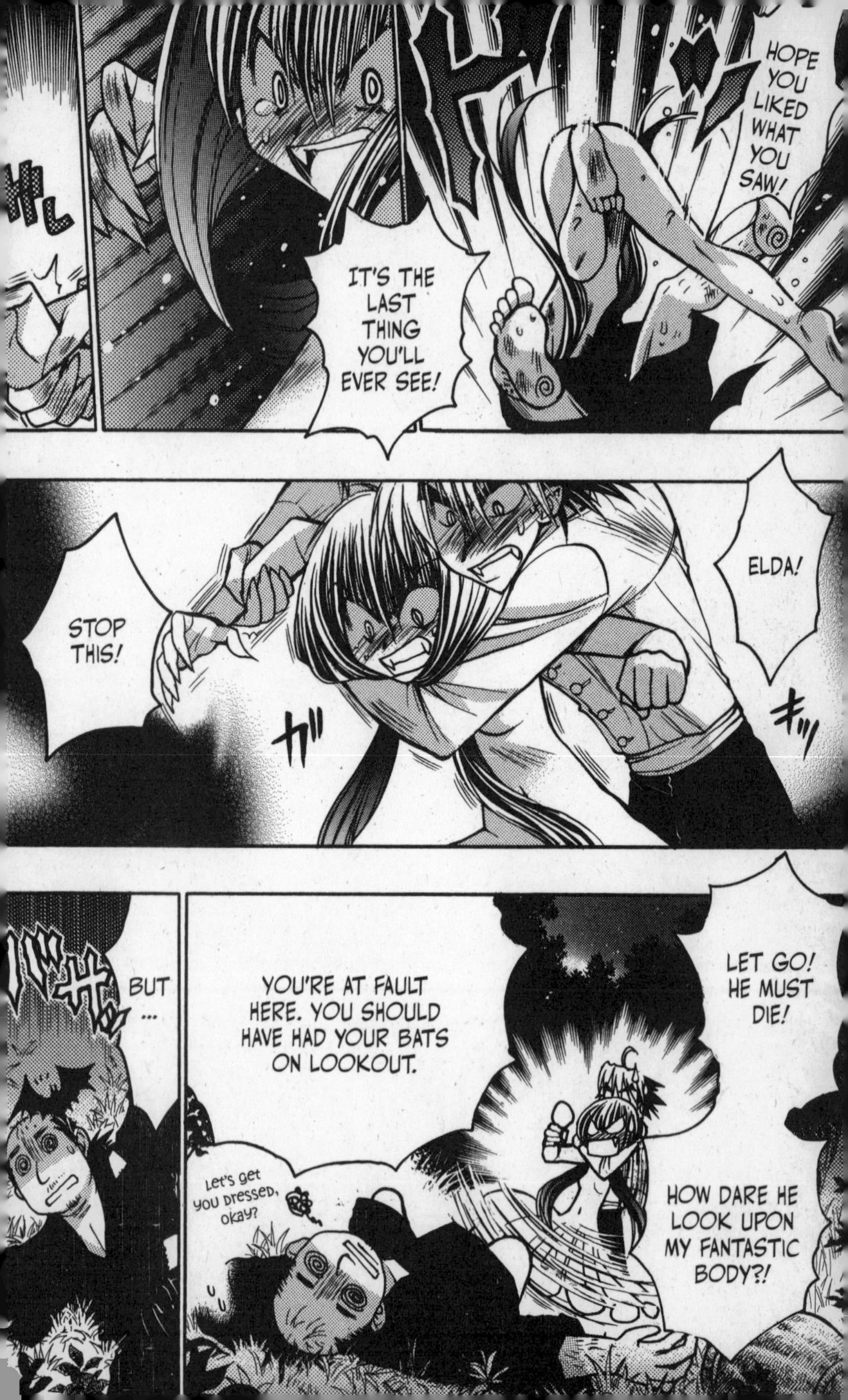
HOPE YOU LIKED WHAT YOU SAW!
IT'S THE LAST THING YOU'LL EVER SEE!
ELDA!
STOP THIS!
LET GO! HE MUST DIE!
HOW DARE HE LOOK UPON MY FANTASTIC BODY?!
YOU'RE AT FAULT HERE. YOU SHOULD HAVE HAD YOUR BATS ON LOOKOUT.
Let's get you dressed, okay?
BUT ...

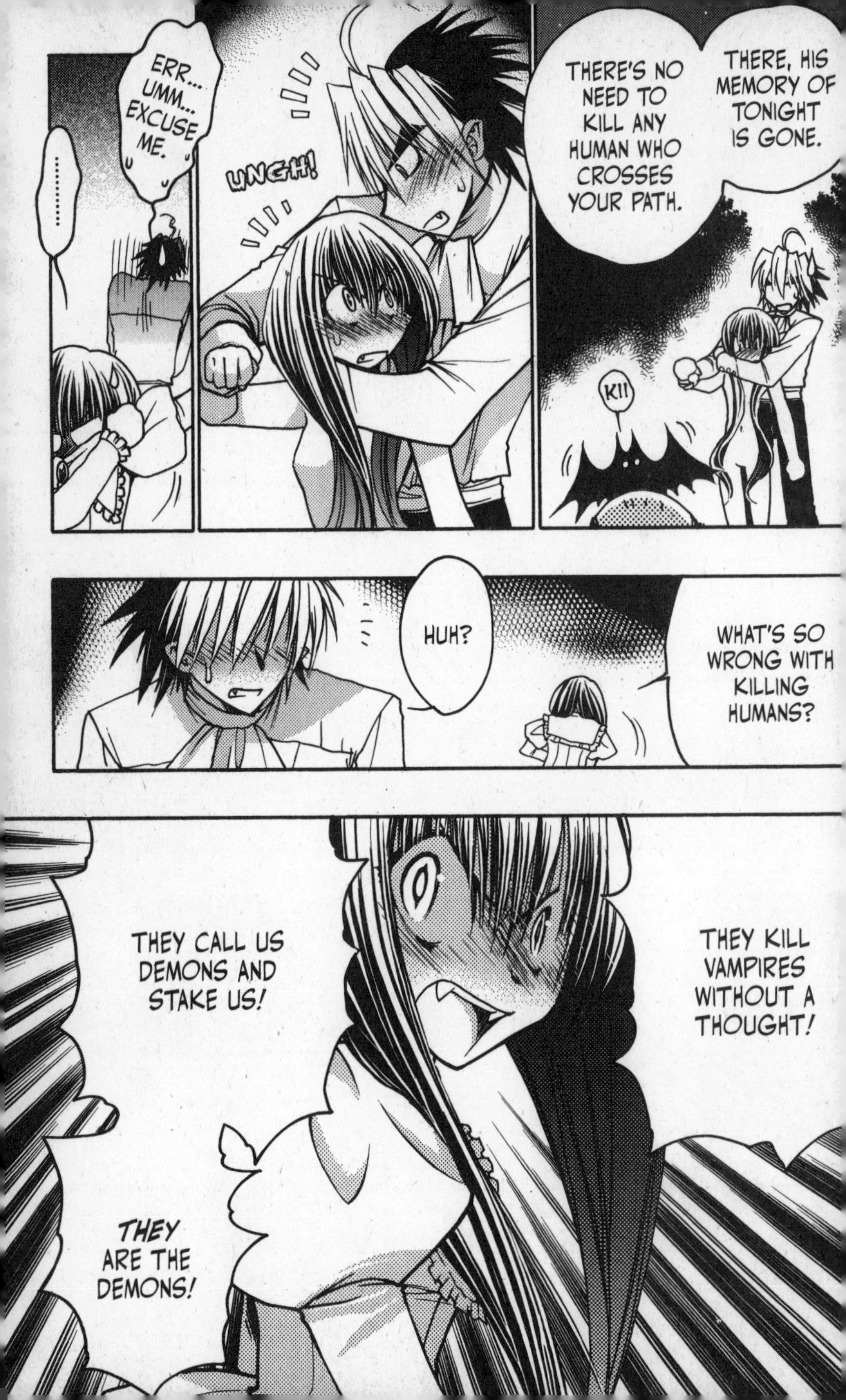
THERE, HIS MEMORY OF TONIGHT IS GONE.
THERE'S NO NEED TO KILL ANY HUMAN WHO CROSSES YOUR PATH.
KII
UNGH!
ERR... UMM... EXCUSE ME.
......
WHAT'S SO WRONG WITH KILLING HUMANS?
HUH?
THEY KILL VAMPIRES WITHOUT A THOUGHT!
THEY CALL US DEMONS AND STAKE US!
THEY ARE THE DEMONS!

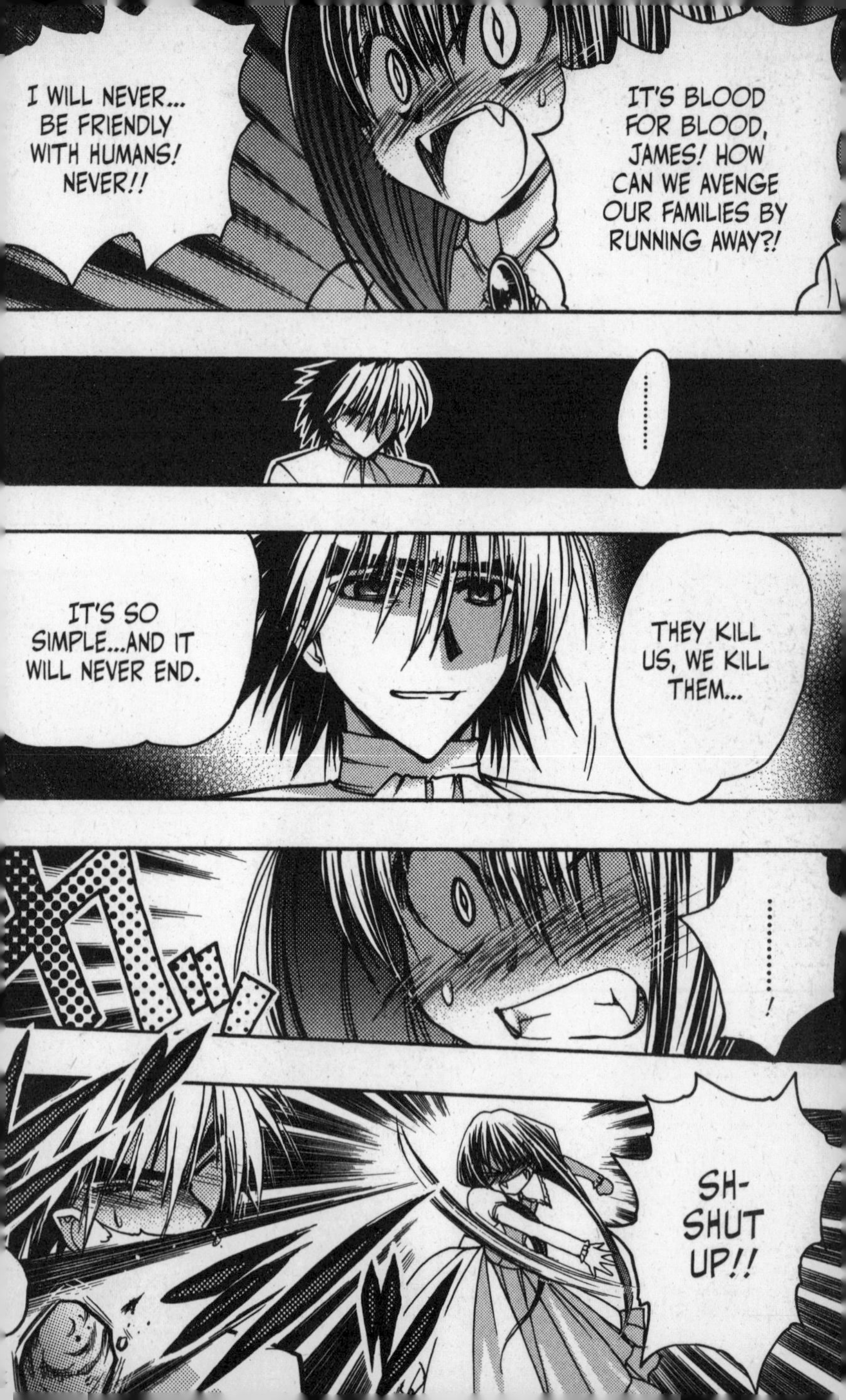
IT'S BLOOD FOR BLOOD, JAMES! HOW CAN WE AVENGE OUR FAMILIES BY RUNNING AWAY?!
I WILL NEVER... BE FRIENDLY WITH HUMANS! NEVER!!
......
THEY KILL US, WE KILL THEM...
IT'S SO SIMPLE...AND IT WILL NEVER END.
......!
SH-SHUT UP!!

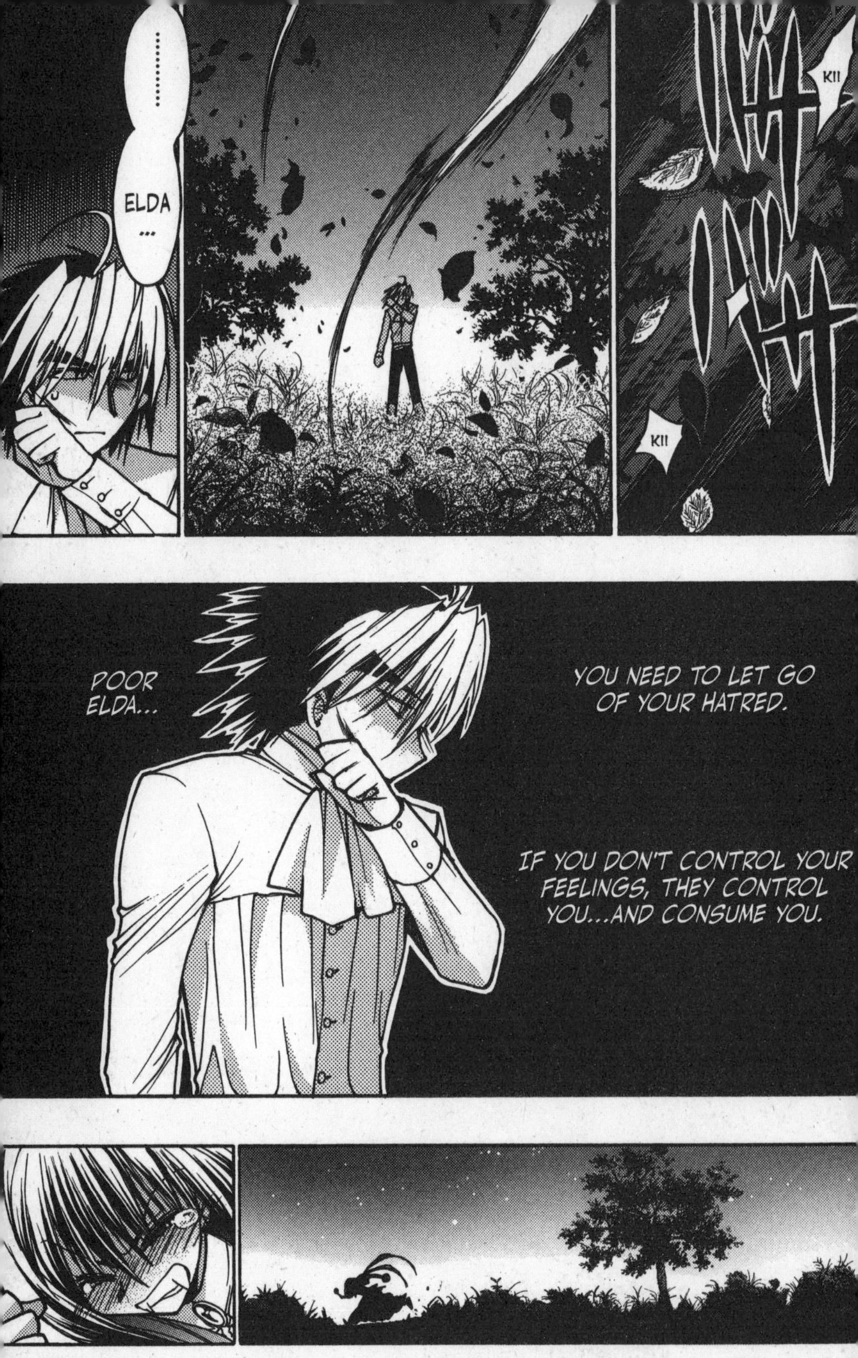
KII
KII
......
ELDA ...
YOU NEED TO LET GO OF YOUR HATRED.
POOR ELDA...
IF YOU DON'T CONTROL YOUR FEELINGS, THEY CONTROL YOU...AND CONSUME YOU.

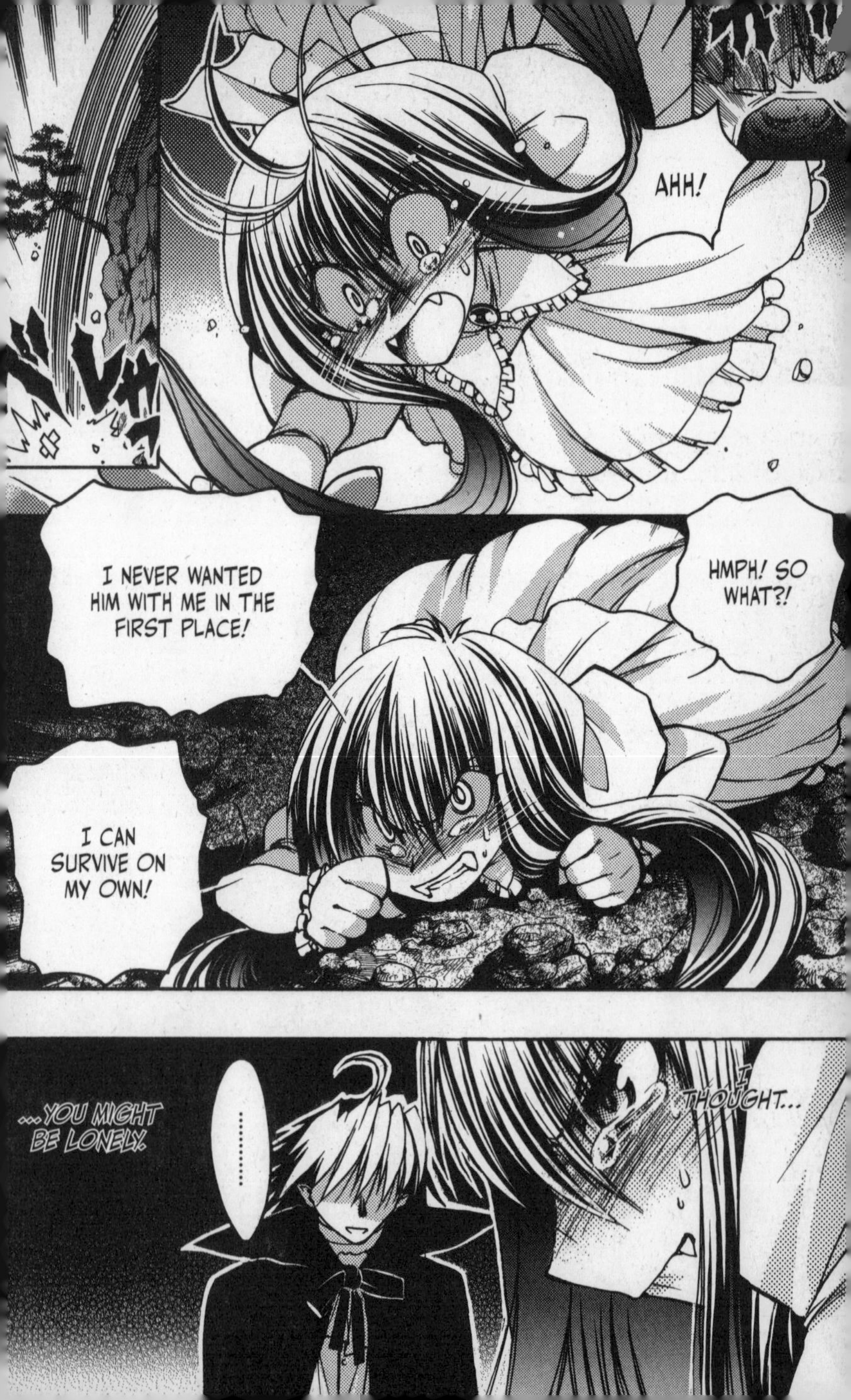
AHH!
HMPH! SO WHAT?!
I NEVER WANTED HIM WITH ME IN THE FIRST PLACE!
I CAN SURVIVE ON MY OWN!
I THOUGHT...
....
...YOU MIGHT BE LONELY.

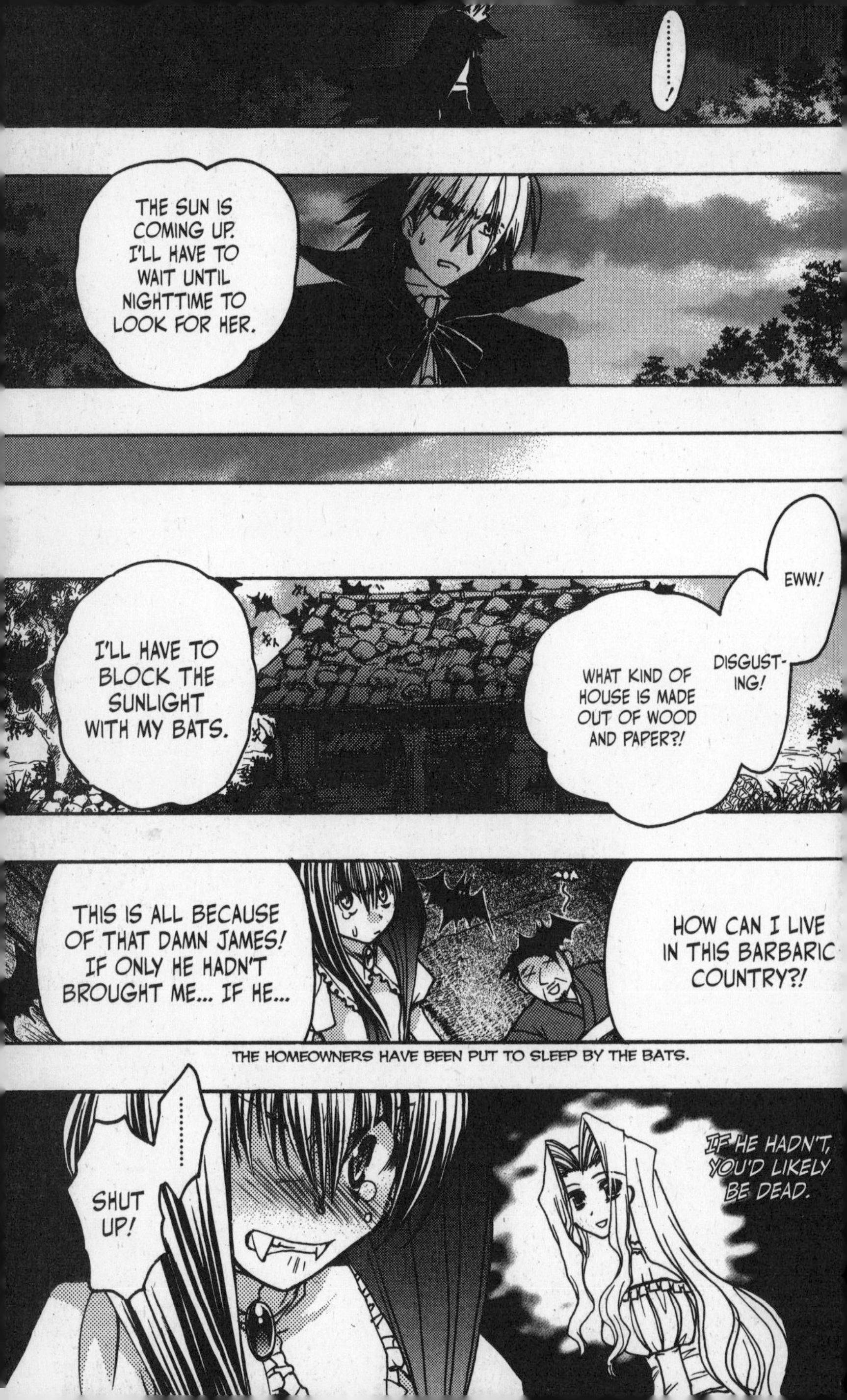
......!
THE SUN IS COMING UP. I'LL HAVE TO WAIT UNTIL NIGHTTIME TO LOOK FOR HER.
EWW!
DISGUST-ING!
WHAT KIND OF HOUSE IS MADE OUT OF WOOD AND PAPER?!
I'LL HAVE TO BLOCK THE SUNLIGHT WITH MY BATS.
HOW CAN I LIVE IN THIS BARBARIC COUNTRY?!
THIS IS ALL BECAUSE OF THAT DAMN JAMES! IF ONLY HE HADN'T BROUGHT ME... IF HE...
THE HOMEOWNERS HAVE BEEN PUT TO SLEEP BY THE BATS.
IF HE HADN'T, YOU'D LIKELY BE DEAD.
......
SHUT UP!

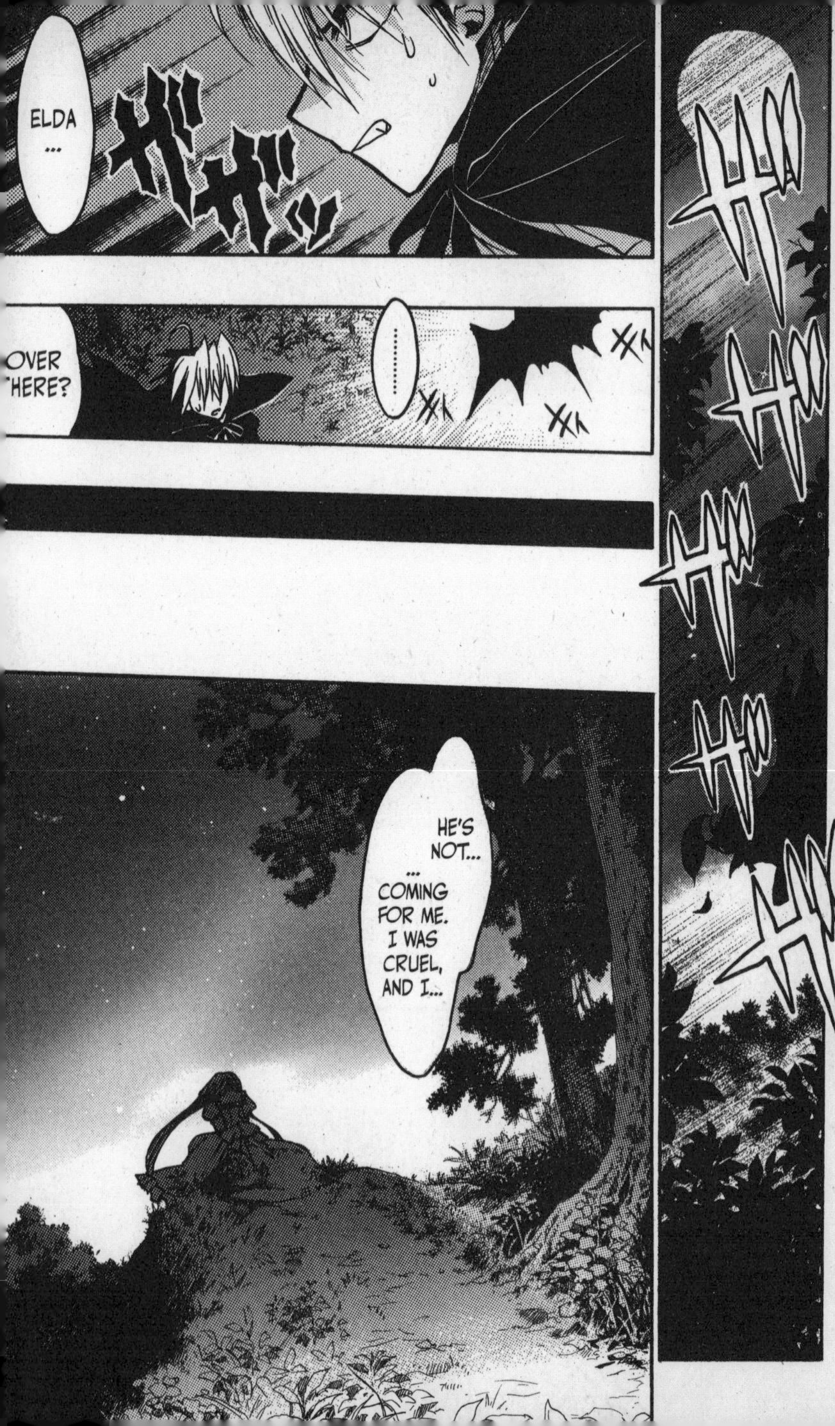
ELDA ...
......
OVER THERE?
HE'S NOT... ... COMING FOR ME. I WAS CRUEL, AND I...

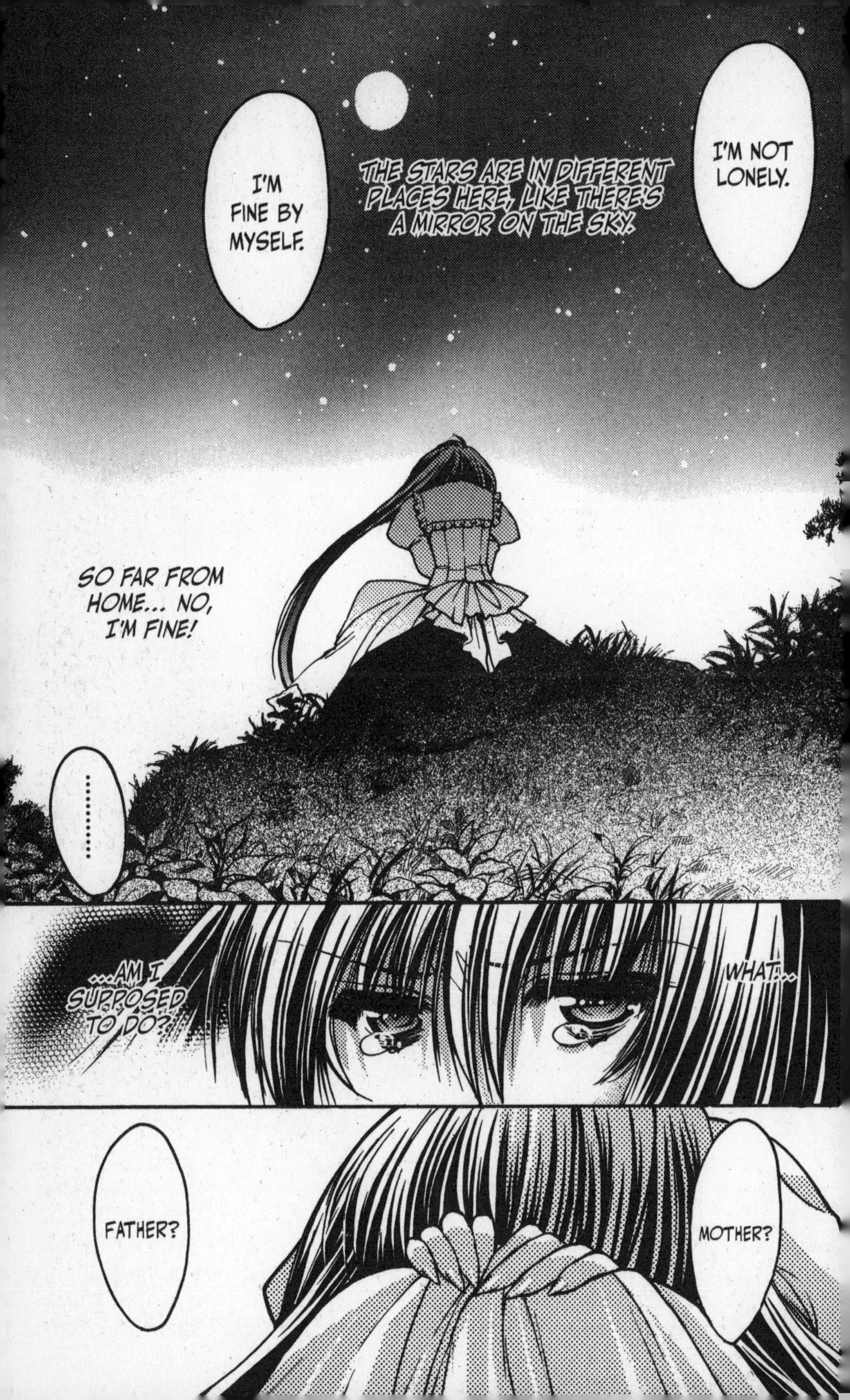

I'M NOT LONELY.
THE STARS ARE IN DIFFERENT PLACES HERE, LIKE THERE'S A MIRROR ON THE SKY.
I'M FINE BY MYSELF.
SO FAR FROM HOME... NO, I'M FINE!
....
WHAT...
...AM I SUPPOSED TO DO?
MOTHER?
FATHER?

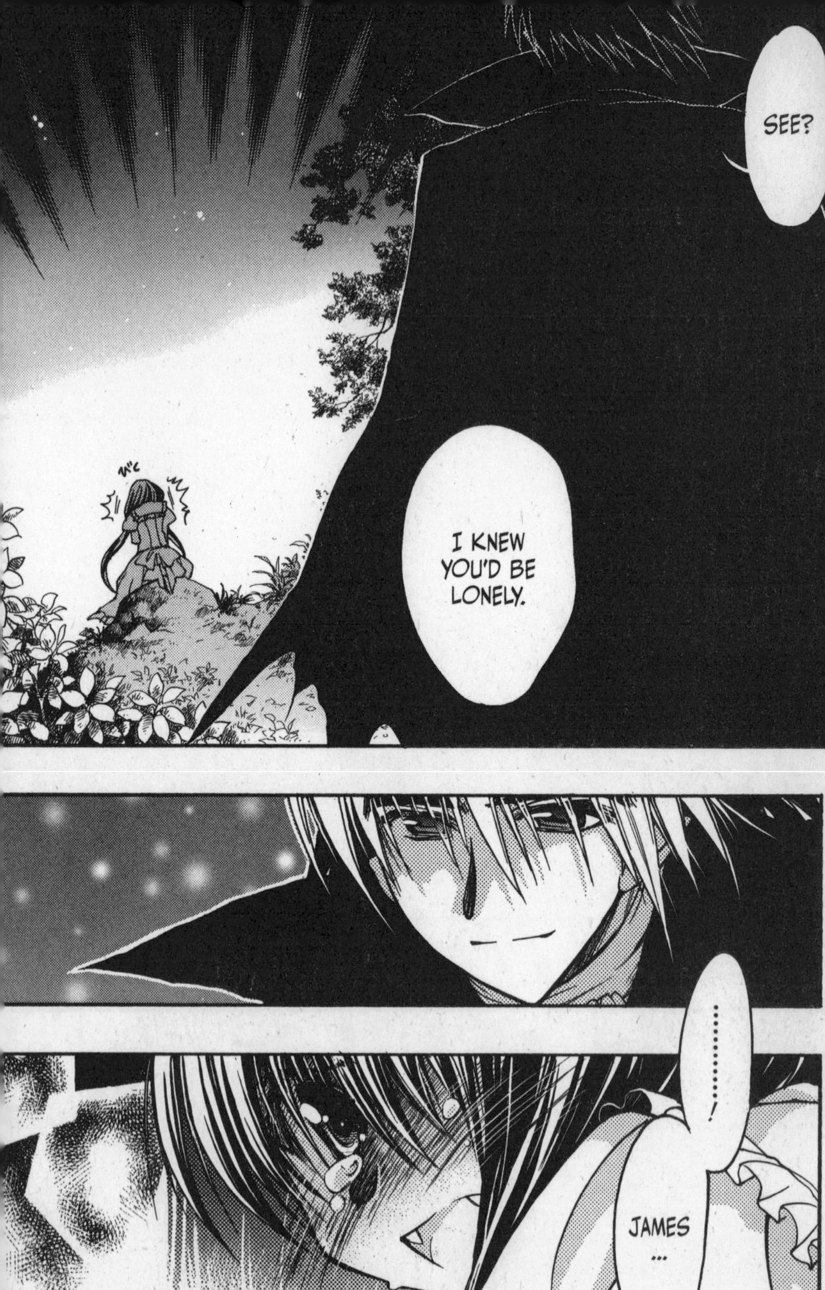
SEE?
I KNEW YOU'D BE LONELY.
......!
JAMES ...

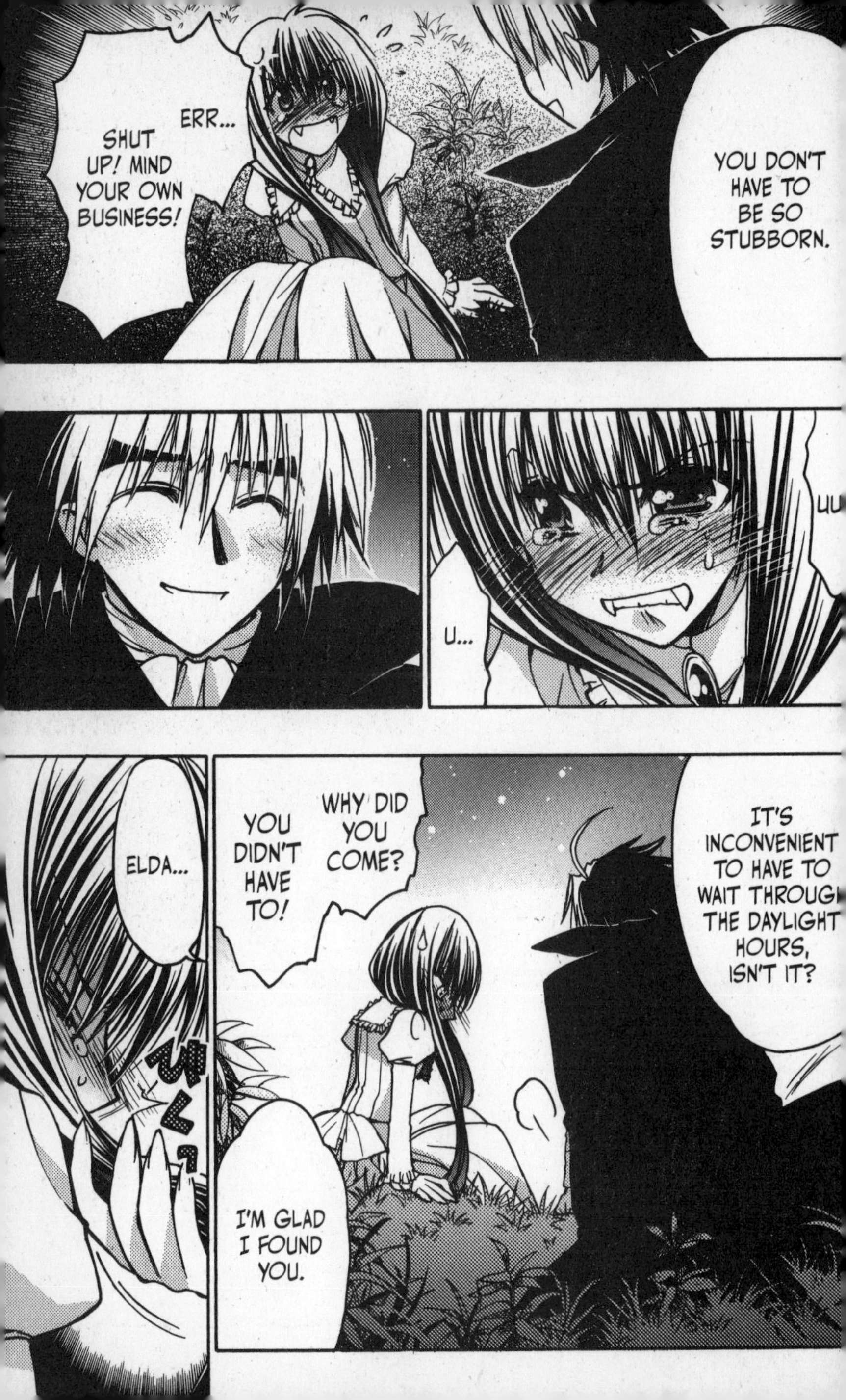
YOU DON'T HAVE TO BE SO STUBBORN.
ERR...
SHUT UP! MIND YOUR OWN BUSINESS!
UU
U...
IT'S INCONVENIENT TO HAVE TO WAIT THROUG THE DAYLIGHT HOURS, ISN'T IT?
WHY DID YOU COME?
YOU DIDN'T HAVE TO!
I'M GLAD I FOUND YOU.
ELDA...

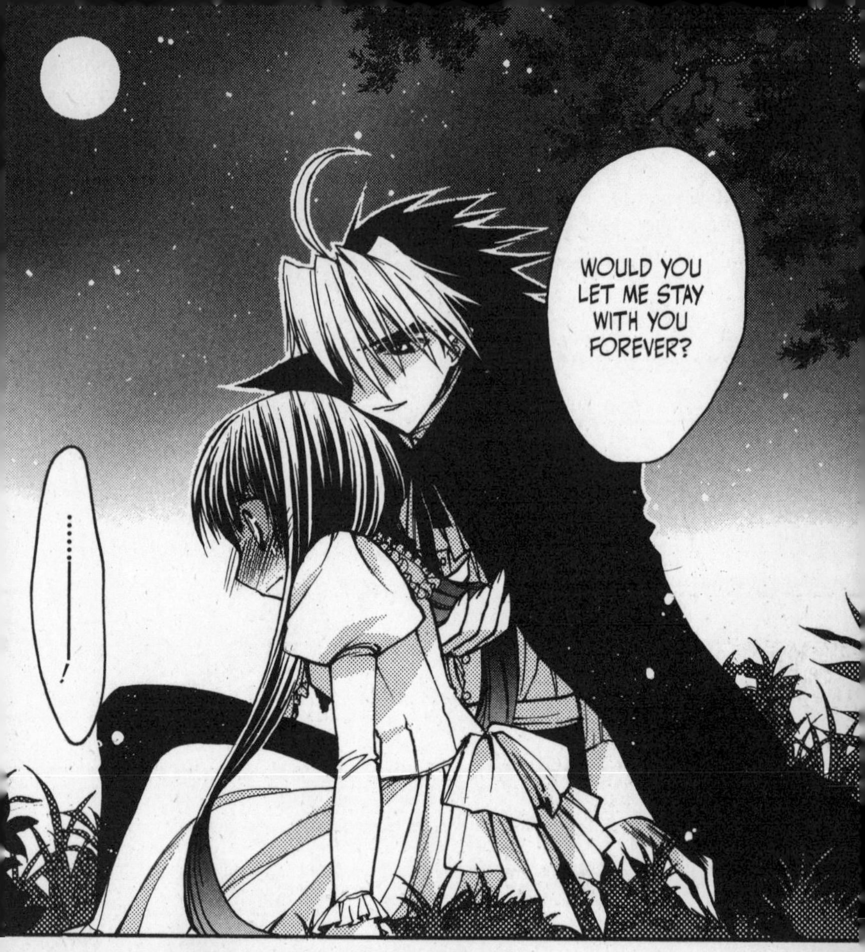
WOULD YOU LET ME STAY WITH YOU FOREVER?
......!

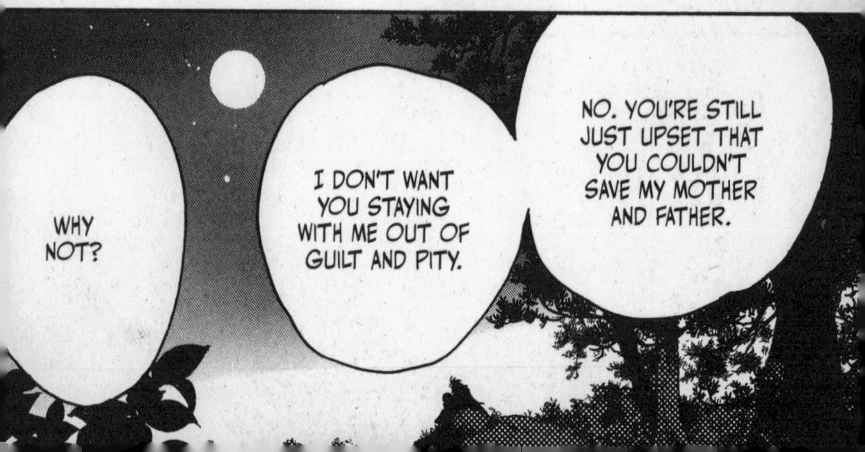
NO. YOU'RE STILL JUST UPSET THAT YOU COULDN'T SAVE MY MOTHER AND FATHER.
I DON'T WANT YOU STAYING WITH ME OUT OF GUILT AND PITY.
WHY NOT?

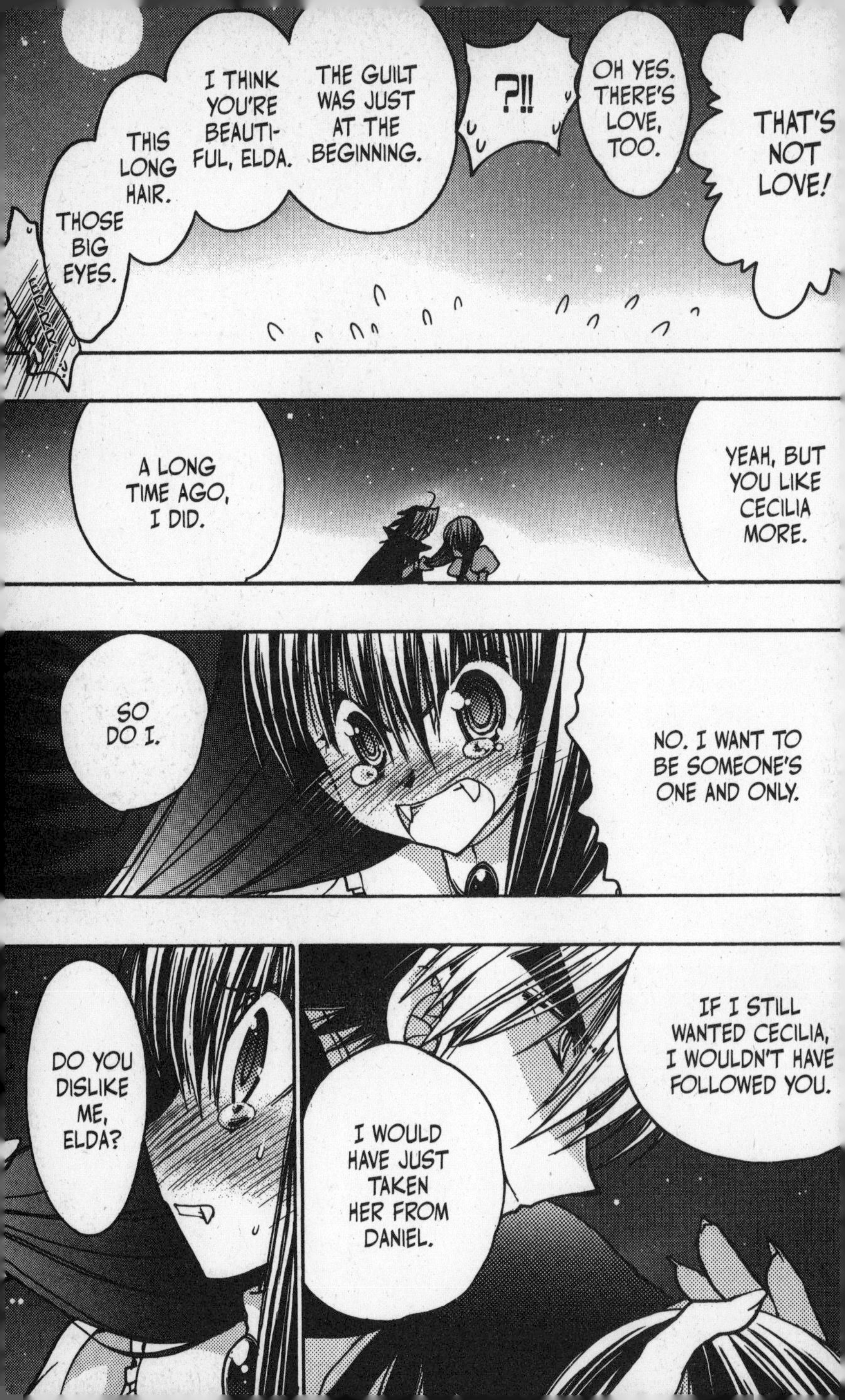
THAT'S NOT LOVE!
OH YES. THERE'S LOVE, TOO.
?!!
THE GUILT WAS JUST AT THE BEGINNING.
I THINK YOU'RE BEAUTI-FUL, ELDA.
THIS LONG HAIR.
THOSE BIG EYES.
YEAH, BUT YOU LIKE CECILIA MORE.
A LONG TIME AGO, I DID.
NO. I WANT TO BE SOMEONE'S ONE AND ONLY.
SO DO I.
IF I STILL WANTED CECILIA, I WOULDN'T HAVE FOLLOWED YOU.
I WOULD HAVE JUST TAKEN HER FROM DANIEL.
DO YOU DISLIKE ME, ELDA?

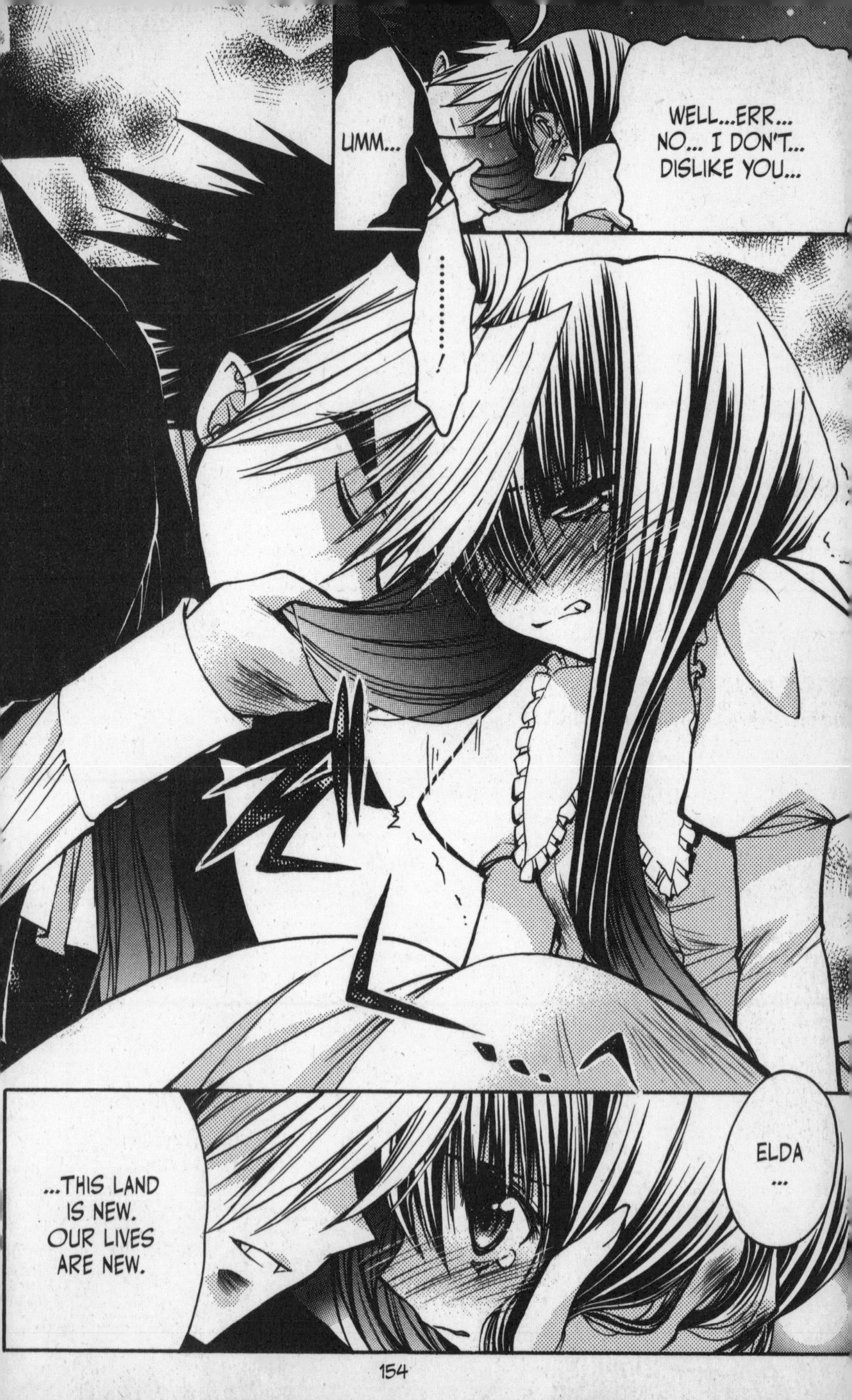
WELL...ERR... NO... I DON'T... DISLIKE YOU...
UMM...
......!
...
ELDA ...
...THIS LAND IS NEW. OUR LIVES ARE NEW.

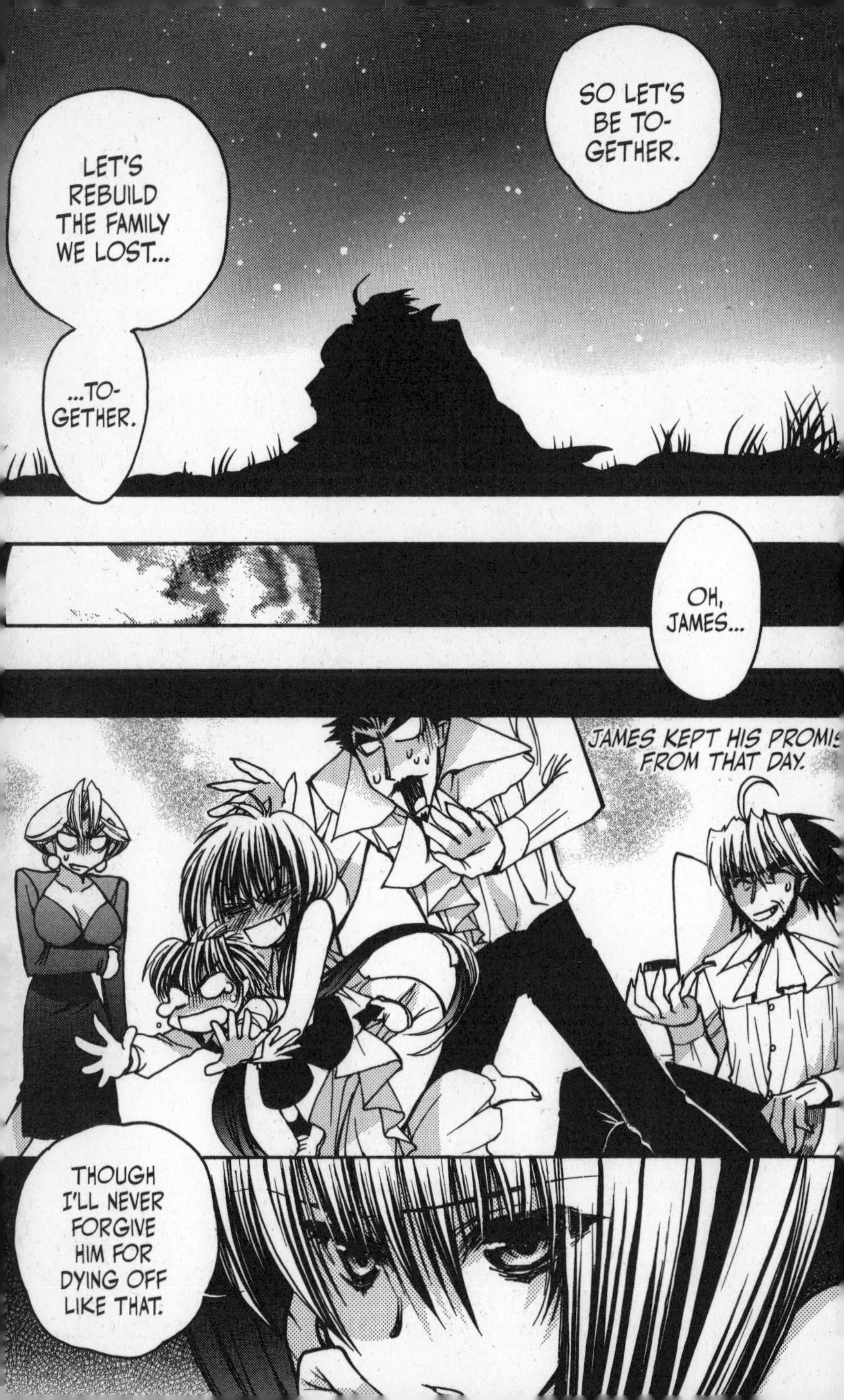
SO LET'S BE TO-GETHER.
LET'S REBUILD THE FAMILY WE LOST...
...TO-GETHER.
OH, JAMES...
JAMES KEPT HIS PROMIS FROM THAT DAY.
THOUGH I'LL NEVER FORGIVE HIM FOR DYING OFF LIKE THAT.

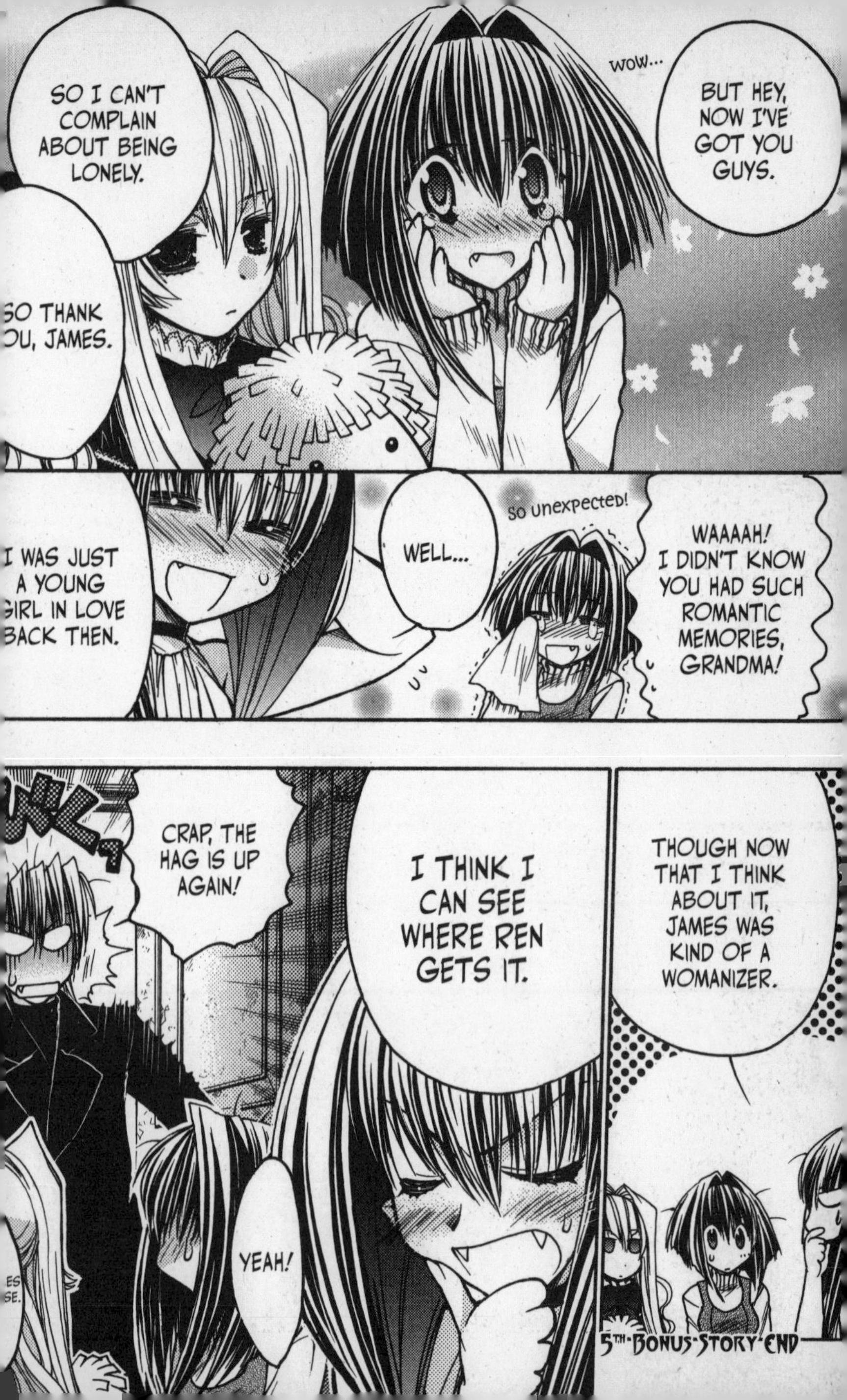
WOW...
BUT HEY, NOW I'VE GOT YOU GUYS.
SO I CAN'T COMPLAIN ABOUT BEING LONELY.
SO THANK OU, JAMES.
WAAAAH! I DIDN'T KNOW YOU HAD SUCH ROMANTIC MEMORIES, GRANDMA!
So unexpected!
WELL...
I WAS JUST A YOUNG IRL IN LOVE ACK THEN.
THOUGH NOW THAT I THINK ABOUT IT, JAMES WAS KIND OF A WOMANIZER.
I THINK I CAN SEE WHERE REN GETS IT.
CRAP, THE HAG IS UP AGAIN!
YEAH!
5TH BONUS STORY END

EXTRAS Soft Bed and Secrets Revealed
~Snug~

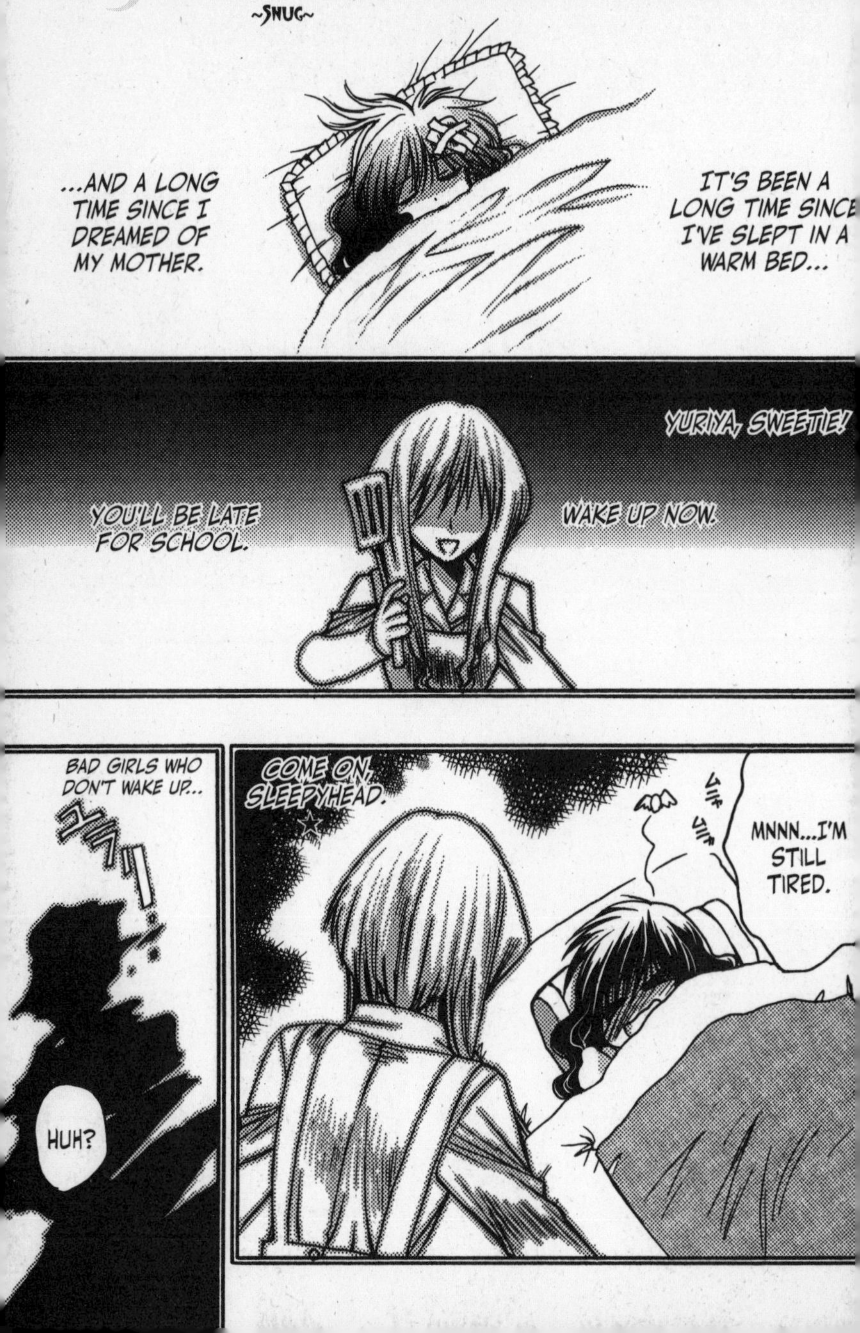
IT'S BEEN A LONG TIME SINCE I'VE SLEPT IN A WARM BED...
...AND A LONG TIME SINCE I DREAMED OF MY MOTHER.
YURIYA, SWEETIE!
WAKE UP NOW.
YOU'LL BE LATE FOR SCHOOL.
COME ON, SLEEPYHEAD.
MNNN...I'M STILL TIRED.
BAD GIRLS WHO DON'T WAKE UP...
HUH?

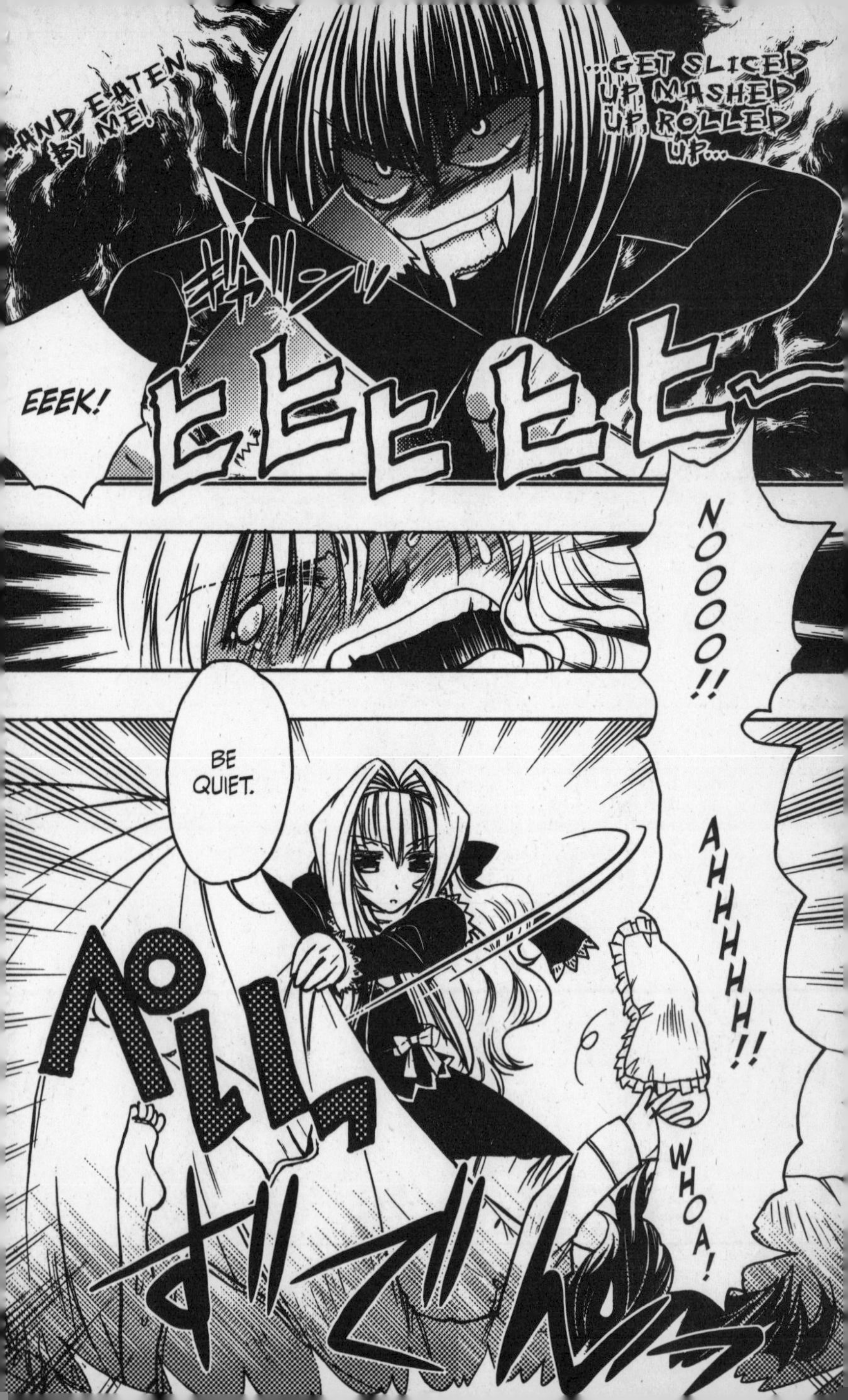
...GET SLICED UP, MASHED UP, ROLLED UP...
...AND EATEN BY ME!
EEEK!
NOOOOO!!
BE QUIET.
AHHHHHH!!
WHOA!

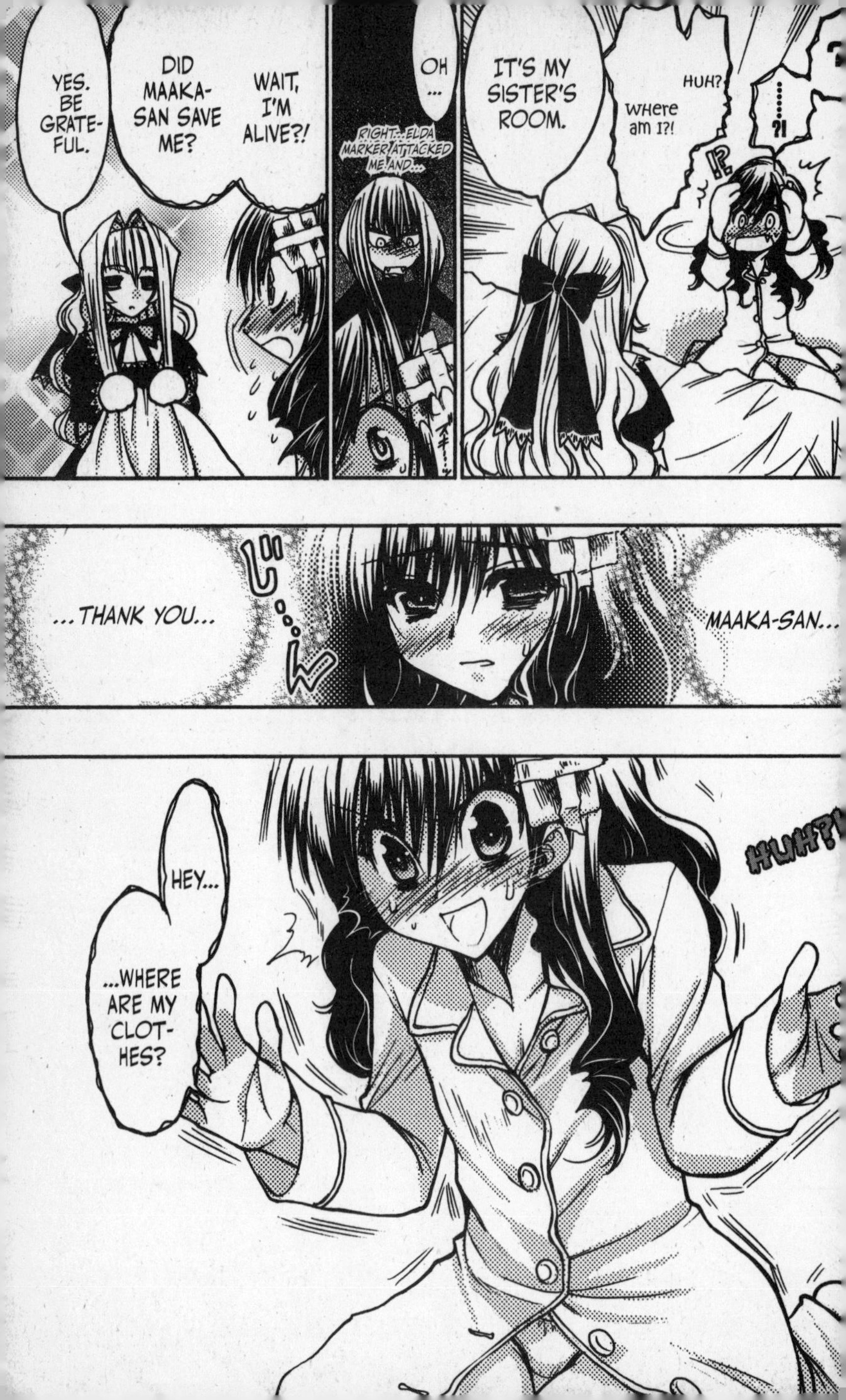

......?!
!?
HUH?
Where am I?!
IT'S MY SISTER'S ROOM.
OH ...
RIGHT... ELDA MARKER ATTACKED ME AND...
WAIT, I'M ALIVE?!
DID MAAKA-SAN SAVE ME?
YES. BE GRATEFUL.
MAAKA-SAN...
じーん
...THANK YOU...
HUH?!
HEY...
...WHERE ARE MY CLOT-HES?

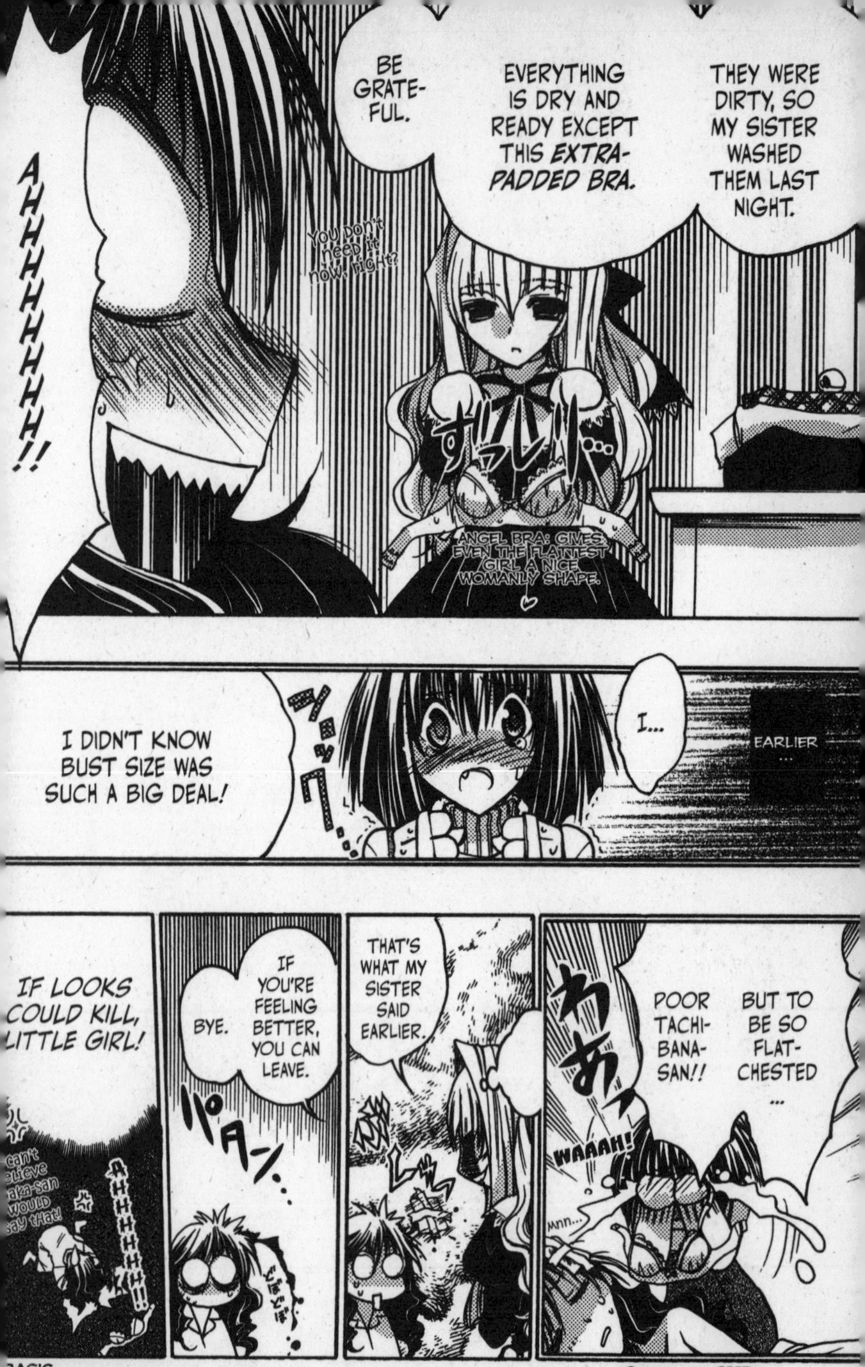
THEY WERE DIRTY, SO MY SISTER WASHED THEM LAST NIGHT.
EVERYTHING IS DRY AND READY EXCEPT THIS *EXTRA-PADDED BRA.*
BE GRATE-FUL.
You don't need it now, right?
ANGEL BRA: GIVES EVEN THE FLATTEST GIRL A NICE WOMANLY SHAPE.
AHHHHHHHHHHH!!
EARLIER...
I...
I DIDN'T KNOW BUST SIZE WAS SUCH A BIG DEAL!
BUT TO BE SO FLAT-CHESTED...
POOR TACHI-BANA-SAN!!
WAAAH!
Mnn...
THAT'S WHAT MY SISTER SAID EARLIER.
IF YOU'RE FEELING BETTER, YOU CAN LEAVE.
BYE.
IF LOOKS COULD KILL, LITTLE GIRL!
can't elieve aka-san WOULD say tHat!
AHHHHHHH!!

EXTRAS END

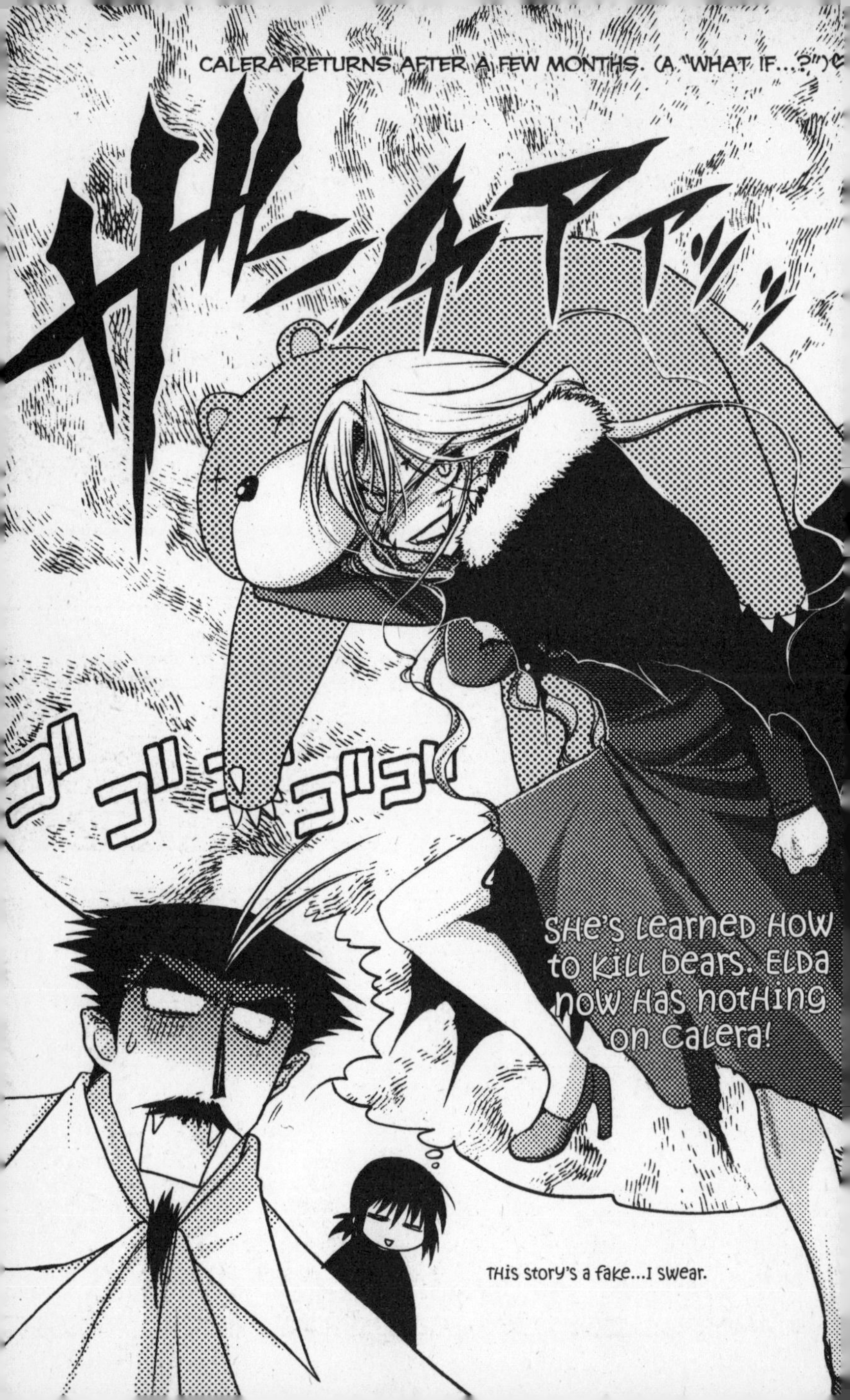
CALERA RETURNS AFTER A FEW MONTHS. (A "WHAT IF...?")
SHE'S LEARNED HOW TO KILL BEARS. ELDA NOW HAS NOTHING ON CALERA!
THIS STORY'S A FAKE...I SWEAR.

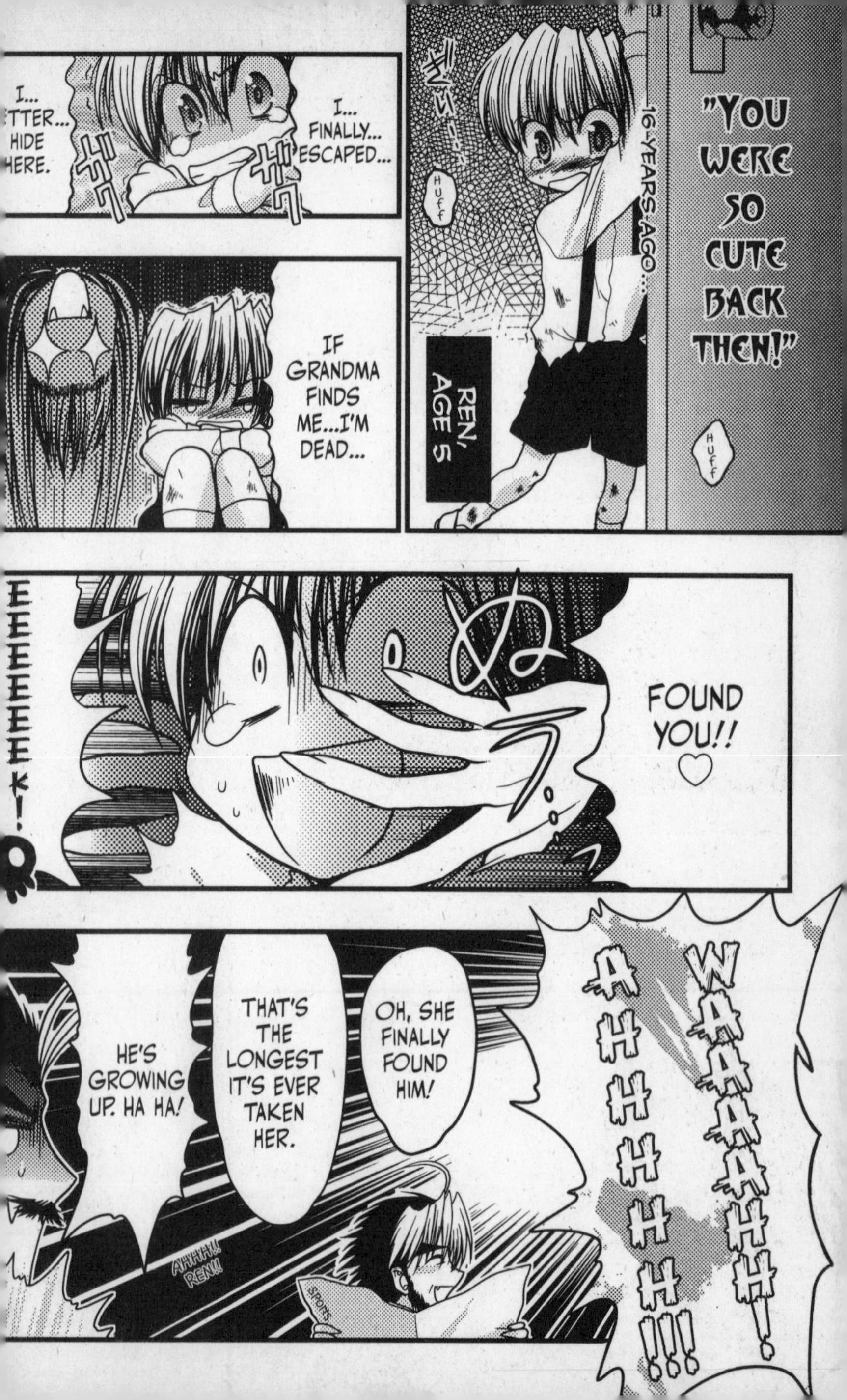
"YOU WERE SO CUTE BACK THEN!"
16 YEARS AGO...
HUFF
HUFF
REN, AGE 5
I... FINALLY... ESCAPED...
I... TTER... HIDE HERE.
IF GRANDMA FINDS ME...I'M DEAD...
FOUND YOU!! ♡
EEEEEEEEEEEK!
WAAAAHHH!
AHHHHHHH!!!
OH, SHE FINALLY FOUND HIM!
THAT'S THE LONGEST IT'S EVER TAKEN HER.
HE'S GROWING UP. HA HA!
AHHH!! REN!!
SPOTS

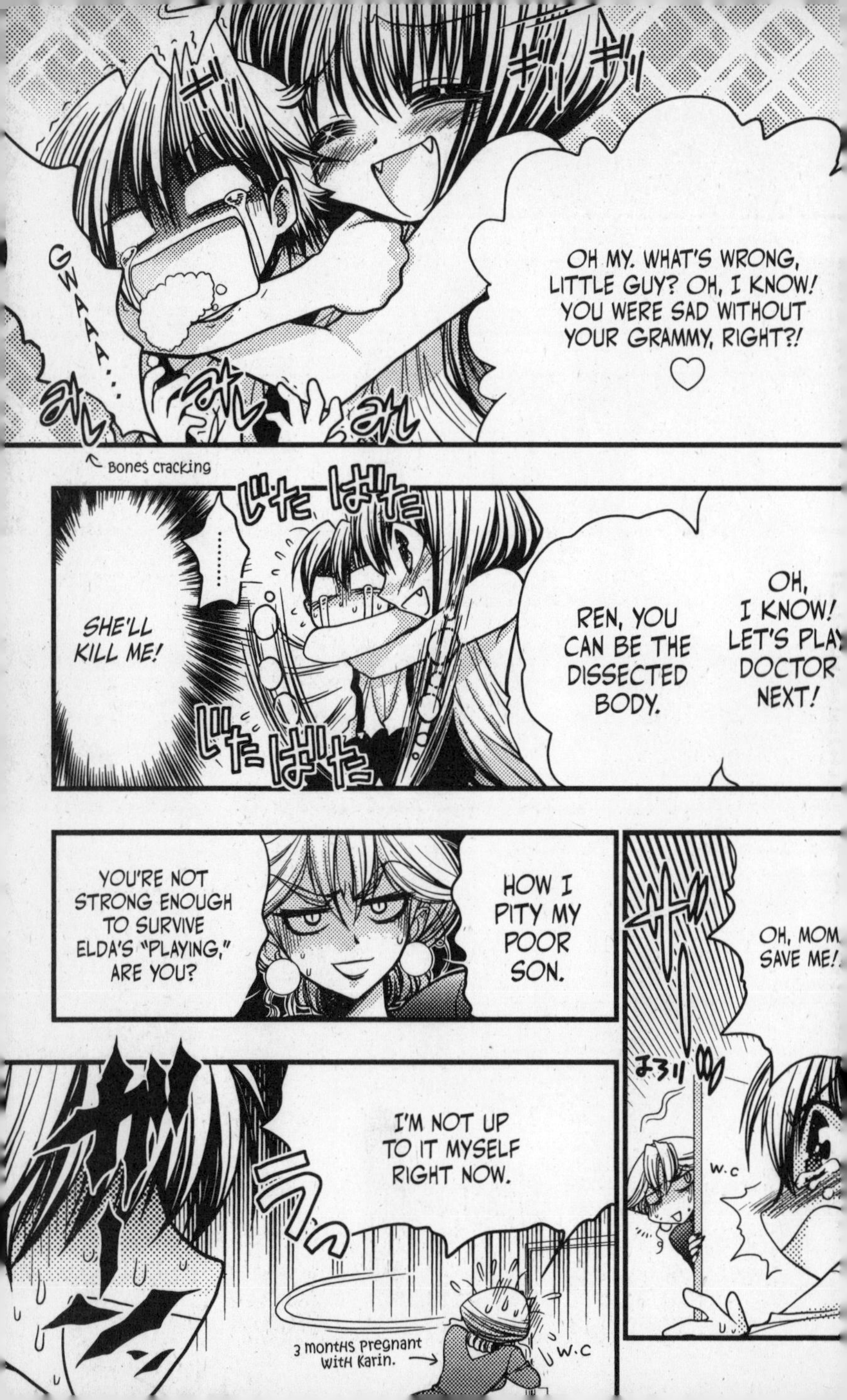

OH MY. WHAT'S WRONG, LITTLE GUY? OH, I KNOW! YOU WERE SAD WITHOUT YOUR GRAMMY, RIGHT?! ♡
GWAAAA...
Bones cracking
OH, I KNOW! LET'S PLA DOCTOR NEXT!
REN, YOU CAN BE THE DISSECTED BODY.
......
SHE'LL KILL ME!
OH, MOM SAVE ME!
W.C
HOW I PITY MY POOR SON.
YOU'RE NOT STRONG ENOUGH TO SURVIVE ELDA'S "PLAYING," ARE YOU?
I'M NOT UP TO IT MYSELF RIGHT NOW.
3 months pregnant with Karin.
W.C

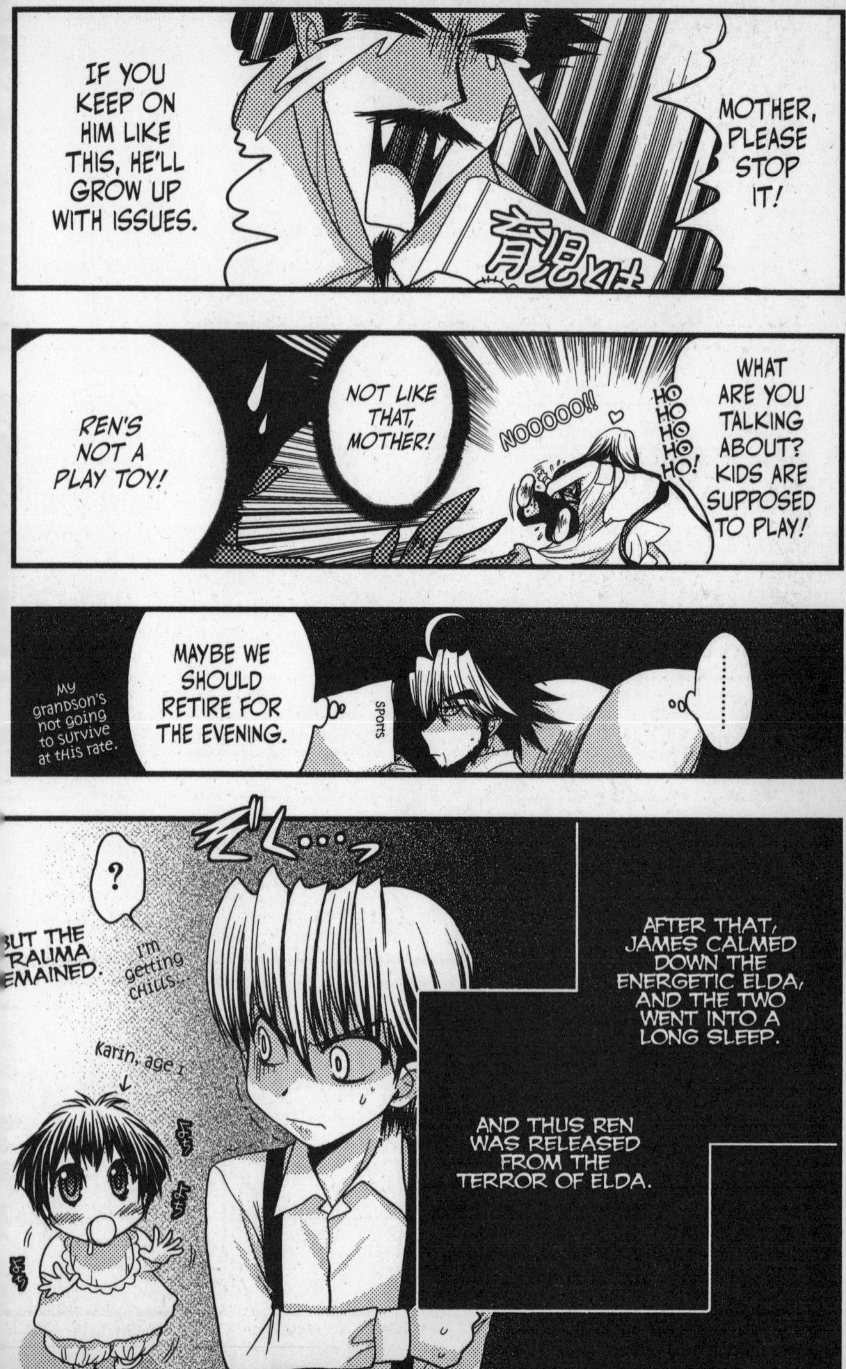
MOTHER, PLEASE STOP IT!
IF YOU KEEP ON HIM LIKE THIS, HE'LL GROW UP WITH ISSUES.
WHAT ARE YOU TALKING ABOUT? KIDS ARE SUPPOSED TO PLAY!
HO HO HO HO HO!
NOOOOO!!
NOT LIKE THAT, MOTHER!
REN'S NOT A PLAY TOY!
....
SPORTS
MAYBE WE SHOULD RETIRE FOR THE EVENING.
My grandson's not going to survive at this rate.
AFTER THAT, JAMES CALMED DOWN THE ENERGETIC ELDA, AND THE TWO WENT INTO A LONG SLEEP.
AND THUS REN WAS RELEASED FROM THE TERROR OF ELDA.
?
UT THE RAUMA EMAINED.
I'm getting chills...
Karin, age 1

COMPUTER TROUBLE

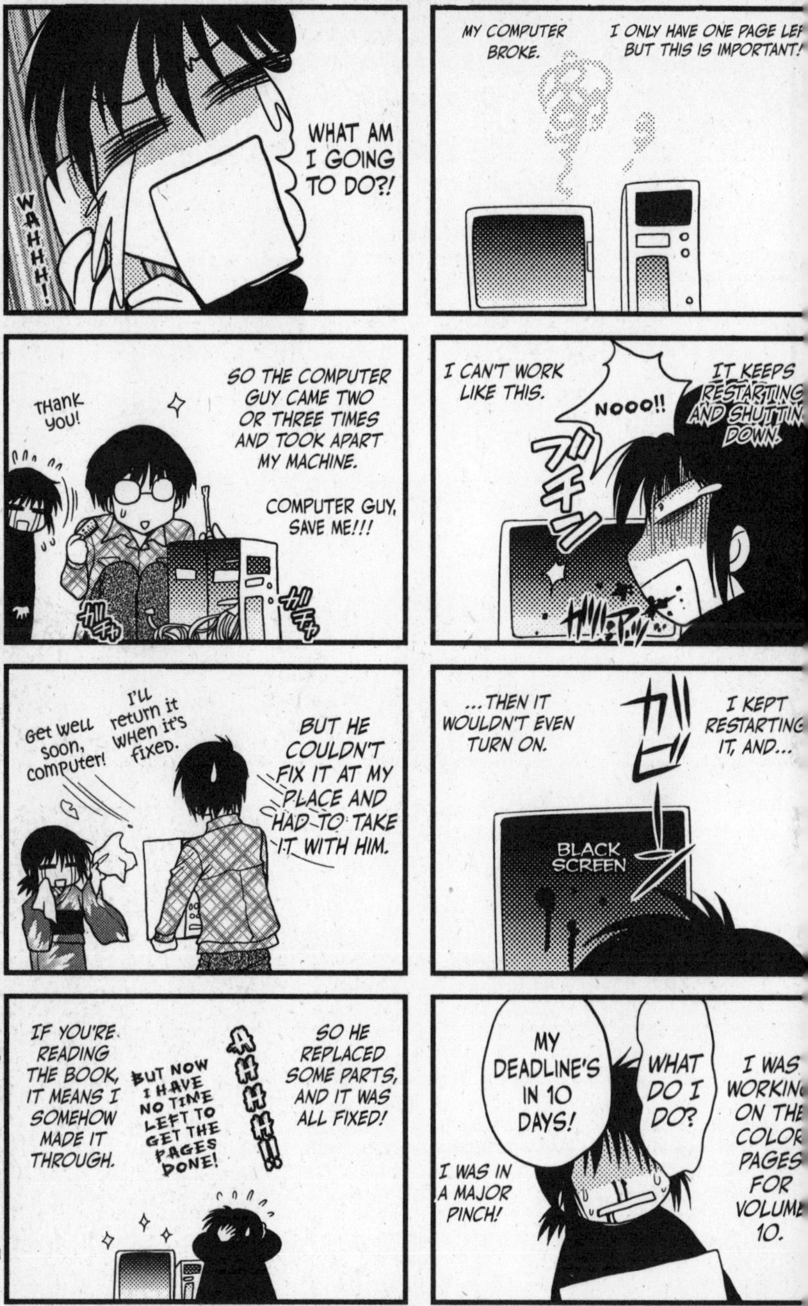
MY COMPUTER BROKE.
I ONLY HAVE ONE PAGE LEF
BUT THIS IS IMPORTANT!
I CAN'T WORK LIKE THIS.
IT KEEPS RESTARTING AND SHUTTIN DOWN.
NOOO!!
I KEPT RESTARTING IT, AND...
...THEN IT WOULDN'T EVEN TURN ON.
BLACK SCREEN
I WAS WORKING ON THE COLOR PAGES FOR VOLUME 10.
MY DEADLINE'S IN 10 DAYS!
WHAT DO I DO?
I WAS IN A MAJOR PINCH!
WHAT AM I GOING TO DO?!
WAHHH!
SO THE COMPUTER GUY CAME TWO OR THREE TIMES AND TOOK APART MY MACHINE.
COMPUTER GUY, SAVE ME!!!
THank you!
BUT HE COULDN'T FIX IT AT MY PLACE AND HAD TO TAKE IT WITH HIM.
I'll return it when it's fixed.
Get well soon, computer!
SO HE REPLACED SOME PARTS, AND IT WAS ALL FIXED!
AHHHH!!
BUT NOW I HAVE NO TIME LEFT TO GET THE PAGES DONE!
IF YOU'RE READING THE BOOK, IT MEANS I SOMEHOW MADE IT THROUGH.

CONTINUED IN VOLUME 11

GOOD THING MY COMPUTER DIDN'T DIE LAST YEAR. I WOULD HAVE BEEN IN HUGE TROUBLE!

IN OUR NEXT VOLUME...

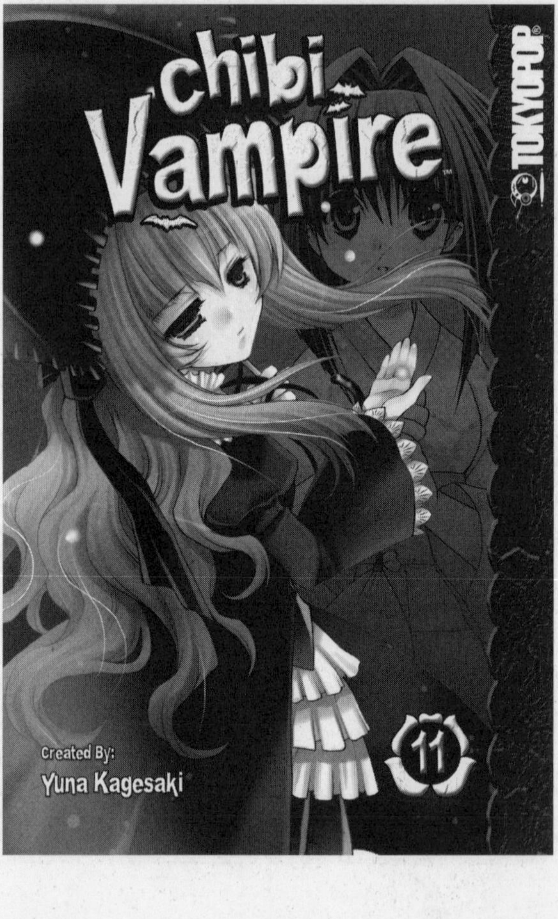
chibi
Vampire
TOKYOPOP
Created By:
Yuna Kagesaki
11

AS KARIN DEALS WITH THE NEWLY REVEALED DEFECTS OF HER OWN BODY AND HOW IT WILL AFFECT HER RELATIONSHIP WITH KENTA, ANJU IS FACING HER OWN SET OF PROBLEMS. ANJU HAS ALWAYS BEEN WEAK TO SUNLIGHT BUT HER AVERSION SEEMS TO BE GETTING STRONGER. COULD THIS MEAN SHE'S CLOSE TO BECOMING A FULLY AWAKENED VAMPIRE? HOW WILL KARIN REACT WHEN SHE FINDS OUT? AND WILL IT TEAR APART THE FRIENDLY SISTERS FOREVER?

Spring is Here

はら
はら
ほと
ほと
WHOA! WHAT'S WRONG?
MAAKA...
WHY are you crying?
sob...
SPRING ARRIVES IN THE NEXT VOLUME... FINALLY!
WE'VE HAD 22 MONTHS OF WINTER ...
...I THOUGHT I WOULD FREEZE TO DEATH.
Crying with them.
USUI-KUN!

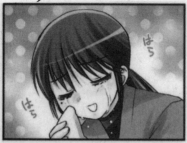

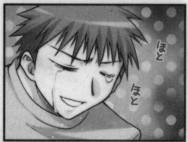

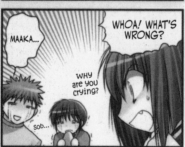

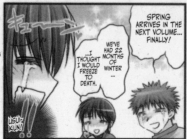

BEHIND THE SCENES, A FAMILY'S UNKNOWN SUFFERING...

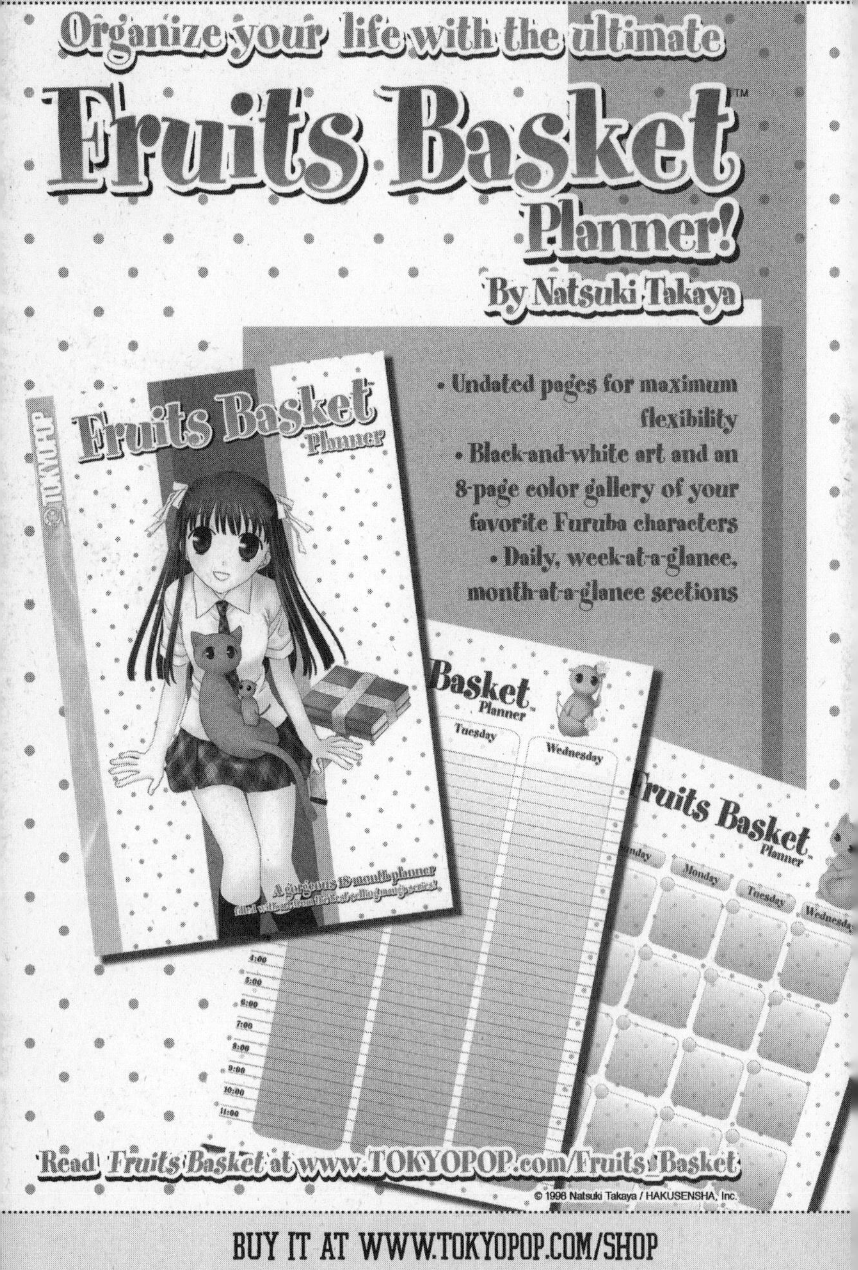
Organize your life with the ultimate
Fruits Basket™ Planner!
By Natsuki Takaya
• Undated pages for maximum flexibility
• Black-and-white art and an 8-page color gallery of your favorite Furuba characters
• Daily, week-at-a-glance, month-at-a-glance sections
Fruits Basket Planner
TOKYOPOP
Basket Planner
Tuesday
Wednesday
4:00
5:00
6:00
7:00
8:00
9:00
10:00
11:00
Fruits Basket Planner
Monday
Tuesday
Wednesday
Read Fruits Basket at www.TOKYOPOP.com/FruitsBasket
© 1998 Natsuki Takaya / HAKUSENSHA, Inc.

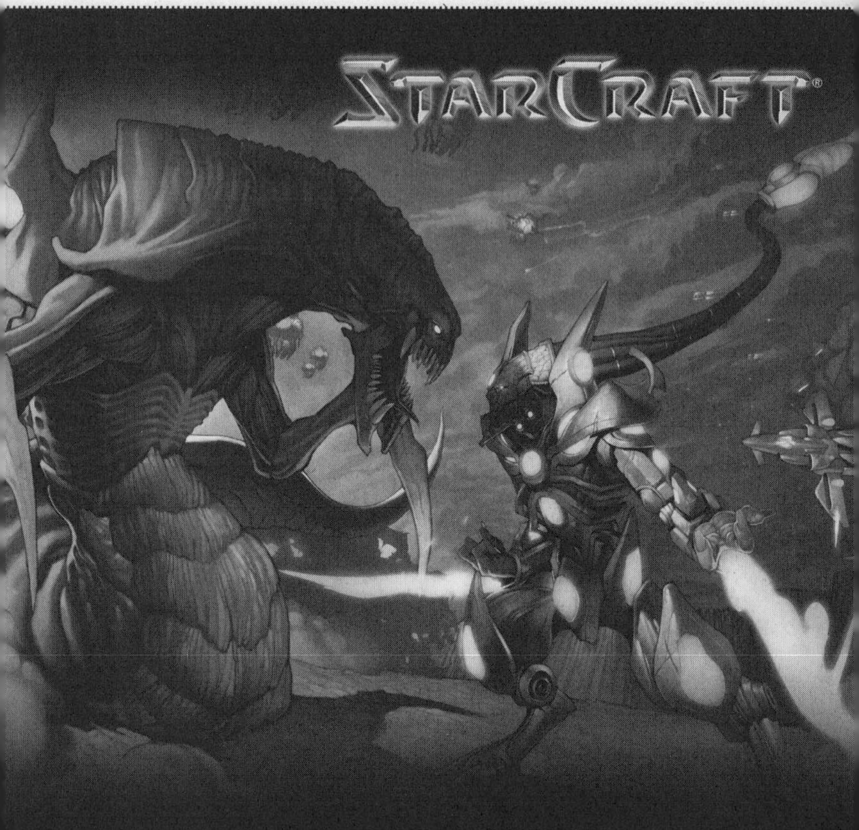
StarCraft®

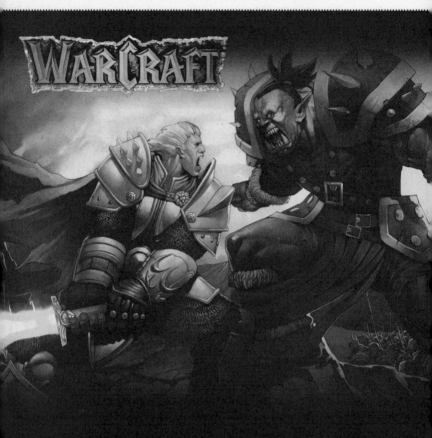

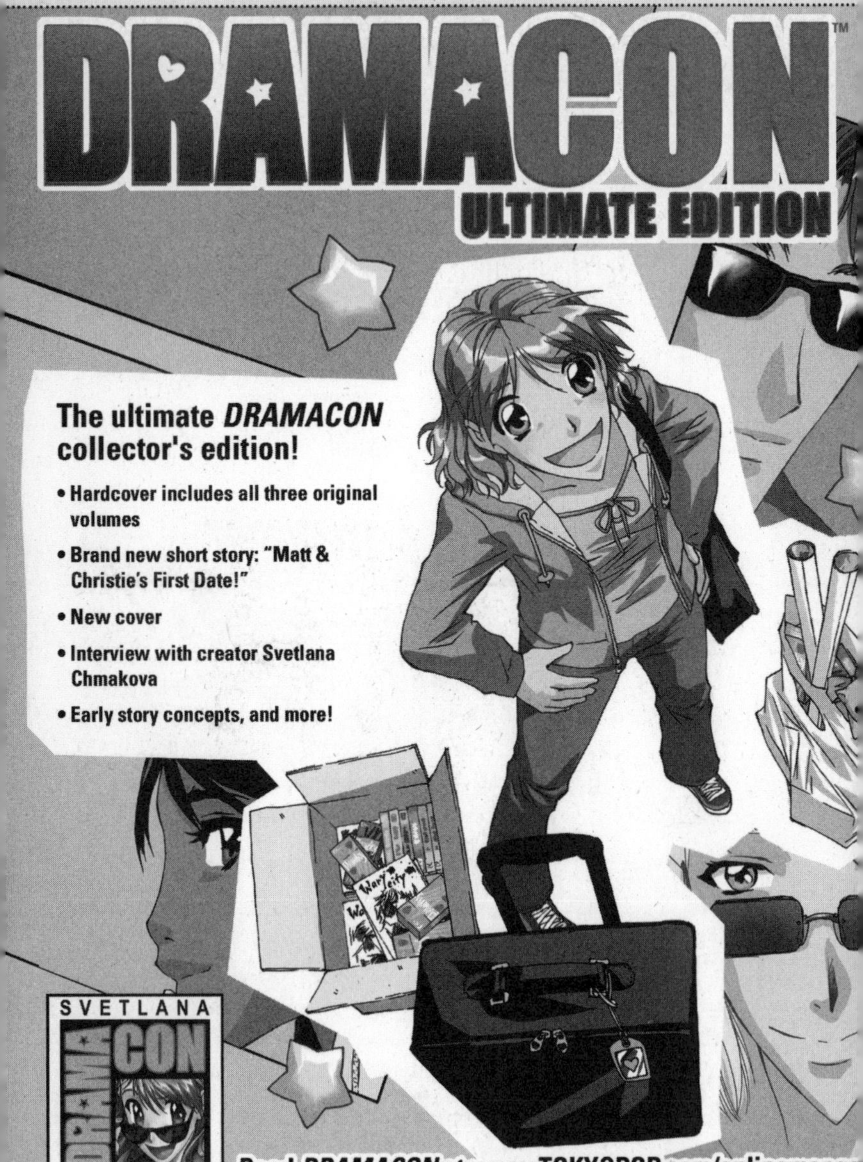
DRAMACON™
ULTIMATE EDITION
The ultimate DRAMACON collector's edition!
• Hardcover includes all three original volumes
• Brand new short story: "Matt & Christie's First Date!"
• New cover
• Interview with creator Svetlana Chmakova
• Early story concepts, and more!
SVETLANA
DRAMACON
CHMAKOVA
Read DRAMACON at www.TOKYOPOP.com/onlinemanga
© Svetlana Chmakova and TOKYOPOP In

STOP!

This is the back of the book.
You wouldn't want to spoil a great ending!

This book is printed "manga-style," in the authentic Japanese right-to-left format. Since none of the artwork has been flipped or altered, readers get to experience the story just as the creator intended. You've been asking for it, so TOKYOPOP® delivered: authentic, hot-off-the-press, and far more fun! RELEASE DETROIT PUBLIC LIBRARY

DIRECTIONS

If this is your first time reading manga-style, here's a quick guide to help you understand how it works.

It's easy... just start in the top right panel and follow the numbers. Have fun, and look for more 100% authentic manga from TOKYOPOP®!